“You’ll recognize lust when it happens.”

The crest of Ethan’s lips brushed against her skin. Charlotte quivered beneath his mouth, and he felt the movement vibrate through the minuscule space left between them. If he pursed his lips, it would be a kiss—a temptation from which he barely refrained. Instead, he allowed himself the tiniest graze of her cheekbone with the tip of his nose.

Nuzzling. He’d just nuzzled her. Of all the ridiculous actions. And that was somehow the sexiest thing he’d done with a woman in years. She was unbelievably soft. The tip of her tongue wet her plump bottom lip, and it was all he could do to not take that as an invitation.

She moved first, turning her head until their noses touched. To kiss her—and God, how he wanted to do that—he’d only have to close that sliver of emptiness between them. Her warm breath, rich with wine, mingled with his, the scent making him feel as if he were tasting her already.

But without her permission, he’d not cross that threshold. Not when that list of reasons why this was a very bad idea awaited them on the other side of this moment. Not when she might soon remember that she didn’t even like him. “May I kiss you, lass?”

Any Rogue Will Do

BETHANY BENNETT

FOREVER
New York Boston

Forever
Hachette Book Group
1290 Avenue of the Americas, New York, NY 10104
read-forever.com
twitter.com/readforeverpub

First Edition: October 2020

Forever is an imprint of Grand Central Publishing. The Forever name and logo are trademarks of Hachette Book Group, Inc.

ISBN: 978-1-5387-3566-4 (mass market), 978-1-5387-3568-8 (ebook)

Printed in the United States of America

OPM

10 9 8 7 6 5 4 3 2 1

To Nicole Locke for asking if I was serious and then holding my hand through the learning curves.

To Daphne Chase for always having my back, occasionally making me cry, and believing in this book even after reading the first draft.

To Alexa Croyle for being the best cheerleader ever. Like. Ever.

And finally, to the high school guidance counselor who assured me I'd amount to nothing: checkmate.

Acknowledgments

I'd never thought of writing as a team sport, but so many people proved me wrong in the best ways.

My incredible husband, Ben, who makes being a writer's widower look hot as hell and accepts discussions about my characters as if they were real people. Every hero has pieces of you.

The Let's Get Critical group, who have poured the drinks to both console and celebrate. Daphne Chase, Catherine Stein, Emmaline Warden, Rosie Danan, Marielle Browne, and Cheryl Tapper: you ladies rock my socks. I love all your words (unless they're anachronistic or make me twitch or…).

Abigail Croyle was a priceless resource when I needed to not quite kill a dude in 1819 England. Thank you for being my herb Google.

The best agent in the universe, Rebecca Strauss—thank you for believing in my imaginary friends. I'd love to say the late-night random emails will stop now, but we both know that's unlikely.

And finally, to Madeleine Colavita and the team at Forever. You guys took my words and somehow made an honest-to-jeebus book out of them. Pure frickin' magic. Thank you.

Chapter One

Somewhere in Warwickshire, Late August 1819

Ethan Ridley—Mac to his friends, Lord Amesbury to everyone else—lounged outside the Boar and Hound. With his face lifted toward the sky, he closed his eyes, taking in the familiar smells of horses and the hearty breakfast served at the inn. Scents of perfectly cooked sausages and fresh bread had him considering a second helping.

Thin wisps of fog would soon give way to the warm August sun, but for now, they clung, hovering in the trees like wraiths. The cool brush of a breeze lifted goose bumps on his throat, where yesterday's cravat hung in a haphazard knot, the linen limp from a second day of being tied. When packing, he'd forgotten a second cravat but remembered the book he was currently reading, so Ethan wasn't terribly upset about the lack of fresh accessories.

He shifted from one foot to the other. Not for the first time this morning, he considered leaving Calvin behind.

They'd traveled all the way from London to visit a highly regarded brewery to see how its processes could be applied to his own budding business venture. After waiting for over thirty minutes past the agreed time, he suspected at least another quarter hour would pass before Calvin appeared looking fresh and annoyingly rested.

Running a hand through his hair, Ethan winced as the strands snagged on calloused fingers. No doubt the unruly curls were assuming their usual vertical position, so he jammed his hat down over the mess. One of these days he'd get a haircut, but today was not that day. Tomorrow didn't look promising either.

The clattering of hooves caught his attention as a wreck of a woman barreled into the stable yard. "There's been an accident! I need a surgeon."

It was the blood that stopped him from acting right away. God, so much blood. It covered her face and the top half of her traveling gown. She rode astride with her skirts hiked up and had the fiercest expression he'd ever seen on a woman. Like a warrior goddess hell-bent on dragging the next poor sod who got in her way into the afterlife, she didn't rein in the mount until they were nearly upon him.

Forcing his legs to move, he shouldered through the taproom's doorway. "We need help out here!" Without waiting for the occupants to jump to attention, he returned to the woman. Ethan swiped a palm over his brow, clearing away fear-ridden sweat, then placed a steadying hand on the heaving chest of the horse. For a moment, his mind had tried to retreat to another accident five years before. Blood had soaked a different roadside while he held his friend, calling for aid until his voice failed. But the past, with its dark, clawed memories, would have to wait.

"My coachman has a broken leg." The woman slid off the horse's back. She touched her forehead, and her fingers came away wet and red. With a grimace, she wiped them on her skirts. One eye had swollen shut, and a cut near her hairline seemed the probable source of most of the blood. "He was unconscious when I left. My maid is with him."

"Where's the accident, miss?" a man from the inn asked, taking the long leather traces she'd used as reins. Men spilled out of the taproom to lend their aid while grooms readied mounts and gathered carts to form a rescue party.

"By my best guess, they are perhaps three miles away. Directly down this road. You can't miss them." She pointed back in the direction from which she'd ridden.

Waving over a fellow whom he'd seen eating with the locals at the morning meal, Ethan said, "We'll need the surgeon. Sir, do you know where tae find him?"

"Yes, milord. I'll fetch 'im." The man donned his hat and scurried down the road toward the village.

The woman swayed on her feet, appearing less warrior-like by the minute and more like a maiden about to faint from blood loss. Before Ethan could say something, Calvin arrived and offered his arm to escort her inside. Just as well. Ethan might want to help, but Cal's particular skill set would be more useful to a damsel in distress. She went with his friend willingly enough, no doubt won over by his charm. Charm wasn't Ethan's strongest trait. Better to stay in the stable yard until everyone had a job and was on their way.

A gentleman with hair that glowed like a halo grasped Lottie's elbow, speaking in the same tone she would use with a frightened horse. "Perhaps you should sit. Your head wound is still bleeding. Frankly, you need help as much as your coachman." Her escort offered Lottie a seat in the public room, which she took, moving with precision to avoid further irritating the bruises making themselves known.

After crawling out of the wreckage, she'd not thought beyond flinging herself atop a carriage horse, then praying she'd stay seated long enough to find a doctor. The shaking in Lottie's legs began, and she feared the rest of her body would follow suit until twitchy, useless nerves overtook her. Lacing her fingers together steadied her somewhat while she waited for her vision to clear. Dear Lord, one of her eyes wasn't working correctly. No wonder her face hurt.

She tried to focus on the man who'd helped her. His striking features and perfect attire seemed more suited to a London drawing room than a Warwickshire country inn. "What brings a pretty fellow like you to a town like this?" A disconnect between her ears and mouth made the words come out slow and slurred. Mercy, her head hurt.

Following his gaze to a sparkling window overlooking the yard, she spied the behemoth of a man they'd left behind deploying volunteers and taking control of the situation with an air of command no one questioned. Ah, he must be here with the man using his impressive presence to get things done. The man's confidence amidst an emergency didn't hurt his aura of competence.

Fresh blood seeped past her lashes. Wincing, she turned from the scene and wiped an already filthy hand over her eyes.

The innkeeper's wife arrived with water and a stack of cloths. "I'm Mrs. Pringle, dearie. Let's look at your head and see what we're about, shall we?"

Lottie waved a hand. "It's nothing. Nothing serious at any rate. I'm sure I'll be fine after a bath and rest. My coachman needs a doctor far more than I do."

Clean tables and the scent of fresh bread made the inn warm and cozy. Hopefully, the rooms upstairs would be as welcoming. She desperately wanted to get her bearings, then find a tub and a bed. A bath would be heaven.

The elegant stranger pushed: "Please, miss, let her clear away the blood—"

Chilly air danced over her cheek as the commanding man from the courtyard entered the room. With a blunt "Give me the rag," he once again took charge, swiping the cloth from Mrs. Pringle's hand.

Her charming escort rolled his eyes. "Fine, Mac. Take over. I'll see if I'm needed outside."

The giant grunted an acknowledgment. Really, were actual words too much to ask? A few moments before he'd been kind, but now surly impatience colored his demeanor. The sheer size of him overwhelmed her—an unusual circumstance for a woman her own father referred to as "sturdy." Even sitting, he dwarfed everyone in the room. Only one other man of her acquaintance had made her feel delicate in comparison, but that had been a lifetime ago.

The man tossed his hat on the table, revealing a mass of dark curls. Another wave of dizziness swamped her as recognition hit. Please, God, let her be wrong. And if she didn't humiliate herself by fainting, she'd tithe double the next time she found herself near a church.

Maybe the head wound caused the buzzing in her ears—

it couldn't possibly be because this man still affected her after so long. But no. Even seven years later, Lord Amesbury, the one who had saved her, then callously ruined her, evoked a visceral response. If he thought to save her again, she'd best remember what he'd done the last time they'd met.

Amesbury leaned forward, sparking an almost-forgotten heat of awareness in her belly. His dark brows were broody slashes under a disobedient lock of hair that fell over his forehead, providing the only softness on his face. Shadows played in the hollows under his cheek-bones, where at least a day's growth of beard made him look as roguish as she knew him to be.

"I know your concern is for your coachman. 'Tis commendable. But you're useless if you don' see tae yourself." That lilting brogue did something funny to her chest, creating flutters she'd rather not ponder. "Now please hold still so you don' make a bigger mess on this good woman's floor."

Mrs. Pringle didn't seem sure if she should leave or stay. The older woman stared at the floorboards while holding the water basin, no doubt wishing to be anywhere else. Lottie felt the same.

Although his exasperated tone rankled, Lottie allowed the examination. Knowing this man, of all people, saw her in such a state set her cheeks aflame with a mix of embarrassment and fury. Fate, that fickle fiend, always tossed her in his path at her worst, casting him as a hero. With a finger under her chin, Amesbury raised her face toward the morning light streaming through the window. His gruff words were at odds with gentle fingers as he brushed the blood-soaked hair off her brow and prodded at a painful area near her hairline.

How had he grown more attractive while she'd merely gotten older? Every year her body grew softer, rounder, despite daily rides all over the estate. As the butterflies in her belly would attest, the small lines at the corners of his eyes and a new hardness to his jaw didn't diminish his appeal. Grossly unfair, in her opinion.

Over the years, she'd imagined a different meeting. In her version, she always wore a stunning new gown—the picture of intimidatingly competent femininity. Lord Amesbury would stop in his tracks, recognizing her in an instant. Then his striking face would flood with regret, evoking her pity—but only for a moment. A strong cup of tea would help the sensation pass once she snubbed him and went on her way.

No matter the scenario, Lottie served witty set-downs while looking ethereally beautiful, then left the man with an unrelenting grief to haunt him for the rest of his natural life. Really, was that too much to ask? In her imagination she would marry a gorgeous duke—even though young available dukes weren't exactly thick on the ground. Especially for spinsters.

Logic had no jurisdiction in daydreams and fairy tales.

Reality was sorely lacking. Her traveling gown's tattered bodice barely clung to modesty, she'd just dripped blood on his boot, and any fool could see Viscount Amesbury didn't remember her.

Perhaps it was immature to wish the circumstances of their meeting were different, but the fact was that she found herself in another embarrassing situation requiring his help and he didn't even have the decency to remember her. Inhaling deeply, she searched for calm and instead filled her head with the scent of him—not the wisest course of action. If only Amesbury favored the usual perfumes or bottled tonics, or smelled of rotten onions with a trace of dock water. Instead, he smelled like a man who bathed, then gave no further thought to his appearance. It reminded her of fresh air, leather, and an underlying warmth she couldn't place. Now her heart pounded for a different reason.

The one thing her old suitor-turned-nemesis did well was confuse her. He always had.

Some things didn't change, even after seven years. Lottie exhaled his essence, pushing the tangle of emotions from her body. A man she hated so thoroughly shouldn't smell so comforting.

Chapter Two

"Heaven's above, lass. What did you hit your head on? Or rather, what hit you?" he asked.

"The sides of the carriage. The floor. Probably the roof once or twice. I woke up after the accident." Their gazes clashed for a heartbeat before Lottie stared down at the table.

"My guess is you'll need stitches tae close this wound." Amesbury brought her hand up to her face. "Press this rag tae your head. There's a good lass. We have tae slow the bleeding."

Lottie winced at the pressure of the cloth but followed his instructions. That commanding presence at work again, convincing everyone around him to do his bidding. But she'd give the same advice to someone else, so Lottie pressed harder and tried not to whine about it.

Clearly, there wasn't much more to be done before the doctor arrived. Which meant nothing forced her to sit here with this man, letting him play hero to her damsel in distress—again. Anger sparked, overriding the myriad pains. "Thank you for your help, my lord. Now I need to check on my horse and secure rooms for my staff." Ignoring her shaking legs, Lottie straightened, forcing herself to move as if she weren't battered and bruised.

As she brushed past him, Lottie deliberately knocked his shoulder with her hip, and he had to grab the edge of the table to keep his seat. A huge man like him probably lumbered through life without expecting women to push him around. A onetime event, to be sure, but she welcomed the petty thrill.

Predictably, he argued. "No, you need tae sit and rest. Wait for the doctor. You've suffered a great deal today." Lord Amesbury looked annoyed. Or maybe that was just his face.

"I'll see the doctor when he arrives." She flicked her skirt hem away from Amesbury, smiling her thanks to Mrs. Pringle, who stood silently by, watching the exchange. "If you'll excuse me, I have things to see to. Mrs. Pringle, I will speak with you privately in a few moments."

The man who'd helped her inside returned to their table. A bit of a dandy and less intimidating than his giant friend, he must be the Earl of Carlyle. The name brought forth vague memories involving a gorgeous gentleman who sent the debutantes' imaginations down church aisles. It would seem Lord Amesbury's circle of friends hadn't changed.

Lord Carlyle's eyes widened, then he reached out to catch her although she hadn't wobbled. "Please, miss, your color is not good. Why not sit? Wait for the surgeon."

"Thank you, but no. I've spent enough time in Lord Amesbury's presence to last a lifetime."

Lord Carlyle rounded on Amesbury. "It's been five minutes, Mac. What in God's name have you managed to bungle in that time?"

Ah, that's right. They called him Mac. Of all the obnoxious names to give a Scotsman. But then, *Mac* had done far worse, hadn't he?

Amesbury's clear bafflement at the situation would be funny if she were not the joke. He didn't recognize her.

Seven years before, she'd sat in her drawing room, wondering where he was, when news that he'd turned her into a gossip-rag headline arrived with the first tittering visitors. Instead of offering the expected proposal, her handsome suitor had ruined her. It should be harder to lose one's reputation.

Back then, she would have bitten her tongue rather than speak her mind, for fear of being deemed unladylike. Now the words flew like barbed razors, and she hoped they cut wherever they landed. "What's the matter, Lord Amesbury? Am I supposed to ooze gratitude like a ninny after you playact the savior? Unlike you, I remember that we've done this once before, and you only impersonate a hero. It's a convincing act, I'll give you that. But I no longer simper, and you're not a gentleman."

Turning to Lord Carlyle, Lottie said, "I thank you for your timely assistance. Please stand aside."

Finally, as if puzzle pieces fell into place, Amesbury's eyes widened with recognition. "Lady Charlotte."

Lottie cocked her head. "I'll accept nothing less than 'Your Highness' from the likes of you. After all, you made me royalty, and the title rolls off the tongue so nicely—the Paper Doll Princess. Oh, so witty. I've certainly never been able to forget it—nor the humiliation of having thought you were a friend." Pouring sarcasm into her voice, she bent her knees in a mocking dip of a curtsy, one hand holding the wadded rag to her wound. "For that, sir, you can go to the devil."

As she swept from the room with her head held high, she heard Lord Carlyle chuckle and say, "Damn. If that was round one, I'm putting five pounds on Lady Charlotte."

When she marched out the front door of the inn, there was an odd empty quality to the stable yard now that aid had been dispatched to the wreckage site. "Is there any more to be done?" she asked the lone hosteler shoveling horse droppings into a pile.

"Nothing, milady. The big gentleman took care of everything. A few blokes should return with news soon, and the doctor will be along shortly." He tipped his cap to her before returning to work.

Well, damn. Was there anything worse than waiting? If only she'd been able to ride back with the men to help her servants. At least that would be *doing* something.

Lottie entered the cool, dark stables and found Samson, the carriage horse who'd served her so well, resting in a stall. She ran a hand down his neck to his withers, then grabbed a fistful of hay, letting him nibble from her fingertips. The soft muzzle hairs tickled the pads of her fingers as if he were petting her too.

Willing her tension away, Lottie leaned against the stall and let the barn scents and sounds work their therapeutic magic. Barns smelled of productivity, hard work, and home. Over the years, barns had been more welcoming than ballrooms. Horses wouldn't mock your mistakes. Sheep didn't care if a dress was a few years old or if a woman wore breeches.

This madcap mission she'd undertaken was foolish but

necessary if she was to have any control over choosing her own future. If Father had his way, she would be announcing the banns now with Mr. James Montague, youngest son of the Earl of Danby. Having never met the man, and with no desire to do so, she'd dismissed a match between them and thought no more of it. Father had other ideas though, deciding that this—her unmarried state—would be the first thing he took notice of since they'd buried her brother and mother. While it might have been easier to cave to Father's wishes, the high-handedness of his demands rubbed her the wrong way. If she absolutely had to marry, she'd do so on her terms, thank you very much.

So here she was, on her way to find a husband before her father's deadline of the beginning of the Season. While summer wasn't a logical time to husband hunt in London, it was ideal when one desired a spouse who wouldn't want to spend any time with her in the country. She needed a city gentleman, preferably one who'd contentedly let her go on her way once the vows were exchanged and a tidy living hit his bank account from her dowry. If she failed to find a fiancé before the House of Lords convened in late November, she'd be forced to marry Mr. Montague. Those were Father's terms.

Either way, she'd avoid the Season—a blessing, considering her advanced age and the utter disaster of her debut.

In the late spring of 1812, while London reeled from the assassination of the prime minister, Spencer Perceval, the *ton* had obsessed over one piece of gossip that gave them reason to laugh—her. And they didn't know the half of it.

They didn't know she'd been caught in the mob on the streets that had formed after word of the shooting spread. More people than she'd ever seen in one place gathered, cheering the actions of a desperate murderer. A frantic chaos had ruled that crowd, creating a danger she'd never experienced before. After being separated from her footman, she'd tried to push against the bodies to find her way to a quieter street. Each second that passed birthed more tension in the air—until a firm hand had grasped her elbow, and the excessively large man who'd danced with her at parties and perched on the tiny chairs in her drawing room had bullied through the throng, guiding her to safety. He'd oozed confidence then too, as his brawny arms anchored her to his side.

There'd been a moment when their eyes locked and the world stopped. She'd swear to it. When he kissed her hand at her door and promised to call the next day, it had felt loaded with meaning, as if his promise held more than mere words.

Instead, she'd waited for a visit that never came. And the day after that, the assassin John Bellingham and the Paper Doll Princess dominated the newspapers. For a while, she'd shared notoriety with a murderer.

Samson's forelock was silky under her hands when the big horse pushed into the caress, shoving away the echoes of shame these memories brought. "Those saddle lessons you had last spring saved the day, my fine fellow." The bay whuffled a response, making her smile. "Extra oats for you. Maybe even a treacle swirl on top. You earned it."

Through a rough timber window, Lottie spied the two men she wanted to avoid walking across the courtyard to where a stable boy waited with their horses. The coast was clear. Time to get a room from Mrs. Pringle, wash, then await the physician.

Lottie tucked a sticky curl behind her ear and wrinkled her nose. She needed a bath as much as she needed her next breath. Perhaps Mrs. Pringle had a soap fragrant enough to induce amnesia and erase all memories of blood and screaming horses. Although, anything would be better than her current odor. *Le parfum du tragédie* was never *en vogue*. A shaky sigh tried to become a sob, but she stifled the sound behind a dirty fist.

Not now. Just a few more moments of pretending all was fine. Once alone, she could let herself cry. Sharp pains all over her body hinted at how many times she'd tumbled around inside the carriage as it careened off the road toward the trees. As if her aches weren't enough, Lord Amesbury's appearance had created another layer of emotional chaos. At least she'd finally said her piece. That was a small comfort.

Tears threatened. The need to rant hammered at her composure. To rehash what she *could* have said when faced with the man who'd treated her so callously during her first Season. But more than anything, she wanted privacy so she could fall apart.

Blowing a lank curl out of her face, Lottie fought for a thin thread of control, squeezing her good eye closed as she counted her breaths. Inhale, one, two, three. Exhale, one, two, three. The pressure in her chest released, and her mask of composure slid back into place. She must not forget why she was London bound. The scandal of her debut wouldn't be repeated. This time, she'd play society's game by her rules.

Chapter Three

The doctor's sewing skills rivaled those of a seamstress. Although he wasn't quite finished, a glance in a hand mirror showed small stitches that would eventually heal and disappear into her hairline.

"You have commendable skill with a needle, Doctor. Does your wife ask you to handle the mending? You would turn out a beautiful seam in no time." Lightening the mood didn't distract her from the pain, as she'd hoped. His flat expression displayed no emotion, which didn't help either. What the physician lacked in personality, he made up for with ability. Better that than a charming quack armed with bottles of mystery tonic and foul river sludge.

Each prick of the needle burned instead of stabbed, as if her body's sensitivities were so overloaded, her brain could no longer accurately categorize individual injuries. She held her tongue against more comments and tried to stay still.

Wishing to be anywhere else, Lottie closed her eyes. In her mind she saw herself at home, at her desk in the sitting room, sunlight streaming through the multipaned windows as she made lists for the week's work. Organizing and prioritizing the needs of the tenants or scheduling the planting and harvest in each field soothed her. An especially painful stitch sent daggers of sensation through her skull, pulling her from the mental retreat.

The inn's maid arrived at the door as the doctor finished packing his case. Lottie invited the girl in as the physician left to await the arrival of Darling and Patrick from the carriage rubble. A moment later, hot water from the servant's buckets splashed into the tub, letting off swirls of steam into the tiny room.

The young woman asked, "Will there be anything else before your bath, milady?"

Just the thought of a bath was enough to make her smile. "I don't think so. I'm very much looking forward to being clean." Sitting on the side of the bed, she was tempted to lean back and fall into the softness of the pillows, but she refused to give in to the urge when layers of grime covered every inch of her. Hot water first, then a lie-down. Checking the maid's progress, Lottie said, "Now that I think of it, would you be so kind as to move that small table beside the tub? If the pitcher and soap are between the tub and fire, the clean water jug will stay warm. It's just a small thing. Thank you."

Exhaustion swept over her. From what she'd been able to piece together at the scene, she thought one of the horses had spooked, snapping a leather line and jarring the carriage. They'd hit a rut in the road at high speed, already teetering from the horse wanting to shy in a different direction. Bad luck. Awful timing. Then shuddering carriage walls cracking and splintering apart. A dirty floor that became a roof, then a floor, then a roof again. Panicked cries from the horses and Patrick's answering call, cut short by an agonized scream. His leg. Lord, his leg. Darling's ashen face, her eyes appearing too large for her skull when she saw the coachman. The disorientation when Lottie lost and regained consciousness at some point.

With closed eyes, Lottie counted footsteps as a parade of sloshing buckets filled the large basin by the fire. One hundred thirty steps. Ten buckets of water thus far. This had been the longest day, and it wasn't even noon. At last, the maid emptied a final bucket, and Lottie stood to savor a moment of silence.

Relative silence. The Boar and Hound bustled with activity. Sounds of commerce and travelers filtered up through the floor. The four walls were her haven from the world as the fireplace blazed cheerily by the washtub, chasing away the shadows in the room.

The earlier waterworks that had threatened to overwhelm her in the stables loomed. Years of experience had taught her the dangers of stifling feelings for too long. A blinding headache with nausea and sensitivity to light and sound would be too much to bear after this morning.

There might be no preventing the pain. But when it hit, she could be clean. If that was all she could do to control the situation, then so be it. A desperate need to get out of the filthy traveling gown overruled the tangled feelings from the day. Although her fingers were clumsy and swollen from repeated impact in the carriage, she managed the tapes and hooks without help. Thank goodness for simple country clothes.

At last, fire-licked warmth from the hearth caressed

bare skin. The idea of touching such a grimy dress, even to hang it on the hook by the door, made her wrinkle her nose, so she left it in a pile on the floor.

Zesty lemons teased her senses when she uncorked the vial of bath oil. It smelled of everything she wasn't. Clean, crisp, and fresh. As she sank into the bath, her muscles protested before loosening under the soothing heat. The water stung her scraped skin, already marked with red and blue splotches. Over the next several days, those would become a colorful road map of abrasions and vivid bruises. What a miserable day.

She'd been in the tub for only a few moments when a knock interrupted her pity party. Lucia Darling poked her head in the room. "We've arrived, milady." Lottie's maid closed the door, then knelt by the tub, gently grasping Lottie's chin to tilt her stitches toward the light. "Once the swelling in that eye goes down, you'll clean up nicely."

"I'll be fine. How are you? Is Patrick awake?" Lottie draped the heavy curtain of her hair over one shoulder and reached for the soap.

"A few bumps. I'll surely feel it tomorrow. Nothing compared to Patrick's leg. He awoke for a few moments before the men arrived, but passed out again when they loaded him in the wagon. The doctor is getting him settled in a bed now," Darling said.

"The physician proved competent with a needle." Lottie gestured toward her own forehead. "Let us pray his bone-setting abilities are as impressive."

"Aye." Darling picked up the discarded clothing, hung it on the hook, then recorked the vial of oil by the tub.

"Darling, maybe you should sit. You have your own bruises and bumps to care for."

Darling ignored the suggestion. She inspected the torn

traveling gown with a critical eye—as if they'd launder and mend the thing. "Mr. and Mrs. Pringle seem nice. The rooms are clean. We'll be comfortable once the men return from the coach with our things."

"The only drawback I can see is our proximity to Lord Amesbury." Lottie wrinkled her nose as if the name itself smelled foul. "We had words downstairs. Now I'd prefer never to see him again."

"Lord Amesbury? Here? Hell on a broomstick, this day is one awful surprise after another." Darling finally sat in the chair near the tub.

Lottie pushed the topic of Amesbury aside with a wave of her hand and a spray of lemon-scented droplets. "We can talk about him later. I'm most concerned about you and Patrick. I can see you're worried. Would you prefer to be with him right now?"

Darling shook her head, but the jerky movement revealed her distress. "My duty is here, milady."

Of course she would say that. "If you wish to keep him company, then go. Let me know what he needs to be more comfortable."

Darling dipped a shallow curtsy, then darted from the room.

Alone again, Lottie skimmed the pitcher beneath the surface, then tipped her head back. Although she attempted to avoid the suture site, water hit the stitches, eliciting a grimace. Clean hair and body would be worth the momentary discomfort, surely.

When the water grew cool, she stepped from the tub before realizing her problem. Her clothes were with the carriage, strewn about the roadside. Lottie eyed the bloody rag formerly known as her traveling dress hanging by the door. No.

The toweling linen wrapped around her ample curves, with a gap of several inches. Lottie scowled at the skin between the ends of the towel. The bedding would have to do.

Wrapped in patchwork colors worn smooth by years of washings, Lottie wrote a letter informing her father—or rather, her father's steward, Rogers—of the day's events. Recounting the facts did nothing to loosen the knot of emotion lodged in her chest. Another note went to her godmother, Lady Agatha Dalrymple. The older woman expected Lottie at her London home this week, but under the current circumstances, the likelihood of that happening was nil.

Even if Patrick's leg set without complications and there weren't any unforeseen traveling delays, a swap of staff and carriages would still take several days. She would not leave Patrick here alone. Once he was safely on his way back to Stanwick Manor, she and Darling would continue on to London. Her father would call her weak for prioritizing a servant over her travel itinerary, but her father wasn't the one making decisions, now was he?

A delay was a better outcome than how the day could have ended. Multiple lives might have been snuffed out like a guttered candle, with such swiftness there would have been no chance to sputter or flare back to life. Just gone. Dead instead of broken. Lottie rubbed at an ache between her brows, then set the letters on a table by the door.

A familiar knock pulled her from gloomy thoughts. Her maid closed the door, then slumped against it. Darling seemed to stare at nothing for several seconds before blowing a lock of hair from her face.

Patrick's leg must be either set or lost. No third option.

Darling's expression fit both outcomes. Clenching her fists around the quilt's corner until her knuckles shone white, Lottie braced for the worst. "How is he?"

Tears slipped down Darling's cheeks in twin trails. "He'll keep the leg for now. As long as it doesn't fester."

"That's a mercy. Better to gain a limp than lose the leg." Lottie slumped onto the edge of the mattress.

"The doctor gave me ground willow bark for Patrick's pain. I'll add it to his tea. He also gave us laudanum, but the stubborn cuss refused to take any. I have it in case Patrick relents," Darling said.

"I can't imagine how hard this ordeal has been for him or for you." The two had been spending more time together in recent weeks, which made Lottie wonder if a romance might be brewing.

"He fainted when the doctor moved the bone." Darling swiped under her nose with the heel of her palm, then dried her hand on her skirt. "I haven't heard from Mrs. Pringle about our trunks. You need clothes." She shuddered as if just noticing the condition of her gown.

"I hope it won't be much longer. I'm sure you want a bath and a change of clothing as well."

"Would you mind if I sat with Patrick until they arrive with our things?"

"Of course not. I'm glad you can be there with him. I doubt the doctor would let me in the room. Especially with my lack of clothing." Lottie nodded toward her quilt.

"I'll report back about our trunks momentarily." Darling snagged the letters on the side table. "And I'll have the innkeeper post these."

Wrapped in the blanket, Lottie flopped on the bed. Each time her eyes closed, her mind filled with fragmented memories of the accident. The aches in her body throbbed as a reminder of the morning, just in case she found herself tempted to think it all a bad dream.

The incoming headache thumped at the base of her skull, setting itself apart from her other injuries. Tucking her chin under the blanket, she surrendered to the imminent agony. If she held still, perhaps she wouldn't vomit this time.

Like an unruly child determined to poke at things with a pointy stick, her mind wandered back to Lord Amesbury. He'd been quite the sight this morning, so tall and broad and oozing confidence. Any average-sized person had to stand with a kink in their neck if they wanted to meet his gaze at a close distance.

She remembered those eyes. The first time she'd crossed paths with him, they'd triggered a longing for her carefree days on the seashore as a child, when the sun lit up the ocean and made the sea match the summer sky. Those blue eyes with their streaks of sunny gold had been the most beautiful things she'd ever seen when he'd pulled her to safety from the mob months later. They'd softened with tender promise when he insisted he would check on her the next day.

Rolling over took tremendous effort, but the way her body sank into the mattress made it worth it.

News of Amesbury had been scarce since Lottie left London. Agatha remained her best source of Town gossip, but she had an understandable bias against the man who'd hurt Lottie. Her honorary aunt and godmother's letters were more reliable and often more entertaining than the *Times*. Surely Agatha would have mentioned if Amesbury married—unless she deemed his marriage beneath her notice. Which was entirely plausible.

Damn. Amesbury might have a wife. What an odd notion. Another woman might even now be choosing her most flattering day dress and debating which sofa in the drawing room had the best light, so she'd be backlit with an angelic glow as she welcomed him home. Lottie sniffed. Yes, she'd been a hopeful fool, preparing for an offer that never came.

"Good luck to the poor girl. She'll need it." The words fell flat. But as she clung to them, her fortress of self-control finally crumbled. Tears wet the blanket beneath her, dripping into the tight curls framing her face.

Everything broke loose with the tears.

This return to London for another Season felt wrong without her mother. After a childhood of forgotten promises, solitary tea parties, and a parade of governesses, Lottie knew where she stood in the grand scheme of things. Mother and Father's passion for one another had eclipsed all else, and any remaining emotional energy had been lavished on her brother, the heir. But when the time came for decorum lessons and preparation for her debut? For the first time in her life, Lottie's time with Mother had no limits. When her debut wasn't a success, they planned to conquer the *ton* a few years later and prove to them all that Charlotte Wentworth wasn't one to be trifled with.

Then her brother, Michael, died in the Battle of New Orleans. The next year, just as they were coming out of their blacks from Michael, Mother fell sick. They never made it back to Town and the infamous Marriage Mart. What appeal did London hold without her mother?

More tears escaped onto the pillow as anger over her father's ultimatum and his insistence that she marry and leave the estate in his hands rose to the surface. Yes, the black cloud of mourning seemed to have lifted, but what if he woke up tomorrow and refused to deal with his responsibilities? How many of their tenants would suffer again under a landlord who didn't care enough to move beyond his library?

After their family's losses, he'd retreated to his bed for weeks. When he eventually moved to the library, she'd thought it progress and assumed he was quietly dealing with estate matters. But no. The library became his sanctuary away from the real world. Their people went without, and the estate fell apart until Lottie stepped in and took the reins. Not that she'd had any clue what she was doing. But she'd learned. And for a few years, all went smoothly. Until her father decided he would resume control.

After she put in years of satisfying labor at Stanwick Manor, making a difference and doing things that *mattered*, she didn't receive so much as a thank-you—just demands that she marry Mr. Montague or someone else suitable before the year's end. The unfairness of seeing hard work torn from her hands stung. Self-pity was a great reason to cry.

She grieved the accident and Patrick's agony as he'd landed in the road like a broken doll, with his leg pointing in the wrong direction.

All this pain and fuss, and she still must face the *ton* with only Agatha as a chaperone, and no friends her own age. If she'd ever needed a friend, it was now. All her acquaintances had husbands and children. Their letters had brimmed with society gossip, babies, and shopping trips, while hers spoke of loss, death, and tenant needs. Understandably, the correspondence had eventually stopped. Lottie had never been so alone.

Pent-up emotion leaked out of her as she cried until the building headache receded, withdrawing its claws for another day. The crackling blaze of the fire and the clean citrus scent of her hair soothed her, leeching the tension away with each shuddery sigh.

Lottie flung the quilt aside far enough to free her legs just as her belly rumbled. Between the doctor's visit, the bath, waiting for clothes, and that brief emotional breakdown, she'd missed the midday meal. A glance out the window showed the skies darkening as the first raindrop hit the glass pane with a *plop*. Brilliant. The weather matched her mood.

Chapter Four

Studying his cards, Ethan wished to be anywhere besides this little inn in rainy Warwickshire. Not long after their visit with the local brewmaster this afternoon, Mother Nature had opened the skies in a deluge that made travel unwise. Several other men stranded by the weather had formed a card game in the public room and provided alcoholic social lubricants, and here they were.

Ethan motioned to Cal. "Your play, my friend."

Two queens fluttered to the floor. After squinting at the remaining cards in his hand, Cal peered down at the queens with a frown but didn't seem inclined to pick them up. Apparently their time at the tables had come to an end.

"I think we're done." Ethan ignored the groans from the other players. In his current condition, Cal was an easy mark. "Move along, Calvin. Let's leave our chairs for a few fellows who aren't as bosky."

"It's fine, Mac. I can play piquet with my eyes closed." Cal clutched a bottle of whisky to his chest as if someone would snatch it away.

Ethan hefted his friend out of the chair and led him to a table near the window. "The game was vingt-et-un."

"Oh. I guess that changes things." Cal collapsed into a chair, the seat barely catching his backside. "Any news on the lovely Lady Charlotte?" Rolling his *L*s must have been vastly entertaining, because Cal sat flicking his tongue for a moment before refocusing on their conversation.

"I haven' seen her since she told me tae go tae the devil." Not that he hadn't looked. Every time he entered one of the public rooms, he searched for her dark curls. During their visit with the brewmaster he'd gleaned valuable insight from the local brewery's layout, but she'd lingered in the back of his mind. All plans to leave for London were washed away when the rain wreaked havoc on the streets. They were stuck here. With her.

"What are you going to do about it?" Cal asked with his typical cheer. "Perhaps this is your chance to grovel—a lot. I would recommend the most impressive level of groveling ever seen by man or beast. A grovel worthy of such a damn spectacular bosom."

"I owe her an apology at the very least." The idea took hold, and he held tight to the hope it brought. His behavior during those early years after inheriting had provided ample reasons to make amends to several people since. If she forgave him, it would be one more piece of absolution toward his pile of sins. If nothing else, he knew the act of apologizing and owning his actions would go a long way toward soothing the painful memories he carried.

"Lucky dog. You have the opportunity to tell a woman

you were a drunken idiot." A hiccup punctuated Cal's teasing.

"Back then I was a drunken idiot with alarming frequency."

"You're sober as a judge now. At least one of us is. In those days, we viewed too many nights through the bottom of a bottle." He held up the whisky as if making a point. "Haven't imbibed like this in a long time."

True. It had been quite a while since he'd seen Cal like this. "I'll have tae wait for an opportunity, I suppose." Ethan held out a hand for the bottle. "Do you think you've had enough? You'll hate your head in the morning."

With a sigh, Cal pushed the bottle of whisky toward Ethan with one finger. "Fine. You may have to run her to ground and make an opportunity. The onus falls on you, my friend. You made her the laughingstock of London. When you tell everyone a girl is dull as dishwater, don't expect a great deal of goodwill from that corner."

"I never said she was dull. I said—"

Calvin raised his glass in the air as if reciting Shakespeare. "*Witless, with nothing to offer but a dowry and a passably pretty face. She's a Paper Doll Princess. Dress her up, then carry her in your pocket—along with the fortune you gained in exchange for a lifetime of boredom.*" Amber liquid sloshed over the rim onto the table. Cal grimaced at the mess and shoved his glass aside. "You, my friend, were a bit of a prick."

Studying his long legs and dirty boots, Ethan winced. "Aye, I was." There had been a clear moment after he'd said those awful words when regret had churned in his belly, threatening to eject the drinks he'd imbibed. Even as he'd tried to backtrack, to call back the foolish words spoken to the men he'd been trying so hard to impress, those so-called friends became wagging tongues. It wasn't long before the gossip rags got wind of his cruelty. The nickname spread faster than anyone could have predicted. Highlights papered shop windows with damning ink sketches. Each morning, as Lady Charlotte's visage appeared in unflattering cartoons, society lapped up every drop of the scandal over tea and toast. And Ethan? The men thought him hilarious, demanding more of his biting commentary. That night had set the stage for both his and Lady Charlotte's reputations, neither of them liking their new role.

The irony lay in the fact that Lady Charlotte had been the perfect debutante. The expectations of her station were clear, and she lived up to them. Set on a course to find a husband, she'd been ready to do her duty to her family and further the blue-blooded aristocratic values of England. God save the king, and all that.

He'd needed her money. The new title had come with crippling debt, and like a young fool, he'd seen her as an easy way to save the estate. It was a cold comfort that he hadn't fallen into the trap of being a full-fledged fortune hunter. Any old fortune wouldn't do—he wanted to like his wife, to desire her. In a perfect world, he'd have a love match like his parents, with a conveniently hefty dowry.

Licking a drop of ale from his lip, Ethan scanned the ceiling. She was up there somewhere, injured, but would be mad as a wet cat if he showed up to check on her. How had the doctor's visit gone? It would take a physician with a steady hand to avoid a scar like the jagged silvery-white line on Ethan's shoulder. For certain, her coachman needed a doctor who would try his damnedest to keep the leg intact. Unlike that drunkard who'd been there after Ethan's accident. That hack had taken his friend and passenger Connor's limb with no more thought than he'd give to carving a Christmas ham.

Although he'd made sure the rescue team brought her trunk to her room, the need to do more nagged at him. But then, many things about Lady Charlotte Wentworth lingered in his brain.

The memory of the first time he'd seen her hadn't faded despite the years. One look at those dark eyes across a dance floor, and he'd proudly scribbled his new title on her dance card at every gathering after that. On several occasions during the following weeks, he'd brought flowers to her home during calling hours, like a proper suitor. But when they spoke outside the confines of a waltz, she lacked the fire he'd witnessed today. Little by little, that initial attraction waned, replaced by disillusionment.

The day after the prime minister was shot, there was that moment when she thanked him for getting her away from the hordes of people clogging the roads. Especially given their previous interactions, he would have expected her to be a shaken mess. Instead, she kept her head in the face of a dangerous mob and worked with him to get out of there. That cool determination made him think perhaps there was more to her. He hoped to peel back those layers and know her better, and his attraction flared back to life.

When he called on her the next day, her father put an end to Ethan's intentions. The earl didn't mince words. Ethan wasn't good enough for the likes of her, and his advances weren't welcomed by Lady Charlotte or her father. The earl called him a fortune hunter to his face—something for which he had no rebuttal. The bouquet he'd brought for Lady Charlotte that morning was much appreciated by the fruit seller on the corner.

If he gave her flowers now, she would probably try to shove them down his gullet.

"You're thinking about her, aren't you? Lord, you're a case. If you could see your expression, you'd laugh." Even drunk, Cal knew him too well. It wasn't only Lady Charlotte in his head now, but the events of the past that haunted him.

The circle of lads he'd called friends had encouraged more foolishness, until that awful evening when he'd agreed to race, wanting to show off for his visiting clansman, Connor. They were drunk. Of course they were. That race and the subsequent accident had nearly killed Connor. All because of Ethan's poor judgment. The same poor judgment that had destroyed Lady Charlotte's Season. Shame wrapped around him with the memories, and Ethan sighed, accepting the emotion as his due. All he wanted to do was go enjoy his quiet room and read a book. "You've dipped a wee bit deep today, aye? Maybe you should go upstairs and rest before dinner."

"Yes, I'm drunk. Drunkety-drunk-drunk. But at least I'm not pouting over a woman." Cal stifled a belch behind a fist, broke wind, then giggled. The Drunk's Trifecta.

Drunkety-drunk-drunk Cal spoke the truth.

Years ago Ethan had been a shallow arse, more concerned with Lady Charlotte's bosom than with her brains, and too lazy to discover what was beneath her faux calm. Moments ago, those same breasts had been a topic of conversation, so perhaps he was a lost cause as a human being. These past five years of living like a monk might have been for naught, because he clearly hadn't become a better person.

Rubbing his hands over his face, Ethan sighed. "Come along, Cal. Let's pour you into your bed. Have a lie-down. Perhaps you'll be sober enough by dinner."

Patrick had awakened long enough for Darling to force one of the concoctions left by the doctor into him, then passed out again.

The warm coziness of Lottie's bedroom had felt comfortable for only a short time after Lottie's trunks arrived. With Darling at Patrick's bedside, the solitude of Lottie's room just felt empty. Noise, chaos, and watching her fellow travelers with a sense of anonymity sounded like the ideal distraction.

Alas, Dame Good Fortune didn't smile on her tonight. There would be no anonymity. As soon as she entered the taproom, Lord Amesbury met her eyes over the rim of his glass, sparking a battle of wills to see who would look away first. Lottie's cheeks warmed, but she held his gaze until reaching a small table, then coolly gave him her back. He could decide if she'd given him the cut direct. Hint—yes.

A movement caught her attention, and Lottie checked the reflection in the window. That distinctive silhouette stood out whether in a drawing room or a taproom. Especially in a drawing room. Here, with the dark wood-planked walls and floor, he appeared to lurk like a storybook giant in his cave. Or an ogre. And he was coming her way.

When they'd first met, he'd been friendly, admiring, even flirtatious. She distinctly remembered a conversation with Father about the young viscount, instigated by Amesbury's heated gaze during their first waltz. Tonight, the weight of his inspection skittered across the back of her neck. The almost-forgotten memory of that dance came alive with ghostlike brushes on her waist and hand where he'd held her a hair closer than entirely appropriate. That lecture from her father had been a humiliating hour of chastisements regarding inappropriate advances and how to bring an *acceptable* man up to scratch.

She hadn't pulled away during that waltz, for fear of losing his attention. But those days of cowering and biting her tongue were over. She would, however, ignore him with studious ferocity.

That worked for all of thirty seconds before he blocked the weak evening light streaming through the rear windows. Lord Amesbury took a seat across the table. "How are you feeling?"

Mrs. Pringle bustled to their table and set a large bowl before Lottie. A hunk of bread rested atop soup, already soaking up the rich juices. Plunking a tankard of ale on the table, Mrs. Pringle gave them a distracted nod, then moved on to another customer.

"I don't recall asking you to join me."

A gentleman would not linger where he wasn't welcome. He grinned and stayed put. Not that she should expect any less. Amesbury propped his elbows on the table. "You're different. In a good way."

"Does unbridled hatred put roses in my cheeks?"

He laughed instead of showing any signs of contrition under her withering look. "See? That's what I'm talkin' about. You're feistier now, lass, an' that's the truth."

"I'm the same woman you courted, then shamed. Not that it matters. Your high regard no longer concerns me." Lottie took a dainty nibble of the bread and nearly moaned. The yeasty bread's crisp crust stood up to the soup juices, as well as a generous slathering of butter. Heaven.

Amesbury swiped the tankard in front of her, then

took a long drink before setting it down again, holding her gaze.

She narrowed her eyes. "Rude. Can't you pretend to be a gentleman for five minutes?"

"You're not the first tae wonder that. From what I understand, I'm one step away from being an outright barbarian. Or at least, I was." He shrugged. "I considered showing up at Almack's with my face painted blue like my Pict ancestors. Put an end tae all the speculation. Alas"—he patted his pockets—"fresh out of woad."

The mental image almost made her smile, despite his general obnoxiousness. It was time to take control of this tête-à-tête.

"Since you've intruded on my meal, perhaps we should keep our conversation to safe topics, such as the lovely weather we're having," she said, gesturing with her spoon toward the rain-splattered windows at the front and rear of the main room. "Or we could sit in silence before going our separate ways, never to acknowledge each other's presence again. I'm sure you can guess *my* preference."

Idiot. He was a blooming idiot. Those noble intentions of issuing an eloquent apology had flown from his head when he was faced with her confidently defiant cut direct. The woman he'd barely known years ago would never have done such a thing, which only sparked his fascination all over again. Commenting on how different she was brought that sharp mouth of hers back to the forefront, and he took perverse delight in her acerbic wit.

He needed to refocus on his reason for approaching her, but damn if her sarcastic commentary on the weather didn't make him smile.

Ethan glanced over Lady Charlotte's shoulder to the large diamond-paned window. The weather was absolute shite. He matched her mocking brow with one of his own. "All we need is some soggy sheep, and it would remind me of home." There. That was moderately amusing.

Lady Charlotte's gaze flitted to his before darting away. Every time she looked at him, he spent a heartbeat or two unscrambling his thoughts. Thick lashes stood out against the olive tan of her cheeks, their delicately curled tips casting shadows in the flickering lamplight. When she used those full lips to spear him with her refreshingly sharp words, it tied him in knots.

If she was as soft as she looked, it would be impossible to stop at one brush of a finger on uncovered skin. Ethan cleared his throat, stuffing down the mental image. Those thoughts belonged locked away with the younger, reckless part of himself. Lusting after a woman in a public tavern room was something Old Ethan would have done. Back then he'd have won the girl—at least for the night. Perhaps New Ethan had spent too many years without a woman in his bed and too many hours poring over account books. Once upon a time he'd poked fun at Lady Charlotte's exceptional manners. Now every day he tried to emulate that level of refinement.

And he failed.

The skin across her décolletage colored, probably with anger or frustration from stifling murderous impulses toward her unwanted dinner companion. The pink skin was bloody glorious. Ethan cleared his throat. Yes, he failed miserably.

"It's possible we'll have similar weather tomorrow," Lady Charlotte said, bringing him back from his thoughts.

It was time to apologize and leave before he made an utter arse of himself. "I think we have other things tae talk about beyond the weather?"

The minx cocked her head to the side, faking confusion. "My lord, I don't know what else we would discuss. As we established all those years ago, a true lady's conversational topics are limited by propriety, civility, and good breeding—all things you lack."

Whether she referred to his commoner upbringing or their scandal, the words elicited a wince. Essentially, Ethan had made her famous for being a dullard. A perfect lady, yes. Everything she ought to be, right down to her frilly bows and lace. Pretty but boring. Sitting before him now in a simple dress, with an eye swollen closed, furious over his very existence—it might be a flaw in his character that he preferred her this way.

"When we met, the problem wasn' you. I hope you realize that. It was my fault. All of it. If not for a solicitor showing up on my doorstep the year before we met, I'd still be a shepherd. I don' have your society training. I didn' know what tae do or expect in the *ton*. Some might argue that I still have no idea how tae go on."

An adorable wrinkle formed between her brows. "Continue. Groveling suits you."

"I'm sorry." It was on the tip of his tongue to throw some blame on her father. If the earl had fancied the match, things might have gone differently. Sure, his interest had only recently been reignited before that awful meeting with her father, but the earl had made sure Ethan knew better than to pursue a lady like her. That might have been what led to his drunken wallowing with his friends that night, but the immaturity driving those choices was entirely on Ethan. If he'd been good enough for an earl's daughter to begin with, this whole conversation would be moot. Bringing up that long-ago humiliation he'd endured in her father's library wouldn't solve anything.

She maintained eye contact while sipping from her tankard. "Thank you for your apology."

For a moment the plump curves of her mouth distracted him. With her bottom lip wet with ale, he would bet his last farthing the brew tasted better when drunk from her lips.

This dangerous path his thoughts insisted on traveling could lead only to trouble. Apology delivered. What she chose to do with it was her business. When he stood, a whiff of tangy citrus followed him. There could be no other possible source for the fresh scent except her. She smelled like his favorite desserts. Lemon ice. Lemon tart. Lady Charlotte. Delicious.

Yes, he had to go—now, before he made a bigger arse of himself.

"Why do you even care? Why make amends now?" she asked as if the question had come as an afterthought.

"I tried tae call on you after…well, before. You'd left Town already. I have much tae answer for, and this was my first opportunity tae say I'm sorry." He'd judged her harshly—and wrongly—years ago. The fact that within moments of her reentering his orbit she'd rekindled his interest made Ethan wonder if there might be something between them worth pursuing—assuming she ever stopped hating him.

On an impulse, Ethan brushed her cheek with a fingertip, needing one touch, however brief. All those years ago he couldn't stay away, and he couldn't seem to stay away now. Lady Charlotte jerked her head away. That was foolish of him. "I'm sorry. But I'm glad there's more tae you than I realized, Princess."

The next morning Lottie awoke to an eerie silence. No raindrops on the roof serenaded her. No splash of water hitting the windowpanes with gale-force winds invaded the sanctum of her bedchamber. The blustery storm had echoed her inner turmoil as she lay awake late into the night. Wiping the sleep from her eyes, she tried to muster enthusiasm for another day at this inn. There would be no traveling until a carriage arrived for Patrick from home. She wouldn't leave him alone, and Darling would probably revolt if she suggested such a thing. At least the weather would be a boon to a schedule that was already a disaster. Small comfort.

The first attempt at standing brought a groan. As a general rule, mornings were loathsome. Anyone who thought differently was touched in the head. With each step she discovered that the morning after a carriage accident was pure torture. Going through the motions of her morning ablutions, she had never been so grateful for simple garments in her life. Stockings, a shift, front-lacing stays, then a petticoat topped with another utilitarian gown.

Patrick's room was three doors down, tucked in the corner of the inn. A knock received no answer, but it was early. Opening the door a crack, she spotted Darling, right where she'd expected her to be. Her maid dozed in a chair beside Patrick's bed, their hands clasped in their sleep.

Lottie smiled. Darling made a wonderful nurse. Patrick couldn't be in better hands—figuratively or literally.

The picture they made—two former outcasts, comforting one another, warmed her heart. Darling had been the town's fallen woman, trading her favors to survive after her husband's death. Patrick had lived in the bottom of a bottle. Yet here they were, sober, happy, both respectably employed, even though Father would have kicked and screamed if he'd known about her hiring them at the time. Sometimes Father's habit of hiding from the world worked to her advantage. By the time he realized what was happening, Darling and Patrick had started over and shown themselves to be model employees.

Easing the door closed, Lottie shuffled toward her room and the stairs beyond, covering a yawn with one hand. Heavens, it was early.

Lord Amesbury stepped into the hallway. They stared at one another for a moment. He'd slept across the hall from her all night. Odd that she hadn't realized.

"Good morning. I'm checking the road conditions and having breakfast," he said a bit too cheerfully given the hour.

Lottie blinked. She didn't care what he did. She needed tea and food. In that order. Their conversation last night had kept her awake, so her natural instinct was to blame him for her exhaustion. To say as much would be telling, and the man didn't need that kind of encouragement. Deciding what to do with him was something that could wait until she'd had tea and she had both eyes open.

In the narrow stairwell, his shoulders dominated the space. "Could you be any wider?" she grumbled. His answering laugh was a low rumble she felt in the air more than heard. Wouldn't it be her luck that he was one of those awful people who were happy in the morning. The mind. It boggled.

The main taproom had filled with patrons and residents for the breakfast service. Through the window, the stable yard looked to be mucky but passable. A large portion of sky shone a bright, clear, beautiful blue that seemed to bully the soggy clouds into a retreat. Lottie searched the room for an unoccupied table, trying to ignore the obnoxiously perky man beside her. He hummed a tune and greeted the patrons. It was unnatural.

"One moment, Lady Charlotte." Amesbury piled the dirty dishes from a narrow table near the wall onto the bar, then brushed a hand over the tabletop, sweeping crumbs to the floor. He held out a chair, waiting with a small smile on his lips.

She cocked her head, a bit puzzled at the casual gallantry. The highest-ranking man in the room had just done servant's work to find her a seat. Clearly, Lord Amesbury wasn't your run-of-the-mill aristocrat. But then, he wouldn't be, would he? During dinner he'd mentioned that before the title he'd been a shepherd. Granted, the last time she'd been in London, the details surrounding his inheritance hadn't been her focus, but she remembered his reception had been mixed.

A maid trotted by with her hands full of plates. "Tea please?" Lottie called. The servant answered with a cheerful smile. As she took her seat, Amesbury pushed the chair into place beneath her like a footman at a dinner party, then sat down across the table.

Lord Amesbury's hair, damp from his morning wash, curled about his head, with one lock falling almost into his eye. She had to clench her hands to stop from brushing it off his forehead. It clearly didn't annoy him as much as it did her, but really—he needed to push that curl out of his face, and she needed tea before her head exploded from dealing with people this early.

When the maid returned with a pot of magical dark brew, Lottie nearly wept in gratitude. After pouring the drink into an earthenware mug, she added sugar and blew on the surface before taking her first sip.

"If you don' mind, I'll take a cup—"

Lottie cut him off by holding one finger in the air. She mutely filled another mug, nudged it his way, then raised the finger again to signal silence.

Tea. She needed tea.

He laughed at her. Not a big belly laugh, but a muffled sort of snort he didn't even try to hide.

When she added sugar to her second cup, he asked, "Is it safe tae speak now?"

"I don't know. Will you continue to be unreasonably chipper?" His responding grin made no promises, so she ignored him and refocused on the tea.

Lottie always loved the second cup more. It was the perfect temperature to drink straightaway, without waiting. The first cup gave her life, but the second was pure gratuitous indulgence. Amesbury's apology last night may have stolen her sleep, but she'd be damned if he stole her tea bliss too.

Mrs. Pringle brought a platter of food and two plates. The older woman grimaced as she looked Lottie over. "How are you feeling this morning, your ladyship?"

"Cranky," Lord Amesbury answered for her.

The glare Lottie shot at him made her wince when her bruised eye protested the movement. "Perfectly fine, Mrs. Pringle. I thought I'd walk into the village later. Where can I purchase more of the lemon bath oil you provided yesterday?"

Mrs. Pringle beamed. "My sister makes the oil, and many others besides. Go to High Street and look for the shop's blue door."

"Well then, I'll explore High Street after I break my fast. Thank you."

Lord Amesbury served himself seconds and handed her a plate of food as Lord Carlyle sauntered to their table. "Well, aren't we cozy? Lady Charlotte, you're looking better than expected." Carlyle lounged against the wall behind Amesbury's chair and stole a sausage from his friend's plate.

"Get your own breakfast, thief. An' leave her alone. She's no' chatty in the morning." Amesbury stabbed at Lord Carlyle's hand with his fork but wasn't quick enough to save the second sausage.

Carlyle grinned at her around a mouthful of stolen goods. "Let me guess. You feel as if you've been thrown in a sack and beaten with a cricket bat?"

Lottie couldn't help laughing. "Something like that. I'll mend. Thankfully, so will my coachman."

"He'll keep the leg?" Amesbury asked.

"Yes. He's tremendously lucky. The doctor is very skilled, as Mrs. Pringle said." Carlyle eyed the empty platter in the middle of the table. "You may have mine if you aren't too picky about from whom you steal." Lottie pushed her plate in his direction. The level of pain in her body seemed to be impacting her appetite. Watching the friends interact was utterly fascinating, though. It revealed a playful side of Lord Amesbury. Yesterday's confidence, then apology, and this morning's teasing conversation with his friend made her wonder how many more layers there were to the man. He wasn't the one-dimensional villain she remembered.

Lord Carlyle grinned. "My endless thanks, Lady Charlotte. Mac, I like her."

Despite the fact that he somehow managed to be even more animated than Amesbury at this ungodly hour, it was difficult not to like Lord Carlyle in return. Lottie smirked when Lord Amesbury rolled his eyes.

That they were sitting here, not only civil but nearly friendly, struck her as strange. Last night's apology must have been working on her years of animosity while she slept, because instead of hiding behind her raised hackles, she'd found this breakfast—well, nearly enjoyable. Though it pained her to say it, she might not hate the man as much as she thought. Trust him? No. Genuinely like and esteem him? A laughable concept. But maybe she didn't wish him to perdition.

In her defense, it had been a great apology.

"Eat quickly, Cal. We should get on the road. Lady Charlotte, thank you for the pleasure of your company this morning. I hope your coachman makes a full recovery and that you're back tae fighting form soon. Perhaps we will meet in London."

Lord Amesbury sketched a shallow bow while Lord Carlyle finished the last bite from her plate. Carlyle bowed over her hand. "You are a gem, Lady Charlotte. Thank you for breakfast. Might I ask a small favor? Don't forgive him too quickly. Watching him grovel is fun."

Chapter Five

As Lottie rattled into Town in one of her father's older traveling coaches, her teeth knocked together, and she bit the tip of her tongue when the coach hit a hole in the cobblestone street.

Darling held tight to a leather strap overhead, looking slightly green around the gills. "If it's this bad for us, how is poor Patrick faring?"

"I gave him the well-sprung carriage, but I'm sure the journey will be hard. His recuperation will be easier at home, though. You gave him the laudanum?"

"Yes. Not that he'll use it. But one can hope." Darling craned her neck to see out the dusty window. "Are we close to your godmother's house?"

"I think so. Although after so long delayed at the inn, just the fact we are in London means we're close." The week had felt like a year. She and Darling had spent their days with Patrick, trying to keep his spirits high while they waited for help from home. His injury was too serious to risk placing him in the hands of strangers in a hired carriage. At least tending to his care had given her something to focus on besides her encounter with Lord Amesbury and the general dread she held for returning to London.

Town was so stifling—and she wasn't used to those restrictions anymore. In the country, a maid was sufficient companionship for sticklers of propriety. But London society saw and judged everything. They gossiped behind chicken-skin fans, eviscerating the next generation over tea, living in the hope that they'd be the first to share the latest tale of misfortune—assuming the misfortune belonged to someone else.

Lottie's days of wandering about as a perfectly capable unsupervised adult were behind her. Lady Agatha would fulfill the role of chaperone through the turbulent waters of the *ton* and with any luck would stomp on Lottie's toes to prevent improper things such as conversations about the works of Mary Wollstonecraft.

Outside the window, the buildings transitioned from sporadic to claustrophobic, one structure built atop another. She probably wouldn't want to wander in London anyway. Only a fool would attempt to navigate these streets alone.

"The town house in Berkeley Square is under construction at the moment. Aunt Agatha leased a home not far away, on Hill Street. The architect assures her they'll finish before winter, but we shall see."

At last, the carriage drew up to the address from Agatha's most recent missive. An ancient man so thin he resembled a walking cadaver answered the door. He stared with a silent, unblinking stillness until Lottie handed him her card.

The butler bowed his head in acknowledgment, no movement wasted. "I am Dawson, milady. Lady Dalrymple awaits you in the front drawing room."

"Thank you, Dawson." Their steps echoed across the tile floor of the foyer, the sound filling the cavernous space before fading into the plasterwork on the ceiling. In the comfortable drawing room, her walking boots sank into the plush carpet.

"I see the prodigal child has returned at last," Agatha said from her chair by the window.

"If you're not serving fatted calf for dinner, I shall be bitterly disappointed." Lottie kissed her godmother's powdered cheek. Although she was still a striking woman, the lines in her face had deepened with time. Agatha had never been beautiful in the classic sense, but then, Lottie loved that about her. Too tall, too thin, and too angular for the popular definition of beauty, yet even at her age, she continued to influence both fashion and society. Lottie's honorary aunt was distinctive and memorable—which was better than beautiful.

"Fatted calf?" The older woman raised an imperious brow. "I am sure we could have tracked down a bit of plump livestock to celebrate your return, had I known to expect you today. I thought you would be here days ago. Instead, here I sat, wasting away for want of a word from you."

"Yes, Auntie, I can see you're wallowing in the depths of despair at the idea of my demise on the road." Lottie gestured to the tin of sweets next to the chair. "All of my best wallowing requires biscuits too."

"Do not distract me with your impertinence. Tell me where you were." Two thumps of her cane on the carpet punctuated the demand.

Lottie settled across from her godmother. The sunlight through the window illuminated the silvery curls peeking from beneath Agatha's black lace cap. "I sent word after my initial post regarding the accident. Some of our fellow travelers ended up staying past their intended departures due to the rain. It must have delayed the post as well."

"God does tend to let his wrath loose on the countryside. Yet another reason I prefer to stay in London. Regardless, it is good to see you, child. I assume you met Dawson on the way in."

"Yes. Do we have guards at night to ward off the grave robbers? I imagine the body snatchers have been eyeing him for some time. He must be as old as Methuselah."

Agatha's bark of laughter had a rusty quality to it. "Mock all you like, but he is frightfully competent at his post."

"He would have to be. After hundreds of years of experience, there would be little new you could throw at him. Wherever did you find him? And more importantly, does Stemson know you're being served tea by another man?"

Agatha leveled a look at her. "Stemson nearly had apoplexy when I discussed moving the entire staff to this residence. One would think the architectural firm staffed highwaymen and brigands, the way he carried on. No, he insisted his place was at his post, keeping an eagle eye on the workmen, even though they came with the highest recommendations." She offered Lottie the tin of biscuits, then waited while she selected one. "Dawson has been a satisfactory addition to my home. This house was leased with staff in place, all carefully vetted by a hiring agency. You do remember the purpose of a hiring agency, do you not? I do not search the gutters for my help."

Lottie rolled her eyes at the old refrain. Her estate was filled with good people, but some of them had needed a second chance. Patrick and Darling were only two of many she'd employed, contracted, and otherwise offered an opportunity to prove to everyone—and themselves—that their lives could be better. People sometimes needed a bit of guidance, that was all. "We have this discussion every time I write about hiring a new staff member. My servants are loyal and appreciate the opportunity to make an honest living. Each of them has redeemed themselves and proven my instinct to help them correct."

Agatha offered a distinct harrumph in reply.

As if on cue, a maid arrived with a rolling tea cart piled high with sweet and savory offerings. Lottie smiled her thanks to the servant, pouring at Agatha's nod.

"Remind me again, girl. Were you in a carriage accident or robbed by highwaymen?"

"Our carriage crashed, as you know. How would highwaymen possibly play into it?" Lottie handed a dainty cup and saucer to her godmother, then self-consciously touched her tender black eye, where shades of green and yellow had lingered that morning.

Agatha placed the tea on the small table beside her, settled her hands on the brass top of her cane, then began an exaggerated examination from the top of Lottie's head to her boots. "It was the only explanation I could think of to explain that ghastly garment you are wearing. I assumed a generous chambermaid lent it to you. Perhaps you have also employed her?"

Lottie's shoulders shook with silent laughter, sending ripples through her teacup. "I'll have you know this dress has served me well for almost five years. I think I even delivered a calf in it once."

"Oh, mercy." Agatha twitched the edge of her skirt farther away from Lottie's hem, despite the several feet between their chairs.

As she shook her head at her aunt's antics, a wave of comfort washed over Lottie. Although the years showed in her appearance, Agatha remained a force of nature. Mother used to say that thunder, lightning, hurricanes, and Lady Agatha were all beyond the control of men.

"Are the workmen on schedule at your house?"

"That seems to depend on the day and with whom you are speaking. I want to be in my own bed for Christmas, but here we are, entering September already. The construction could have waited had I known this would be the year you finally decided to show your face again."

Knowing her presence inconvenienced Agatha churned waves of guilt. "The timing was not my decision, I'm afraid. I'm only doing this because Father decided to make a match with the Earl of Danby's son and I refused. I have until November to find an acceptable husband, or I will be forced to accept Mr. Montague."

Father couldn't leave his library to fix the tenants' roofs or myriad other issues, but her marital status was suddenly more than he could tolerate. Lottie swiped two fingers between her brows, smoothing all sign of emotion from her forehead. Mother always warned about such displays causing lines.

"The Earl of Danby's youngest? Rumor says he is handsome. But those are not the only rumors about him, my love. Be careful with that one. We will find a better match. You were wise to come to London."

"I hope you're right. Father promised an estate of my own in addition to my dowry. Let's pray that is incentive enough to overcome my past." With her own property, the decisions she made, the improvements and modernizations, would benefit the lives of *her* tenants. She'd be making a difference, proving once and for all that she wasn't the vapid Paper Doll Princess anymore.

"You were a scandal, my darling girl. Unlike some of these debutantes, who are witless as a sack of hair, you were innocent of wrongdoing. In these seven years, countless scandals have come and gone," Agatha said.

"Whether they love me or loathe me, I'm prepared to face the *ton* again."

"Your mother would be proud of that decision." They shared a moment of silence at the mention of the woman Agatha had thought of as a daughter. Agatha sighed, then clapped her hands once, as if to scare away the glum mood. "We can catch up while I show you to your room. You look ready to drop, my dear."

The town house dated from the century before, standing tall, elegant, and narrow, like so many others on the street. The houses stood in a line like beautifully decorated toy soldiers, ready for inspection by the king.

Inside the home, carved woodwork framed brilliant silk-covered walls, making each room colorful and opulent. In her bedroom, a canopied bed dominated one wall. It would be hard not to be content here.

"I apologize for the uninspiring view of the stonework on the house across the way. But let us count our blessings. We have a corner lot, and any space in Town is precious." Agatha parted the drapes, letting natural light flood the bedroom.

"This layer of sheer curtains for privacy is rather ingenious." Lottie fingered the delicate cream fabric. "The effect is so welcoming with the sun lending a glow to the blue walls."

Agatha smiled, but looked a bit weary. "Without them you could see right into the house next door. Lord knows what things you might witness when looking in the windows of Lord Carlyle's home. Do you remember him? He is quite fashionable despite his reprobate father's reputation."

"I can only imagine the kinds of bachelor goings-on." Lottie peered out the window just in case there was something to see. A few dark windows reflected the pattern of Aunt Agatha's stone walls. "Lord Carlyle was at the inn too. In fact, after the accident, he made certain of my comfort. He seemed an affable fellow."

"How remarkable. A handsome, eligible bachelor, right next door, with whom you experienced a harrowing journey." Agatha raised a brow.

Instead of pondering their charming neighbor, Lottie's mind wandered to the dark-haired friend of the eligible bachelor in question. The fickle one who apologized oh so neatly and had touched her cheek at dinner. That path of skin tingled at the memory.

She should have bitten his finger.

"Lord Carlyle is not the man for me. Whoever I marry cannot be prettier than I am. My ego won't allow it." She mustered a grin for Agatha's sake. Carlyle's appeal wasn't in question. Being so blasted cheerful, he would make a congenial spouse to anyone. The man could probably make friends with a wall if he tried. But she wasn't on the lookout for a love match, and good-natured Lord Carlyle deserved a real wife.

Lottie tested the thickness of the pillow on the padded seat. It would be perfect for drizzly autumn days with a book. Those would come soon, followed by winter winds that whipped down streets and through corridors of buildings. With any luck she'd be gone before then. "Thank you, again. I don't think I could do this without you."

Agatha leaned on her cane in a way that made Lottie wonder if her larger-than-life godmother's age was starting to have effects other than simply wrinkles in her skin. "To be honest, child, having a companion will be a joy. The years are exhausting and not as enjoyable without a similar mind with which to pass the time. I miss my Alfred." Her wistful sigh told its own story. "That man laughed at anything. I could not have asked for a better friend to spend the last forty years with. We shall do our best to find you a loving marriage as well."

Lottie shifted. In her experience, love meant ignoring everyone else around you—even your children—in favor of one person. Her father was proof that even in death the damage didn't end. He'd spent years grieving, to the detriment of everyone who relied on him. She had no interest in opening herself to that kind of pain. "My reasons for needing a husband are practical, not emotional."

Agatha appraised her with the direct intensity of a woman who knew she could say anything. Choosing to embrace tact, she changed the subject. "I am happy you are here now. It has been too long. Over the years, I hoped to see you at other events, if not the Season. When your friends married, I expected you would attend the weddings, yet you remained in the country."

"Those friendships have died off. I don't know if I'll see any of my old acquaintances while here, but if I do, it will no doubt be awkward. They're married, and here I am still hunting for a husband to suit my needs." At her age, most women donned a cap and settled into life with cats for company. Come to think of it, she would enjoy a cat.

It would be a good companion, since she had no intention of keeping a husband nearby for entertainment.

"And what needs are those?" Perched on the window seat in her black dress, Agatha eyed Lottie with interest, like a crow spotting a shiny object.

"The man I marry will be content to stay in London with his cronies and clubs and leave the management of the estate to me. Then, finally, I can work on building *my* future with *my* dowry. That money is rightfully—if not lawfully—mine. An apathetic spouse shouldn't be hard to find with a dowry that's nothing short of vulgar."

The silence stretched between them until Agatha finally said, "I trust you will not mind if I hope your plan fails spectacularly." Ah, there was the blunt Agatha she knew and loved. "There is no better gift in this world than to have a marriage based on affection and love. To that end, tomorrow we visit Madame Bouvier. Now that you're in Town, we must at least try to make you look as if you have not been traipsing through a cow field."

Chapter Six

Ethan spent a week at his estate, buried under the duties and responsibilities it took to keep Woodrest running smoothly. Account books needed updating, the hops required inspection after wet weather swept through the region, and plans for his new business enterprise were coming to a satisfying conclusion.

Joseph, the local pub's landlord, had the idea to create a beer using Woodrest's hops. From there, the concept had grown. A separate brewery would mean more jobs for the town, making a name for Woodrest, as well as opportunities to sell in London and the surrounding areas. The town would have a source of income and the ability to thrive outside the largesse of whomever the current viscount happened to be.

Woodrest and the tenants had lived with strict economies while he built the estate back into a profitable property. Years working the fields and tending livestock as a commoner had served him well, since it had taken the same hard work and skills to bring the estate back to health. Little by little, Woodrest began to see profits. Those precious funds were barely enough to split—with half invested in the Exchange, under the advisement of Cal's Midas touch, and the other half poured back into the estate. The brewery was a fresh start but also a risk he was sinking most of his money into. If it worked—and it had to work—the town would thrive, the estate would benefit, and he'd have made a difference for the better. If it failed... well. Best not think on that for too long.

This was everything he'd worked for since inheriting. It also meant ironing out mind-numbing contractual details, hiring laborers, and doing backbreaking work to clear the land for a new building.

Even with all that on his plate, the days since leaving the inn had consisted of near-constant thoughts of Lady Charlotte. He'd left her at that breakfast table at the Boar and Hound, yet she followed him everywhere, even into his sleep.

After the fifth night of bizarre dreams, Ethan would have volunteered to single-handedly construct the brewery if it meant working himself to the point of being able to sleep. If the dreams had all been erotic, he'd have had no complaints. But he wasn't that lucky.

The first night's dream starred Lady Charlotte, blooming with passion, as he filled his hands with every delicious inch of her. He'd gasped her name as he awoke, hard and needy. The next night, his carriage accident with Connor played on repeat. The dream had him stuck on the side of the road, holding his broken friend, while his da looked on disapprovingly and his mum wailed to the skies, asking how she'd failed as a mother.

Those two extreme dreamscapes mingled into a messy, angst-ridden nightly disaster he had to live through over and over. A week of this meant he slogged through the days foggy and cranky with exhaustion.

After dinner he fell asleep by the fireplace with a book open on his lap. In this dream, his teeth explored the delicate skin on Lady Charlotte's tanned neck with light nips, then soothing openmouthed kisses. Thready breaths feathered against his ears while busy hands roamed his back. Ethan raised his head, needing to see her eyes half-lidded with desire, but instead saw the black toe of an evening shoe beside her hair. And above that, a white stocking with silk knee breeches. Then other people surrounded them, his dead cousin's cronies hiding their laughing faces behind masquerade dominoes. One man's mask became the sneering face of Charlotte's father, chastising her for debasing herself with an upstart Scotsman who smelled of damp sheep. In his arms, Charlotte drew away, with an expression to match her father's.

The man beside the earl, leading the mocking crowd, could be easily recognized by the bleeding, empty pant leg that hung useless and tattered beside his other healthy limb.

"Lord Amesbury. Milord? Get up, Ethan. You'll wake the maids with your caterwauling."

"Connor?" Ethan winced against a bright lantern shining in his face.

"Aye. You're knackered, your lordship. Go on up tae bed." Connor jerked his head toward the library door and the dim hallway beyond.

Ethan rubbed his neck. Of course it was Connor. After the accident, his stubborn clansman had refused to accept guilt money and a cozy place back in their village on the Solway Firth. Instead, he'd taken a job managing Woodrest. Providing a livelihood was the least Ethan could do, since his drunken recklessness had nearly killed the man. At the time, they'd figured that if Ethan could learn to be a lord instead of a common shepherd, then Connor could learn how to be…whatever his job title was. Butler, head footman, valet, and general pain in the arse most days. As luck would have it, Connor excelled at both running a home and reminding Ethan that despite a title, he was still just a shepherd. It was only by dumb luck that he had a nicer house these days and more sheep.

Clapping a hand on Connor's shoulder, Ethan grumbled a "good night," then stumbled toward his chambers.

The next morning found Ethan holding his third cup of tea, staring out the window, waiting for the energy to face the day. The grounds of Woodrest were particularly beautiful as the trees put on their autumn dresses one by one. It would be a few weeks before all the leaves changed, but the first colors were appearing.

"Have ye gotten used tae it yet?" Connor's voice interrupted a period of staring out the window for God only knew how long.

Shaking his head to clear the brain fog, Ethan turned around. "Used tae what? The view?"

"All of it, I suppose. 'Tis a far cry from our village, aye?" The thump of Connor's gait was more uneven than usual as he swung a cylindrical bundle from beside his feet to the floor by the desk.

"Aye." The view outside was as green as their village on the Solway Firth. The cottage in which he'd spent his youth had been made of stone, just like Woodrest. But that was where the similarities ended. Although he stood as lord and master of a mansion on a hill, there were days when he longed for that small cottage. Ethan couldn't part with it. A family leased the property now, so he had the comfort of knowing someone else could grow up happy in that corner of Scotland.

"Yer mum and da would have been tickled tae see you runnin' this place. Ever think of that?" Connor said.

Ethan rolled his shoulders under the sudden weight he felt. "If Da were here, he'd be the viscount, not me." And Ethan would be grateful for it. If given the choice, he'd much rather be a viscount's son than hold the title himself. "He'd have done a better job of it. One year in London and he'd have had them all eating out of his hand. Da was the charmer." After eight years, Ethan remained an outsider. Perhaps his son or grandson would have the dubious distinction of finally finding acceptance in the *ton*.

"Ach, don' be so hard on yerself. Yer da was a sweet talker all right. But ye have skills of yer own. Yer makin' good changes here." Connor pulled a stack of letters from his pocket and set them on the desk. "These people are lucky three blokes died, so ye got the title. None of those Englishmen would be so hell-bent on building this brewery. They were busy spending more money than they had. Yer makin' honest work of it."

Ethan shot him a small smile while he sorted the mail. Maybe today would bring more scathing letters from peers damning him for sinking a noble title into trade. Investing in a venture he hoped to expand into a retail endeavor was raising eyebrows and ire.

He divided the correspondence into a stack regarding the estate, an invitation, and a lone personal envelope. A letter from Cal.

Part of Connor's statement needed correction. "Four.

Four men died. Two I'd never heard of—a father and son, second or third cousins I didn't know existed—my gran'da, and my da." His family tree was more of a spindly twig, with Ethan clinging to the end of it. No one underneath supporting him, and no one waiting to inherit should he die.

Changing the subject, Connor nudged the bundle he'd brought in with him. "What's this, then?"

"That must be the rug I ordered. It will fit here along the desk and reach the door."

There was a beat of silence while Connor stared at the rolled rug. "Which of the footmen told ye I fell while ye were gone?"

Shooting him a glance, Ethan said, "Doesn' matter which one told. You should have said something. Your leg doesn' like the hardwood floors."

"My leg likes them fine. It's my wood peg tha' has an issue with things." Connor smirked.

"I don' understand why you won' get fitted for a wooden leg, Connor. Why use a peg like some kind of bloody pirate?"

Connor's short huff of breath clued Ethan in to the fact that this conversation wouldn't go well. The earlier humor had disappeared at the mention of a prosthetic limb. Each time he'd brought up the subject in the past, Connor had shut him down, and Ethan didn't understand why.

"Pretendin' I have two legs doesn' make it true. A peg is good enough. It's better than the crutch, aye? Ye don' have tae cover the house in carpets. I'm no' an invalid, milord." He threw the title with as much force as a weapon.

Ethan shook his head. "This is your home. I don' want you falling."

Connor left the room without further comment.

Somehow, he'd bungled that spectacularly. Sighing, Ethan opened the letter from Cal.

Mac,

Lady Bartlesby is hosting a dinner this week. She insisted I encourage you to attend. Odd, considering your history with her husband. Perhaps he's had a change of heart? I promised I would send a note.

Behold! My note.

Come to London. Have dinner with that arse Lord Bartlesby. Meet my new neighbor.

Regards etc.,
Calvin

Ethan rubbed at his eyes. They burned with exhaustion despite the early hour.

Speak of the Devil and he appeareth. Sort of.

When alive, the heir to the title, Ethan's distant cousin Jerome, lived with his wife and son in London, surrounded by friends and accepted by society. Lord Bartlesby had been a particular friend. Understandably, the loss of not only Jerome but his son as well, only three months apart, had hit Lord Bartlesby hard. When Ethan met him in London, it hadn't gone well. Chance encounters since had been frigid at best, especially after Jerome's widow left London for the continent. What she was doing in Greece was anyone's guess, but that was where her widow's pension went. Since establishing the generous fund, he'd heard not a peep from her.

Maybe Cal had it right. Maybe Lord Bartlesby wanted to make amends. Enough time had passed; perhaps the man could move beyond his grief and accept that Ethan held the title instead of his beloved friend. One more ally in the *ton* certainly wouldn't hurt, especially with this new business venture. Getting Woodrest's ale into the finer houses of London would be a massive boon to sales when the brewery was ready.

If nothing else, Cal would be with him at this dinner, so the forked tongues in the room might behave. Cal's combination of influence and good looks tended to bring out the best in their peers. And perhaps a change of scenery would help with these damned dreams. Crossing to the doorway, he called, "Connor."

The Scotsman poked his head out of a room two doors down. "You bellowed?" The sarcasm, a sign that Connor's earlier annoyance was either dealt with or forgotten, made Ethan grin.

"Calvin demands I come tae London for a mysterious dinner party at the Bartlesbys'."

"Isn' he the one who kicked ye out when ye went tae his house two years ago?"

"And then had me thrown from a club the next month. Yes, he's a charming fellow. His wife sent an invitation."

"Intriguing. Will ye be wanting a valet?" Connor refused to wear livery, but he kept his clothes in sharp condition, ready to stand for an inspection that never came. Like Calvin, Connor openly despaired over Ethan's utter lack of concern with fashion.

"No' this time. You're in charge, as usual. Send a messenger should any issues arise. Have one of the lads saddle Ezra in an hour."

"Consider it done." Connor hollered for a footman to notify the stables of the master's departure. "Oh, and while yer galivanting about the city, try tae find a brewmaster, would ye? Martin took another offer. I just got word."

Damn and blast. Martin Peterson was the best brewmaster he'd found thus far. He finished his tea in one gulp and set the cup down with a clatter.

A few hours later, Ethan handed his hat to Cal's butler, Higgins, then sauntered down the hall to Cal's elegantly furnished library lined with books that hadn't been opened in half a century.

"Don' think you can summon me like your lackey. That said, here I am, as requested. Now what is this about?" Ethan leaned against the doorway, slapping a rhythm with his gloves on one thigh.

Cal looked up from the correspondence on his desk. "I'll try not to make it a habit. Have a seat." He gestured toward a leather chair.

"What is so special about this event that the Bartlesbys would open their doors tae me?"

"I don't know, Mac. I was more a messenger boy in this scenario. I received an invitation—"

"Because London is short on decent company these days."

"No, because I'm a handsome devil who is not only entertaining but highly decorative at any gathering." Cal waved in a servant with a refreshment cart, then poured himself a cup of coffee. He was midsip before he nodded toward the teapot to tell Ethan to get his own.

Ethan snorted in amusement. Thanking the maid, he made himself a cup of tea.

After swallowing his coffee, Cal picked up the conversation once more. "Also, yes, company is quite thin during these months. I happened upon our hostess in the park, where she mentioned dinner, then quizzed me about your whereabouts. It was the strangest thing."

Ethan settled deeper into his chair, stretching his legs out in front of him. "Why would she want me there? Her husband made his opinion of me quite clear." Sipping his tea, he tried to puzzle through it, but the situation didn't make sense. "Ach, I suppose we'll find out soon enough. Anything else of note since we last spoke?"

Calvin shrugged. "I received another letter from Emma. She detests school. Can hardly wait for her Season. The usual."

"A Season already? I still think of Emma with a dirt-scuffed face and tangled hair full of twigs from running through the woods."

"She'll make her bow at eighteen, but she's already wailing as if I'm holding her back. This is my last year to enjoy myself before I need to be the adult in the family and beat all the scoundrels off with a stick. Lord knows my father won't be of use there." Calvin sighed, taking a drink. "Lady Agatha Dalrymple leased the house across the lane. From what I hear, she's having some rather extensive remodeling done to her home. Now she's deigned to grace our neighborhood with her presence, instead of merely managing the next street over."

Ethan grinned. "Ah, Lady Agatha. I've always enjoyed her. Can't say the feeling is mutual, though. She's given me the cold shoulder since that blunder with Lady Charlotte. If I remember correctly, Lady Agatha is her godmother."

Cal wiggled his eyebrows, grinning at Ethan.

"Wait. Are you telling me she's next door? Lady Charlotte is the new neighbor?" A shiver ran up his spine, and he had no idea if it was excitement or instinct warning that everything was about to change.

"Unless you know of another buxom, dark-haired woman who looks as if she's gone a few rounds in a boxing ring, then yes." Cal's expression was far too smug.

Both men stared out the window at the gray stone facade of the house in question.

"London just got more interesting, aye?" The woman who'd been running circles through his thoughts had moved in across the lane from his best friend. What a small world. If he was given the opportunity to see her again, would his disturbing dreams die down? Perhaps his body was telling him there was unfinished business with the brunette. "Uh, you may choose tae read more into this, but brewery business may bring me tae Town more often before the Season. Connor informed me before I left that we need a new brewmaster."

"My guest room is available for your use, as always. Stay as long as you like. I enjoy the company. The Puppy shows up in the mornings to fence in the gallery and shuffle papers about on the desk over there. But once he leaves, I rattle around the place with only Higgins for conversation," Cal said.

"I can't believe you call Hardwick the Puppy. Some friend you are."

"It fits. You know how he's all legs and floppy feet? Puppy. Hardwick's a good sport. Besides, I pay his salary, so I can get away with it. The lad is wet behind the ears but solid." No doubt the young steward in charge of a small forest Cal refused to do anything with tolerated the name in exchange for a paycheck. "Between the two of you, I might not die of boredom before the Season."

"So what you're saying is, you keep me around for the entertainment value."

"Never doubt it, my friend."

Chapter Seven

"What a pleasure to see you again, Lady Charlotte." Lady Bartlesby greeted her like a long-lost friend while Lottie struggled to find a single memory of their hostess. "I heard someone saw you shopping with your godmother, so of course I couldn't resist inviting you to dine with us. Thank you for accepting my invitation on such short notice. I planned this dinner at the last minute, but it simply would not have been the same without you."

A sense of foreboding struck Lottie. Overly friendly strangers usually had an agenda of their own—and she was almost certain this woman was a stranger.

"Our numbers weigh heavily on the side of the gentlemen this evening. We ladies will have to soldier on while surrounded by some of the finest men in London." Lady Bartlesby winked.

"That may not be saying much with the lack of company

in Town. But keep an eye out, girl. Your dream wastrel may be present this evening," Agatha teased Lottie in a whisper.

In their hostess's warning that the numbers were uneven, she did not clarify that the only women present besides Lottie and Agatha were herself and a daughter of marriageable age. Naturally. Because why wouldn't she throw her innocent daughter into this den of hungry bachelors. Although as dens of hungry predators went, this was a small gathering. For that Lottie was thankful. Agatha stopped to greet an acquaintance while the lady of the house towed Lottie along in her wake.

"You'll remember Lord Bartlesby, of course." Her hostess gestured to an older gentleman with the beleaguered air of a man used to swallowing his opinions with copious libations. Lottie had never seen him before. The alcohol fumes surrounded him in a noxious perfume.

Lord Bartlesby gestured to a man at his side. "May I introduce Mr. Leopold Lurch, youngest son of Baron Ellery."

Mr. Lurch's eyes were a lovely shade of blue, with lush thick lashes sure to be the envy of any woman. A few excessively long, lonely strands of hair attempted to cover his shiny bald pate in a swirling pattern held in place with pomade. His nose had an unfortunate upward tilt at the tip, giving him an undeniably porcine air, with perpetually flared nostrils. Mr. Lurch's eyes were sharp, leaving Lottie with the feeling she'd already been scrutinized and found wanting. A strong odor of onions came from him as he muttered something about being charmed and kissed the air above her fingers. Thank goodness for evening gloves.

When Lottie and her hostess turned away, Lady Bartlesby

leaned close. "Quite a decent catch, if you ignore the nose. Good family."

There was bitter truth in Agatha's earlier teasing. Could she stomach adding Mr. Lurch to her list of potential matches? This wasn't about attraction. A husband who would be content to leave her in the country in charge of the daily management was just as likely to resemble a farm animal as not. Besides, his padded, sloped shoulders lacked the blunt-force impact on her senses Lord Amesbury caused, which could only be a good thing.

Why would she think of *him* at a moment like this? There should be no comparison.

A footman opened the door behind them, and Lottie's earlier sense of foreboding returned with force. As if her wandering thoughts had summoned him, Lord Amesbury stood in the doorway in evening dress beside Lord Carlyle. Lord Bartlesby crossed the room to shake Carlyle's hand, then greeted Amesbury with a stiff nod.

Her unease deepened when their hostess joined the men at the doorway, looking awfully pleased with herself, eyes darting between Amesbury and Lottie. This was a setup from the beginning.

Of course. It made sense now.

As the first hostess to get the Paper Doll Princess and Lord Amesbury in the same room—at her table, no less—Lady Bartlesby held the trump card of hot gossip. Their hostess winked at Lottie with a glittering diamond-hard smile, her earlier friendly facade nowhere in sight.

For a moment, Lottie was that awkward debutante again—a young woman who chose to run from London rather than endure the laughter of her peers. The gossips, led by tonight's hostess, would feast for weeks on the loaded silence that fell over the room as the guests realized what was happening.

Possible plans of action presented themselves. Leaving immediately, remaining silent, or simply pretending she wasn't bright enough to grasp the situation might work but smacked of cowardice. One by one she rejected her options until only a single clear path remained. This time, Lord Amesbury was a victim of the circumstance as much as she. That put them on the same side of this war, so to speak.

Amesbury and Aunt Agatha wore twin expressions with hard eyes and tight lips. He didn't exactly appear welcoming, but she'd have to act quickly and hope he played along.

As fast as the feeling of impotent panic arrived, it fled. This situation could be managed, thank you very much. She'd handled worse. If Lady Bartlesby intended to create drama, they would try their best to disappoint.

Donning her most enthusiastic smile, Lottie greeted the new arrivals with her hands held out, as if sure of her welcome. "Gentlemen, what a delight. I hadn't expected to see you again so soon."

Lord Carlyle bowed first. "Lovely as always, Lady Charlotte. I trust the rest of your trip to London was uneventful?"

"Thankfully, yes. I think we've all had enough dramatics to last for a good long while." She raised a brow meaningfully at the men. Behind her friendly mask, Lottie counted to three on each inhale and then three again for the exhale as she waited to see if the gentlemen would cooperate with her ruse. If they appeared to be friends, there would be nothing to gossip about, now would there? It was only conflict that fed the chatty cats, and she would *not* give their hostess any more fodder to share over tea tomorrow. Even if it meant allying herself for a time with a man who waffled between hero and villain.

All eyes were on them. Amesbury looked panicked for a moment, as if on stage with no idea of his lines. No doubt trying to stall, he kissed her glove, claiming the top of her hand with the pressure. No polite air kisses for him. "A pleasure, Lady Charlotte. Your injuries seem tae be healing nicely. How fares your coachman?"

"He's home in Westmorland recuperating, thank you for asking." Their friendly exchange needed to appear authentic, as if she were entirely at ease in his company, so Lottie slipped her hand into the crook of his elbow. He froze for an instant, then tucked her against his side. Gracious, there was a lot of him. The lapel of his coat sat at her eye level. Although his smile was easy when he spoke to her, his body was taut with tension. With any luck, they would appear as a united front as she addressed the room at large.

"On the way to London, my traveling party suffered a horrible accident with grave injury to my coachman," she explained to the other guests. "Lords Carlyle and Amesbury were staying at the nearest inn and lent their aid with the situation." Lottie patted Lord Amesbury's arm for good measure. He was a solid wall of muscle in an evening coat, radiating heat beside her. Something under her skin began to hum.

The top of her head would fit right under his chin. Everywhere he was hard, she was soft. Under her clenched fingers, the tendons of his arm felt like warm steel. Lottie's senses swam as she drank in his unique scent, with a trace of lemon reminiscent of her bath oil.

"Lady Charlotte is being modest." Amesbury's deep burr brought her back to the moment. "She sustained injuries yet bravely rode for help." The sharp lines of his face softened when he smiled, making a shallow dimple play peekaboo beside the corner of his mouth. Somehow, she hadn't noticed that dimple before now. But now she couldn't *unnotice* it.

"How fortunate that you were there! Travel is such a chore these days." Lady Bartlesby appeared nonplussed. The expression sent a thrill through Lottie. The lack of drama was undoubtedly a bitter disappointment, but it served her right.

A gong sounded, signaling the dinner hour. Lottie let Amesbury lead them into the dining room. Her skirts occasionally brushed against his pantaloons, making a sensual swishing sound of wool rubbing silk.

"Well done, love," Agatha whispered as she passed.

It wasn't a surprise to anyone that Lottie's and Amesbury's name cards were side by side on the long table, right in the middle, where everyone could keep an eye on their interaction. Now she and Amesbury needed to make it through dinner while convincing everyone present that no ill will remained between them.

For all her faults, Lady Bartlesby set an elegant table. The linens glowed in the candlelight as flickering flames danced off cut-crystal faceted stemware and gleaming silver.

Lord Amesbury held out a chair, ignoring a footman who stood at the ready to assist guests. The gesture was so similar to their breakfast at the inn when he'd cleared a table for her.

The inn where she'd told him to go to the devil after he hadn't remembered her.

Lottie stifled a sigh. She would need to set aside their differences this evening for the sake of preventing gossip. "Thank you, Lord Amesbury."

That didn't mean she had to like it.

Dining with the enemy was one of Dante's levels of hell, right? If not, it should be. This night might be one of the oddest social events he'd attended in months. Lord Bartlesby's greeting had been cool, and that was being generous. In Bartlesby's defense, he was three sheets to the wind and lucky to still be upright.

If this wasn't supposed to be an olive branch from his cousin's friend, then why invite him? The whole situation had baffled Ethan until he'd encountered his hostess. Once he spotted Lady Charlotte and the gleam in Lady Bartlesby's eye, it all made sense. Lady Bartlesby had seen an opportunity for gossip and taken it. Lord Bartlesby clearly didn't make decisions in this house beyond his bottle of port, so he'd gone along with the plan.

Ethan often received invitations to join men carousing after hours, but invitations to respectable dinner parties like this one were rarer. If tonight opened the doors to more events, that could mean building connections with peers who might eventually buy Woodrest Ale for their households. He thought of his host and the other guests as prospective customers—if he played his cards right. After dinner, when the men retired with their port, he would determine if that was realistic or if this evening was an utter waste of time.

Bartlesby jostled Ethan's shoulder, making him bump into Lady Charlotte. Their host continued on without apology, finding his seat at the end of the table without a backward glance. Lady Charlotte shot Ethan a look. Yes, their host was decidedly in his cups and rude. The chances of this invitation being a sign of goodwill dwindled.

It might have been a month after Ethan arrived in

London that he'd met Lord Bartlesby for the first time. Before London, he'd stayed at Woodrest to grapple with this new life he'd had thrust upon him.

The charming oddities of the estate had made him curious about those who'd lived there prior—this extended family who'd been out in the world all along but hadn't reestablished contact after his great-gran'da left for Scotland. Who were the people that had celebrated christenings, marriages, funerals, and holidays within the walls of his new home? Since none of them survived, he asked around to determine who was closest to Jerome and his son, George.

George's friends were happy to open a bottle and reminisce.

Jerome's closest mate, Bartlesby, made it clear in the first three minutes of their interview that while Ethan might not have heard of Jerome, Jerome had known exactly who Ethan was, and apparently had spoken about his relief that George was there to prevent the "mongrel shepherd" from dragging the Amesbury title through the muck. The meeting went downhill from there.

At the opposite end of the table, Lord Bartlesby signaled for another glass of wine while Lady Bartlesby pretended she didn't notice. The man would pickle himself from the inside out at this rate. As the footman poured, Bartlesby lifted his bloodshot gaze to meet Ethan's, and any fool could see that no part of this evening had been a gesture of peace. With a raised brow and a slight sneer, Bartlesby dismissed Ethan and began conversing with the guest to his left.

If indeed the purpose of his invitation had been to create gossip fodder for Lady Bartlesby's sewing circle, then Ethan had Lady Charlotte's quick thinking to thank for saving the day.

But it wasn't only her level head holding his attention now. The Lady Charlotte sitting beside him bore little resemblance to the quiet woman of his memory. This lass wouldn't have given a second glance to the immature man he'd been back then. Had she always been this way and been forced to remain silent? If so, that was nothing short of tragic. It was as if she'd debuted as an ink-sketch portrait but had come into her own now, painted over with the vivid oil hues of wit, opinion, and intelligence.

"The papers are calling the events in Manchester the Peterloo Massacre, and you think we should be proud of the actions taken? Are you utterly mad?" she was saying to Mr. Lurch on her right.

"It's a pun, milady. I hardly expect a woman of your refined sensibilities to grasp the connotations—"

"I grasp them quite capably, Mr. Lurch. My sex does not hinder reading comprehension." Lady Charlotte's eyes were bright, and the roses in her cheeks made her appear warm and soft—much like the deceptive camouflage nature often gave predators to lure their prey. Ethan curled his fingers into a fist. If he touched her hand in a show of support, she'd snap at him.

The conversation around the table petered out when the other guests noticed the unfolding conflict.

"I understand the newspapers are making a play on words with the Battle of Waterloo. I've been following the issues that started this rather closely, sir. The strife has been documented in the papers building to this tragedy." The muscles in Lady Charlotte's jaw twitched, and Ethan tried not to laugh, sure she was ready to weaponize her words. When she got angry at someone besides himself, it was rather fun to watch.

"Rebellious agitators." Mr. Lurch shrugged. "Industrial workers in Manchester. No one of note. Nothing that affects you."

"They are subjects of the crown, suffering from gross underrepresentation in our government. The last time a population rose up regarding their lack of representation, a war broke out and they formed a new nation. *America* is what happens when you don't listen to the people, Mr. Lurch."

Mr. Lurch spoke as he chewed, masticated meat showing with each word. "Leave politics to the men, Lady Charlotte. Although I concede you are the authority on satirical cartoons in this room, so I understand if you feel entitled to an opinion on Cruikshank's work." A titter of amusement rippled down the table. Ethan's fingers tightened around his fork. "Settle your head on the subject. Else you risk sounding like a revolutionary, yourself. Clearly Lady Agatha should restrict your access to anything beyond the society pages. One must guard a young lady's impressionable mind from too much information." Mr. Lurch returned to his meal as if he wasn't the biggest arse in Christendom.

"I doubt you'd recognize an impressionable mind if it bit you," Ethan said loudly enough for Mr. Lurch to glance over at him, but the other man didn't engage. Bartlesby shot him an acrid look of reproach. To lose favor with his host when he'd never had it to begin with was no loss at all. Perhaps he'd throw Ethan out of the house. Again. The lost potential social connections would be worth it if he could defend Lady Charlotte in this small way.

Bartlesby remained seated without calling for a footman. It would seem this dinner wouldn't be ending right away.

As the next course arrived, cueing the guests to shift

focus to their other seating partners, Lady Charlotte turned to him.

"After all that, it shouldn' be hard tae be the best dinner companion you've had this evening."

Lady Charlotte blinked, gaped for a second, then laughed.

In his chest, Ethan's heart stalled. A wide grin creased her cheeks. If she lived a happy life, she'd form permanent lines at those creases. The thought made Ethan smile in return. This woman, with her opinions and defense of the less fortunate masses, was breathtaking. And he—Ethan Ridley—had made her laugh.

Pure.

Magic.

She'd bewitched him.

Lottie dismissed Darling and tightened her dressing gown's sash. A silver tray on the vanity held her mother's brush, comb, and hand mirror set and the vial of lemon oil she'd acquired from Warwickshire. She tugged the brush through her long curls, wincing at her reflection in the mirror as she worked through a tangle. The black eye had faded entirely, and a doctor would visit tomorrow to remove the stitches. She cocked her head, then sighed. While not a great beauty, she wouldn't scare small children now that the bruises had faded. Things could be worse.

It wasn't her first black eye. She'd been a rambunctious child, whom Mother had tried to mold into submission during short visits to the schoolroom. Tonight, when she'd been deciding on a plan to control the events unfolding around her, Mother's training had come in handy. She'd pretended that Amesbury's presence hadn't affected her in the slightest—which couldn't be further from the truth. Or at least, she'd appeared unflappable until that awful conversation with Mr. Lurch ruined her plan to not make a scene.

Oh well. If tongues wagged tomorrow, it would be because she was well read on the current political climate and had opinions. Better that than everyone laughing because they thought her empty-headed.

Her heart rate doubled for a second or two at the memory of how Amesbury had looked at her this evening when she'd finally torn her attention from Mr. Lurch's condescending conversation. The expression on his face had sent shivers of…something along her limbs.

Then he'd spoken up in her defense. Just the one comment to Mr. Lurch—but that single sarcastic bon mot in solidarity had meant so much when she'd realized how far her heated conversation had carried down the table. Feeling the weight of everyone's attention, then turning to him and seeing an ally, of all things, was the oddest sort of comfort. He hadn't judged her for debating politics at a dinner party. Instead, he'd seemed to, well, enjoy her.

The rest of the dinner she'd ignored protocol and engaged Amesbury in conversation instead of swapping back to Mr. Lurch when the courses changed. They'd managed to maintain their charade of friendship, and by the end of the night it had almost felt real—if not for the occasional awkward lag in conversation when she remembered he wasn't a friend and was only playing along with the game she'd started.

Those periods between the pauses, though, when she

didn't check herself and simply let the conversation flow, were confusing. Laughing at the low-voiced comments he'd made for only her ears had been easy for a while. That ease confounded her, because if she were quite honest with herself, it shouldn't have been possible. Not with their history.

Now her head hurt, and she didn't know which way was up with that man. One week of social engagements in London and she was already exhausted by the pretense—reminding her once again that she wasn't cut out for this.

Enough. She set the brush back on the vanity and dug in the drawer for a ribbon.

These thoughts would spin through her brain all night if she let them.

Lottie subdued her curls into a plait, tying the end with the lone silk scrap she'd found. Snuffing the candle in its brass holder, she hoped the morning would bring clarity. If not clarity, then opportunities to handle the *ton* in a way that didn't mean partnering with a man she couldn't trust.

Hours later, in the light of morning, Lottie opened her eyes with a groan of frustration. Rested, she was not. A strong cup of tea, then a dose of the great outdoors was needed. Or rather, as close as she could get to the great outdoors while in London. The park would have to do.

The new riding habit's snug jacket hugged her waist, creating an hourglass shape different from the high waistlines that had been popular for years. Turning in front of the mirror, she thought the effect flattering despite the dark circles under her eyes. The new silhouette was worth every moment she'd spent at the modiste's shop.

At Madame Bouvier's, ladies enjoyed tea and gossip

and trusted the modiste to determine what garments best suited them. To achieve whatever plan Madame Bouvier created, one had to strip down to a chemise while being poked with pins by a stranger. Outside the fitting rooms, the shop had possessed the hushed, reverent air of a chapel for worshipping Chantilly lace and fine muslin.

After securing her hat at a jaunty angle, Lottie gathered her leather riding gloves and hurried out the door to meet a groom, who led two mounts down the lane from the mews. The horse he'd chosen for her, a leggy bay with intelligent eyes, sighed heavily and leaned into her hand when Lottie caressed the mare's soft nose. "Who's this beauty?"

"Dancer, milady." The groom tightened the girth strap one last time, then patted the mare's side.

"Nice to meet you, Dancer. Shall we explore a bit, pretty girl?" The horse lipped her glove, which Lottie took as permission to carry on. With the groom's help, she mounted and settled the swath of velvet skirt over her legs.

Oh, how she missed the ease of riding in breeches. When she returned to Westmorland, she'd spend the first day home astride a horse, flying over the fields. For now, she would count her blessings and try to appreciate the park in all its man-made, handcrafted beauty. The trees were beginning to hint at autumn, which would be breathtaking given time.

Settling deeper into the saddle, Lottie found her seat with Dancer's swaying stride. The clip-clop of the horse's hooves echoed off the stone houses as she made her way out of the neighborhood. The green expanse of the park opened up before her, and Dancer sidestepped in a move Lottie chose to interpret as enthusiasm. A glance over her shoulder showed the groom keeping pace behind her, giving Lottie the illusion of freedom. With a nod she signaled her intent, then let Dancer have her head. This early in the day the park was nearly empty, so an unladylike run would go unnoticed.

Dancer's gait was a dream. While the exhilaration of a hearty ride blew the lingering cobwebs from her brain, Lottie shuffled and reorganized recent events in her head, trying to align everything with her reasons for being in London.

As soon as that first new gown from Madame Bouvier had arrived, she'd stepped back into the role of society lady. Dinners, game nights, intimate gatherings of friends—every night there were new faces. And every night, she met new men who could, in theory, be husband candidates. Agatha's steady flow of invitations meant the pace wouldn't be slowing anytime soon.

All those matrimonial options, yet the man dominating her thoughts happened to be the one who'd sat beside her last night and defended her.

As she spurred Dancer to stretch her legs even more, the park became a blur.

Hell on a broomstick—as Darling would say. This trip to London was supposed to be about finding a husband, not about a giant Scotsman who'd already shown her his slimy underbelly. Never mind that the underbelly in question hadn't seemed slimy during their last several encounters.

She and Dancer were nearly upon another rider before his presence registered. With nimble feet, her mount veered around the man and his horse, snapping Lottie from her thoughts. Slowing Dancer, she reined around to call out, "Are you all right? I was woolgathering and didn't see you. I'm so sorry."

Nudging his mount closer, the man tipped his hat and met her with a grin. Sunlight lit him from the side, setting him aglow like a hero in a painting. Good Lord, he might be the most beautiful man she'd ever seen. Albeit a bit tired looking around the edges.

"I hope your ruminations were on good things, Lady Charlotte," he said.

Lottie paused, cocking her head as a ripple of disquiet rolled through her. "Do we know one another, sir?"

"In a way. Although we've not met before now. Someone pointed you out in the crowd on Bond Street earlier this week. Our families share ties, you see. Last I heard, our fathers want to deepen that connection. I'm the Earl of Danby's son James Montague. I believe you are the woman I'm planning to marry."

Chapter Eight

Two days after Lady Bartlesby's dinner, the gossip columns featured a small square of cramped text speculating on the relationship between the Paper Doll Princess and MacBrute. According to the snippet, given their history, it was noteworthy that they'd passed the remaining courses of the meal engrossed in conversation.

It seemed they were damned if they appeared friendly and damned if they hissed at each other like cats. Ethan dropped the newspaper on the breakfast table. At the sight of his full nickname alongside that awful moniker he'd given Lady Charlotte, a sharp pain pierced his temple. His appetite gone, he pushed his plate away.

Those damned nicknames. When he'd arrived in London, he'd discovered that while his size had been an asset back on the farm, in a ballroom he'd been an unpolished bumpkin towering over everyone. They'd named him MacBrute, and now everyone except Connor called him

Mac. It didn't usually bother him, but seeing it in this context left a sour taste in his mouth.

Lady Charlotte's father had particularly relished the name, beating Ethan's unworthiness home with well-placed verbal jabs, including his cousin Jerome's favorite, "mongrel shepherd."

At the time, he'd wanted to defend himself any way he could, and Ethan remembered holding himself back from spouting off on several things. Like informing the earl that English ladies preferred their men with thin necks and padded shoulders only in the ballroom. Behind closed doors, they seemed to appreciate a larger man-scape. Considering he'd been dealing with the father of a woman he'd only just decided to court in earnest, none of those arguments would have won favor. So he'd taken the verbal lashing, removed himself from the property, and then proceeded to get exceedingly drunk. That night his wounded pride and whisky tongue had created the Paper Doll Princess.

Apparently, it didn't matter that he'd left the philandering, racing, and drinking behind him. After one innocent dinner they were feeding the gossips again.

"Are you all right?" Cal asked, sipping his coffee.

"Aye. The rags got wind of Lady Charlotte's return tae society, and dinner the other night. They're already pairing us in the gossip columns. A small notice today, but we both know that won' last."

"Just like old times," Cal murmured. "So what's your plan?"

"I could woo the girl tae show the *ton* I was wrong about her appeal. This Paper Doll Princess nonsense will persist if we don' do something. I apologized, but I can't help wondering what else I can do."

"Or you could run away to the country and focus on the brewery."

"There's nothing saying I can't help make things right while I'm in Town finding a brewmaster, aye? If I can find one. The two gentlemen I spoke with yesterday with experience weren't keen on leaving London." Ethan picked up the newssheet to reread the short column. Lady Charlotte had tried so hard to minimize the gossip at the Bartlebys', and they'd still landed in the paper. "Could you do me a favor? Send a footman next door tae Lady Agatha's, and find out if our neighbors will be at an event this evening."

Servants knew everything, and anyone who thought differently wasn't connected to reality. Maybe talking to Lady Charlotte would shed some light on how he could help make this right. Their names being in the paper was proof that the damage he'd done years ago lingered.

Later that night, Ethan found a seat at a musicale. The delicate chair squeaked under him and he froze until he felt confident the spindly legs weren't going to break.

Two rows away, Lady Agatha loomed tall and regal in silk and black lace, with a black ostrich feather bobbing from her pale silver hair. Beside Lady Agatha, Lottie acknowledged him with a cool nod before facing the front of the room.

The olive-toned column of her neck distracted him throughout the performance, although she didn't look back again.

The gathering wasn't elaborate. A soprano of moderate talent finished warbling something in Italian, then curtsied to mild applause from the small audience. Their hostess rose, signaling an intermission.

Calvin had other plans this evening, so Ethan was on

his own in this crowd. Whatever they were up to, Cal and Adam "the Puppy" Hardwick were probably having a grand time.

During moments such as this, standing a head above the others in the room, Ethan was aware of how alone he was in London. Sure, there were friendly nods with inquiring smiles, but no one stepped forward to converse beyond an offhand greeting.

After eight years in society, he had yet to figure out how to be one of them. The rougher crowd from his younger days would accept him into their fold again, without a doubt. One of them invited him out each time he stayed in London for more than a day or two. But the man they wanted to carouse with and the man he chose to be these days were not the same.

He rolled his shoulders and ignored the curious looks his presence drew. Evening coats never fit comfortably, even when made by a reputable tailor. They hugged him until he felt constricted instead of fashionable, and collar points were so high as to be ridiculous. Properly tied cravats were an exercise in slowly choking to death. He fought the urge to tug at the length of linen for the umpteenth time as he scanned the room for Lady Charlotte. She'd vanished. Taking a cup of no doubt watered-down punch from a nearby footman, Ethan sought out the closest source of fresh air.

Beyond the double doors at the far end of the great hall, he found a balcony, which was not empty as he'd hoped. It was hard to complain, though, because there she was—stunning in an emerald gown. The moonlight and lamps created patches on her dress, illuminating the skin above the deep neckline he'd noticed and kept noticing since the evening's first aria. When she turned away from the house to lean on the balustrade, those lights cast her face in shadow.

Lady Charlotte hadn't done anything but stand on a balcony, seemingly in want of the same fresh air he desired, but his skin prickled with awareness. The silky gown slithering over her body was temptation itself, akin to the foliage covering Eve in the Garden of Eden. He'd never related to a serpent so much in his life. Much like the snake and Eve, Ethan wasn't worthy of her. But he couldn't deny he craved her attention anyway.

The door closed behind him with a low *snick*. Lady Charlotte snapped from her relaxed pose against the stone railing and whirled to face him. When Ethan stepped farther onto the balcony, her posture relaxed infinitesimally and he nearly smiled. Perhaps his presence wouldn't drive her away after all.

At a loss for words, he took a drink of the punch and nearly spit it out.

She settled against the balustrade, crossing her arms in front of her. "Not to your liking?"

Setting the glass aside on a windowsill, he wrinkled his nose. "'Tis three-quarters brandy, and the rest tastes like piss. Pardon my language, Lady Charlotte." God, she'd think him a crass idiot. And she'd be correct. "I don' drink strong spirits. Haven' for years." This bloody cravat grew tighter by the second. Running a finger between his throat and the linen, he pulled just enough to loosen the knot a tad.

Lady Charlotte shot him a glance but did not say anything for a long moment. "I suppose one of us should go in. There will be talk otherwise."

"I assume you've seen the papers." Ethan took a step closer until her citrus scent filled his head. "Thank you, by the way. For the way you handled things at the Bartlesbys'. They're talking anyway, but we both know it could be worse."

"Hmm. That we do."

Reminding her of their history like that was a dunderheaded move. Leaning back against the balustrade, he took a deep breath and forged ahead. This was why he'd come, after all. To speak with her, not just enjoy looking at her. "Is that how you prefer tae go on? In public, at least, pretend you don' hate me?" Her direct gaze led him to believe she was considering his words, but her expression wasn't exactly friendly. "I apologized back at the inn, and I meant it, lass. I'd like tae make this right between us if I can. Business has me in London. If there's anything I can do while I'm here, I'd like tae do it."

She cocked her head. "What business?"

The question caught him off guard. "I'm building a brewery. Someday all the fine houses in Town will drink Woodrest's ale, made from my estate's hops." Saying it out loud shot a burst of pride through him. "I accepted the Bartlesbys' invitation hoping tae make connections with future customers, but we both know how quickly that evening veered from plan."

She laughed softly, so he took that as encouragement to continue talking. "But before all that happens, I have tae find a decent brewmaster—which is proving tricky."

Lady Charlotte worried at her bottom lip with her teeth, and Ethan forgot the thread of conversation entirely for a moment. "I might know someone. Our brewery was famous in Westmorland once upon a time. The brewmaster left when things...changed a few years ago." A flutter in her voice implied that there was a story there.

"Last I heard, he'd moved to London. I can see if he's looking for a new position if you'd like."

Ethan blinked. Could it really be that simple? "That's incredibly generous of you, Lady Charlotte. If he'd be willing tae leave the city, it would certainly solve my problem." An awkward chuckle rose unbidden, and he shifted on his feet. "Is that your plan? Make me indebted tae you tae make things right between us?" He winced. "That was supposed tae be a jest, but I sound like an arse, don' I?"

She made a *little bit* motion with her thumb and finger. "A simple thank-you would have sufficed."

"Apologies, lass." He cut a small bow. "If you'd be so gracious as tae send along your former brewmaster's direction when you discover it, I'd be very grateful."

She rolled her eyes. "That's your idea of a simple thank-you?"

The air shifted between them at her teasing. Tension in his shoulders eased, and he found himself grinning. "Is there anything I can do in return? Help with while you're in Town? Speaking of, why are you in London, lass?"

"I suppose it will be public knowledge soon enough." She stared down at her fingers, then knotted them in a fist at her waist. "I'm looking to marry. If all goes well, I'll find someone suitable, set a wedding date for next year, and be home before the Season begins."

Calmly stating a plan of that magnitude might as well be waving a red flag at fate. Ethan couldn't stop a laugh. "Easy as that, aye? The romantic in you is showing."

"Who said anything about romance?" It was her turn to laugh, but the sound held sharp edges hinting at things he didn't understand. "Love does not last, Lord Amesbury. Even if an emotional attachment persists, life will find a way to interfere. My parents are proof of that."

Ethan cocked his head. That was unexpected. "If not love, then what about other reasons tae marry? Affection, companionship . . . lust?"

Her dark eyes widened and her breath caught.

The last word became a tangible thing between them, coming to life at the mere mention of its name. Lust. Possibly the only thing stronger than the history they shared.

His senses focused on her. The light and shadows playing on curves of soft flesh. The tang of lemon, tempting him to taste. Her exhale whooshed out, warming the air between their faces. She might be light-headed after holding her breath for so long, but it was proof that she was reacting to him. Pleasure bloomed in his chest. He wasn't alone in this attraction. At least, not in this moment.

"Don' you want someone tae woo you? Quote Byron like a fool? 'She walks in beauty,' et cetera. An appropriate quote for this evening." He smiled, daring a compliment. "You look lovely, but I'm sure you already know that."

"Are you trying to seduce me, Lord Amesbury?" The question retained some of her teasing tone, as if to downplay the shift between them.

He leaned an elbow on the stone balustrade, canting his body closer. This conversation wasn't going to plan at all, but he wasn't inclined to course correct. After several years of living like a monk, separating himself entirely from his old rakehell habits, it felt marvelous to flirt again. Especially with her. "If I attempted a seduction, I think we both know you'd find some way tae put me in my place." That drew a smile from her. "I admit, I'm curious tae hear your thoughts on marriage, lass. You seem tae have settled on a plan."

The way she met his eyes boldly, despite the flush spreading across her skin, shot straight through his blood. Arching a brow, she said, "You mentioned affection and lust. Neither is a prerequisite for marriage."

"That's a shame, lass. Being familiar with both, I'd hate for you tae miss out on them." Something compelled him to push her on the subject. Maybe it was his way of testing her boundaries to see if she'd relax with him.

The pink dusting her chest deepened. More proof that he wasn't the only one affected by the conversation. "I have other priorities, my lord."

"As much as I admire a woman with a plan, emotions have a habit of overriding our intentions, aye?"

"I wouldn't know." Her hands clasped the stone railing in front of her like a lifeline, but she didn't shy away from his gaze. If anything, she straightened her spine, standing with perfect posture in this new conversational minefield.

He wanted to make things right between them, but the possibility of more bloomed. If they acted on this tension, what would happen? It would cause a cascade of problems. Not the least of which was her intention to find a husband, when he wasn't the man for the job. Her father had already made that abundantly clear, even if Ethan were inclined toward matrimony. Not that he was disinclined, but his focus had to be on this new business venture—which wouldn't be helped by an extended stay in London, wooing a woman.

And yet those warnings came from his rational mind, and that part of his brain wasn't as compelling as the temptation pounding through every heartbeat thumping in his ears.

Lady Charlotte took one step toward him along the

banister, until her gown pooled in soft folds around his feet, and he never wanted to untangle himself. The swell of her breasts pressed against his arm and chest, making him wish there weren't so many layers between them. His voice came out rough when he said, "You'll recognize lust when it happens. And it might change your mind about those plans." The crest of his lips brushed against her skin. She quivered beneath his mouth, and he felt the movement vibrate through the minuscule space left between them. If he pursed his lips, it would be a kiss—a temptation from which he barely refrained. Instead, Ethan allowed himself the tiniest graze of her cheekbone with the tip of his nose.

Nuzzling. He'd just nuzzled her. Of all the ridiculous actions. And that was somehow the sexiest thing he'd done with a woman in years. She was unbelievably soft. The tip of her tongue wet her plump bottom lip, and it was all he could do to not take that as an invitation.

She moved first, turning her head until their noses touched. To kiss her—and God, how he wanted to do that—he'd only have to close that sliver of emptiness between them. Her warm breath, rich with wine, mingled with his, the scent making him feel as if he were tasting her already.

But without her permission, he'd not cross that threshold. Not when that list of reasons why this was a very bad idea awaited them on the other side of this moment. Not when she might soon remember that she didn't even like him. "May I kiss you, lass?"

She held her breath and stared back without answering. When her breathing resumed, he sensed the measured cadence. Inhale for a count of three, exhale for a count of three. The deliberate control brought the balcony around them, with its dappled lantern light breaking the shadows, back into focus.

Perhaps she too was considering her own list of reasons why this was a bad idea, because she silently shook her head. Just once. Her full bottom lip grazed the corner of his mouth as she denied him.

Ethan nodded, unable to speak around the disappointment in his throat. She was right. Flirtation on dark balconies was a game best saved for widows and women who knew the score, not unmarried ladies with every reason to hate him. Even if they'd somehow stumbled into a moment when the emotions between them felt like the opposite of animosity.

A glance over her shoulder at the windows showed no gaping faces, so perhaps no one had witnessed their conversation. Beyond the doors separating them from the rest of the musicale, voices murmured over the lilting melody of stringed instruments.

Closing his eyes, he took a last draw of lemon-scented air and stepped away. "May I escort you back inside?"

For a woman who'd just rebuffed his advances, she didn't seem angry or disgusted. However, the earlier signs of softening—even, dare he say it, arousal—were gone. Lady Charlotte seemed to have shaken off the oddly intense encounter and regained control of herself. With a polite smile lacking teeth or emotion, she said, "No thank you. I'll make my own way."

That was for the best. Grabbing the punch cup from where he'd set it down a million heartbeats before, he turned back to the lights and chatter of the intermission.

A glance back showed her to be the picture of composure. At least one of them was.

Darling said good night, leaving her alone. Going through the motions of her bedtime routine, Lottie couldn't hide from one pertinent fact: she'd almost kissed him.

Out there, on that balcony. As she looked back on the evening, it was like watching strangers in a play. There'd been a strange intimacy in the shadowy space as they'd acknowledged having landed on the same side of the gossip rags. Uncomfortable allies, as it were.

He'd apologized again, and perhaps it was the repetition, but she was more inclined to believe this time that his remorse was genuine. She'd softened further, remembering how he'd spoken up for her and then managed to be a charming companion at dinner a few nights ago. What had begun as a pretend friendship for appearances against Lady Bartlesby had felt real by the end of the night.

In the two days since then, she'd caught sight of him coming and going from Lord Carlyle's house. There'd been nods of acknowledgment, a small wave in greeting, and even a polite exchange about the weather.

In short, he was trying. And tonight, he'd reiterated that apology and his desire to make things right between them.

Acknowledging his role in her life as something other than an enemy complicated things. She didn't know how to go about finding her feet if she didn't hate him, so she'd defaulted back to what she knew. They'd gone from polite conversation to talking business. To his credit, he hadn't seemed put out when she'd offered opinions and assistance. In fact, he'd thanked her.

There'd been none of the ego she often encountered when discussing business matters with men. No verbal pat on the head, with a condescending request to let the men handle things. He hadn't even once questioned whether she was qualified to recommend someone worthy of his time.

Yes, that threshold between enemies and friends had appeared between them, and she'd found herself stepping into unknown territory. He wasn't exactly an enemy anymore. But then, he wasn't precisely a friend either. She strongly suspected that neither of them knew what they were doing.

The flirtatious conversation had been a pleasant surprise. Entertaining, until—like their conversation at dinner the other night—it'd felt very real. And she'd almost kissed him.

Almost. Thank God common sense had stopped her. Well, common sense and years of self-control wrapped in layers of hurt. Her distrust was not so easily eradicated, although the evening had muddied the emotion.

Maybe she didn't hate the man anymore. Or at least, not all the time. And she might occasionally want him to touch her in a non-sworn-enemy sort of way, knowing full well he could incite an impulse to hit him over the head with the nearest blunt object.

Which was the last thing she needed to deal with while handling the appearance of Mr. Montague.

Montague had called this morning and asked to take her for a drive. She'd pled a headache and a need to write her father, then sidestepped his leading questions about her plans for this evening. Something about him set off alarms in her head. Unfortunately, she hadn't been able to get out of committing to a picnic tomorrow. At least a picnic meant Agatha would accompany them.

Objectively speaking, Montague was a gorgeous

specimen of male beauty. More so than Amesbury, whom she'd classify as distracting and masculine rather than beautiful.

Charm seemed to be Montague's native tongue. His eagerness to move forward with the engagement would be flattering if she wanted a marriage in the traditional sense. However, compliments and charm were a decided drawback in light of her desire to have a disinterested spouse. Come to think of it, so was flirting on balconies, but this evening she hadn't been thinking of that. Amesbury might have a point, that emotions could override plans. Damn the man.

Most problematic of all was that Montague was somehow unaware that she'd already declined the match. Father was being less than forthcoming with someone in this situation, and she suspected that she was the one in the dark here. It incited a fury she'd struggled to keep tucked away since meeting Montague. It wasn't Montague's fault Father was practicing subterfuge, after all. But without her knowing why Father had kept that pertinent information to himself, she couldn't outright tell Montague no. At least, not yet.

She'd written to Stanwick Manor today—one note to Rogers the steward and one to her father. Rogers would end up handling both letters, but it was the principle of the thing. Demanding answers held less dramatic appeal when it would be nearly two weeks before she received a letter back.

Knowing at least part of Father's reply would involve giving Montague a chance to pay his addresses in person, she'd resolved to go on a few outings with the man. Who knew if he was merely making the best of the situation and might actually be amenable to her plan? That wasn't exactly a line of questioning she could spring on him a mere day after making his acquaintance.

Bottom line, she'd told Amesbury she was on the hunt for a husband, and it was the truth. Father had told her to choose either Montague or another man equally acceptable.

And then she'd nearly kissed Amesbury of all people. Hating him had been far easier than this emotional muddle.

Exhaustion swept through her. She draped her shawl over a chair, snuffed the lamp, and made her way by moonlight to close the curtains.

Across the narrow lane, Lord Carlyle's home remained illuminated. When someone crossed in front of a second-story window, she paused. There, directly opposite her, stood one of the men on her mind. Without a cravat, coat, or waistcoat, the open neck of Amesbury's shirt drew her eye to the wide expanse of his chest. Stifling a gasp, Lottie pulled back from the window. She shouldn't peek. But if the darkness hid her, would one more look hurt?

Just as they had this evening, the tiny hairs on her arms stood at attention, pointing toward him, like a compass guiding to true north. Muddied feelings aside, the look of him still made an impact. Dark and broad, rough around the edges, with those ridiculous curls in need of a trim softening his appearance. He wasn't the epitome of male beauty like Montague. But what he was appealed to her more than Montague's perfection.

A chill from the glass met the heat of her body, which seemed to creep up by degrees the longer she watched him. Her nipples pebbled against the fine linen of her night rail as a tendril of warmth spiraled around her belly in a lazy swirl.

In the window across the lane, Amesbury craned his head toward the small portion of sky between their roof lines. Clouds and soot impeded any of the celestial views she found so familiar back home, and she had to wonder what he looked for.

With unhurried movements, he gathered his shirt, pulling it from his waistband. An inch of his stomach showed above the top of his dark breeches. His navel was a shadowy dip, hemmed in by grooves of musculature forming a V, pointing down to things she'd only ever seen in books.

With that thought, she almost snapped the heavy drapes closed. Almost. All it would take was a forceful flick of her wrist to bring this voyeurism to an end. And yet she didn't move.

The rhythm of her heart pounded in a song she'd never heard before as she clung to the shadows, watching.

His shirt was gone now. There was just…so much of him. Were all men built like that? Surely not. Montague was lean, not bulky. And at dinner the other night, Mr. Lurch had seemed downright squishy. She'd bet ten pounds that Lurch padded the shoulders of his coat. Whereas nothing on Amesbury needed padding or filling out. He was all angles and planes, with a deep color to his skin that suggested he worked outside bare-chested—wasn't *that* an intriguing mental image.

With his arms braced against the window frame, every inch of him seemed to ripple and bunch into new shapes. The shifting lines of his body were rather delicious, to be honest. He leaned on one arm, using his free hand to unbutton the fall of his silk breeches.

"I refuse to peek. I refuse to peek." Turning from the window, she forced herself to march like a dutiful soldier to bed. She flipped back the counterpane and slipped under the covers, blocking out the temptation to see just how naked he'd get before leaving the window.

No, but really—how naked *would* he get before stepping out of view? Would her imagination be capable of envisioning how he'd look when his breeches slid down his heavily muscled legs? This would be a long, hard night. So to speak.

Lottie threw an arm over her face to muffle her groan.

Ethan blew out the light, then indulged in one last look across the lane. "Sweet dreams, Lady Charlotte." The minx might have been invisible if he hadn't noticed her bedroom's lamplight and the shadows moving about the room. Filmy curtains preserved her privacy, although his windows had no such layer of protection—a fact he'd used to his advantage.

He usually considered his brain an orderly space where logic ruled. He'd made it that way after living through the aftermath of rash decisions several years ago. Tonight, the habits he'd built to think through every action, to weigh and measure the risk, had disappeared on that balcony, and it would seem they remained absent. Exhibitionism wasn't something he'd ever indulged in, but knowing she watched, remembering the heat of their encounter earlier this evening—he'd wanted just a few more minutes of her attention.

But now he ached with need. She occupied a bed a few dozen feet and a narrow lane away, and his body knew it. The previously comfortable mattress seemed made of rocks when he rolled over yet again.

Lady Charlotte planned to marry. An empty society union by the sounds of it, which would be a bloody shame. Tonight he'd glimpsed beneath her layers of composure and known for certain that she was no longer the society debutante from years before. It wasn't only her personality that had changed. Everything about her was…more. Time hadn't just been kind to her. It had caressed and sculpted her from a lovely young lady into a lass with strong opinions and a wicked sense of humor that fascinated the hell out of him.

She'd been beautiful tonight, so polished and coiffed. But that first meeting at the inn, when her hair had been a mass of dark tangles reaching her waist, haunted him. With the trauma of her accident passed, his mind veered off the Good Samaritan path. He'd give anything to sink his hands into those waves of silky hair, wrap the strands around his fingers, and tether her to him. Those curls would flow like ink spilling over his pillow as he lowered his body to hers.

They'd stood so close tonight, their bodies aligned in a way that stayed with him. She would fit. Her curves would meld with him like an erotic puzzle piece, linking and tangling until neither could tell where they began or ended.

Lord, he wanted to trace the incredible blushes that danced over her skin. The pink flush followed the same path each time, beginning at her cheeks, then blooming across her collarbones and stretching down to the low neckline of her gown. Where the delicate color traveled from there was the stuff of fantasy.

The tent in his bedding would have been awkward to explain if he were sharing a room. Ethan lifted the blanket, glancing down in exasperation at his rigid erection.

"Really, lad? Of all the women in the world, you want this one?" He rolled his eyes and dropped the covers. There was no denying it. His body wanted her. His mind craved her.

Tonight they'd been so close to a kiss, and now he had questions. Would her breathing change with increased arousal? What noises would she make when she climaxed? Were her breasts heavy and pendulous, or tight globes? Would they bounce as she found her satisfaction atop him or sway with the rhythm they found together? Lady Charlotte in the throes of passion would be a vision as her body milked him with each shudder of pleasure.

Under the sheet, his erection twitched, but he absently stroked his chest instead of sliding a hand under the blanket.

He'd asked tonight and she'd said no. Although he didn't know her taste, he could have her scent. Back in Warwickshire, Ethan had purchased the same lemon oil the innkeeper had given Lady Charlotte. Since then, he'd smelled the oil with alarming regularity, as if trying to conjure her from the bottle like a djinn. Ethan uncorked the small bottle beside his bed. With the tangy citrus on his skin, he could almost imagine her here, instead of next door.

Finally, he reached under the blanket to spread the bead of fluid weeping from his cock over the thick head. Oil-slicked hands sliding over flesh stole his air. One stroke. Two. He hummed with pleasure as the fantasy took hold.

The fingers on his sack became her delicate hands in his imagination, small fingernails gently abrading skin that tightened with building need. His grip worked faster, squeezing until he kicked the covers away from his body because the room was altogether too hot.

More. His brain supplied the gasps and panting pleas of his imaginary lover, and he answered her aloud. A bellow roared up his throat, muffled with his arm over his face. Teeth sank into his meaty biceps, even as his back arched off the bed with the force of the orgasm.

He lay there a moment, chest heaving. The air was thick with their two mixed scents—an intensely satisfying combination.

The fantasy had been so real, but now the room felt emptier than it had before.

Chapter Nine

"How was the picnic, milady?" Darling placed Lottie's pearl necklace and earbobs in their velvet-lined case.

Lottie wrinkled her nose. "Mr. Montague seems thrilled with a match between us, but my intuition says encouraging him wouldn't be wise."

"He's certainly a fancy piece to look at."

"Oh, no doubt he's attractive. I admit, when he touched me, I considered going along with Father's plans. Then he started talking and ruined it."

"Touched you?" Darling raised a brow. "What kind of picnic was this?"

Lottie chuckled. "Don't get your hackles up. Nothing inappropriate happened. When he helped me out of the carriage, he kissed my wrist. Inside, here." She brushed her skin absently. "Right above the edge of my glove. Agatha was there, so any liberties were minor. He is a gentleman, after all." A gentleman hell-bent on wooing. She'd tried to steer the conversation toward practical matters, to determine if he was a viable candidate for her plan, but the man's answers fell firmly in the category of flirtatious lothario. He was like a porcelain figurine—decorative and utterly useless.

"I thought a true gentleman wouldn't take liberties at all. If there's one thing I know, it's men. Don't expect him to treat you like a lady later if he treats you like a hussy now."

"How lovely to know I have a friend looking out for my interests," Lottie teased. "That is wise counsel, although not needed. I don't plan to spend much more time with him if he won't answer a few simple questions."

"You're decided, then?"

Lottie paused, then shrugged into her dressing gown and tied the ribbons. "The potential is there if he'd let me manage the estate. Lord knows he doesn't seem to have a head for business." Sliding her feet into cozy slippers, she contemplated the situation aloud. "After all, I don't have to like the man—I only have to marry him. He seems to have no interests or abilities beyond a surface level of charm, but a handsome husband wouldn't be a hardship." That charm had worn thin by the time they'd finished the picnic. He'd spent the outing drinking the lion's share of a bottle of champagne while bemoaning the lack of options available to a younger son.

Darling gathered the last items of Lottie's toilette and put them away. At the door, she turned, with her hands full of laundry. "Perhaps it's none of my business, but don't you think you deserve better than that? No matter how handsome, if he can't offer at least companionship, I'd mark him off your list."

Lottie sat at the vanity table and picked up her hairbrush. Not because her hair needed attention, but because her hands had a case of the fidgets, and brushing her hair gave her something to do as she mulled over the day.

While Agatha appeared to nap under a nearby tree, doing her best impression of a cat in a sunbeam, Montague had brought up the Paper Doll Princess scandal. Of course he had. She couldn't escape that stupid moniker. In an unforeseen twist to the conversation, he'd dismissed it, claiming Amesbury had far more to answer for. According to Montague, after several flutes of champagne, Amesbury had almost killed a man. A friend, at that.

Somewhere between gossip and outright fabrication, there could be a kernel of truth to his statement. The implications of that didn't sit well.

Lord Amesbury might be a bad romantic risk, which she'd learned seven years ago—never mind how appealing he looked framed in a window—but the man wasn't a threat to anyone's life. She was sure of that. So where, then, was the truth amidst the fable?

The next morning dawned, illuminating wet cobblestones. For once, Lady Luck was smiling Ethan's way, because the groom who'd brought him Ezra had been only a few feet in front of a groom leading a mount for Lady Charlotte. Their horses splashed through puddles as he and Lady Charlotte rode toward the park. Fog lingered along the grassy trails within the park's gates, lending the quiet space a reverent quality that he preferred not to break.

They'd hardly exchanged a handful of words since

meeting on the street and awkwardly setting off in the same direction. Remembering her desire for silence in the morning from their encounter at the inn, he didn't press for conversation. Since she appeared fully functional, he assumed she'd enjoyed at least one cup of tea already. The habit she wore fit snug as a glove, showing her assets in such a way that rational thought and blood flow left his brain for a second every time he looked at her—and he couldn't stop looking. The modiste responsible deserved a hug and his eternal gratitude. Every curve of her body showed to perfection.

A small satchel he'd slung crosswise over his body contained a pair of breakfast pastries he'd packed for himself. Without a word, he offered one to Lady Charlotte, leaning his body as far over in his saddle as his balance would allow to pass the warm bread.

Another five minutes passed before she broke the silence. "Thank you."

"You're welcome." He cleared his throat, not entirely sure what to say.

Before he came up with a conversational gambit, she said, "I have two orders of business to discuss. Have you something to write with in that satchel?"

"I do." They drew to a stop, and he dug out a scrap of paper and a pencil.

"Write this down. I sent a query yesterday, and the messenger returned with a reply. Wallace Macdonell, the brewmaster I told you about, is expecting to hear from you."

Grinning, Ethan scribbled notes as she rattled off the man's direction and pertinent details. By God, the lass had followed through with her offer to help. Not a moment too soon, because Connor's missive this morning pressed for a return date and news about the search for a brewmaster. Every day delayed, every setback they'd experienced was money wasted. Frankly, he didn't have the funds to throw pound notes into the wind like that. He clutched the precious piece of paper. "Thank you, lass. This means a great deal."

"Don't thank me yet. The next order of business is more personal. I heard a bit of disturbing news about you yesterday."

That didn't bode well. "Sounds ominous. Gossiping about me, were you?"

She raised a brow his way, as painfully beautiful as she'd been in his dreams last night. "I think it's safe to say we share a mutual disdain for gossip. However, these allegations are dire enough that they deserve an answer."

"Dire, eh? Yet you helped me with Mr. Macdonell's information. I'm touched," he said, hand over his heart.

"I didn't say I believed the gossip, only that I wanted to hear your defense. One of my suitors claims you tried to kill one of your friends."

Well, there it was. He sighed, then navigated Ezra around a patch of late-blooming flowers. This was progress of a sort. A month ago, she'd have unilaterally believed the claims. However, with his dirtiest laundry hung before her, he wasn't sure if the heavy emotion settling in his gut resulted from the accusation or her casual reference to a suitor. "Your, uh, suitor is catching you up on all the news you missed these past few years."

"You don't deny it? He's accusing you of attempted murder." Lady Charlotte gaped at him as if outraged on his behalf. That weight in his belly lifted a tad.

"Nay. A charge of attempted murder implies forethought

and planning. There wasn' forethought given tae anything back then. Not much thinking, period, if we're being honest. I ran wild through London." So much he could say. Explain. Excuse. Best to stick to the facts. A quick glance showed he had her attention as their horses plodded sedately down the path. "Connor planned tae join the army, you see. We grew up together. No' best friends, but we ran with the same lads in the village. Anyway, before Connor got his uniform, he wanted tae see London. Everyone back home thought it a great lark when I inherited. I was showing off my fancy life, because I tended tae be an insufferable twit. I'm sure you remember."

"And Connor never made it to the army," Lady Charlotte said.

Ethan shook his head. "Nay, he didn'. We were drinking, gambling, actin' the fool. Someone proposed a race. It was an asinine bet, but we were drunk. Rather, I was drunk and the one at fault. The carriage crashed. Connor lost his leg—nearly died on the side of the road beside my horses."

Lady Charlotte pulled her mount to a stop. "That's why you cared so much about my coachman's leg."

He reined his horse to circle back. "Aye. I'm grateful you had a good doctor." It was tempting to reach over and brush the curl from her forehead where it covered the red scar at her hairline.

Her brows scrunched together when she was deep in thought, and it was adorable. He hoped she'd considered what he'd said, and heard the truth. "Where is Connor now?"

"Yelling at masons today. The construction isn' going tae plan on the brewery."

She cocked her head. "He works for you?"

Ethan shrugged. "He refused money, so I gave him a job. Connor pretty much runs Woodrest."

Her smile rivaled the sun melting the last of the surrounding fog. "Woodrest is your estate, right? Everything turned out all right, then."

Ethan went cold. No, it wasn't all right. He'd robbed a friend of his career in the army, in addition to a limb, for God's sake. Having free run of a rambling manor house was hardly a worthwhile trade-off. Yet things could have been so much worse. He cleared his throat, tamping down the emotions. It would ruin the morning if he went down that conversational path. "At least people can only accuse me of *attempted* murder. I'm curious—who is your chatty suitor?"

"Mr. James Montague, son of the Earl of Danby. Our fathers are friends."

He'd heard of the man—none of it flattering. Ethan tried to keep his expression benign but probably just looked bilious.

If her father had a connection to the Earl of Danby, one could assume that he'd look upon their match with favor. The stab of jealousy wasn't unexpected. Ethan wasn't good enough for his daughter, but somehow Montague—with a reputation that was nothing short of infamous—passed muster for the earl.

On top of that injustice, most women found the man appealing. Montague might be a scoundrel, but he was a handsome scoundrel. They would make a beautiful pair, with Lady Charlotte's dark beauty acting as the perfect foil for her golden partner. Even Cal looked—well, normal—in comparison to Montague. When had the other man earned the title of suitor? Without thinking, Ethan blurted, "You can't add Montague tae your husband list."

That he'd mishandled the situation became clear when she stiffened and shot him a glare. "Of all the presumptuous, rude..." She gaped as if struggling for words.

Damn. Trying to lighten the mood, he said, "Is 'rude' the best you can come up with? You disappoint me, Lady Charlotte."

Teasing banter wouldn't soothe her ire. "What makes you think you have a voice in my 'husband list,' as you call it? For all you know, Mr. Montague already made an offer and has been accepted by my father."

"Has he?" Please, no.

"You miss the point, my lord. That's none of your business."

That wasn't a no. "You're right, it's not. I only say something because Montague is not a man you want tae saddle yourself with for life. I don' want tae dirty your ears with details—" This ride had been going so well, and now the morning was shot to hell.

Her short laugh couldn't be mistaken for amusement. "This from the likes of you? Might I remind you of our conversation not three minutes ago? If his character is so vile, I deserve to know the charges against him."

"In plain terms, the man lives on credit. He rarely greets a morning sober or with the same female companion. In fact, I'd bet he wasn't entirely sober when you met him."

"You know this to be fact?" she challenged.

"His reputation speaks for itself, Lady Charlotte—"

"So does yours, my lord," she snapped.

He winced. There was no defending that. "You deserve better."

With a deliberate look, she perused him from the top of his head to his dirty boots, then back up to his eyes. "Yes, I do."

Without waiting for him, she spurred her mount to a canter in the opposite direction, and moments later a groom passed Ethan, giving him a quizzical glance.

"Damn it."

"You have a letter," Agatha said.

Lottie looked up from her book. "I wonder if Father finally found a moment to write." Yes, that busy schedule of drinking port and reading in his library.

Fine, that wasn't fair. He'd been coming out of his decline these last few months, trying to do more with the estate—which was why she'd been ousted to London for a husband hunt.

Mr. Montague might be sending more poetry, but that was unlikely, since he was due any minute for a drive in the park. He'd visited every day since the picnic, but she'd managed to delay another outing until today. Perhaps he'd written to cancel their plans? Hope sprung eternal.

During yesterday's call he'd mentioned being lucky to marry for love, and she'd nearly gagged. That made her decision easier. Lottie would tell him the engagement was off—not that it had ever been on—during their time today. Father wouldn't be happy, but if Father liked the man so much, he could marry him.

Lord Amesbury had disappeared after their disastrous ride a week ago. Not that she'd looked for a light in his window every night since. It was merely an observation.

"It does not resemble the earl's hand." Agatha handed over the letter.

The precise handwriting was familiar. "This is from

Rogers, the steward. I wonder if today's post has a letter for Darling. That would make her happy."

"Who would be writing your maid? One would think she would be a social outcast after her time as the town's feather mattress."

The term made Lottie grit her teeth. "That's an awful turn of phrase, Godmother. To answer your question, she and Patrick have exchanged letters during his recovery. I think there may be a budding romance in our midst."

"Do you encourage relationships between servants? It could make the workplace awkward. Considering that workplace is your home, I would discourage such a thing."

"I think they'd be a good match," Lottie mused. "After all, it's been several years since Darling's husband died."

"Some might consider them an odd pairing. The former drunk with the former prostitute," Agatha commented.

"'Former' being the most important word." How lovely it would be to have her own household, where she could handle servant affairs the way she wanted to, without answering to anyone. Of course, Agatha would still have opinions, because she was Agatha. "Perhaps their history is common ground. Their pasts aren't a secret." It would be hard to hide Darling's history, and everyone back home knew about the schoolteacher who used to teach while three sheets to the wind. "Despite their colorful pasts, they are wonderful people, with much to offer the right person."

Agatha seemed content to let it go at that, so Lottie opened the letter. Rogers's elegant script felt familiar, like a friend, although Rogers himself had never earned that designation. She read it through once, then again. "Father may have found a house for me. There's a view of the sea and an established rose garden. Can you imagine a more lovely property?" It sounded perfect. Fertile land, a house with modern amenities, and a thriving nearby town—what could be better?

"This would be the property with which your father intends to entice you to marriage?" Agatha sipped her tea with a raised brow, staring over the teacup's rim.

Lottie sagged in her chair. The house by the sea came with strings. Best not forget that, no matter how appealing it sounded.

"Not a subtle push, is it?" Agatha said.

No, her father's lack of subtlety didn't surprise her. Rogers would have written at her father's direction. At least it meant Father was preparing to keep his side of their bargain. Now she had to keep hers—not an encouraging prospect when she lacked suitors other than Montague, whom she hoped to never see again after today, and possibly the absent Scotsman. Lottie neatly folded the letter back into its rectangular shape, creasing the edges with precise movements.

Dawson entered the room. "Mr. Montague is here to collect Lady Charlotte, madam. He's awaiting her in his phaeton."

"In my day, gentlemen came inside when they called. They did not wait on the street or expect a lady to come to them," Agatha said in a *what is the world coming to* tone.

"Times change, Auntie." She bent to kiss Agatha's cheek. "I shan't be long. When I return, I'll take extra time dressing for this evening. I have to look my best if I'm to catch a husband."

Hopping down from the high seat of the carriage, Mr. Montague swept a grand bow and kissed the inside of her wrist. "A vision, as always, Lady Charlotte."

"You're in a good mood today, Mr. Montague." When he flashed that grin, Lottie couldn't help softening toward him. After all, she had depressingly few friends in Town. The list of annoyances and doubts regarding him were bound to surface again when they parted ways, but the man could weave a charming spell when he wanted to. It was too bad their friendship would end after today.

"I had brilliant luck at the tables last night. Now I have the prettiest creature in London for company." He helped her up into the seat, where she gripped the edge and tried not to look down. Goodness, these seats felt unstable.

Forcing a laugh through a suddenly parched throat, she said, "Mr. Montague, you are too kind."

He swung up beside her, making their perch sway to a terrifying degree. Gathering the reins, he paused to tip his hat at a rakish angle with one finger. "Oh, I'm quite serious, as you know. But that's fine. I'll wait. Eventually, you'll realize there's no one better for you than me."

"Sir, I must insist you cease with the flattery." She'd wanted to ease into this conversation, but they might as well do it now, while they sat outside her house. "You see, I've given this some thought and—"

"You'll come around." Montague sent her a heated look. "Until then, I shall make do with stealing you away for times such as this." He clicked his tongue, setting the horses in motion.

Obnoxious man. On paper, Montague checked every box on her list. But his apparent desire for her made her own plans for marriage entirely incompatible. No matter how handsome he was or how beautiful their children would be, she didn't want that life. She didn't want his adoration. Or his babies, come to think of it.

She tried again as the carriage sped toward the park.

"As you know, our fathers desire a match between us. However, after some reflection—"

"The earl was ecstatic when I wrote him. I sent an express messenger the day I saw you on Bond Street. He's given his blessing."

"Excuse me?" She gaped at his presumption. Surely her father would never give consent without first consulting her. Not after she'd already declined this exact match. The disquiet in her heart stirred when Montague ignored her question in favor of navigating the phaeton through the streets of Mayfair. The verdant expanse of Hyde Park sprawled before them. Without a pause, Montague guided the horses past the park gates as they approached Oxford Street.

"Wait, I thought we were going to the park." Over her shoulder, the bustling acres of Hyde Park shrank behind them.

"I have a different drive in mind for today. Trust me." Montague signaled the team to a higher speed, away from Mayfair.

Trust him? Not bloody likely. Amesbury's warning about Montague rang in her head. "Mr. Montague, I insist you take me home. If you don't plan to drive in the park as planned, then this outing is finished." City blocks of businesses passed, then houses. Hedgerows dotted the distance, and still they continued.

"You worry too much. We're almost there," Montague insisted.

"Sir, turn these horses around at once." Who cared if her voice was shrill when the blasted man continued down the road in the opposite direction of where they should be going.

"Not to worry, pet. I'm sure you're concerned about

your reputation. But as an engaged couple, we can enjoy a nice drive in an open carriage." He snapped the lines, pushing the horses to go faster.

"Not out into the countryside! And we aren't engaged. We will never be engaged, which is what I was trying to say, but you kept interrupting!" There. Her chest deflated as she sighed with relief at finally getting the words out. She could have been more diplomatic, but the man was obstinate to the extreme. There was no way to misinterpret her wishes now.

"That's not what your father says. Sit back and enjoy the drive. You said you prefer the country, so I planned this just for you." Montague turned off the main byway, onto a rutted path.

"My father is not the one who'd have to marry you, and I've just said that I won't. We aren't getting married. Not now, not ever." She bit the words out while her brain scrambled for a plan. At least they were off the main road, thus not going farther from London.

The phaeton didn't handle this terrain well. But then, a rocky trail with nubby clumps of grass and soil couldn't be what the engineers had had in mind when designing it. Lottie gripped the seat edge until her knuckles were white, and counted her breaths. In, one, two, three. Out, one, two, three. What was she going to do?

At what point did a situation become kidnapping? There had to be a way to get him to take her home. She could guess at how far they'd gone, but she didn't know for sure. If she jumped down and made a run for it, there was only the road back—which left her open to him following her. If she played along long enough to get out of here, she need never see this man again.

The horses slowed, coming to rest in a grassy clearing

surrounded by trees. A serene pond reflected the vibrant colors of autumn. Montague nimbly jumped down, then turned to lift her out of the carriage, but she tightened her grip on the seat and stayed put. "Mr. Montague—"

"James. My name is James. I ache to hear you say it." He gripped her hips, dragging her to the edge of the seat, sending the whole contraption rocking again.

"James." She gritted her teeth and held on tighter to the wood. "You brought me out here even though I asked to go home. We're here. And yes, it's lovely. Now I'd like to return to London immediately."

"This isn't how you were supposed to be," Montague grumbled.

"Terribly sorry to disappoint," she snapped. Staring him down, she waited for him to climb back into the phaeton. Instead, he glared, then walked toward the trees and stood with his back to her. When he widened his stance, she grimaced, then looked away.

While Montague took a piss a few feet to her left, Lottie stared at the bucolic view and wrestled her irritation under control. This place was beautiful, even though she didn't want to be here. It reminded her of home, which brought to mind the letter from the steward. Her new house might have a view accompanied by the sound of the sea crashing on the rocks below her window.

If Lottie could make herself say yes to this man, then write to her father this evening, that house would be hers. She shook her head and stored away the serene scene in a corner of her mind to relish later.

Someday she'd have that house. But she wouldn't marry Montague to get it.

The horses shifted, sending the phaeton swaying again. The reins slid off the seat, where he'd left them. Before she lost them entirely, she looped the leather around a brass anchor by her feet.

Eyeing the horses, then the man buttoning the placket on his breeches, she weighed her options. She'd driven the gig back home. But that was one horse. A phaeton was double the horseflesh, plus an unstable carriage design, and she was off the beaten path.

Montague clambered up to join her on the narrow seat, and the opportunity was lost. "Mr. Montague, I would like to leave. Now."

"We agreed you would call me James."

"You insisted, then I relented. That is *not* coming to an agreement. But fine. Yes. James." She rolled her eyes. It was like negotiating with a surly child. A cool breeze whistled through the trees, making her shiver despite her heavy spencer. Changing tactics slightly, she sweetened her voice. "This pond is lovely. Thank you for sharing it with me. But I am rather chilled. Could you take me home, please?"

He loosened the reins and held them in his hand. "Before we go, there is one thing I need to do," Montague said, then sealed her mouth with his.

Her first kiss. Kind of shocking, really. To be twenty-six and have never experienced this. It was, well, wet. Warm. Different from how she'd imagined it would be. But then, she'd always imagined her first kiss would be given, not taken. Wrenching her head away, she wiped her mouth with a gloved finger.

"Come now, love," he said with a silky, firm voice. "Don't turn missish now. We aren't leaving until you kiss me properly."

The charming man she'd thought she knew had disappeared. Instead, his flat eyes were set in a face that used to be handsome and now appeared to be carved from stone. The sneer he wore fit him better than a smile ever had. Everything Amesbury had warned her about was true. This man was a bully, a cad, and a reprobate.

Montague held the reins, literally and figuratively. By refusing to set the horses toward home unless she kissed him back, he'd trapped her. At his mercy, she felt a cold pressure behind her ribs, limiting her air to shallow sips.

Not knowing what else to do, she shook her head. Denying the situation, denying him a kiss, denying that she'd somehow landed here, outside London, with no way home besides him. When Montague kissed her again, it was a second invasion she hadn't asked for.

This had nothing to do with romance. Even a woman with her nonexistent romantic history knew that. His fingers pinched her upper arms. If she bit his tongue, he might do worse than a kiss.

But then, if she vomited on him, perhaps that would speak for itself too. A whimper clawed up the back of her throat as she tore her face away, twisting to use a shoulder to create precious inches between them.

"Please, sir. I don't feel well." Truth. Her stomach rolled with acid waves fed by fear.

"So formal, my love. I told you to call me James." The fingers on her arms tightened. There would definitely be marks to commemorate their time together. But in that split second, she saw an opening. He'd dropped the reins to hold her arms, trying to turn her body to face him.

She trapped the leather straps under her boot so they wouldn't fall off the driver's perch. If she was going to get herself out of this, she'd need those reins. As a girl, she'd wrestled with her brother, and one particular tussle they'd had in the stables surfaced above the panic flooding her mind. She wasn't helpless.

Mustering every thread of strength and rage, she moved her head and hands at once. Slamming her forehead into Montague's face, she pushed against his chest. The seat was narrow and high, made of slick polished wood, and Montague sailed right off it with a cry that rang like music to her but spooked the horses. It took precious seconds to grab the reins, and only sheer dumb luck sent the carriage moving in the right direction. Sending a quick prayer of thanks for her rough-and-tumble big brother, she slapped the reins against the backs of the matched pair and let loose a whoop of triumph when the phaeton jarred and lurched its way out of the clearing.

The journey back to the road was worse than coming in, because all she cared about was speed. A quick glance back showed Montague running after the phaeton with a bloody nose, limping slightly. One irate dandy was no match for two horses, even with a driver who had no idea what she was doing.

Once on the road, she gave them their heads, wanting as much distance from him as possible. Lottie focused on the horizon. There were buildings. They weren't too far out of town, then.

How she'd erred, thinking Montague manageable, when she couldn't even convince him they weren't getting married. In the distance, those buildings grew taller. The horses slowed, and she eyed the reins, tracing which lead went to which side of each horse. As she threaded the leather through her fingers, Lottie released a sigh, and with it the panic that had gripped her.

That's when the shaking started. It began in her thighs and traveled up her belly to her arms. As she pressed her hands to her knees to steady them, her throat closed around a sob. Her brain was a jumble of emotion, so she focused on one thing: driving. One unemotional thing, because she couldn't handle more than that or she'd fall apart. On the way to London, she would learn to drive with twice the lines she was used to. And by God, she wouldn't cry yet.

After what seemed an eternity, she arrived at her house, a few streets away from their original destination of the park. If only she'd raised more of a fuss when he'd passed those gates, she would still have a first kiss to give, and her arms wouldn't have finger-sized bruises. Before the self-recriminations could settle in, she said aloud, "Yes, and that bastard wouldn't be walking home."

She jumped down from the swaying seat and clutched the side of the carriage, waiting for her legs to support her.

Montague would never touch her again.

As she climbed the stairs, keeping her footfalls steady, tears pooled in her eyes. Counting her steps, she clung to control. *Five.* Then to the door. *Eight.*

Dawson opened the door. The first tear fell with her stuttering exhale as her feet crossed the threshold, and his concerned expression loosed the rest of the tears.

"Thank you, Dawson. Please have the carriage returned to Mr. Montague's address."

"Are you all right, milady?"

She ignored the tear trailing down her cheek and summoned a smile. "I will be, Dawson. My association with Mr. Montague has come to an end. Under no circumstances is he welcome in this home."

Dawson straightened to attention. "Mr. Montague shall never be permitted entry, milady. I'll notify the staff." The man might be older than Moses, but Lottie understood why Agatha liked him.

"Thank you. I'll be in my room, if you'd be so kind as to send Darling to me." Lottie turned on her heel with precise movements while her heart fluttered in her chest like a panicked bird in a cage. The last bit of fight seeped out of her. She needed to sit down soon, before the trembling overtook her entirely.

Steady on.

Just a little farther.

The fragile composure lasted until she closed her bedroom door. Clenching her hands into fists until her fingernails stung her palms, she repeated one thought like a mantra. No matter what she'd lost, in the end she had won. It was vital she remember that.

Chapter Ten

Ethan leaned a shoulder against the wall, crossing one foot over the other. The antics in front of him were the perfect entertainment on his first morning back in London.

"Admit defeat, Puppy. I've been doing this far longer than you," Cal taunted, advancing toward his opponent on the red carpet of the long gallery.

Adam Hardwick's grin flashed fast as his rapier as he countered each move with whip-thin arms that seemed to be an extension of the sword. At first, Ethan worried for the younger man—Calvin would trounce him with complete disregard for Adam's obvious case of hero worship.

Turned out, he should have saved the concern for Cal. Obnoxious bravado aside, everyone in this gallery knew Adam was going to win. It was just a matter of time.

"You're flapping your jaw an awful lot for someone

who should be conserving his energy," the Puppy replied. Blades flashed through the sunlight from the windows. Hardwick's tightly shorn red hair atop his thin, freckled frame made him resemble a lit candle as he held his own, occasionally dodging a shiny sword with nimble alacrity. What he lacked in finesse, he made up for with speed and dogged determination. The lad had his fair share of raw talent as well.

"Did you just imply that I'm old?" Cal sounded almost wheezy.

"If the shoe fits," the Puppy said, not a bit of breathlessness interrupting his chirpy impudence.

Ethan laughed, shaking his head. Yes, this was so much better than arguing with masonry workers. A moment later Adam disarmed Cal with a flourish, leaving Cal with his chest heaving, staring at his sword five feet away.

Cal bowed to his grinning opponent. "Well played, Puppy. Let's go downstairs to the breakfast room. If I have to endure you rubbing this in my face all morning, I'll need sustenance. Join us, Mac?"

Ethan shook his head. "I thought I'd go next door and coax Lady Charlotte out for a ride. The last time I saw her, we parted ways under unpleasant circumstances."

"Lady Charlotte?" Adam asked.

"Mac is on a mission to make an arse of himself over the lady next door. Again," Cal explained as he wrapped the swords in oilcloth.

Ethan rolled his eyes. "I'm trying tae make amends. I destroyed her first Season with an unflattering nickname."

"Oh, you mean that Paper Doll nonsense. I read something about that. How do you propose making up for ruining her Season?" Adam had a face full of freckles and kind eyes. No judgment, just curiosity.

Ethan could see why Calvin liked him. "I have no idea, but—"

Cal interrupted, "The entire thing is a disaster waiting to happen. It's great fun to watch. I'll try to get you an invitation the next time we go out."

"Does this woman have dark curly hair? Pretty?" Adam asked.

Ethan nodded.

"I passed her when I arrived. She looked to be on her way out for a ride."

Ethan straightened. "Which way was she headed? Perhaps I can run into her." He owed her an apology for butting in about Montague last week. Besides, call him a glutton for punishment, but he wanted to see her.

Adam jerked his head in the direction of every decent park in the area. Green Park, St. James's Park, and Hyde Park. Hundreds of acres of green space. Hyde Park alone was over three hundred acres. It would be a happy coincidence if he found her.

A short while later Ethan entered the Grosvenor Gate of Hyde Park. As if manifested from his mind, she sat in profile, confident and entirely at home atop a beautiful bay several yards away. She held her mount in place, looking out at the park trails. What she searched for, Ethan didn't know, but she certainly made a pretty picture. Like a painting titled *Lady on Horseback*. A groom waited patiently behind her. Several curls escaped down her back from what might have once been an elegant coiffure, so perhaps she'd already been for her run this morning.

Ethan waved. "Lady Charlotte, might I have a word?"

Drawing closer, he noticed the dark smudges beneath her eyes that hinted at a sleepless night. She didn't answer, but she waited for him to join her.

"I owe you an apology for my behavior the last time we spoke. You were right tae tell me tae mind my own business. I'm sorry for upsetting ye and sorry for my rudeness."

Her blink was slow, as if she'd taken a few extra seconds to process his words. "You were right to warn me about Montague, even if you were rude."

Beyond the exhaustion, her eyes had a dull, defeated look that was unlike the woman he'd met before now. Had her suitor shown his true colors? Concern overrode etiquette, so he said, "I know I just apologized for sticking my nose in your affairs, but are you all right?"

She nudged her mare into a leisurely walk. "A headache kept me awake all night. It's made me quite cross, I'm afraid."

"I'm sorry tae hear that. Did something happen with Mr. Montague?" A flock of birds left a nearby tree in a feathered swirl, their squawking filling the pause as he waited for her answer. He'd wait all day if need be. They headed off the trail toward a copse of trees.

"You were right about him. Now's your chance to say, 'I told you so.' Go ahead."

"I won' do that, my lady. Especially if he hurt you." What had happened? Possible scenarios crossed his mind, each worse than the last. "I know we aren' exactly friends, but I am worried for you, lass."

She pulled her mount to a stop and turned to him. "I can't believe I'm saying this—to you of all people—but I could use a friend. The only person outside my house who cared enough to warn me away from Montague was you."

"Are you certain you want tae befriend the man who made you flee Town for nearly a decade?" Emotions piled into his chest in a happy mess, but he couldn't quite believe the offer of friendship was genuine.

"Please, you give yourself too much credit, my lord." For the first time this morning she smiled at him, like the sun coming out on a gloomy day, warming everything in its path. "That Paper Doll Princess nonsense knocked the wind out of me but not for long. I retreated, cried, then plotted your demise—"

"As one does," he teased, and she laughed.

"Mother finally convinced me that rather than murder you, a better revenge would be to return triumphant and publicly reject you as a potential suitor for anyone of merit. Show everyone you were wrong."

"I *was* wrong. So what happened?"

Her smile turned bittersweet. "My brother, Michael, died. Then Mother followed soon after from a fever. Father couldn't handle the loss. He retreated to his library, and I stepped in to run things."

That sank in as he stared at the sky's reflection off the Serpentine stretched out before them. He hadn't driven her away for nearly a decade. Life had intervened in her plans, not shame or embarrassment. No wonder she'd changed since her debut. During the interim years, Lady Charlotte had grieved nearly everyone. That was a situation he understood all too well. Mum, Da, his gran'da, cousins...only he remained. "'Twas a tremendous loss for your family. I'm sorry."

The black plume on her hat bobbed with her nod. "The one bright spot was learning where I belong. Running the estate, implementing changes, and taking care of the tenants—that means something. And I'm good at it. Or I was, until Father pulled out of his grief and took it away."

The horses passed through the trees, the morning light

kissing her cheeks. Ethan was content to listen to her talk, since she obviously needed to get a few things off her chest.

"So here I am, an old maid searching for a husband just so I can have a home of my own to do what I love."

"You're not an old maid. You may not be fresh from the schoolroom, but you're hardly ready for caps and yarn crafts." Their conversation at the musicale, when she'd described her idea of marriage, made sense now. "If your goal is tae have your own estate tae manage, then marriage is a means tae an end."

She looked surprised. "Of course it is. Why else would I want a husband?"

His laugh came out a bit too loud, scaring a bird out of a nearby tree. "I'm not so foolish as tae guess at the female mind. Especially yours. I suspect it's mostly twisty bits and dark corners."

"You aren't wrong." She shrugged with a smile.

That pile of emotions in his chest settled into one clear thought. "I would like tae be your friend, my lady. Very much."

"Good," she said. "Because hating you is downright exhausting when you're right in front of me. You're much easier to despise from afar. Speaking of which, where have you been for the last week?"

It was on the tip of his tongue to ask how she'd noticed. Checking his bedroom window, perhaps? Ethan cleared his throat. "I went home. Mr. Macdonell agreed tae meet this week, so I took the time tae visit Woodrest."

"You made contact with Macdonell, then? He's a good man. I hope he will be an asset to your estate."

"I hope so as well. We have an interview tomorrow afternoon. If it works out, I'll owe you a great debt."

"We're friends now. I'm sure I'll collect on that debt soon enough," she said.

In Ethan's opinion, one thing London did well was bookshops. The shops crammed with aisles, rows, and stacks of stories and information just waiting for a reader were the best part of Town. While these literary riches did not make up for the abject poverty, the sooty air, and a river that ran thick with sewage, they provided a haven he could return to whenever the world outside the shop door grew too dark. In a way, the proprietor of this shop in particular had borne silent witness to the ups and downs of Ethan's entire history in society.

A small bell tinkled over the door as he entered, then it faded back into quiet stillness. The smells of ink and paper, of dust and leather bindings, never failed to soothe.

"Good day, milord. The book you ordered arrived this morning. I was just preparing it for shipping." The shopkeeper, Mr. Matthews, held out a heavy encyclopedia for his examination. The binding was tight, and the leather wasn't worn at the corners yet, although it had to be an older copy, since the bookseller had hunted it down from an estate parceling off its private library. Hundreds of pages detailing livestock ailments and cures, both common and rare.

"Excellent, Mr. Matthews. I'll take it home with me today."

Ethan wandered the familiar rows, brushing his hand along the spines as if greeting old friends. When he found what he sought, he couldn't suppress a grin. Gold lettering on the cover contrasted perfectly with the dark leather binding.

The last time he'd brought a gift to Lady Charlotte, years ago, he'd chosen a small posy of peonies, if he remembered correctly. Innocuous blooms that in no way implied anything beyond *I think you're a nice person. Here, have some flowers.* Tucking the slim volume under his arm, Ethan took the long route back to the counter, where Mr. Matthews wrapped the encyclopedia in paper and twine.

Since their ride yesterday, this situation with Lady Charlotte had been rolling about in his mind. Considering where they'd been less than a month ago, her offer of friendship was nothing short of miraculous. The problem was him. Yes, he wanted to be her friend—almost as much as he wanted to kiss her and hear her moan his name. Somehow, he didn't think that was the level of amicability she sought. While being her completely platonic friend, he'd have to ignore his growing desire for her while she searched for a husband.

That might drive him mad.

Even considering impossible scenarios in which Lady Charlotte desired him in return, there was no getting around her father. The earl's feelings regarding a match between them were clear—and that conversation had happened before Ethan went and spouted off in a bout of drunken idiocy. If Lady Charlotte ever decided she wanted him as much as he wanted her, they'd be in quite a pickle. The earl was a formidable man in both power and reputation.

He smoothed a hand over the leather volume he'd selected and set it on the counter. Friends gave one another gifts, especially when one of those friends had been dealing with something upsetting. Whatever had happened with Montague, it had cost her a night of sleep. Hopefully, the book would make her smile.

"Found something else, milord? You usually do." Matthews grinned, his straight white teeth bright against his umber skin. The shopkeeper tallied the total, and Ethan paid on the spot, as he always did.

"This store never fails tae hold something I have tae bring home. How's the missus? An' your daughters? I've no' seen them in the store the last few times I've come in."

Mr. Matthews had a special smile reserved for the mention of his family. The man exuded sheer joy, and damned if it wasn't impossible to not envy him a little. "Oh, the missus keeps me on my toes, but she's a gift. The girls are both married now, one just last month, and the other is making me a grandfather in the new year. I'm a blessed man, milord," the bookseller said.

"Sounds like it. Congratulations. Please pass along my best wishes tae your family." Ethan gathered the two wrapped parcels and donned his hat again. "Until next time, Mr. Matthews. Be well."

Outside, he paused to let a hackney pass before he dodged across the road. Only a couple blocks to the south stood Cal's Bond Street tailor, where Ethan had left his horse. He stole a glance at his pocket watch. He was due to meet Mr. Macdonell at a nearby coffeehouse in an hour.

A little girl selling violets at the corner turned her large eyes on him. With a little juggle, he tucked the books under his arm and tossed a coin to the girl. He had grossly overpaid but didn't care a whit when her smile stretched to show the gaps in her teeth. Crouching low, he let her pin the blooms to his lapel. With a tip of his hat, he swept a bow as she giggled.

Rather than fight the congestion of the shopping district all the way to the end of the street, where Cal's tailor had been in business for decades, he ducked into the newly opened Burlington Arcade. With some of the shops standing vacant, there were fewer people in the covered shopping area. The riffraff tended to avoid the area, as the arcade's beadles were most enthusiastic about their job. Passing the shop windows with their frills and high-priced wares, he wove through the shoppers to where the arcade opened on Piccadilly.

The tailor shop had the kind of air to it that said, *Yes, we've been here longer than the king has been alive. Wipe your bloody feet.* Ethan did just that, then looked over to see one of the tailors watching him. He recognized that scrawny face. This man, back when he was a lowly assistant, had refused to wait on Ethan the first time he'd met Cal here years ago. When Cal had explained that this was the newly titled viscount and a dear friend, the disbelieving stare would have been comical if directed at someone else. For a brief time, the assistant had thought to transform Ethan from bumpkin to fashion plate. Once the man had realized the new Viscount Amesbury didn't care if his cravat was pressed, much less tied in a perfect waterfall knot, they'd each retreated to their respective corners, and now they eyed one another like wary ex-combatants.

Ethan followed the sounds of his friend's voice to a lush carpeted salon, where Cal stood with another tailor's assistant kneeling before him. Thank God everyone concerned wore clothes, otherwise this might have been awkward.

"No, sir. I always hang left. If you kink my cock with a misplaced seam, we shall have words, you and I," Cal said.

Never mind. Still awkward.

"The poor lad's ears are bright red, Cal. Apologize for embarrassing him," Ethan commented, taking a seat and resting an ankle on his knee.

Cal glanced down at the man who held a measuring tape snug against what one would assume to be the left-dangling member in question. "Do conversations about cocks embarrass you? So sorry to offend. You might be in the wrong business, though. I imagine there are a great many cocks in your line of work."

Ethan muffled his laugh with a hand and shook his head. The tailor's assistant stammered something that seemed to appease Cal, then went back to making notes and taking measurements.

"Don' they already have your measurements on file? You've been coming here since you were in nappies."

"These will be Cossack trousers in the new style. Looser fit for my fencing bouts with the Puppy," Cal said.

"You'll look utterly ridiculous and probably still lose. You know that, right?"

"They're the height of fashion," Cal said.

"Right, as you said. If nothing else, they'll allow plenty of room tae dangle left while your young friend runs circles around you."

"Never underestimate the importance of the dangle. And I long ago gave up any hope of you understanding fashionable dress."

"About damn time. Are we done here, or will you be a while yet?" Ethan exchanged a look with the tailor's assistant, who scuttled back so Cal could step down from the dais. "I need tae get tae my meeting with Macdonell and don' want tae be late."

"I'm famished, so I'll come with you. You're meeting at the coffeehouse, right?" Cal asked, accepting the tailor's assistant's help shrugging back into his coat and boots.

"Aye. A kidney pie sounds perfect. I've spent the last week asking around, and Lady Charlotte didn't exaggerate. The brew he made in Westmorland is spoken of very highly, but from what I've heard, his methods differ from the gentleman we met in Warwickshire. I'd like your read of him. I'll have tae work with the man, after all, and we both know I'm getting desperate tae fill the position." Ethan gathered the small bundle from the bookstore. "Maybe after a pint I can convince you tae rethink those trousers."

Chapter Eleven

Lady Agatha stood before the window, tapping her cane on the floor in an agitated rhythm. The sun backlit her silver hair and black dress, giving her the look of an elderly avenging angel. The way she twisted the brass knob of her cane, it wouldn't surprise Lottie to discover a sword stashed inside, ready to burst into flames, channeling the vengeance of God.

Heavenly vengeance would be useful right about now. She'd been expecting fallout since leaving Montague by that pond and borrowing his phaeton—fine, she'd stolen it. But she'd given it back. With his wounded pride, and possibly broken nose, she'd known he wouldn't let the situation stand, even though she'd hoped he would choose discretion and slither back under whatever rock he'd come from. Even so, she hadn't expected blackmail. At the window, she swung back to traverse the room again until she reached the sofa.

"I should have listened to my gut. I knew something felt off about him. But no, for Father's sake, I tried to give him the benefit of the doubt. Agatha, you told me he wasn't suitable. Darling—hell, even Lord Amesbury—warned me off the man. Montague is nothing but a low-life, scummy, awful pile of excrement. *Bastard.*" Clutching the letter she'd received in one hand, she nibbled at her other thumbnail—an anxious habit from her childhood she'd thought eradicated.

"I should chastise the language, but frankly, my dear, you understate the matter," Agatha said.

Waving the letter in the air, Lottie wailed, "What am I going to do? He's sending an engagement notice to the *Times*. I won't marry that man, and I told him as much. But Father gave his blessing, in writing. Father is drawing up contracts, and that house Rogers wrote about must be part of it. Montague and Father have me cornered. He wants to call on me and discuss wedding details, as if Dawson hasn't already turned him away several times."

"I would never ask you to let him call. I do not know what happened between you, and I do not need to. If you cut ties and he is responding with this blatant manipulation, I know you are in the right," Agatha said.

Lottie slumped onto the sofa, resting her forehead in her palm, and tried to think through the situation. Hard to do when all she wanted to do was rage and cry. Father appeared to be ignoring her wishes by going forward with the engagement. Montague was more wily than expected, and she had no idea how to get out of this. She'd dispatched a messenger as soon as the letter arrived, but she didn't have much faith that it would do any good. Even riding hell-for-leather, the messenger would take several days to reach Stanwick Manor, and the engagement notice would be in Friday's *Times*.

A tap on the door interrupted her downward spiral. Dawson entered. “Pardon me, milady. Lord Amesbury is here. Would you like him to return at a later date?”

Before Agatha could reply, Lottie said, “Send him in, Dawson.”

Aunt Agatha gave her a concerned look, and Lottie shrugged. “I don’t know what to do. You don’t know what to do. Maybe Amesbury will have an idea.”

“Since when are you two friends?”

“It’s a recent development. I feel like I can use all the friends I can get right now, don’t you?” She didn’t regret her offer of friendship, although thinking of Amesbury as a friend didn’t feel natural yet.

Lord Amesbury took one tentative step into the room. He’d taken care with his dress before calling, and the effort made Lottie smile, despite the events of the morning. The dark-blue coat fit him to perfection, and his cravat was simply tied but bright white and starched. The dark shadow of his beard remained, but she suspected that was because of thick facial hair, not a lack of shaving.

Agatha headed toward the door. “Welcome, Lord Amesbury. Lottie, I’ll be back shortly. I need refreshment stronger than tea, and Dawson moved my brandy decanter again.” She left the door to the hall open to observe proprieties.

Amesbury watched her go, then turned to Lottie. “Am I interrupting?” He held up a brown wrapped parcel. “I brought you something, but I can come back later.”

It seemed too great a task to sit up and play her part in drawing room etiquette, so Lottie stayed where she was, in her unladylike sprawl. She waved the letter in the air and said, “Montague played his hand, and I might be outmatched.”

Raising a brow, Amesbury took a seat beside her on the sofa, setting the parcel aside. "You, outmatched? I can't believe that. What has he done?" He eyed the mangled paper as if it might burst into flames at any moment.

The vote of confidence soothed her emotional turmoil somewhat. "I have to figure out something, and fast." Straightening, she smoothed her hair, tucking an escaped curl behind her ear. After pacing and ranting, she likely looked a mess. "I'll read it aloud. *Since you have made yourself unavailable*—I refuse to see him, and Dawson has denied him entrance multiple times, on my orders—*I must carry out our plans without your assistance. Our engagement announcement will appear in Friday's edition of the* Times. *If you wish input on our nuptials, you must deign to see me in person. Your future husband*—he's signed it James, but I've been calling him more colorful names."

Amesbury exhaled with a great sigh, leaning back on the sofa beside her. "You may have tae catch me up. Are you two engaged? Were you?"

"Like I told you before, his father and mine are friends. They proposed the match, and I flatly declined, back before I came to London."

A maid arrived with a tea cart, and Amesbury waved for Lottie to sit back. Ignoring etiquette entirely, he poured her a cup, then one for himself. "Two sugars, right? That's how you took it at the inn."

Lottie cradled the delicate teacup and stared down at the liquid. He'd paid attention to how she liked her tea, and at the moment, that was the sweetest thing she could remember anyone doing for her. "Thank you. I can't believe you remembered."

Amesbury blew on his beverage and waved for her to

continue her tale. "Carry on. The earl arranged the match, and you refused."

"Yes. There was a big row until he finally agreed to let me come to London to find a husband, with one stipulation. I have until Parliament convenes in November. If I don't find someone suitable by then, I have to accept Montague."

He furrowed his brow and swallowed. "But Montague seems tae think there's a different timeline."

"Exactly. Also, I told Montague in no uncertain terms that I'd never marry him. And apparently, Father never passed along my original answer to the match. Montague is pushing forward, and Father is too far away to handle any of this in a timely manner. It's a disaster."

"Manipulative bastard." Amesbury ran a hand through his hair. "Sorry for the language."

Lottie shrugged. "Think nothing of it. Had you arrived five minutes earlier, you would have heard far worse."

"He has the earl's permission. Can he force you?"

"Father can certainly try to pressure me, but I'm of age. I refuse to marry Montague. Suffice it to say, he showed his true colors, and I found the shade did not suit me. My concern at this moment is more for exiting the immediate situation and then handling whatever underhanded dealings my father and his friend have been up to. We had an agreement, and by accepting the match, Father has broken that deal."

Sighing, Amesbury shook his head. "What can I do?"

The fact that he'd offered to help in any way made her smile. "I bet you didn't know agreeing to be my friend would involve all this, did you? I don't know what to do. Every option I think of ends in scandal, shame, or a lifetime of dealing with that man."

"You're a better person than I. The plans I've considered in the last few minutes all end with a body disposal," Amesbury said.

Her laugh felt wonderful after a day of darker emotions. "Do all Scotsmen have this homicidal bent?"

He grinned, and a bit of hope speared her. As allies went, this giant man was a good one, if only to lift her spirits. When his expression turned serious, she could practically see the wheels turning in his head.

"You have an idea. What is it?" She tilted her head toward him, and he met her halfway, with mere inches of sofa between them.

"How far are you willing tae go tae get rid of Montague?" he asked, and his low voice felt like a caress.

Lord, his eyes were blue. The thought distracted her for a moment, sending a fizzing sensation loose in her chest. They'd been closer than this on the balcony but not by much. Memories of their near kiss and then watching him disrobe from her window heated that fizzy feeling into a warmth settling low within her. Friends probably weren't supposed to think of one another that way, but with the memories replaying and him so close, Lottie was having a hard time shoving the emotions back in place. "What are you thinking?"

"Montague can't publish an engagement announcement tae you if you're already promised tae someone else." He grinned, bringing the dimple out.

Lottie blinked, connecting his suggestion to the situation. "You? You're asking me to marry you?" Granted, she'd instigated friendship, and she might have just been admiring his dimple, but marrying him was a bit of a stretch. Not an abhorrent thought, oddly enough, but not the answer she'd expected either.

"You don' need tae follow through with it, lass. When we're ready, you end it. Quietly or publicly. I'm at your mercy. Or we can set a time limit if you like. Maybe a month? Then you will be free tae find a man the earl will accept."

She cocked her head, resting it against the back of the sofa. "You'd do that?"

He moved first, breaking the odd tension that had risen with their noses almost touching. Leaning his elbows on his knees, he laced and unlaced his fingers over and over, as if nervous. "Aye. What better way for me tae show society how wrong I was about you than tae tell the world I want you?" His voice was rough as he stared at his hands. "Montague said he's posting the engagement announcement in Friday's paper, aye?"

Straightening, Lottie grappled with the details of this plan. A fake engagement might work. "I believe he is giving me time to come about to his way of thinking."

Amesbury shot her a grin. "I might not know you well, but even I know you won' be changing your mind on this." He pulled a pocket watch from his waistcoat and flipped open the cover to check the time. "The print deadline is rapidly approaching. But our announcement doesn' have tae be in tomorrow's paper. We can still spike his guns if we get the news into Thursday's edition. That gives you until this time tomorrow tae make your decision."

It was the only choice she had, and for reasons she wasn't willing to explore now, the idea of an engagement to Amesbury wasn't abhorrent. Yes, she'd still have to deal with Father. But she could slay only one dragon at a time, and this would neutralize Montague's threat. "We bring our close friends in on the plan. I won't lie to Agatha."

He nodded.

"And even though this engagement will be temporary, this is my first proposal—"

"Montague didn't?"

"Not in person. So since this is my first proposal, I want you to do it right. Even if it is a sham." She primly folded her hands in her lap and waited.

His expression softened. "Well, let no one ever say I can't fake propose with conviction." Amesbury eased off the sofa, then took a knee at her feet and held out his hand, palm up.

As she laid the tips of her fingers across the rough pads of his, a worry niggled at the hope bursting through her. "Are you sure? By starting down this path, knowing I'll end it, you're opening yourself to the ridicule of the entire *ton*."

"We're friends. I don' have many of those. I value the few I have," he said with a shrug.

"I don't think either of us expected this when we decided to be friends."

His fingers wrapped around hers, anchoring them together. "We're partners in this now." He cleared his throat. "I wasn' raised tae be a fancy gentleman. And I've already failed you once. I won' betray you again, lass." He donned a serious expression, but the twinkle in his eye ruined the effect. "Lady Charlotte Wentworth, will you do me the honor of being my faux fiancée?"

A giggle bubbled up, even though she knew this wasn't a real proposal. Romance and true love weren't in her future, by choice, but this moment of friendship and having an ally was precious. "Yes, Lord Amesbury. I'd be happy to be your faux fiancée."

He grinned, then got to his feet and pulled her up to

stand. “Let’s go write our engagement announcement and ruin Montague’s plans.”

It wasn’t until he’d left for the *Times* office that she noticed the parcel abandoned on the sofa. She set aside the note tucked into the string, unwrapped the paper, and began to laugh. He’d brought her a beautifully bound volume of Francis Grose’s *Dictionary of the Vulgar Tongue*. Still chuckling, she read the note, written in scrawling penmanship.

So your tongue may be as sharp as your wit.

Looking forward to crossing swords again soon.

Your friend,
Ethan

Chapter Twelve

The *Times* announced the engagement on Wednesday, two days before Montague's threatened date. There it was in black and white. The longer Lottie stared at it, the stranger it became. She'd saved the paper, as nonsensical as that action was, stashing it in the drawer beside her bed. It wasn't as if any of this was real, after all. On the seventh morning of her faux engagement, she read the announcement for the thousandth time, then girded her proverbial loins for that day's gossip columns. The rags, being the upstanding informational tools to the masses that they were, had been going wild with the story.

"How bad is it this morning?" she asked Darling.

"The papers or the servants' gossip network?" Darling laid out a dress for the morning, then took the paper from Lottie and tucked it back in the drawer.

Lottie winced. "Both, I suppose. Are the servants saying worse things than the papers?"

A lord offering for the woman he'd once shunned was too juicy a tidbit for people to resist. The old satirical cartoons resurfaced from the archives and were published alongside new ones. Even people who couldn't read knew the alleged details of her love life. The most popular image showed a pathetic groom walking down the aisle of a church with a life-sized cutout of her tucked under one arm like a newspaper as he trudged toward a bishop holding out a bag of gold. It wasn't even a flattering likeness—if such a thing were possible when speaking of mocking caricatures.

"Some love the romance of it, you know? A man ruins a woman, then wins her back, and they fall in love. Word is, you have a heart of gold and the patience of a saint."

Lottie snorted. That was one way to interpret it. Not remotely true. But creative. "What's the other side say?"

"You broke Mr. Montague's heart by choosing a title over love. Those people think you're a moneygrubbing hussy. We don't like those people." Darling shook out a chemise and placed it with the day dress on the bed.

"No, I suppose we wouldn't like those people. Is Montague still flapping his jaw all over Christendom?" She tried to laugh it off, but it stung to think of strangers passing judgment on her based on false information.

"The man should be on the stage from what I hear. A more wounded martyr for love you've never seen. The cartoonists are having a grand time, let me tell you. Between you and me, I think he's selling these stories to pay his gambling debts," Darling said.

"Too bad I can't tell everyone he's the real brute here, not Lord Amesbury. Have you heard back from Patrick regarding our little subterfuge?" At her request, Darling had sent a letter to Patrick the same day Amesbury had brought the announcement to the *Times*. With any luck, by the time the edition of the paper announcing their engagement arrived at Stanwick, Patrick would have prepared the staff to follow her instructions. The servants ironed the paper before Father read it over breakfast—although he didn't always read the news, since the world beyond his library was of little interest. The papers ended up passed around the servants' hall and eventually burned as kindling. But just in case, they'd enlisted Patrick in making that particular edition disappear. As long as Father hadn't developed a taste for gossip pages, they should be able to contain news of her engagement until Montague had moved on and she was ready to figure out her next step.

"Not yet. Patrick will have taken care of it, don't you worry. As to you and Montague, and what went on—I've held my tongue. But it's hard," Darling said.

"On what side are our servants?" Lottie flipped back the coverlet, then crossed to the vanity table for her hairbrush. She'd expected there would be talk, but Montague casting himself as the victim fed the flames of the gossip columns, making the chatter that much worse.

"This staff has a righteous fear of Dawson's wrath, and Dawson's taken a shine to you and Lady Agatha. None of us would speak against you. But servants talk at the market, over the back gate, couples stepping out together." Darling shrugged, leaving the rest unsaid. There was nothing they could do about the talk.

Darling handed her the day's papers. Lottie perched on the window seat to read the newest fabrications, innuendos, and allegations delivered to their door. Today's columns reported seeing Mr. Montague visibly distraught. Not news. She snorted indelicately, then flipped to the next page.

Some reports said while he was out with his friends, he'd furiously ranted about the situation. Entirely plausible. He did love to monologue. Others claimed he wept inconsolably while declaring his heartbreak to anyone who would listen. Ah, there was the fiction. "I'd love to see that," she muttered.

Three broadsheets later, she surmised that the papers all agreed—no matter his mood, Montague always spoke of his lost love. More like her lost dowry, but that would make *him* sound like a money-grubbing arse.

The treatment he'd received from MacBrute and his Paper Doll Princess was nothing short of abominable, the papers declared. To be thrown over after beginning marriage contracts in good faith was too tragic for words, said another paper. "Never mind that he shared plenty of words on the subject. This is the same rubbish, just using different phrases each day," she told Darling. "Listen to this nonsense: *How could the lady in question choose the hulking Scottish MacBrute over the Adonis-like perfection of the Earl of Danby's son?* I'll tell you how. Lord Amesbury doesn't have to pad his coats, and he probably doesn't kiss like a gasping trout."

"I bet you a week's pay you find out for sure sooner rather than later. Lord Amesbury might be a friend now, but he's still a man," Darling teased.

Lottie made a noncommittal noise but held still while her maid tightened the short stays. It was her and Agatha's at-home day, which meant an entire afternoon loomed ahead, filled with endless rounds of tea and onlookers. If she must endure a parade of curious faces, probing questions, and subtle inquiries, she'd prefer to do so while comfortable. The day dress was fashionable but looser than anything she'd wear outside the house. While smiling her way through visitors, she'd miss the buffer of Darling's cheerfully snide commentary regarding the gossip columns.

"Can I ask you a question, milady?"

"Of course, Darling. What's on your mind?"

"Wherever we live after London, would you be willing to bring on Patrick instead of leaving him at Stanwick Manor?"

Lottie focused on her maid in the mirror. "Are things with Patrick progressing in that direction? Has he declared himself?"

Darling shook her head. "He's not said it in so many words. I think he's waiting to have that conversation face-to-face. I need to be sure he's thought it through. Marrying someone with my history—that takes a special kind of man."

Lottie turned to squeeze her hand. "You both have histories to consider. Patrick would be the luckiest man alive if he won your heart. If you want this, then I am happy for you." She turned around and lifted her heavy hair away from her back so Darling could fasten the line of silver buttons. "To answer your question—I would create a position for him no matter where we lived. Do not fear that I would separate the two of you."

"That sets my mind at ease. Now, what gown do you want to wear this evening? It's your first outing with Lord Amesbury since the engagement, so you should look spectacular."

"How about the scarlet silk? If they're going to talk, we might as well give them something to talk about." Lottie winked. The red gown in particular would tell everyone she didn't care about what the papers said. Even if she wasn't entirely immune to the talk.

That night, light and chatter spilled from the townhome into the street, acting as a beacon for the line of carriages. With an entire evening stretching before her, Lottie closed her eyes a moment and wished desperately for a cup of strong tea to help her get through the rest of the night.

Having dealt with the expected afternoon parade of callers, wearing the red gown felt like donning a facade—an alternate personality who courted notoriety, not caring that her love life was under dissection in the papers.

Again.

On top of dreading the speculation of her peers, there was the ever-present worry that she'd have to deal with Montague face-to-face. There was no doubt in her mind he was behind the news stories, so thinking he'd avoid the opportunity to make a fuss in public was naive. When she thought of her last encounter with him, she tried to dwell on his expression as he'd flown off the seat and not the way he'd kissed, threatened, and made her feel helpless. Events by that pond couldn't be changed, but she could celebrate the way she'd fought back and won.

Now she'd have to deal with whatever the evening brought. Hopefully, she worried for nothing, and it would be a lovely night with Amesbury, her godmother, and Lord Carlyle.

Taking a deep breath, she placed her hand on Lord Amesbury's arm. He covered her gloved fingers with his as if having her beside him was the most natural thing in the world. "You are lovely this evening."

She looked up from under her lashes as they ascended the steps. "Thank you, my lord. Flattery is an admirable characteristic in a fiancé. Feel free to continue in that vein."

When he grinned, that dimple flashed, crinkling the corners of his eyes.

The butler opened the door, releasing a chorus of voices that swelled through the air, buzzing in a way that resembled a hive—complete with their hostess, the queen. Sharp laughter occasionally broke above the din. Lottie wished she were comfortable enough in this environment to laugh so freely.

The Blanchards had no ballroom in which to entertain. Instead, guests flowed from one room into the next, with the largest room cleared for dancing. As the great number of bodies crowded into a relatively small space, the air grew stale with each degree the temperature rose.

Lady Blanchard greeted them with a broad smile, her eyes darting to Lottie's hand tucked through Amesbury's arm. "The happy couple! I do hope you'll enjoy the evening."

Amesbury smiled down at Lottie, playing his role to perfection. He winked, and the deep blue of his eyes distracted her from her earlier worries. Since he'd entered the carriage this evening, there'd been a quiver low in her belly. With that wink, it grew from tiny flutters into a rapid pulse, like the wings of a hummingbird.

Leading her away from their hostess, he leaned down to her ear. "If Montague is here, remember you aren't alone. We are partners, lass." The look he gave her made the hummingbird flutters calm until everything within her quieted. A blooming liquid warmth spread over her as he held her gaze for a moment. A few heartbeats.

Too long.

She blinked away the intimate spell and searched the room for something to distract her from this inconvenient attraction to her faux fiancé. A blond halo of curls held ruthlessly in check with pomade caught her eye an instant before she felt Montague's glare.

"Speak of the devil."

Amesbury stilled beside her. "I see him. You're more than capable of handling him. But I'd like tae stay close."

Lottie hugged his arm as an answer. Moving away from Montague, they greeted acquaintances, sipped champagne, and fielded the questions underlying each innocuous exchange. People smiled and laughed in a friendly way while hissed conversations swelled in their wake all around the room.

"I thought Montague signed contracts with her father..."

"Did poor Mr. Montague realize she was considering MacBrute?"

Several women looked her way with envious stares. Lottie couldn't say she blamed them. The sharp, simple lines of an evening coat suited her escort's frame. The muscles bunching and releasing in his thighs showed through the fabric of his pantaloons. So many men needed padding to enhance their figures. When faced with the real thing, one tended to stare.

Amesbury tapped her hand, then flicked his finger toward the doorway. Mr. Montague approached them. High collar points framed an elaborate cravat of snowy linen, from which a gem winked in the candlelight. The man who'd pushed himself on her resembled a fairy-tale prince except for the faint bruising under his eyes. Whether from too many late nights or the blow to the face she'd delivered, Lottie didn't know. With every step he took toward them, her mind screamed for her to run, while her feet froze in place as if she'd grown roots.

"Lady Charlotte." Montague bowed over her hand. When he attempted to turn her wrist up for a kiss in his customary greeting, she jerked her hand away.

"Mr. Montague." Ice crystals should have formed in nearby champagne flutes from her tone.

"You used to call me James. I suppose such intimacies aren't appropriate now." His eyes turned glassy, as if on the verge of tears. What a handy trick, to summon tears on cue.

Amesbury stood as a quiet pillar of support next to her.

"I wish you nothing but happiness, of course, pet." Montague grabbed her hand again. She tugged, but he held firm, increasing the pressure of his grip with brutal force.

"Release me at once, sir." The quiver in Lottie's voice betrayed her, but with any luck no one would notice. She dug the tips of her fingers into Amesbury's arm in a silent cry for help.

Montague ignored the demand and smirked at Amesbury. "When you marry, what shall we call her? Lady Amesbury or Lady MacBrute?"

Amesbury covered Montague's wrist, his fingers easily encircling the bone, as well as part of his forearm. "I don' care what you call me. However, you'll listen tae the lady and release her now."

At last, Montague let her go. As blood rushed back to her fingers, she swallowed a gasp. Goodness, that hurt. Refusing to let him see her pain, she raised her chin and channeled every lesson in decorum Mother had pounded into her brain. "Goodbye, Mr. Montague. I see no reason to speak again."

Anyone watching would think the whispers didn't matter as she and Amesbury made their way into the next room.

Ethan couldn't get them away from that smug golden bastard fast enough.

"Where are we going?" Lottie trotted to keep up with his long strides.

"Someplace private. If such a place exists in this house." A corner by the back windows looked appealing. One wall sconce illuminated the small nook, and a potted plant of some kind hid them from the rest of the guests. "Take off your glove, please."

The "please" was a formality. Ethan would not be swayed in this. Lady Charlotte pulled her glove off carefully, wincing now that they were away from prying eyes. Her hand was already swelling at the knuckles, discoloring in places. Ethan cursed low, keeping his fingers gentle while examining the damage.

"I only understood half of what you said just now. Did you know your accent gets heavier when you're upset? The 'sheep-loving son of a whore' reference is self-explanatory. But what is a 'feartie'?"

"'Feartie' means 'coward.' The least offensive thing I called him, I think. Apologies. I shouldn' speak like that in front of a lady."

"Oh, pish. I don't mind your language one bit. I even learned something," she joked, then gasped when he tried to put her fingers through their full range of motion.

"He hurt you, lass. I want tae rattle his skull."

"When I tried to remove my hand, he squeezed harder. Thank you for intervening." She grimaced at the blooming bruises. "At least my glove will hide it."

"Lass, one day I hope you'll tell me what happened

between you, so I can determine exactly how bad a thrashing he needs. No one should hurt a woman. Ever."

Her smile was a bittersweet thing. "Thank you for the sentiment, Lord Amesbury. Actually, may I call you Amesbury? We are engaged, after all. And friends. Perhaps we can drop the formality."

"Call me Mac. Everyone does."

"I most certainly will not." A glance at her face confirmed he'd somehow misstepped. "That's the name everyone gave you because the *ton* couldn't be bothered to call you by your proper title. Your name is *not* Mac or MacBrute or any variation thereof."

Long ago, he'd felt the same way about the name. Hearing those old feelings come from her mouth made him blink. When had he accepted the pejorative name? "Ethan. My name is Ethan Ridley."

She smiled for real this time, lighting her eyes. "Ethan, you may call me Lottie."

Hearing his name—his real name—from her lips felt impossibly precious and intimate. "Thank you, Lottie." Lifting her injured hand, he lightly kissed each knuckle. "I should call out Montague. This is not acceptable."

Arching a brow, she worked her glove back on, then tucked her arm into his. "I want your word as a gentleman that you won't. I don't need the scandal, and you don't need his blood on your hands—because I have every confidence you'd win."

He growled. Montague had hurt her. The bastard deserved a thrashing, then execution at dawn, followed by dumping his body unceremoniously in the river. Let the fish have whatever remained after Ethan was done with him. Lady Charlotte—Lottie—stayed him with a hand on his chest, and his growl became something closer to a purr.

"I mean it, Ethan. He's not worth ruining our lives simply to get even. Promise me."

"Fine. I promise I will not call him out." Dumping him in the river might be an option, though.

"Thank you. Now, I am going to freshen up a bit. Don't kill anyone while I'm gone. You appear quite fierce." Lottie patted his chest one more time, then walked away, leaving a lemony tang in the air.

While Montague didn't appear in the immediate area, every protective instinct within Ethan reared its head, so he followed at a distance just in case, keeping an eye on the people in her path. As she sailed with the confidence of a queen across the room, then down a hall, she smiled at a few acquaintances.

Leaning on the wall several feet from the doorway, he waited for her to emerge from the retiring room. Female voices approached the door. None of them were Lottie's.

"She must be a fool to give up such a treat for a fatter purse. Especially with a hefty dowry of her own."

"She has to have a huge dowry if her father ever expects to unload her on some poor fellow. Her bank account isn't all that's plump."

"Doesn't Lord Amesbury care he's getting used goods? I overheard my brother saying Montague described exactly *how* pink her bits were—if you understand my meaning. The words *eager* and *enthusiastic* were used. Repeatedly."

"Poor Paper Doll Princess. Amesbury isn't that much of a catch. Not with his past..."

Sometimes Ethan was grateful for his ungentlemanly build. As he straightened from his casual stance against the wall, he didn't feel even remotely gentlemanly. The tittering laughter cut off when they caught sight of him.

Curling his lip with disgust, he stared each of the three women down—he couldn't call them ladies after that shameless display of vindictive tongue wagging. One by one, the women avoided his gaze, then scurried away as if he would release hellhounds after them.

One minute passed. Then two. Finally, Lottie emerged from the room. Ethan snaked an arm around her waist, gently pulling her toward a nearby passageway. The small dim space, intended for servants, had only a single lamp on the wall, near a set of narrow stairs.

"Ethan—"

He towed her deeper into the shadows, then used his body to protect her from the view of those passing by. "Now. Look at me, lass." Flat eyes stared at his cravat, lacking her usual spirit. "Sweetheart, look at me." The endearment slipped out, but it felt so right he couldn't regret it.

She firmed her chin until her jaw set in a mulish line, then raised her gaze to his. There was no use biting back a smile. Lottie's stubborn streak made an appearance in that narrow little point of her chin, which was too adorable for words. His girl had a spine of steel, even if she occasionally forgot that.

When had he begun thinking of her as his?

"How much did you hear?" she asked.

"I'm a beast, which we both knew already. They have grossly inaccurate opinions about your beautiful figure. And every one of them deserves tae be courted by that rat Montague."

"All of it, then. Or most of it. I doubt they knew I was in the room. Not that my presence matters, I suppose."

"It's rubbish. Every bit of it."

"How are you certain it isn't true? Montague is saying

I—" She gulped. Tears shone in her eyes in the low light. "He's saying I—"

Ethan brushed a finger down the side of her face, as he had that evening at the inn forever ago. Still impossibly soft. "We both know you didn' drop Montague for my fortune or because you're fickle in your affections. You barely tolerate me on the best of days." That got a watery smile. "I don' care how far things went between yourself and Montague. He's a bastard and a rogue tae say such things about you, no matter the circumstances." The siren song of her luminous skin called to him in the dim light, drawing him a half step closer.

"For what it's worth, they're lies. He kissed me. I didn't care for it. I tried to push him away. But he refused to take me home without another kiss. I think he likes to hurt women. I had bruises, but by the end of it, so did he. Since then I've refused to see him."

Bracing an arm above her head, he closed his eyes and pulled her close with a hand around her waist. The move wasn't meant to be an embrace for anything but comfort. "Oh, lass, I'm sorry. If I could take away that memory, I would."

The hug changed when she raised her face toward his and rested her hands on his waist. Air grew scarce, but that might be because he held his breath. The expression on her face looked an awful lot like welcome.

"Maybe we can't take it away. But you could replace it. Can you kiss me, please?"

He hung his head, then grazed his lips along the juncture of her neck and shoulder, because by all that was holy, he'd just been asked to kiss Lady Charlotte Wentworth, and those were the closest body parts to his lips. Lottie's nearness, the dramatic dip of her waist, her unique scent cueing his body to the intimacy of the moment—all of it would be forever lost to him if he made a mess of this.

As she'd told him of Montague's assault, every bit of him had wanted to rage, to pound a fist through something, to hunt the slimy toad down and ensure he never touched another woman. But he had an excellent reason to not do any of that—Lottie in his arms, warm and willing, asking for a kiss. With one hand pressed so firmly into the wall, it was a wonder he didn't leave a handprint behind in the plaster. Ethan tried not to pounce on her like a man offered his fantasy, although that was exactly what was happening.

Their breathing dominated the narrow passage, muffling music from distant rooms filled with guests. Opening his lips slightly, Ethan allowed himself a small taste of her skin at the shoulder—salty, complex with rich flavors he'd crave after tonight. As he placed slow, openmouthed kisses along the arch of her neck, her body softened against his. When he kissed her jaw below her ear, Lottie's breathing grew shaky. She liked that.

He finally reached the corner of her mouth, and she turned her head and met him halfway.

She would think about the consequences later. Plans for the future, the list of qualities she needed in a husband—she set all that aside. Right now this mattered more. The heat coming from his body set off an unsettling buzzing under her skin she realized was *need*. Desire. That lust he'd mentioned on the balcony, then inspired as she'd watched him from her bedroom window. She knew how he looked under these well-tailored evening clothes.

This decision would throw them off course, away from the familiar. The danger of that, the unknown, made something within her come alive.

He finally kissed her lips. Usually, her brain assessed every moment, searched for ways to handle situations, prepared for any outcome—from the worst-case scenario to the best. All that went silent. There was simply her and him. And they fit.

His mouth moved over hers, and that part she'd only just discovered—the desire for *more*, for him, flared brighter. The gentle scrape of his teeth on her sensitized bottom lip drew a noise from her somewhere between a moan and a whimper. This was nothing like the bruising mashing of faces she'd experienced with Montague. Where Montague had roughly taken, Ethan was asking, gently coaxing as he gave pleasure.

Kissing him was like learning a new language. There was a call and answer between them made of breath and sounds that weren't words but somehow still created a conversation—the most erotic conversation of her life.

If his hands caressed her, she'd probably purr. But he kept his palm firmly against her lower back, straying neither north nor south. The contact was both too much and not enough. She arched her body into him, chasing that need for *more*.

When the kiss ended, her small groan joined his heavy sigh. He rested his forehead against hers, exchanging air for a few more seconds. Their mouths were so achingly close. It took all her remaining self-control not to lick that dip at the top of his lip.

"You taste like heather honey, lass."

"Is that a good thing?" Her world shook a bit, so it made sense that her voice would shake too.

"Aye." Ethan eased his body away in small increments. One of her hands skimmed up his chest, and his blue eyes fluttered closed. After a moment, he stepped away and offered a hand. "I believe, my lady, that you owe me a dance."

That was that, then.

In a daze, she returned with him to the rooms full of people. He hadn't run his fingers through her hair or mussed her gown. Nothing of her outside appearance gave away the internal shift she'd just experienced. There was *more* to be had, and while she hadn't had time to unravel the tangle of emotions inside her, her heart and mind agreed that the feeling was significant. That this would complicate things but perhaps for the better.

They lined up for a country dance as if nothing untoward had occurred.

As if he hadn't just caused an emotional earthquake making her question every unsentimental piece of her perfectly planned future. Because those plans didn't make room for *more*.

Lottie curtsied when the music began and sent him a sunny smile, as if he hadn't just potentially ruined everything.

Chapter Thirteen

Calvin dropped the paper next to Ethan's breakfast plate. "Either you're living an alternate life I'm not aware of, or the gossip columnists are getting desperate with their conjecture."

Ethan flicked the edge of the newsprint out of his eggs. "What are they saying this time?"

Calvin pointed. Today's headline declared "Paper Doll Torn Between Love and Money" in bold print. A sketch below showed Lady Charlotte as a one-dimensional cut-out caught in a tug-of-war between two men. Montague's perfect face shone as the hero in the picture, while Ethan's hulking form sported an ill-fitting coat made of pound notes.

"Charming. Only accurate in that Montague is one gambling note shy of debtor's prison." Ethan folded the paper to hide the cartoon. One bright spot in all this was that the gossips weren't aware of his financial situation if he'd been cast as the rich suitor who'd wooed her with his money.

Calvin flopped in the chair beside him. "People are mocking you, Mac. Is all this worth it? You don't even get to marry the girl in the end."

"She's worth it." They'd kissed last night, and he couldn't help feeling that the landscape was changing beneath his feet. They'd gone into this engagement with clear boundaries: which people would know the truth, how long it would last, and who would end it.

Now he didn't want her to end it. Whether that translated to actually desiring marriage, he didn't know. But he sure as hell desired Lottie.

After their kiss he'd blurted out the first thing on his mind and told her she tasted like heather honey—sweet, earthy, and precious. Heather bloomed for only a short while, so the honey produced by the bees was all the more treasured for its rarity. She tasted like the best parts of home, and the knowledge had kept him awake late into the night.

Whether this new territory was a good thing or a disastrous mistake remained to be seen. And if by some miracle they blew up their plan and actually headed down the aisle, convincing the earl to give his blessing would be its own challenge. He set that particular problem aside. Best not to borrow trouble.

"Think the engagement will be enough to discourage Montague?" Cal asked.

That was a question he'd been considering since last night. The man's boldness to hurt her in front of everyone while smiling and expecting her to smile too—Montague was worse than he'd thought. "I don' know. James Montague isn' known for his accommodating nature."

"He's a sewer rat, plain and simple. We need to find a way to protect her beyond a phony engagement," Cal said.

"I'm open tae ideas."

"There's something off about him, you know?" Cal sipped his coffee.

Ethan flipped the newspaper open and studied the cartoon again. "Money. He's in debt up tae his eyeballs. If we control his finances, we control the man. Maybe we get Danby tae call him home tae rusticate in the country."

Cal nodded in agreement. "We buy up his debts. I shadow him at the tables and buy his markers. Then we dun him all to hell and back."

Ethan sighed. This was going to be expensive, tapping into what he had saved in case the brewery project went awry, but if it meant Lottie would be safe, it would be worth it. "I'm goin' tae ask Lottie tae join me at Woodrest for a few days. The new brewmaster is moving in, and I need tae check in on the worksite. It gets us away from Town for a while. Are you fine with following him while I'm gone?"

"Absolutely. I'll turn it into a learning experience for the Puppy. We'll call it 'An Idiot's Guide to the Underbelly of London: What Not to Do.' We'll have a grand time," Cal said.

Silence descended between them. Years of friendship meant Ethan could recognize a comfortable silence—and this wasn't it. "What else is on your mind, Cal?"

He took his sweet time answering. But finally, Cal sighed and said, "It's been one of those weeks where I want to run away from home. I fear the problems would find me again eventually, though."

"Sister or father?"

"Both," Cal said without humor. "Emma's plans for her Season grow more intricate and expensive with every letter. You'd think finishing school would teach common sense or budgeting, but apparently not."

"Is the estate having financial difficulties?" Ethan's brow wrinkled. "And here I am making expensive plans tae take down Montague. I hope you know that's something I'm financing, not you."

"No, I'm fine. And I'll happily help with taking down Montague. I know you're good for it eventually. This is nothing more than the usual frantic bailing measures to clean up my father's messes—which I also had to do yesterday." Cal's relentlessly chipper personality usually kept his face alight with laughter, but right now he looked tired and about ten years older.

"The usual problems with your father?"

"Indeed. That man couldn't keep his pecker to himself if his life depended on it."

"Let me guess—another jilted mistress." A jilted mistress was always preferable to the heartbreaking interviews with younger servants in the family way.

"This time it was an opera dancer. Father pulled his old trick of gifting paste jewels, then barred her from the house. As per usual, the next person she called upon was me. Why can't he simply remarry and be faithful? Mother's been dead for a decade. And you can't tell me the man is grieving her. They hated each other."

"How long did it take her tae proposition you?"

"About fifteen seconds," Cal snorted. "As if I'd consider my father's leftovers. Ugh." He shuddered and Ethan laughed. It wasn't the first time they'd had this conversation, nor would it be the last. Even though there were few things more pathetic than an aging rake, it would be foolishness to expect the Marquess of Eastly to change. While Cal accepted that, he still—more often than not—had to clean up his father's messes. Whether that meant a payment and a cottage somewhere for a servant and the Marquess's by-blow, or situations with an angry lover, Cal stepped in and did the dirty work.

"The Marquess doesn' deserve you."

"He's the only father I have. Even if he is utter rubbish at it," Cal said.

"At least Emma only wants a pretty dress."

"Or twenty. But you're right. She'll only debut once. After that her wardrobe will be someone else's problem."

Ethan wiped his mouth with a napkin, then finished the cup of tea he'd nursed over breakfast. "I'm going next door. Would you like tae join me?"

"No. Hardwick is coming by. My tailor delivered a new coat, so I'm passing one on. I need to work on my *you'd be doing me a favor by taking it off my hands* face."

"You're dressing the lad now?" That explained why Adam's coat had looked familiar a few days ago.

Cal shrugged. "He lives on pennies. Insists on saving his pay for a rainy day. What kind of rainy day is he expecting that warrants living like a pauper? I pass along what I can and try to convince him it's not charity. Then he makes the clothes over to fit. Which probably means he cuts the bloody thing in half and sews it back together. The boy is painfully thin."

There was something in the way he'd taken Adam Hardwick under his wing that reminded Ethan of Cal's determination to befriend him years ago. "Adam and I are both lucky tae have you as a friend. I have a few cravats I can add tae the donation if you think he could use them."

"Nice sentiment, but I'll pass. Your linen is a disgrace." Cal poured himself another cup of coffee. "Enjoy the lovely Lady Charlotte. Charm Lady Agatha for me."

Shrugging into his overcoat, Ethan laughed. "Is such a thing possible?" As he pulled on his gloves, he paused, clearing his throat. "Since we're catching up, there's another thing. Lottie said something last night. She refuses tae call me Mac."

"But we've always called you Mac." Calvin rested his elbows on the table and cocked his head, listening.

"Don' you remember? Some of the lads called me MacBrute that first year. That shortened tae Mac. She says the nickname is disrespectful."

Cal sat back. "Huh. Never thought of it that way. Always thought it was in good fun, but I see your point. I call you Mac all the time. I don't mean any offense by it."

Ethan drummed his fingers on the back of the chair. Ethan was positive Cal, more than anyone, would understand that he wanted to be called by his rightful name. "I know you don' mean tae offend. Before Lottie brought it up, I'd accepted the name. But she's right. They called me Mac so no one would forget I don' belong here. Not really. Just another Scotsman puttin' on airs, taking a title from a good English family."

"What are you talking about? You're worth ten of these young lordlings born with silver spoons in their mouths. What happened with your cousin and his son is tragic, but no one can blame you for being the next in line to inherit. You belong here. Never doubt that," Cal said.

"Thank you." Those doubts sometimes crept in, especially when he spent a lot of time in London. A wave of homesickness for Woodrest flooded him. He wanted to bring Lottie to Kent. See if she liked Woodrest and the people who mattered most to him. That might be courting heartache, when their relationship had a time limit. Of course, if he convinced her to give them a chance, he'd have to deal with her father. That man hated him. As it was, once word reached her father, all hell would break loose.

"I feel I should mention, *Ethan*, that in most relationships, it's the woman who changes her name."

Hearing the name his Mum and Da had given him caused a strange feeling of wholeness to settle in him. There might be more to a name than he'd thought. With a grin, he tipped his hat at a rakish angle and stole the last piece of bacon off Cal's plate before he left.

Dawson entered the breakfast room. "Milady, Lord Amesbury has come to call. Shall I have him wait in the drawing room?"

"This early? No, Dawson. I'm unwilling to go another moment without tea. Show him in here." Sharing breakfast at her table was intimate, but what was the fun of having a fake-fiancé neighbor if she couldn't break convention?

Ethan walked in, bringing a chill that clung to his coat. The cold dissolved with the look he gave her as he took off his hat. Heavens, his eyes were blue. Somehow brighter this morning. The smile he gave her was another intimacy. Not just friendly but carnal. Seeing that smile, no one would doubt he'd tasted her mouth and he wanted to do it again. Warmth flooded her, and those flames he'd stoked the night before flickered back to life.

"Good morning." Lord, she was blushing, wasn't she? Like some schoolgirl instead of a woman of the age to adopt ten cats and a lace cap. "Have you eaten? Would you like chocolate or tea? You're welcome to join me."

"I would love a cup of tea," he said. "You look beautiful this morning."

The simple compliment somehow made the warmth growing within her worse. "Thank you. I was just, ah, admiring you as well. Oh, how awkward and childish that sounds." She pressed her hands to her cheeks, which, yes, were on fire. Pulling herself together, she took a bracing breath and focused on breakfast. "Forgive the informality, but as you've already dealt with me in the mornings, you know I'm a bit of a termagant before food."

She spread strawberry preserves on toast, then took a bite. Agatha's cook did amazing things with preserves. The strawberries tasted of summer, prompting a happy little sound, which drew a glance from Ethan. She ignored it for the moment. Fresh cream butter with strawberries was the best way to start the day. Ethan poured himself a cup of tea, then sat beside her.

"So what do you have for me this morning?" She sipped from her teacup and waited.

"I come with a proposal. As predicted, the *ton* won' stop talking about our engagement," he said. "I don' know about you, but I'd prefer tae just escape it all."

"Escape sounds lovely. What do you have in mind? I hear Trinidad is beautiful, no matter the time of year. Think they would have forgotten about us by the time we sailed there and back?" She bit into her second piece of toast and washed it down with a sip of tea.

The way his eyes crinkled at the edges when he smiled never failed to charm her. "I've always wanted tae see that part of the world. But I was thinking Kent. Woodrest specifically."

"You want to take me to your estate?" This time, her sip of tea was more of a gulp. Goodness, he wanted to bring her home? That felt like something a real fiancé would do with the woman he planned to marry—not the lady with the temporary role.

"Lady Agatha as well, obviously. We must observe the niceties, after all. Word around London is that we're so enamored of each other, we'll be the love match of the Season." Ethan winked over the rim of his teacup.

"Gossip also says I'm a scheming tart who broke Montague's heart to marry you for your money. I wouldn't put too much stock in what people say." Ethan's low laugh hit her, making her body vibrate like a tuning fork.

"True. I must like tae love dangerously. Hold still a moment." He tilted her face toward him. "You have a bit of jam right…here." Their smiles touched as he nibbled on the corner of her mouth—close, yet not quite on her lips. Giving in to the urge she'd been dealing with since he walked in the door, Lottie turned her head. Kissing him hadn't been far from her mind since last night, and tasting him again was both familiar and new.

They remained close for a moment, mingling air. "Lottie?"

"Yes?" Her toes were tingling. Were toes supposed to tingle?

"Your bacon smells almost as good as you. Is the offer of breakfast still open?"

Lottie laughed at the subject change. "Of course. Help yourself to whatever you desire."

Ethan wiggled his eyebrows lecherously.

"Bacon, sir. As much *bacon* as you desire."

He rose to get a plate for himself. "One must specify these things when given carte blanche from a scheming tart. This looks excellent. My compliments tae your chef and the pig. Speaking of pigs, what are we tae do about Montague?"

Lottie shook her head. "I imagine that segue was smoother in your head."

"In my mind, I sounded witty." Taking a seat beside her, he grew serious. "Lottie, he hurt you. On purpose and in a public place. You have bruises. We can't know what he's capable of. You made me promise not tae call him out, so I'm assuming maiming him would be frowned upon. And by that look, I'd say I'm correct."

Raising a brow, she shook her head as if chastising a naughty child. "Your solution is to visit Kent for a few days?"

"Cal and I came up with a plan, if you're agreeable. We go tae Woodrest, help your old brewmaster—who's my new one, so thank you for that—settle in. You're free tae traipse about the countryside. Meanwhile, Cal will visit some of Montague's favorite haunts. He'll keep an ear tae the ground and let us know if the man is planning anything. We said we'd give this a month. Might as well escape tae the country if we can, aye?"

They'd agreed to a month. That left three weeks before they'd return to simple friendship and she'd have to revisit her plan. Imagining the house by the sea didn't bring the comfort it usually did. "I'll speak to Agatha about Kent. When Montague finishes his little tantrum, he'll move on to more low-hanging fruit. Surely there will be an indiscriminate heiress or two running about this Season for him to play with."

"Indiscriminate heiresses are surprisingly hard tae come by—not that I've made a habit of looking for them. But I assume if they were common as ugly hats, then everyone would have one."

Chapter Fourteen

Few things were more glorious than Kent in October. Lottie sighed and settled against the padded velvet seat, angling her body so she wouldn't lose the view out her window. The road wound through gently rolling hills lined with orchards and fields peeking through fog. The bounty had been gathered, leaving vast acres ready for winter. It reminded her of home in many ways. This place embraced simpler living and the toil of agriculture.

"The mistress of Woodrest would be conveniently located to entertainments, modistes, and the best society in Town. She'd be close enough to visit friends and family in Berkeley Square." Agatha kept her voice even, although the twinkle in her eye gave her away. "Perhaps she'd even stay current with fashion. No more livestock-birthing gowns in her godmother's drawing room. Imagine."

"Does that mean if I were mistress of Woodrest, you'd leave London of your own volition?" Lottie teased.

Agatha harrumphed but the twinkle remained.

"That's what I thought. In the past ten years, I think you've left London only a handful of times. Two in recent history were because you had to chaperone me."

"Surely more than a handful," Agatha said.

Ticking the list off on her fingers, Lottie said, "One picnic on the heath where you complained of the wind and the flat champagne—"

"But the pudding was passable."

"Yes, the pudding was decent. Then there's the much-dreaded annual house party at the Clemens estate over Christmas, and Mother's funeral."

"I couldn't miss that, now could I?"

Lottie smiled at the bittersweet memory. "That day would have been impossible without you. Even if you did stand at the graveside fussing at Mother for dying in the depths of Westmorland instead of someplace civilized."

Outside the window, Ethan rode Ezra back to her side of the carriage. With a look he asked a silent question, which she answered with a nod. Yes, all was well. He pointed to a spot in the distance.

"We are almost there. Or at least, I think that's where Ethan is pointing."

"Perfect. My old bones are done rattling around in this box on wheels."

The damp low-lying fog shrouded the lines of a stone house, making it appear as if the battlements and rooflines rose out of thin air.

"It reminds me of a castle from Arthurian legend." Lottie smiled at the utter ridiculousness of the architecture, with its frivolous curves offset by crenellations and gargoyles, all hovering above the mist.

"One of his ancestors must have been of a fanciful bent

when designing this estate," Agatha said. "If you were to give me babies to spoil, I might resign myself to spending quite a bit of time here."

Lottie rolled her eyes. "You know this engagement is temporary."

"And you know that brawny gentleman out there would make it real in a heartbeat. He has ridden in the rain and drizzle for the last few hours just so we would have more room in this coach. You should keep him." Agatha pointed a bony finger toward Ethan, who appeared soaked to the skin despite a hat and caped overcoat.

Dark curls had tightened in the damp, and no doubt they'd wind around her fingers if she ran a hand through his hair. The white shirt he wore would be transparent without the coat, clinging to each line of his muscular torso. Maybe, if she was lucky, she'd see him without the coat soon. Lottie blew out a slow breath. The restriction of her stays grew uncomfortable at the mental image.

The coach rolled to a stop before stone steps and a massive wooden door. The huge knocker, made to resemble dragon's teeth holding a metal ring, looked ready to bite the next unwelcome visitor. In line with the whimsical architecture, even the entryway embraced the dramatic.

The door eased open, and a well-dressed wiry man with a peg leg stood in the doorway. He greeted them by saying, "Welcome home, Ethan. Ge' those London birds out of the rain before they melt, aye?"

Although Ethan shook his head, his smile implied this cheeky behavior was expected. "Lady Agatha and Lady Charlotte, this is Connor. He runs Woodrest and drives me crazy while he does it. In case you couldn' tell, we're an informal household."

Lottie grinned at Connor. "A pleasure to meet you, Connor. Ethan told me how indispensable you are to his home."

Connor nodded a bit coolly. "If ye need anything, jus' ask. Let's get ye settled in rooms."

Taking her hand on the stairs to the great door, Ethan asked, "What do you think of my house, lass? 'Tis a wee bit of a mishmash after all the ancestors left their mark."

"If a squat castle indulged in an unholy union with a Gothic cathedral, this house might be the result. I rather like it."

He laughed. "Aye, I think you have the right of it."

A curving staircase opened up to the hall inside. Their fingers interlaced as he led her to the next floor in silence. She bit her lip to hide the smile at how the simple action affected her. Every brush of fingers or casual show of affection pushed her further from her comfort zone. Yet the bubbling sensation beneath her breastbone compelled Lottie to discover that tantalizing *more*—that lust and everything it could contain—and with every touch, the curiosity grew. It might be time to have a frank conversation with Darling, and fast. Darling's advice on physical matters between a man and a woman would be unvarnished truth. This time away from London might be the best time to explore this feeling that had grown between her and Ethan. Once the thought crossed her mind, she couldn't get rid of it. Truth be told, she didn't want to get rid of it.

He walked ahead of her down the long hall, and she took the opportunity to let her eyes linger. Long powerful legs, confident stride. The deeply tanned nape peeking out beneath dark, damp curls. And lord, those shoulders. She knew how that torso looked without clothing, and now she knew how it felt under her hands. Lottie pressed a palm low over her belly as if to hide the heat growing there.

What if she treated this time away from London as a sort of escape? Here they could do whatever they wanted. Indulge in a mutually satisfactory exploration of lust and get this desire out of their systems. If, in a few weeks, she did her duty and agreed to marriage with someone her father approved of, at least she could do whatever she wanted first. This was her chance to make memories that would keep her warm for the rest of her days.

Pushing open a wooden plank door, he lingered in the doorway. Lottie forced herself to focus on her assigned bedroom instead of her wayward thoughts. The wooden floors gleamed with a high polish, while plush rugs by the bed ensured her toes wouldn't freeze when she awoke in the morning. Gold and yellow walls with white floral-print linens made the space feminine and comfortable. If the tapestries flanking the window were a bit threadbare, it was because they were likely hundreds of years old and fine quality.

"This is so bright and sunny. You'd never know it was drippy and gray outside."

"Aye, I'm wearing a wee bit of our English liquid sunshine. I'll be down the hall, changing. There's a rope pull in the corner if you need anything. Would you meet me in the library in a half hour?" He began unbuttoning his coat, and she couldn't tear her gaze from his chest. Standing close enough to touch, with his fine lawn shirt transparent from the rain, she couldn't think of a single reason not to do whatever she pleased. As she smoothed her fingers over his damp shirt, along a deep crevice of musculature, her heart rate quickened.

"If you're wanting me tae kiss ye, you're doing it right, lass," Ethan said with a low rumble.

A quiver raked over his body at her touch, and she smiled. Such simple contact, yet this giant of a man responded readily, at her mercy. At the opening of his shirt, below the bedraggled cravat, she slipped two fingers inside to feel the crisp hairs on his chest. Springy but oddly soft. Finally skin to skin.

Already heated from her blatant ogling in the hall, her core went molten. Lottie knew if she met his gaze, he'd see the effect he had on her. Boldly, she did just that, smiling her welcome. Ethan caught her around the waist, pulling their hips together as her back hit the wall with a controlled push. When he covered her mouth with his, she had to wonder if he wasn't at her mercy at all. Perhaps in this way, they met as equals.

He sighed into her mouth, as if it were a relief to kiss her, and she understood. Eager fingers made quick work of his cravat until finally the V of his shirt opened to her hands. Their groans mingled while his hand explored up her side to cup one breast.

He pulled back, sucking her bottom lip until the very last second. "You're killin' me, Lottie. I need tae go before I make an utter arse of myself." He dived back in for a fast kiss. "You're delicious. Library. Half hour." One more kiss, with a whimpered moan on her part when he removed his hands from the shiver-inducing torture they'd created.

Leaning against the doorway, Lottie struggled to think clearly. She was in his home. Not a single London hostess or gossip-rag spy to be seen. Agatha might go to bed early. There was no delaying this if she wanted to seize the opportunity. It was definitely time to speak with Darling.

Lucky for her, Darling arrived only a few moments

after Ethan left. Flanked by a couple of burly footmen carrying Lottie's trunks, her maid shot her a questioning look. Lottie grinned. If the staff had arrived three minutes earlier, there'd have been far more to see besides one slightly rattled, aroused woman lounging in a doorway.

The staff departed, leaving Darling and Lottie alone. They set to work removing gowns and underthings from the trunks. Selecting a simple day dress to change into, Lottie stepped out of her traveling costume and gathered her courage.

"Darling? I'd like to discuss something with you."

"What's that, milady?"

"It's about Ethan. Lord Amesbury, I mean. I can't help wondering if this time away from London is a chance for us to get to know one another more intimately."

"You want him," Darling said casually, as if discussing the weather.

Hearing it said aloud made all the tension leave her body, and Lottie sank to the edge of the bed like a deflated balloon. "God, yes. And I don't have the foggiest idea what to do about it." At Darling's look, she corrected herself. "Fine, that's not true. I know exactly what I want to do. But I can't risk pregnancy."

"I can teach you preventions, but nothing is guaranteed. Do you plan to actually marry him, then? Sounds like he's won you over."

Shaking her head, Lottie said, "No one's won anyone over, and my plans stand. We have three weeks left of this engagement, and part of it will be here, in the privacy of Woodrest."

Darling slid the clean dress over Lottie's head and reached for a brush while Lottie tied the tapes. "So this is more scratching an itch?" Darling asked.

"That's a rather crass way to put it, but yes. It occurred to me that if I'm trying to find a marriage on my terms, then I should be free to dictate the circumstances. There's no great love match in my future, so why save my virginity for a husband? This could be my one chance to experience lust to its fullest, and I'm taking it."

Darling finished brushing Lottie's hair, then coiled it into a simple knot, letting a few curls wisp free at the front. "You'll need a sponge and French letters. I'll send to London for them. Enjoy other methods until then."

Lottie shot her a questioning look. Darling wagged a finger and said, "Never expect a man to be prepared. Rule number one: make sure you're taken care of, no matter what."

"What other methods?"

Darling grinned. "Milady, let's you and I have a talk, yes?"

A half hour later, her mind swimming with new knowledge, Lottie sent a message to Ethan to apologize for not meeting him in the library, claiming a need to rest until dinner. It wasn't entirely untrue. The big bed with the soft floral blanket called to her like a siren song, and frankly, it was the perfect place to hide.

Darling, bless her, was a thorough teacher. She'd left after their talk to send for the supplies they'd discussed, which meant the bedroom was empty except for Lottie and her swirling thoughts battling between what she wanted and what she needed.

Everything came back to the plan. When she'd left Westmorland, there'd been a clear path laid out, a pros-and-cons list made in her head, and a firm idea of the man she'd marry. He would, firstly, be a man Father found suitable—otherwise this entire exercise would be a waste of time and money.

Secondly, he'd be a man who would be content to stay in London, living his own life, leaving her to run her home and land as she deemed fit. Having seen what Town had to offer in the summer, she now realized that would require a unique combination of disinterest and affability.

Thirdly, he didn't have to be rich, but he couldn't need her fortune so desperately that she wouldn't be able to use it to further her property. A man content to live on an allowance would be ideal, but she'd begun to doubt such a man existed.

Finally, she refused to end up with a relationship like her parents'. While they'd been happy together, their bliss had come at the expense of their children and eventually their tenants. Giving one person the power to destroy her, like Mother's death had leveled Father, wouldn't be wise. That would never be a choice she'd make, having already survived it twice. First as a child, excluded from the warmth they'd shared, and then as an adult, left to pick up the pieces. No, a love match wasn't for her. Let another fool fall in that trap.

Wrapping her arms around her waist, Lottie hugged herself as she'd been doing since childhood and rolled onto her side. The pillow dipped under her head, smelling of a fresh herb sachet from whatever linen closet the bedding had been stored in. Staring out the window, she let her gaze wander over trees and vast stretches of green fields. In the distance a stone-and-timber structure stood in midconstruction. Probably the new brewery they planned to visit after Mr. Macdonell arrived.

Reviewing her plan and making lists usually calmed her. But the list wasn't the problem today. The list was comprehensive. For once, it offered no comfort. Because instead of the man she'd set out to find, she had Ethan. A fiancé who was none of those things, except wealthy in his own right.

Logically, that was reason enough to return to her plan, as she'd told Darling she would, and let this temporary arrangement expire in three weeks.

Yet despite her best intentions, she wanted him. The man who was the antithesis of everything she'd set out to find.

Disinterested? Not even close. He walked in a room, and her body tingled, sensing him. By the time she caught sight of him, his eyes were already on her. The sensations she experienced when he kissed her were headier than brandy.

And lest she forget, Ethan was the one man Father would never approve of. Assuming she decided to keep him and he wanted to marry her—which was a giant leap from their current agreement.

That was the reality. The truth without emotion.

All this worry might be for nothing, because who said Ethan wanted her for longer than three weeks? Sitting up, she pushed a curl off her face and scrubbed her palms over her eyes.

If she wanted to create the life she dreamed of, she needed a husband who checked the boxes on her list. She had three weeks to enjoy Ethan, then they'd end it.

And if this month-long detour from the original plan meant she didn't find a suitable candidate by the end of November, well, she'd deal with that when the time came. Father would have to see sense and recognize her efforts to find a husband he'd agree to. Or perhaps by then she could convince him to let her remain on the shelf and use the dowry to establish her own house.

Either way, it would work out. She'd make it work out.

Chapter Fifteen

After dinner, Lottie perused the shelves of his library, moving ever so slowly toward him, section by section. Geography. Poetry. Agriculture—a large section and a shared interest. That was an area she could have lingered in for a while, if her goal hadn't been to eventually make her way to the fireside.

She could feel the weight of Ethan's gaze from where he lounged in a chair by the fireplace. Since arriving at his home, he'd made no effort to hide how much time he spent watching her. Sometimes with a light of arousal in his eyes, sometimes curiosity, and sometimes simple enjoyment.

And he didn't just watch. The man loved to touch. All day while they'd visited the brewery site, talked to workmen, and greeted Macdonell, he'd maintained contact. Whether a brush of a finger, holding her hand, or touching her where no one could see. As a result, her body had been simmering with awareness that could flare into desire at any moment.

"I dreamed of you in this chair once," he said.

"Was it a good dream?"

"Started that way."

The firelight illuminated his features, while the dimple in his cheek played with shadows. The dark evening beard gave him a devilish appearance, reminding her that Lucifer had been the most beautiful angel. That low simmer rose to a steady flame, and she couldn't resist touching him.

Knowing she wanted more than kisses from him lent her a boldness she might not have had otherwise. Ethan's eyes grew wide when she stepped between his knees and sank her fingers into his curls. His hands wrapped around her waist, and he held her gaze as he slid his palms down to her hips. If he waited for her protest, he'd find none forthcoming. For the moment, she was content to simply touch him. Seducing a man wasn't something she had experience in, but one could assume that touching was a good start.

When her fingers wove through his hair, playing with the curls and gently tugging the strands in a strange kind of scalp massage, he closed his eyes and made a low happy sound. His silky wayward curls tickled her hand with warm flicks that still held on to his body heat. The fingers at her hips flexed, pulling her closer until she swayed farther into him.

"You need a haircut," she mused.

Ethan shrugged. "My hair has a mind of its own no matter how long or short. The curls do what they want. Cal wanted his valet tae cut it, but his man scares me."

She chuckled. "Scares a big guy like you?"

His hands smoothed up to her waist, then down to the bottom of her hip, fully traveling the curve of her bum. "Aye. He wants tae put a linen noose around my neck and make me wear coats that pinch my shoulders. If I wore a queue like Cal, I'd never have tae cut it."

"I like it longer, but it could use a trim in some places. You're bordering on unkempt." Lottie wrapped another curl around her finger. "Would you let me cut it?"

The hands at her hips paused in the slow caress she'd been enjoying. "Have you ever cut a man's hair before?"

"I've sheared sheep. How different can it be?"

A beat of silence stretched as he stared at her. Finally, she couldn't contain the laugh. Giggling, she gasped out, "Don't worry. I used to cut my father's hair. Mother taught me how. He preferred she do it instead of his valet."

Ethan seemed to think it over for all of three seconds. "All right. Have a go. But in the kitchen, or else the maid will complain about sweeping the hair from the rug."

"You want me to do it tonight? Now?"

"No time like the present. I'll get Connor's shears and meet you in the kitchen." With a final squeeze, he let her go.

The kitchen—much like the rest of the house—had its own sense of order in a comfortable, welcoming way. A maid finishing her duties jumped when Lottie entered the room.

"Beggin' your pardon, milady. Do you need something?"

"Lord Amesbury will join us in a moment. While I stoke the fire, will you find a stool for him to sit on? I'm cutting his lordship's hair."

The maid raised a brow but fetched a short stool. "Will you be wanting help, milady?"

Lottie shook her head, placing the fireplace poker next to the hearth. "No thank you. I'm sure we can muddle through if anything comes up."

The maid left her with a shallow curtsy. Footsteps echoed down the short hall beyond the open door. Lottie brushed damp palms on her skirt, then warmed her fingers by the fire. There was no need to be nervous. She'd cut her father's hair dozens of times. Perhaps hundreds. But then, it wasn't the haircut she was nervous about.

Would Ethan take her to bed tonight if she asked? What if he said no entirely? It might be a matter of honor to him, after all. Trying to calm the butterflies, Lottie focused on her breathing. Inhale, one, two, three. Exhale, one, two, three.

The stool scuffed on the stone floor. Ethan sat, then shifted his weight as he untucked his shirt. Was he going to—yes. Bless him, he was. The shirt sailed to land in a lump under a wooden chair.

Lottie gulped. Any possibility of keeping her composure disappeared when she was faced with all that sun-bronzed skin within arm's reach.

"I won' bite, lass. Not hard anyway." Ethan winked, then handed her a pair of scissors and a small comb.

"Thank you for trusting me to do this." She gave him a light kiss, intending to keep it short, but lingered at his rich, warm taste. He'd had wine with dinner and fruity notes lingered on his tongue. The butterflies in her belly swirled lower. Forcing herself to focus on the matter at hand, she drew back and ran the comb through his hair. Glossy curls parted, then sprang back under the comb. There was a whorl near one ear that would no doubt give her trouble. The firelight caught on a silvery-white line marring his shoulder.

"This must have been a significant injury. What happened?" Lottie traced the line with a finger. Goose bumps rose on his skin.

"That's my reminder tae be a better person. Connor lost his leg and career. I walked away with this. Barely anything, really," he said.

Barely anything? "This scar is sizeable, Ethan. You didn't walk away unscathed." The roll and shift of his muscles when he shrugged paused her brain for a moment. Lord, the man's body could distract a saint. "Having seen Connor in action these last few days, I'd say he's adapted admirably to the circumstances. He may not be in the king's army, but he's certainly the general of this house."

"Shouldn't I be the general in my home?" Ethan asked with a short laugh.

Lottie tugged at the lock of hair she'd just combed. "Let's not kid ourselves. Connor is in charge here. He may be unorthodox and informal to the point of rudeness, but the man has Woodrest firmly under control."

"True enough. Are you planning tae play with my hair all night, or cut it?"

"If you rush me, it's on your own head." Lottie gathered a handful of hair and made one giant snip in the center of his head. There. No going back now. For several moments the only noises in the kitchen were the *snick* of the scissors and the pop of firewood. "Do you think Connor's forgiven you? For the leg, I mean."

"How could he? That's no' something a man just moves past." His quiet but firm voice suggested he'd already decided the concept was impossible. As if he believed he'd never receive forgiveness.

"He doesn't seem to be wallowing in misery. From

what I've seen, he appears to consider you both an employer and friend."

"What are you getting at, Lottie?"

She nudged his head to drop his chin down for better access to the nape. "I'm just saying I think he'd have mentioned it if he hated his life and blamed you. Connor strikes me as the direct sort."

"It was my fault," he said.

Stubborn man. "Yes. That is not up for debate." Lottie brushed loose hairs from his shoulder and inspected her work thus far.

"Do I want to know what's happening here?" Aunt Agatha appeared in the doorway.

Lottie tilted her head and fanned her fingers through his curls to see if the hairs were relatively even. "I'm cutting his hair. My virtue's safe. I'm armed with scissors."

"And even sharper opinions," Ethan said.

"Why are you down here, Auntie?"

"I'm feeling peckish. Lord Amesbury—if I may be so formal while you're half-naked—do you know where your cook keeps something sweet to nibble?" Agatha wandered over to the shelves and began opening crocks and canisters.

"The jar on the far right with the blue lid usually contains shortbread." Ethan stood. "Here, let me." With his long arms, reaching the high shelf was easy. Behind his back, Lottie exchanged a glance with her godmother, who winked in return.

"Thank you, young man." Agatha bit into a biscuit and closed her eyes with a happy sigh. "Bliss. My compliments to your cook. This is excellent. Now, you two. As the chaperone, I should be on the verge of apoplexy about all this." She waved a biscuit in the direction of

Ethan's bare chest. "However, you two *are* engaged." She plucked a few more pieces of shortbread from the jar and fluttered a hand over her shoulder as she left the room. "Carry on."

"I think your godmother likes me," Ethan said.

"You may be right. Come sit. I'm almost done." His skin was hot under her fingers when she gently pushed him toward the stool before the hearth. The heat radiating off him was intense, and she didn't want to remove her hand. Such a simple choice to indulge in the pleasure of touching him. Trailing her fingers from the heavy bulge of his shoulder, toward the side of his neck, then down the deep indent of spine and sinew, she followed the lines delineating muscles she didn't know the names of. Delicious maximus, surely.

Under her touch, Ethan's skin erupted in goose bumps. Like a giant cat wanting to be petted, his muscles bunched in response to her as he leaned into her hand.

What was it about firelight hitting this man that scrambled her wits? She'd begun the evening with a plan—a practiced speech that laid out the reasons he should indulge her in exploring this passion between them. Here she was with her careful mental script set aside in favor of running her fingers over every available inch of him. Lottie couldn't even find it in herself to feel bad about taking advantage of the opportunity to touch him, although any chaperone worth her salt would be having a conniption at this situation, and no lady of good breeding would be in this situation to begin with. Besides, it could be argued that she was here with her chaperone's blessing—not that it mattered, when the whole point was that she'd make her own decisions during this stay in Kent.

Settling into the soothing rhythm of combing, measuring the hair with her fingers, then evening the ends, she tried to find her carefully prepared script amidst her enflamed senses. "Agatha might be onto something. Perhaps we should enjoy the time we have." She cocked her head, enjoying the picture he made with freshly trimmed hair. The sides and back were shorter, but she didn't have the heart to take too much off the top. Those floppy curls did something to her equilibrium, and the only place she wanted to see them spread out was a pillow—not cast aside on the floor.

"What are you saying, Lottie?" He turned to meet her gaze, pulling her to stand between his legs like she had in the library. His hands found their place on her hips, and she wished he'd take the chance to explore her, as she was him. The fingers digging into her curves told their own tale—Ethan was clinging to self-control as tightly as he was her hips.

She set the scissors aside, then brushed the stray hairs off his shoulders. "I'm propositioning you. You know I don't want a love match. But I'd like to experience whatever this is before I settle into a society marriage. I spoke with Darling, and she sent away for French letters. It may be a day or so before they're here and we can fully indulge, but she's assured me that there are plenty of other ways to enjoy each other in the meantime. Unless you have a supply of French letters?" Unexpected nerves made her chatter. Lord, if only she could remember the words she'd prepared. There was mention of French letters and precautions in her carefully worded proposition she'd practiced, and the whole thing was supposed to sound worldly and sophisticated.

His eyes lit with humor. "I'm sorry tae say I don' have

any on hand, no. It's been a long time since I've needed one. That must have been quite the conversation between you and your maid."

The teasing made her relax somewhat. With a sigh, Lottie admitted, "She made me sit, then paced and talked for a half hour. It was like a sexually graphic schoolroom."

A low laugh rumbled from his chest, and Lottie would have sworn she felt it vibrate through her core. "Did you take notes? Were there sketches involved?"

She swatted his shoulder playfully, shaking her head. "No. Are there sketches available? I should find the shelf in your library devoted to reference texts of that nature. I'm sure if I search long enough, I'll find something." It felt natural to place a small openmouthed kiss on the side of his neck, then another on the sharp blade of his cheekbone.

His hands encircled her waist, drawing her closer. "You were on the right wall earlier. Far corner by the window. Third—no, fourth row up. Educate yourself at will, lass. I can join you for hands-on lessons if you prefer."

As a child, she'd placed colorful river rocks in a canister with water, gravel, and sand. When they'd all rubbed together, the result had been shiny colorful stones that she'd believed to be gems at the time. His voice was rough like the gravel, carrying an acceptance of her desire that was as precious as the gems she'd treasured.

Perching on one of his heavily muscled thighs, she marveled at the look of him. Everything about Ethan was solid and wide. In comparison, she felt delicate—a novel experience. With one hand on the back of his neck, Lottie pulled him close for another taste, nipping the corner of his lip. "I'm afraid I'll have to insist on *very* hands-on lessons, my lord. You'll find I'm an eager student." A soft noise escaped her when he sucked her lower lip, letting his teeth graze the sensitive flesh. Giving herself over to the heat between them, she explored the angles of his face, enjoying the stubble of his cheek as it roughed the pads of her fingers.

On a moan, he took command of the moment, tasting her as if she were a treat and he a starving man. Fumbling for her hem, Ethan skimmed one large hand up her leg until he gripped the curve of her hip.

Desire coiled low in a tingling heat that settled between her thighs, demanding contact. With her leg free of her skirts, she shifted, straddling his lap to press their bodies together, soothing that ache. The movement brought his hand to cradle her bottom. An appreciative hum sounded from his throat. She nipped his lip in reply, skimming her hands over every inch of sun-kissed skin within reach. Touching him was a pleasure in itself, but knowing he received pleasure from her touch fanned curiosity into passion.

At the juncture of her thighs, she pressed against the ridge of him. Breathless, she pulled back from the kiss enough to ask, "Is this a yes to my proposition?"

He pulled her against his hardness, and she lost her breath all over again. Ethan's gravelly voice rumbled. "We only do what you're comfortable with. Agreed? There's much we can do without French letters."

The urgent friction between her legs made her moan. Her fingers clutched his shoulders, using his body as an anchor. "Agreed. But I think we'll need them. God, that feels amazing. Don't stop."

Pulling her hot core against him in a rhythm, Ethan used his teeth to pull aside the neckline of her bodice.

His hot groan at her collarbone vibrated through her chest as he gasped expletives with openmouthed kisses on her skin. Goose bumps skittered over her flesh, and that coiled tension built until it threatened to burst from her skin. “Lesson one. Come for me, lass.”

Chapter Sixteen

Breakfast the next morning was a study in avoiding eye contact and not blushing. There'd been the worry at the back of Lottie's mind that she would feel awkward the next time she saw Ethan. After all, the evening before he'd brought her to orgasm, and she'd reciprocated by opening the placket of his breeches and taking him in hand. The size of him had made her pause, wondering how they'd fit together should things progress enough to need a French letter. The thought hadn't stopped her for long, as each encouraging noise he'd made had inflamed her own arousal.

All in all, it had been a successful experiment in pleasure—even though she'd gone to bed feeling as if she'd been primed but not entirely satisfied. One would think after an orgasm one's body would be content and return to a sense of normality. Not so. She added that to the list of things she'd learned last night.

So what happened when you faced that person over sausages and eggs the next morning? If you were her, you grasped the bottom of your chair with one hand to keep yourself seated and resisted the urge to repeat the experience of the night before in the breakfast room. It turned out Lottie had a streak of lusty physicality within her, and she didn't know what to do with it when indulging wasn't an option. They were alone at the moment, but that wouldn't last long with servants entering and exiting the room.

Dropping sugar into her tea, Lottie stirred the dark brew and blew over the top. She studied the subtle pattern of the tablecloth. The piece was of good quality. A local weaver, perhaps?

Wondering if Ethan was terribly attached to the blue wallcoverings or if he'd consider a bright spring green instead occupied another few minutes. The morning light would be lovely against walls colored like sprigs of rosemary. The blue really was too dark for this small room.

"Are you all right, lass?"

"Hmm? Yes. Why do you ask?"

Ethan cocked his head. "Because you're on your third cup of tea and haven' started talking yet and won' look at me."

She sighed, setting the cup down. "I'm sorry. Truly, I'm fine."

"If you're regretting last night, I would understand. It doesn't need tae happen again."

"No," she nearly yelled. Lottie closed her eyes and counted to three, then repeated, softly, "No. I don't regret it. Quite the opposite, actually. I'm acutely aware that we could be interrupted at any moment. Agatha might join us, or a footman will enter the room to refresh the teapot, or a maid will come in to stoke the fire. I'm trying to be circumspect instead of mooning over the lord of the manor like some ninny."

The dimple in his cheek made an appearance, wreaking havoc on her nerves, which were already humming from her confession. "So we'll talk about something else," he said. "I'm visiting the tenants today. The Thatchers are expecting a babe any day, and I wanted tae check in. Would you like tae join me?"

Estate matters she could focus on. Hearing the schedule—all things well within her comfort zone—steadied her. "I'd like that, thank you. How do you feel about green for the walls in this room, instead of blue?"

"Planning tae redecorate already, milady? Don' ye need tae marry him first?" Connor said from the doorway. His tone was light and breezy, but there was a hardness about his smile that made Lottie uneasy.

She smiled tightly. "Merely making conversation."

"What can I do for you, Connor?" Ethan asked.

"Were ye planning tae visit the worksite today? I've heard from the workers, and Mr. Macdonell seems tae have sent ahead a list of ideas about changing the building already," Connor said.

Ethan gulped the last of his tea, then wiped his mouth on a napkin. "We are going by today, yes. And don' worry about Macdonell. I brought him in this early in the project for exactly that reason. If the building won' work for what he needs, better we find out now when we can build tae suit, aye?" He stood and made his way to Lottie's seat. He kissed her cheek and said, "I need tae grab a few things before we go. Take your time. I'll wait in the library."

She and Connor watched him go. At the last minute,

Ethan called over his shoulder, "And for the record, I think green is a grand idea."

Lottie chuckled, then returned to her breakfast before she remembered that Connor remained in the room. "Have you eaten? The water is still hot if you'd like some tea."

Crossing his arms, he studied her. "No thank ye, milady."

Uncomfortable under his scrutiny, she set her utensils on her plate and dabbed her mouth with a linen napkin. "I'd best join his lordship."

"How long do ye plan tae stay, your ladyship?"

Lottie smoothed a curl in place, trying to determine how to handle him. Connor and Ethan had a special, complicated relationship, but she didn't quite know what to do with him—especially when his direct way of speaking came across as rudeness. "We haven't set a date for our return to London yet. I'm sure Lord Amesbury will inform you when we know."

Connor gave her a short nod, then headed for the door. "I only ask because this brewery is important. We don' need our viscount gallivanting off in Lon'on when he's needed here. You're an expensive distraction, and ye already hurt 'im before."

Well that put her in her place, although it was a confusing version of their history. The door closed behind Connor, leaving her alone. Standing by the table, she plucked the last sausage off her plate, then finished her tea and wiped her fingers on the napkin. Glancing around her, she said, "It really is too blue."

It may have been his plan to include Lottie in his business in order to show her how she might fit in here at Woodrest, but today hadn't been the best day to bring her along. Connor was in a mood, the arrival of Macdonell had thrown the masons and carpenters into chaos, and Lottie rode beside him, suspiciously quiet for the last hour. "What's on your mind, lass?"

"Connor doesn't like me, does he?"

He furrowed his brow. "Connor is grumpy today. Don' take it personally. Was he rude tae you? I'll no' let him make you feel unwelcome, Lottie." If Connor and Lottie didn't figure out how to get along, there could be problems ahead—assuming he brought her around to the idea of a shared future.

She smiled, but it didn't reach her eyes. "I'll keep that in mind. Maybe it was nothing."

They'd just left the Thatchers' house—where Mrs. Thatcher seemed beyond ready to have the baby, if only the baby would cooperate—when Lottie spoke again. "Is the local midwife one you trust, or should we bring someone in for the baby's birth? I was going over the date calculations with Mrs. Thatcher, and the babe is overdue. With such a large child, there could be complications."

"The midwife in the village is very experienced. Mrs. Thatcher is in good hands." Watching Lottie interact with the building crew and tenants was a new way to get to know her. It was obvious she felt deeply, cared about details—and yes, sometimes managed everyone around her. Usually those people needed managing, though, so he could hardly blame her.

He reined Ezra under a tree. When he dismounted and held his arms open to her, she slid off her horse without protest. The dip of her waist seemed custom made for his hands. Flashes of memories from last night flickered behind his eyes, as they had all day. How Lottie had looked when she'd come apart in his arms—her long throat working for breath as she cried out, causing her neck to vibrate under his mouth. The satisfied expression she'd worn when she'd made him come in return—an endearing blend of sexy smugness and fascination at the process. "I've been thinking about what you said last night. About being lovers."

"From your tone, I feel I won't like where this is going."

This had been running through his brain all day, but it was still a tangle to speak the words in order. "I want you. Don' doubt that. Ever. Not ever, you hear me, lass? I can't believe I'm even saying this. But as long as our agreement stands and this engagement ends in three weeks, we won' be needin' those French letters." Tightening his grip on her waist, he drew her closer. "I want so badly tae be the dishonorable bastard you used tae know. If I were, I'd tup you on the grass right now and not leave your thighs for days."

She remained quiet, but Lottie was rarely still. Her fingers worked the linen of his cravat, adjusting the folds of the knot while he spoke.

"Maybe it's splitting hairs, tae assuage my conscience. But here's what I offer instead. We explore other ways tae bring each other pleasure. My body is yours tae enjoy. But I won' do anything that risks a babe." If she fell pregnant, they'd have to marry, and the last thing he wanted was to force her hand. Even though the hands in question felt better than anything he'd ever experienced—and there he went, back down the hot slide toward arousal.

Her sigh puffed against his chest. "This is your final answer? Do you think you have the self-control to not need a French letter?"

A choked, self-deprecating laugh worked past his throat. "I've no bloody idea, but I'll try my damnedest."

A devilish glint in her eye alerted him to a change in her mood. "How close can we get before you lose control, do you think?" She leaned against the tree, pulling the lapels of his coat so he followed.

"That's a dangerous question, lass." Pressing his body to hers, he loved how she instinctively shifted, welcoming him into the cradle of her hips. There was no disguising his body hardening against her. With an impish smile, Lottie wrapped her foot behind his knee and pulled him that final inch until there wasn't any space left between them. He caught her leg at his hip, then dipped a hand beneath her skirt to skim up her calf until he found skin above her garter. Exactly how close to this line in the sand could they play before he had to pull back? Lottie was a physical woman with a deep well of untapped passion; he'd be a fool to ignore their shared desire—especially when he suspected it might be the key to her considering a future together.

She raised a brow in challenge, even as the pink blush of arousal crept across her chest. "Touch me like you did last night but without clothes in the way. If I can't have you inside me, let me feel you." The words ratcheted his desire to a new level. He wanted to be in her in the worst way. Perceptive, Lottie tilted her head. "You like it when I tell you what I want."

"Aye," he ground out. "I want you tae tell me what you need." Her thigh was smooth under the rough pads of his fingers, and it felt forbidden, like fondling a priceless marble sculpture. Except marble wasn't molten and wet like she was behind the curls he parted. Lottie's eyes fluttered closed as she leaned her head back against the tree, offering her neck to him. Settling his mouth on her rabbiting pulse, he inhaled the lemony scent of her and smiled at her moan when his fingers entered her heat.

Her submission lasted only a moment before she sought his mouth and he felt the buttons on his breeches give way to her hands. "I need more of you. Please, Ethan. I don't want to go over that edge without you." Wrapping her hand around his length, she rose on her toes to press her cunny against his cock.

They froze, skin to skin, petal soft to hard. His breathing sawed out of him as Ethan held her wide-eyed gaze and hitched her higher against the tree, dragging the length of his erection against her heat. Out of instinct, her hips tilted to try to bring him inside. He held her in place, then slipped against her again. It might kill him, but he wouldn't enter her.

"You're so wet. God, you're perfect, love." Ethan savored her cry as he used his slick length to rub the bundle of nerves at the top of her slit, traveling her outer channel over and over. With one hand under her thigh and the other behind her neck, he tried to protect her from the rough bark of the tree, pinning her with the pressure of his hips. Their foreheads touched, and he locked gazes with her as they panted together. So close, her wetness pillowing his cock without letting him inside, it took everything in him to not notch the head of his erection into her.

As if she read his mind, she whimpered, "Just one stroke inside. Just one, please." The desperate plea of *please* was on her lips when her orgasm overtook everything else. With one more stroke—alas, outside her body—he followed with his own climax.

Whether through self-control or lucky timing, he spilled on the ground between them. Ethan had to wonder if he'd have caved to temptation and slipped inside her if she'd lasted another thirty seconds.

Placing gentle kisses on her jaw, Ethan worked his way toward her mouth, stealing a few quiet moments before the real world intruded on them. While seconds ago she'd been begging, it was on the tip of his tongue to ask for more from her now. Lottie was willing to share her body with him, but even as he shook from his release, Ethan suspected what he really wanted was her heart.

Chapter Seventeen

The mount Lottie had chosen for the day's ride pranced with a skittery side step to avoid a tuft of grass waving in the breeze. There was an ease to how she collected the gelding beneath her, murmuring soothing noises while she brought the horse under control. The country was her natural habitat. She was comfortable here, and he didn't want to think about her leaving soon.

They'd spent the afternoon visiting the construction site and helping Mr. Macdonell settle in to his cottage. After a day on horseback, Lottie was windblown, mussed, and distracting. He'd pulled her behind two stone walls and a tree so far today to steal kisses, and each time she'd gone willingly. He'd tried his damnedest to stop at kisses. The encounter by the tree the day before had been thrilling but dangerously close to the point of no return. Now, on their way back to Woodrest, a feeling of contentment washed over him.

"Where are your land borders?"

"Do you see way over there, the sun reflecting off the water? Woodrest runs tae where the bit of the Thames meets the River Cray, and about a half hour's ride tae the south beyond us." He pointed to the landmarks.

"Is it very different from Scotland? I'd think to go from a smaller homestead to this with no preparation or training…how incredibly overwhelming."

That was the understatement of the day. "A solicitor showed up on my doorstep, claiming I was an English lord of all things, and I didn' know what tae think. My family—no' this English branch—we were sheep farmers. And damn good ones too. I didn' know anything else."

"Very different from the future you'd imagined, I suppose," she said.

Peat smoke from the tenants' hearths scented the breeze, not quite covered by the scent of fresh earth after last night's rain. "God and the English king conspire against those who make plans of their own." He laughed a little, shaking his head. "When I saw Woodrest the first time, I panicked. I thought I was doing well for myself, aye? I could support a wife with the land my parents left me. But my entire childhood home would fit inside one of the drawing rooms here."

"I'm surprised you didn't run away from it all."

Frankly, so was he. Sometimes the urge still hit him to leave it all behind and go back to his quiet corner of Scotland. They let their horses pick their way across a small stream, navigating rocks and uneven ground. "I nearly did. Excused myself from the staff and the solicitor, then sat on the floor of the smallest closet I could find. I remember thinking there wasn' enough air tae breathe while I waited for my heart tae beat out of my chest."

"How old were you?"

"Young. Twenty-two. Sitting in a scullery closet, panicking like a child." They were cresting a small hill, with the fields spread out before them, and pride shot through him. The estate's success was evidenced by harvested land and well-maintained buildings. A tenant cottage stood to their right, tidy and charming, with a small kitchen garden off the side farthest from the west wind, and a heavy wood door worn smooth from decades of hands coming home. He shot her a glance and was gratified to see Lottie taking it all in.

"I might have panicked too. Where were your parents in all this? How did you not know you might inherit?"

That was a question he'd often wondered himself. In the beginning, he'd struggled with resentment that Da hadn't prepared him for the possibility. No one could have foreseen an entire line of men dying off, though. Or maybe Da would have mentioned it when Ethan was older. "We were the black sheep branch and had been for a few generations. No one cared that we were there, and some English title wasn' important tae us in the village. Mum and Da had passed on by the time I inherited."

"So what you're saying is that underneath the wild young buck in London, you had a lot of adjustments to make," she said.

The reminder sat heavy. His past actions would always be between them, no matter how close they became. "Aye. I didn' always handle it well."

"About that. I have a question. It's personal. And none of my business," Lottie said.

Ethan raised a brow, waiting. "I thought anything personal was open for conversation by now."

It didn't take long for her to sigh and say, "Well,

it's like this. The brewery you're building—aren't you worried about it?"

"Worried? Did you notice something on the worksite?" He'd thought everything was in order, and Mr. Macdonell had agreed. Had they missed something?

Lottie looked uncomfortable but, being Lottie, continued anyway. "You avoid spirits. My coachman, Patrick, has a compulsion to drink alcohol as well. He conquers that need daily, as I assume you do, since I've never seen you have more than a single glass of ale or wine."

"I see." Ethan studied the horizon, where the main house, with its ridiculous gargoyles, canted rooflines, and chaperones, awaited them. Lottie deserved honesty, even if she might judge him for his answer. "I don' have compulsions or cravings for liquor like your coachman. But I learned the hard way that I don' like who I become when I drink that much. An occasional ale or glass of wine is fine. Never more than one or two in a night. And no whisky. I haven' been drunk in five years."

Her brow furrowed as she mulled over what he'd said. "If you don't have Patrick's issue with stopping, then why not enjoy one glass of whisky and leave it be, like you would ale or wine?"

Because he was a coward. And now she'd know it, which couldn't help him win her over. Rubbing a hand over the rough stubble of his jaw, Ethan tried to find the right words. "I'm scared, Lottie. I don' trust myself. When I hurt you, I was drunk. When I injured Connor, I was drunk. I don' want tae make more mistakes and hurt people."

She nodded but didn't respond before they arrived at the house. A groom rushed to hold their reins, and Ethan took the opportunity to help Lottie dismount.

"You just wanted an excuse to hold me for a minute, didn't you?" she whispered from his arms.

He winked. "Guilty as charged, my lady. I'd kiss you if we were alone."

"And if we were alone, I'd let you." She stepped away, straightening her hat. "I'm going to meet with Cook and arrange a delivery to your new brewmaster. Mr. Macdonell might appreciate a basket from the kitchens as he settles in. Do you mind?"

"Not at all, lass. Thank you for thinking of it." He watched her go, shamelessly admiring the sway of her full hips as she climbed the steps to the door. She was all curves and competence, and he couldn't look away.

After dinner they relaxed in the library, as had become their custom. They were already settling into patterns and habits.

All day he'd received compliments from masons and carpenters on his choice of bride. It had been bittersweet. His feelings had grown beyond what she offered in return, so he shied away from putting a name to them.

Her fingers caressed the spines of the books on the far wall of the library. What she was looking for, he didn't know, but the quiet was comfortable, so he didn't ask.

A glass of brandy warming in his palm would be nice. It wasn't often he longed for alcohol, and this wasn't really a craving per se. But if this were a painting, the lord of the manor would have a glass of brandy and a dog asleep at his feet while his lovely woman perused the bookshelves of their library, feeding her curious, nimble mind.

He could imagine them like this. Being able to so clearly see a life with her should have scared him, considering their arrangement. They didn't have a future—they had three weeks.

It was a nice fantasy. "Have you found what you needed yet?" She'd moved out of his field of vision.

"Almost."

Several minutes passed before she joined him with a book in hand. Instead of taking the chair beside him, she knelt at his feet with a wicked gleam in her eye.

"What are you up tae, lass?"

"Educating myself." She winked. "I found a reference text," Lottie said, holding up the book. He glanced at the title and gripped the arms of the chair tighter. So she'd found that section of the library after all. And now she knelt at his feet. God help him.

"It says here that I...well. That doesn't sound so difficult. Sounds rather fun actually."

She wasn't talking to him, but he was intrigued to see where this was going. Given the title of the book in her hand and her position between his knees, Ethan's body was already warming to the myriad ideas running through his head.

When her fingers loosed the first button of his breeches, he muttered an expletive and she froze. "Is something the matter, Ethan?"

He shook his head, praying she'd continue. In the open placket, his cock stood at half-mast to meet her. Watching Lottie wrap her lovely mouth around him starred in many fantasies, so breathing evenly was rather difficult. For her to instigate this left him at a loss for words—polite words, anyway. Giving the head of his erection a small kiss, she gently sucked the tip into her mouth, watching his face for a reaction, and the need for being polite disappeared. "Bloody fecking hell," he whispered.

Fully in the playful role of educating herself, she sat back on her heels, holding the book in one hand and perusing the page while the other stroked him to full hardness with a slow, torturous rhythm. The urge to lean his head back and enjoy overwhelmed him, but Ethan didn't want to miss a moment of watching Lottie. Just her hand felt a thousand times better than his own, and Lord knew he'd spent enough time holding his dick lately.

"I think I can take it from here." Setting the book aside, she grinned saucily up at him. With a deliberate lick, she traced a line from the base to the plump head of his penis, stopping to suck his shaft along the way, sending ripples of pleasure vibrating down his legs. "Ethan, why do you smell like lemons?"

Of course she'd notice that—Lottie missed nothing. He huffed out an embarrassed laugh, rubbing a palm over his face. "You talked about the bath oil in front of me with the lady innkeeper. I bought a bottle, and I, uh, use it when I take myself in hand. It reminds me of you."

She rested her cheek on his thigh, looking up at him through her lashes. One hand leisurely stroked him. "You've wanted me that long? Even when I hated you?"

Sinking his fingers into her curls, like he'd imagined doing so many times, he caressed her cheekbones with his thumbs. "Aye, I always wanted you. Always." The rough timbre of his voice might have been arousal, but he suspected a different emotion compelled his admission—one that would scare her away if he named it aloud. It scared him a bit, how completely she'd conquered his heart.

She fidgeted with the hem of his shirt, running fingers over his stomach. "Confession time, I suppose. I watched you undress at the window the night of the musicale."

He grinned. "I know."

Laughing, she raised herself to her knees once more

and pulled his head down for a kiss. Their flavors melded together, and he could have lost himself in her for the rest of the night if she hadn't left his mouth to kiss his stomach. Working her way down, trailing fingers and lips, she explored his body until—finally—her mouth sank over his cock once more and he lost rational thought.

This woman was a dream. Hot, wet, and playful, she never let her hands rest. Noises rose from his throat in time with his hips as he met her in a cadence set by squeezing strokes of her fingers and sliding suction between her lips.

His grip on her hair tightened, not enough to pull, but acting as a tether to tie him to her lest he fly away under her wicked mouth. And he would come apart soon. Her fingernails grazed his tight sack, and that was it. "Lottie, love, I'm close," he managed to gasp before his eyes rolled back in his head and pleasure sang through his blood, stealing his breath.

Lottie gave his cock one last pull with her mouth, then finished with her hands, gentling her grip as he came down from the climax. When he finally opened his eyes, she looked awfully pleased with herself.

"See? I told you I was an eager student."

He laughed, letting his head fall back. "I do love a woman who reads."

Chapter Eighteen

There goes your faux fiancé," Agatha commented from the window.

Lottie's hungry gaze followed his broad silhouette as he guided a cart and horse down the lane. After these last few days, the sight of him impacted her senses. She knew the feel of his skin, tanned from working outside, the salty taste, the smell of him. There were firm lines he insisted they not cross, but her fingers twitched, wanting more time exploring the smooth warmth of muscle and bone of those impressive shoulders.

This insistent craving for Ethan made her suspect she might be in over her head. Yesterday afternoon she'd visited the library for a book and ended up spread over Ethan's desk with his mouth between her legs. A flash of heat accompanied the memory, making her clench her thighs together.

A day apart would do her good. Time away to remind

herself of her list, her plan, and the insurmountable hurdle of Father's hatred for the man who'd brought her to orgasm atop his account books. Twice.

"He's calling on a tenant. The Thatchers. The midwife sent word this morning. Their babe was born late last night. A healthy little girl." Lottie couldn't help a smile. Who wouldn't be happy about a healthy delivery, after all? "Cook and I assembled a basket for the family, and Ethan helped me sort through the blanket cupboard after breakfast. He's distributing warmer linens to the Thatchers and a few other families. The local farmers are claiming it will be a brutally cold winter."

Agatha cocked her head. "You seem to know everything that is going on around here. Is he winning you over? You could do far worse for a husband than Lord Amesbury."

Lottie set her book down, then picked it up again in an effort to *not* watch Ethan's back as he disappeared down the lane. "He is nothing like the man I envisioned marrying." It felt disloyal to say such a thing, given their new intimacy.

Agatha's short laugh ended on a delicate snort. "They never are, dear. I suppose you mean he is not incompetent, easily cowed by you, or able to be managed, as you manage everything else in your life."

"Auntie!"

"Oh, pish. I am old, not blind or senile," Agatha said, rolling her eyes. "A woman of your brains deserves an equal, not whatever it is you seem determined to settle for."

It sounded so cowardly when her godmother said it that way.

Since the night of Ethan's haircut, Lottie's perspective

on intimacy had undergone a change. Desire had been theoretical for so long, yet now it waited beneath the surface, always ready, when Ethan was near. With each encounter they shared, the passionless years loomed empty and cold—and guaranteed if she ended things in a few weeks. As she did whenever the thought crossed her mind, she shoved it aside and tried to focus on the here and now.

Lottie set the book down again and craned her neck for one last peek at Ethan before he disappeared around the curve and trees hid him from view. Seeing him, touching him had become a source of comfort. Like a talisman she didn't want to need.

This was supposed to be only physical. But now she had a constant craving for the little things. Mundane things. Like reading together in the evening and riding the estate during the day.

Like it or not, she had a clearly outlined future. Even if she were to throw away her entire plan and discard the list into the wind like some heroine in a romantic novel, she still had Father to contend with.

"Lord Amesbury could be a good partner for you," Agatha said.

Partner. Lottie wrinkled her nose. What an unwelcome word. She'd have her own property soon, and she wouldn't have to share it with anyone. The plan ensured that.

Ignoring the lack of response, Agatha continued her one-sided conversation. "For someone of your disposition, learning how to be a partner in return could be a lifelong endeavor. You may have noticed you're a managing sort." Lottie shot her a look and pointedly picked up the book again and pretended to read. "He doesn't seem to mind, though. You could have something real with Amesbury. What your mother and father shared, and what I had with Alfred. That is what your mother wanted for you, after all."

The warmth seeped out of Lottie, leaving her with a cold knot of anger and frustration in her chest. There wasn't an easy answer to her problem—she should know, because her brain had dwelled on little else for days—and Agatha pointing out Ethan's bloody perfection didn't help the situation. Slamming the book closed with a thump, she snapped, "I know what Mother wanted. A dutiful daughter as refined as she was. But as I'm learning, we can't always get everything we want, can we?" Tears threatened, but she beat them back with her anger. "She and Father may have shared something special, but they didn't include their children in that happiness. And with her gone, Father has no love left for anything except his books—even his grieving daughter." Every thud of her heart echoed in her ears, but the tears stayed put.

Agatha sighed. "You need never be alone again, child. Even if you choose not to marry, you will always have a place with me. Your father loved your mother with the last fiber of his being, but I can see that his attention to you has not been as constant as it should have been. I will not push. I will not pry." When Lottie snorted, Agatha conceded, "Fine, I shall *try* not to push or pry more than I already have. I will say this—even if you never grow to love Lord Amesbury, you could do far worse than a viscount for a husband."

There was no way to answer that.

The autumnal colors dressing the trees outside shadowed the path down which Ethan had ridden. She would have agreed to coo and cuddle the Thatchers' new baby, except the thought of Ethan's large hands holding an infant had turned her insides to goo, and she had panicked. Lied. Claimed Agatha needed her for something. It was a matter of self-defense, really. Anything to avoid having memories of him snuggling a baby.

He'd be an amazing father. Patient and doting and kind. Someday.

To someone else's children.

Which was none of her concern, since she wasn't marrying the man—even if the throaty burr in his voice did turn her knees to butter.

"Lady Agatha, you've somethin' in the post today. Do ye have a beau writin' tae ye?" Connor entered the room, tapping an envelope against his palm.

"I do hope everything is fine at home." Agatha broke the seal. "Oh my. Stemson writes that the workmen are in their final stages of cleanup. The Berkeley Square town house will be ready for our return by the end of the week. Excellent news." Agatha practically glowed with happiness.

A move would mean they'd no longer be neighbors to Lord Carlyle and, by extension, Ethan. No more private shows at the windows or impromptu visits. Not that Aunt Agatha's townhome was a great distance away, but there was a kind of intimacy that came with being direct neighbors.

They'd originally come to Woodrest to escape Montague's slanderous tales. She'd chosen to avoid the gossip pages from the London papers while here. If talk had died down in their absence, then great. But she'd not let avoiding her notoriety in society be the reason Aunt Agatha delayed returning to her home.

Lottie addressed Connor. "That answers your question

from the other day. We will return to London as soon as possible. No more female distractions for his lordship." She let the sarcasm speak for itself. Gathering the forgotten book from her lap, she rose, shaking out her skirt, and turned to Agatha. "I'll tell Darling to begin packing."

"Yes, dear girl. We have much to do. When Lord Amesbury returns, we must inform him of our departure. We leave tomorrow," Agatha said.

"Of course, Auntie." Lottie left the room as her aunt requested a pen and paper from a footman. There were lists to make. Focusing on that might distract her from the thought that leaving Woodrest meant leaving the freedom she'd shared with Ethan while here.

Connor met him at the door. "Yer lass an' the old lady are goin' home."

"What happened? Are they all right?" Ethan's heart dropped. Delivering the blankets and visiting the Thatchers had taken most of the day. He'd missed the evening meal, and now his houseguests were leaving him.

"Aye, they're right as rain. Just a bit worked up after gettin' word from Lon'on. Lady Agatha's home is ready. No' sure what that means, exactly, but they're packing."

"Lady Agatha's home has been under construction, leaving her tae rent the house next door tae Cal. I suppose they'll move back tae Berkeley Square, then." No more Lottie next door. No more window views. But he'd be damned if she'd back out of their morning rides. Seeing her grumpy morning face at the beginning of each day was something he looked forward to.

Connor took Ethan's overcoat and plucked the hat from his head. "She's in the library right now."

Ethan squeezed Connor's shoulder in thanks and hurried down the hall.

Tonight's gown glowed like an ember in the firelight, with the flickering flames casting her olive skin and inky hair in stark relief. Sitting in his chair reading, she seemed right at home. This time had essentially been a break from reality. A tease of what life could be if only things were different. "I hear you'll be leaving me soon, lass."

Lottie looked up from the book with a start. "I didn't hear you enter. We missed you at dinner." She closed the book, then crossed to where he stood. "How are the Thatchers?"

"First, kiss me. I've no' tasted you in hours." She was smiling when his lips met hers. Again, the rightness of the moment struck him. Unable to let her go quite yet, he placed a light kiss on her forehead. "The Thatchers are tired but healthy, and besotted with their wee one."

"What did they name the babe?" Lottie resumed her seat, leaving him to follow.

"Beatrice." Ethan sighed and sank into the chair beside hers. After his time in the cold wet, the warmth of the fire was heaven. "I wish you'd seen her, Lottie. Such a wee bit of a thing. Her head fit in my palm. She's only as long as my forearm. Didn' cry the whole time, except tae eat. Mrs. Thatcher thanked you for the basket."

"I'm glad she liked it. Beatrice sounds precious."

"Aye, she is. Now what's this Connor tells me about you leaving tomorrow?"

The book in her hand caught her attention. Her long fingers stroked the spine in a habit he'd become familiar with this week. When he stilled her fingers with his hand, she flipped her hand, intertwining their fingers as if they'd been doing it for years instead of days.

"I'm sure Connor told you. Agatha's home will be ready for us to move in by the end of the week. Much remains to be done before we move house. We leave for London in the morning. Darling is packing my things as we speak."

"The real world intruded at Woodrest, aye?" Ethan rested his head on the chair back but kept his gaze and hand on her. "Thank you for sharing my home for a short while."

Her posture mirrored his, with her smile just as tired as he felt. "I've enjoyed my time here. Particularly how you've included me in your duties and business discussions. Thank you for not expecting me to sit in the front parlor and knit."

"Ach, lass, I know better than that. You've run things for years at Stanwick. Why wouldn' I include you?"

"I've been trying to determine if there's a way to fit you—us, I mean—into my plans. I'm not saying I expect you to actually marry me—that would be presumptuous, wouldn't it? But our time here has me questioning everything—even my plans. And my plans have perfectly sound reason to support them." She appeared flustered, shaking her head at her own words. "Never mind. Ignore all that."

A bittersweet ache pierced him at seeing her unsure of herself. "I don' want our time together tae end either. You know I want you. But no, I'm not a man who fits in your plans. If I married you, I'd want you in my bed every night. I'd want you by my side, not in some far-off estate living alone. The future you want and the one I'm making here don' fit together, lass. One of us would have tae change everything."

"Let's just say for argument's sake that we did marry," she began. Her face was so serious, he could almost see her labeling and organizing thoughts, puzzling a way through this conversation. Hope bloomed, even though he knew odds were against them finding middle ground. "Would you still treat me that way? Including me in estate matters, I mean."

Ethan squeezed her hand. "'Tis what you've trained for."

Lottie studied him. "Easy as that? No arguments or masculine posturing?"

"Where I come from, the women work as hard as the men. I'd no' expect you tae sit and lounge your days away unless you wish it, lass. You're no' the type. But even if you changed your plans tae include me—which is a big if—the earl hates me."

She sagged back in her chair. "Yes, he does."

He pursed his lips and nodded. There wasn't much more to say. The earl was her last remaining relative. Ethan would not be a wedge between them. Having no family of his own, he couldn't ask her to alienate hers.

The weak evening light outside didn't reach the far wall of the library, where the fire roared near their chairs. The dim atmosphere, warmed by the flames, created the perfect scene for seduction. If they came together this evening, the passion would be colored with desperation, given the reality of their situation. But stealing one last taste of her was a temptation impossible to resist. He rose from his chair, reaching for her despite the knowledge that goodbye loomed. "Lass, we only have—"

Lottie had already lifted her chin for a kiss they both

wanted when Agatha burst into the room. "We're hosting a ball—a grand event celebrating your engagement and the completion of the construction. All those who flee Town in the summer will regret missing it. If invitations go out by the end of the week, a few families might find their way back to London early. We only have a few weeks before Parliament sits again anyway."

Lottie shook her head at her godmother and shot him a look. "Isn't an engagement ball deceptive? Not to mention expensive?"

A ball sounded like a lot of fuss to raise expectations he knew would be dashed—along with his foolish hopes that somehow he and Lottie might create a future together. But if Lady Agatha wanted a ball, she'd get a ball. That woman was a force of nature.

"Darling girl, never discuss finances in mixed company. Terribly crass, love. Since I am your guardian while you are in London, celebrating the engagement will let everyone know the family supports this match."

"But Father won't actually—"

Lady Agatha swept out of the room as quickly as she'd come, leaving Ethan and Lottie staring after her. A few moments before, the air had been thick with possibility, then the harsh sting of reality. Now silence fell, each retreating to their thoughts—someplace the other couldn't follow.

With a tight smile, she let go of his hand. "Good night, Ethan."

Her book lay abandoned on the chair. Plucking the book from the seat cushion, Ethan glanced at the title. *Fanny Hill*. Of course his curious lass would find an erotic novel.

The fire crackled, the only sound besides his breathing

in the library. The room had felt cozy and comfortable. Now it just felt lonely. Over the years, the books, with their smell of ink and leather, had been friends enough. He had to wonder if he could return to being content without her sitting in the chair beside his.

Chapter Nineteen

Seeing Ethan again sent a thrill through her. She and Agatha had returned from Woodrest a week before, but Ethan had returned to Town only this morning. There'd been work to do, as Ethan had explained in one of the letters he'd sent this week. Connor had put pressure on him to stay at Woodrest, citing the myriad obligations of the estate. She hated to think his duties were falling to the wayside, but seeing him again felt like a physical relief to an ache she'd been only half-aware of carrying.

The open carriage meant she didn't need to bring Darling on this outing, but it also limited the kind of greeting she could offer. They'd been gloriously free at Woodrest, and by comparison, London felt like a cage. It felt like he hadn't touched her in years instead of days. His eyes were admiring when he helped her into the carriage, and she was grateful she'd chosen a new dress for the outing. Vivid green, trimmed with embroidered leaves and birds, the design had arrived the day before from Madame Bouvier. "You're beautiful, lass. 'Tis good tae see you."

She bit her bottom lip and stared at his mouth. What she would give for a few moments of privacy, instead of a greeting on the public street. "It's good to see you too. If we were alone…"

"Aye," he said, his voice husky. He cleared his throat. "Gunther's for an ice?"

"I may be a lunatic to want ices when it's so cold, but yes."

As they headed toward the fashionable tea shop, she stared at Ethan's profile, drinking in his features. Goodness, she'd missed him. Their last conversation in the library had played over and over in her head since she'd returned. They'd left things with a feeling of hopelessness for the future, and it didn't sit well.

The drive was short, not nearly enough time for the jumble of words that wanted to fall off her tongue. Yes, she craved the taste of him, but more than anything, she'd longed for her friend—hearing his voice, making him laugh, seeing him interacting with his tenants. It seemed simplest to say, "I missed you. Thank you for writing."

"I missed you as well. The whole week, I didn' stop thinking about you. Do you mind if we take a few wrong turns? I'd like tae talk privately."

At her nod, they made two turns and headed back toward the parks.

Ethan's side pressed against hers, hip to hip. Their arms brushed every time he signaled to the horses, but neither moved away. "Our month is nearly up. If you want tae continue with the original plan, I will honor my word, step aside, and wish you happy." He drew the horses to a stop on a stretch of gravel path in Green Park and faced her with a serious expression. "But Lottie, if you want a life with me, I'll write your father and beg. I'll make an arse of myself and grovel. I can't make him agree, but I can try tae convince him that I'll make you happy."

A war arose within her, and she didn't know which side should win. It felt like no matter what, she'd lose a part of herself.

On one hand, she wanted to let this proud Scotsman beg her father, then spend the rest of her days living how they had during their time at Woodrest—taking care of the estate, then coming together with that combustive passion they'd discovered. But would that be fair to him? Whether by choice or chance, he'd not mentioned love, but she knew Ethan wanted something that resembled it. When he spoke of his parents, it was clear they were a love match, though his experience differed greatly from hers. Sure, she cared about him. Desired him. But love? How did someone determine that emotion without good examples?

Setting aside the scary concept of love, he deserved partnership at the very least. A marriage built on friendship and lust could be a happy medium between their two visions for a future.

On the other hand, that house by the sea, with its siren song of freedom, called to her. She wasn't convinced that kisses—no matter how toe curling—were worth losing that independence.

Her silence stretched for too long, because Ethan set the horses in motion again, heading back toward Gunther's. Helping him understand what was in her head would be a challenge when the thoughts weren't clear even to her. But opening himself to her like that had taken courage, and he deserved an answer. She only wished she had one that felt definitive.

"I want you, but I want the future I've worked for too. If there's a compromise, let's try to find it. After all, if our passion burns out, we might share enough common interests to live peaceably. Or I can retreat to my estate, and you to yours, then we can coexist miles apart without rancor. We might even manage an heir before the attraction fades."

"Your inner romantic needs work, lass," he said, but his tone wasn't teasing. Had she hurt him with her honesty?

"Please understand, I'm trying to be pragmatic about this, Ethan. Have you considered that Father is someone you'll have to deal with forever? He isn't a dragon we slay once, then never have to see again. That assumes we get him to agree to the match—which we both know is against reasonable odds."

They arrived at numbers 7 and 8 Berkeley Square with its signature pineapple décor visible through the window. Resting the reins on his knees, he stared down at his boots, avoiding her gaze. "It's a gamble. Any relationship is. But I think you're worth the risk. Or you can end it. Our month is up the day after the ball."

She squeezed his fingers. "I don't want to hurt you. If we married, what if you came to resent our agreement in a few years? Can I think about what you've said for a bit?"

"Aye. Take all the time you need, lass." Their fingers interlaced for a moment before he released her and stepped down from the seat to tie off the horses.

When she stepped down from the carriage, a leaflet blew onto her boot, then stuck. Lottie kicked, trying to dislodge the newsprint. Grasping Ethan's arm for balance, she peeled the paper off her shoe, along with a wet autumn leaf acting as glue between boot and leaflet. The edge caught on her glove and wouldn't budge. Flicking her hand only made it worse.

"Ethan, would you mind? This paper seems far more enamored of me than I am of it."

It was only when he'd removed the soggy mess from her hand that she registered the blurred picture on the newssheet. Caricatures of Lottie and Ethan stood at the altar, while another man, who was clearly meant to be Montague, knelt behind her, clutching her hand desperately, looking forlorn. Another sketch starring her private life.

A cold lump of resignation settled in her belly. The scandal continued, and there seemed to be nothing she could do about it. Would her time in London always be plagued by these kinds of mocking sketches? Sending up a quick prayer that the gossip hadn't reached her father in Westmorland, she attempted a joking demeanor. The newspapers would not ruin their day.

"Well, that's just rude. Is my bum really that huge? Please tell me there's been creative license taken by a particularly vile artist." Ethan's solid presence reminded her that she wasn't the only target of the gossips. Having an ally helped alleviate some of the frustration.

"These damn cartoons are getting worse. Your bum is perfect—not as it's portrayed here. See how they've drawn my chin? If it was that blocky in real life, I'd cut myself on it while shaving. The caricaturist was not kind. Although that pathetic expression on Montague's face is a perfect likeness." Ethan crumpled the soggy paper in his fist, then threw it aside. "Enough. What flavor of ice do you want? We can share one if you prefer."

"Chocolate. And I'm not sharing—even if my hind end does resemble a horse in that horrible cartoon." She picked her way across the slick cobblestones to the door without waiting for his assistance. "Do you think the rags will find another target soon? This is getting tiresome."

Ethan hurried to catch up, then held the door open. "We might have a bit of storm tae weather out just yet. You're more interesting than you thought, Princess."

He winked as she passed in front of him and into the warm, fragrant tea shop. An ally. A friend. A man she craved more than the delicious chocolate ice she would order in a moment. She'd said it a few minutes before, but it repeated in her head now. If there was a compromise, she'd like to find it.

At the base of her spine one of his fingers traced a hidden caress. Shivers of longing flowed from that small contact. Could she marry another man, when Ethan affected her so? The thought brought a wave of nausea that made her press a fist to her stomach. No. Compromise had to happen. "Ethan? Yes. Write him. I'll write him too."

"Are you saying you'll marry me, Charlotte Wentworth?"

A breath escaped that she hadn't realized she'd been holding. "I think so."

Chapter Twenty

It had been a week since Lottie and Agatha had moved out of the leased townhome. The room in Agatha's home she'd occupied on previous visits remained largely unchanged. Although the linens and draperies were new, the lemony shade remained. The space was both comforting and nostalgic, overlooking the cook's herb garden and the mews beyond.

Berkeley Square was like the rest of London—cramped. Even if the house itself might be spacious, neighbors frequently either shared a wall or were close enough to pass a pot of jam from one breakfast room's window into the next. In theory, the view from this bedroom was far superior to the one from her room at their previous house, since she didn't face a giant wall of stone. Yet she rather missed that stone wall with its window framing Ethan like a milliner's tempting shop display. At least she knew her weakness now—

half-naked viscounts and French lace were beyond what any woman should have to resist.

Below her window, a kitchen maid bustled through the garden, clipping the last remaining sprigs from the thyme patch, clutching a shawl around her shoulders. Lottie's sigh fogged the windowpane. On a whim, she drew *E+L* on the glass, then surrounded it with a heart. Silly, really.

Over the past week Lottie and Ethan had crafted eloquent letters to Father pleading their case. Agatha kept her busy with plans for the engagement ball, drawing her into intense deliberations over the difference between white and ecru linen. Wouldn't the white linen be ecru by the end of the night? Yet even with the details she found absurd, Lottie couldn't deny the thrill over the event. It might have begun as a farce, but their engagement felt more real by the day.

Like clockwork, Ethan appeared at her door for their morning rides, even when October lived up to its drippy gray reputation. The horseback excursions were the only thing keeping her sane amidst the ball preparations.

Parliament would commence shortly, which meant the men of the aristocracy were returning to Town. The Season itself would not begin in earnest until the spring. However, each day more knockers hung on the doors of Mayfair, signaling the family was in residence.

With only a few weeks to prepare, while also moving house, Lottie had initially expected a small affair.

She should have known better. Agatha never did anything by half measures. Not only would this ball celebrate her engagement, but at some point, it had become a masquerade. Ironic when you considered how their relationship had begun.

The door to the dressing room opened, and Darling stepped through, covered by yards of brocade fabric. The top of her hair peeked above a starched, lace-trimmed ruffle that stood at attention like a satin soldier.

"How can you see what you're doing?" Lottie laughed. "I want to help, but I don't know where to put my hands."

Darling's reply came through the heap of dress as an unintelligible muffled exclamation.

They heaved the mass of fabric onto the bed, then sighed in unison.

"Can you imagine having to wear this many layers of skirts every day? And you haven't even seen the wig yet." Darling shot her a look with an arched brow. "Being a lady's maid is easier these days—that's all I'll say. Once we finish the shepherd's crook, you'll be the loveliest shepherdess anyone's ever seen."

"I'll look ridiculous and we both know it. But thank you. I'm just glad we were able to find something suitable in the attic. Agatha and I are hardly the same size."

Darling shrugged. "When your bodice is pinned in place and laced together, wiggle room is easy to find. I nipped a bit from the skirts for extra fabric where needed, not that you'll notice. This gown is fifty years old, but the quality is exceptional. Do we know what Lord Amesbury is wearing this evening?"

"No, he's been left to his own devices. But he's an enterprising sort. I'm sure he'll manage. I told him I'm dressing as a shepherdess, which he found as amusing as we did. If this fabric is appropriate for tending sheep in *any* century, I'll eat the wig that goes with it. Utterly preposterous."

Three hours later, with Lottie's hair tightly coiled to

make way for a towering wig of ridiculous proportions sure to fall off if she moved her head too quickly, she muttered, “This is a fresh hell I’ve never experienced before.”

Behind her, Darling snorted a laugh, then secured a flashy necklace around her throat. “There we go. Let the pendant settle between your lady friends, and Lord Amesbury won’t be able to tear his eyes away. Poor man. He’ll be running into walls tonight if he doesn’t manage to see past your neckline.”

“How is it I’m wearing the fabric equivalent of every garment I own, yet still have this much cleavage on display?”

“Because I have your best interests at heart. I’ve seen the way that man looks at you. These are your weapons. Use them—but try not to sneeze. You risk loosing a nipple above the neckline.” Darling stepped back to admire her handiwork.

With perfect timing, a footman arrived with the shepherd’s crook. Someone had painted the curved staff to match the powder blue of the dress, then wrapped it all around with greenery and white blooms from the décor downstairs. She would match the decorations. God help her.

“What do I do if the wig falls off?”

“Send a footman. I’ll meet you in the retiring room to fix it. But try not to let the wig fall off.” Darling smiled, then waved her out of the room, giggling a bit when Lottie had to turn sideways to fit the wide panniers through the door.

The view from the top of the staircase was designed to impress. Beeswax candles illuminated the foyer with a warm glow that carried the faintest scent of honey to where she stood. White flowers were draped from everything stationary. Her aunt did know how to make an impression.

Standing a head above most of the others in the foyer, Ethan made it awfully easy to admire the picture he made in his black coat and costume. Sauntering down the steps and grinning like a fool, she met him halfway when he bounded up to meet her.

Ethan swept a courtly bow. "Fair shepherdess. You're a bonny vision, as expected."

"A wolf? Really, Ethan?"

Fuzzy gray wolf ears poked from Ethan's wayward curls. She might not have taken enough off the top when she cut it. That, or his curls truly had a mind of their own. The memory of that first night together, exchanging orgasms before the kitchen hearth, ignited the now-familiar burn of desire in her belly. His gaze behind the domino mask felt like a caress as he blatantly perused her costume and gave an appropriately wolfish grin. Lottie petted one of his costume ears, rearranging a curl to cover the fastening clips.

"Should I be quaking in the presence of the Big Bad Wolf?"

"The Big Bad Wolf will eat you up at the first opportunity, I promise you." Ethan's mask almost hid the wicked glint in his eye. "Look, I even have a tail." Sure enough, a matching length of gray fur trailed out from beneath his coat.

The earliest guests trickled through the door. Mindful of the eyes on them, Lottie offered her hand. "I wish I could greet you properly." Truly, the weeks since leaving Woodrest had been the longest of her life. This last week especially—waiting for a reply from Father and wondering if her mad plan to marry the man who'd ruined her would come to fruition—had taken its toll. Sleepless nights wanting the comfort of his arms while she concocted contingency plans for the likely event that Father wouldn't see reason.

Ethan placed an openmouthed kiss on her palm, pulling her from her musings. His lips against the white of her glove sent curls of sensation up her arm. "We'll steal a moment tae ourselves as soon as we can, lass."

The trickle grew to a steady stream. As hostess, Agatha was in her element, greeting friends, then directing them to the ballroom without ever letting on that she'd essentially herded them like cattle. Lottie took her place at Agatha's right hand, with Ethan beside her.

When the arrival of guests trailed off to a trickle once more, Agatha said, "Amesbury, if you would be so kind, please open the floor for dancing."

"I don't know how I'm going to manage dancing in this gown." Lottie shook her head and immediately regretted it when the wig shifted precariously. She froze, afraid to move.

"Nonsense." Agatha sniffed. "I danced at court in that gown. Several of the Russians copied the design, I'll have you know. Turn sideways through doors when needed, hold your head steady, and try not to think too hard. You will be fine."

Lottie took Ethan's arm, which shook with his barely contained laughter. "The best advice she could give was 'Don't think too hard'?"

In the center of the ballroom, beneath a chandelier heavy with swags of white flowers, Ethan drew her closer. "I have faith in you, Princess."

At the nickname, Lottie stuck out her tongue, then

heard a titter travel through the room. Ah, yes. The ever-present spectators to their courtship. She huffed under her breath and tried to lengthen her neck under the weight of the wig. Her aunt's faultless posture made so much more sense now.

"I don' envy you the task of navigating in that dress, but you look beautiful." Ethan placed a palm at her waist as the opening strains of music floated through the room.

Lottie scanned the faces around the edges of the ballroom.

"Who are you looking for?"

"Just making sure Montague hasn't found a way in. He wasn't invited, of course. But you never know. Can you believe he's just *happened* to be in the square three times in the last few days? He doesn't live near here as far as I know. Didn't try to call or anything. He knows we wouldn't allow him inside. Instead he just *watches*. It makes me nervous."

Taking their cue from the music, they began to dance. "Calvin has eyes on him tonight. Montague won' ruin our night, lass. Cal and I have been buying debts from the gaming tables, and today we wrote his father, calling in the lump sum. Danby will insist Montague retreat tae the country, and he'll no' be around tae cause trouble for you. But still, take a large footman when you go out until he's no longer a threat. Please? I don' like that he's loitering outside."

"Fine. We will enlist the burliest footman we can find. Do I want to know how much this plan has cost you?"

His dimple flashed. "Didn't Agatha say we shouldn't discuss money in company?"

Lottie squinted, giving him a false glare. "Fair enough. For now."

By the time they'd completed one circuit of the room, other guests were joining them on the dance floor. Ethan was a confident, although not terribly graceful dancer. He tended to charge through the steps with little regard for musicality. But he held her gaze as they worked through the turns of the dance, focusing all that determined energy on her, which made her almost dizzy. Lottie's internal temperature rose another degree, while the air thickened with something she could not name. It was as close to magic as Lottie had ever experienced in public. When she was a little girl dreaming of her debut, this was the stuff of her young hopes.

Closing her eyes for a moment, she let him pull her through another spin.

Guests danced, musicians played, wine flowed, and if he didn't get Lottie alone for five minutes to kiss her properly, he might scream. The damned skirts were too wide to allow him a place by her side, so he held her fingers, tugging her along the edge of the room toward the balcony beyond the windows of the glittering ballroom. Lady Agatha had outdone herself. The house was almost as lovely as the woman who'd finally agreed to marry him.

Their visit to Gunther's and her abysmal timing of consenting to marry him—while standing in a public venue—was so very Lottie, he'd been smiling like a fool since. She was a woman of surprises, and it was pointless to deny that his heart was hers. Entirely. Even if he couldn't tell her in those specific words, because she would run away, he knew he loved her.

Somehow, he'd managed to win her hand. *Him.* Lady Charlotte Wentworth, daughter of the Earl of Brinkley, had agreed to marry a Scottish sheep farmer. Such an odd thing.

They'd written to the earl, but they hadn't received a response. Not a huge surprise given the distance the letters had to travel. It felt a bit like tempting fate to celebrate so openly without her father's blessing. While writing their letters, they'd shared their plans with Lady Agatha. The older woman had encouraged them to continue with the engagement ball on the grounds that creating a public spectacle of the match might corner the earl into agreeing to the marriage.

A memory of the earl's sour face crossed his mind. The years had changed Ethan. Perhaps they'd softened the earl too.

If not, this could be the last time he had Lottie alone. Tomorrow might bring a letter—or even the earl himself—to her door, ending everything. No matter how he spun the possibilities, Ethan didn't have a plan beyond begging if that happened. Any other action risked separating Lottie from her last family member, and he couldn't do that to her. Especially not if there was a chance her relationship with her father could be repaired now that he was coming out of mourning.

When Ethan had told her she looked beautiful, he'd understated it. Yes, maneuvering in the gown was a chore, but he heartily approved of the style if it meant acres of skirts and a minuscule bodice.

"You have a habit of cornering me on balconies. Have you noticed?" She was teasing and laughing, and *his*.

"They're the closest thing tae privacy I can find, and I need tae kiss you before I go mad." She didn't protest when Ethan pulled her toward the corner farthest from the ballroom lights.

At last, her body pressed against his, and something inside him released on a sigh of relief. "I've missed holding you," he said. The back of her neck warmed his palm through his evening gloves.

"Careful of the wig," she whispered.

If she couldn't tilt her head, he'd have to come down to her. Grinning at the ridiculousness of it, he bent so they were on eye level and finally kissed her.

Lottie tasted sweeter when she smiled. That he knew something so intimate about her had him thanking whatever god was so lax as to let Ethan stumble his way into favor. Again, the earl's face flashed in his mind, intruding on the moment of happiness. The love match between Lottie's parents was well known in the *ton*. There was a chance the letters could sway her father. Shoving away the worry, Ethan lost himself in the kiss until she pulled away a long moment later.

Her breath feathered against his face on a sigh. "What if he says no, Ethan?"

Their thoughts traveled the same path, then. "I've been wondering the same thing. You're the master planner. Do you have any ideas?"

Beyond the garden walls a night watchman called the hour as one by one gaslights flickered on down the street, filtering light through the trees lining the balcony.

The sight of her worrying her bottom lip with her teeth distracted him from her words for a moment. "Elope? We'd probably forfeit my dowry, though, and he might never forgive me. But I am of age."

He brushed a thumb over her lip, soothing the skin her teeth had nibbled. "He's all you have left, lass. I don' want tae jeopardize that. But as tae the dowry, Woodrest will support us—although not in a lavish lifestyle. At least, not for a few more years. Tae be honest, nearly everything I have is invested in the brewery."

"He is all I have left. Well, Father and Agatha. I don't want to lose him. But it's the principle of the thing, Ethan. That's *my* dowry. It isn't right that he could deny me what's mine."

Leaning against the balustrade, Ethan interlaced his fingers with hers. "What are you saying, lass?"

"I'm saying, he needs to see reason and let me marry whom I choose." The frustration in her tone was clear.

Ethan would do everything within his power to make her never regret marrying him. Even so, the future wasn't set in stone. Nothing had been resolved, and it sounded like she wasn't going to be moved from her stance. Those last precious pieces of her plan—the dowry, her own estate, having someplace to run away—were hers to cling to. And they might be the deciding factor that kept them apart.

Saying that aloud would make it real. It would mean giving voice to the fear. That in the end, she'd choose her plan, the future she'd envisioned, over him. If she did, it would hurt like hell.

No matter his gloomy thoughts about the future, the balcony remained blessedly empty, and she was in his arms. This might be their last chance to steal a moment together, and the urgency to have her come apart one last time overtook his worries for the future. By God, if the earl shut them down, he'd do his best to give them both warm memories.

Ethan's focus narrowed to her skin exposed to the night-time air. "This neckline will be the end of my sanity."

Her laugh turned into a gasp when his teeth found the sensitive spot on her neck. After their time at Woodrest, he knew she loved that. But only the right side made her breathless, not the left.

If given the chance, he would be a husband who paid attention.

Husband. Ethan grinned against her skin, relishing her light giggle. A very un-Lottie-like sound, made all the more precious because he'd caused such a girlish noise. "I can't stop thinking about that night in the library with your mouth on my cock. Remember the next day, when I returned the favor?"

The grin she shot him played with every wicked thought in his brain. He set her hands on either side of him, to grasp the stone railing he leaned against. "Keep your hands here. Don' let go, lass. You'll be needin' the support. And try tae keep that wig on."

"What? Now? Ethan, where are you— Oh mercy!"

The layers of her costume muffled sound when he dived under her skirt, tucking his costume tail behind him so it wouldn't give away his location should someone pass by. Surely, he wasn't the only man in history to think of this. These skirts had to be good for something beyond making walking a hazard.

"I didn't know you meant *now*." The hissed statement reached him loud and clear, cutting through the layers of fabric without a problem. However, she didn't step away from the edge of the balcony, and she widened her stance to make room for him. The trust she offered and that willingness to explore passion were two things he loved about her.

Grinning, he kissed the inside of one knee. There was plenty of room under here to maneuver. It would be nice to see the landscape, so to speak, but beggars can't be choosers. If he couldn't find everything in the dark by feel alone, then he had no business being under a woman's skirts in the first place.

Ethan tugged off his evening gloves, tucked them in a pocket, then used his fingers to see her, beginning at her knees before traveling north. Her garter ribbons were silk. Kissing one bow, Ethan hoped he'd have the chance to determine its color another day, then continued on, tracing the line of her legs with eager fingers.

When he greeted the plump curve of her inner thigh with an openmouthed kiss, her body quivered for an instant under his lips. But then—oh, beautiful lass—she leaned into his mouth.

Holding her open, Ethan blew lightly across the top of her slit, where her bud waited. Her body jolted, but not away from him. Drawing in her scent, he placed an almost-chaste kiss on the triangle of curls before letting himself go further. Lord, he'd missed her.

Finally, the taste of her coated his tongue again. Years seemed to have passed since he'd last savored her unique flavor.

Ethan grasped her legs, curling his long fingers at the crease of her buttock and thigh, then he encouraged her movements against his mouth with light presses and squeezes of his fingertips. Similar to leading a dance, except that this was something more intimate than a waltz. And just like on the dance floor, she was a brilliant partner.

The soft, willing body under his hands froze.

A woman's voice filtered through the lusty haze clouding his brain. They were no longer alone.

Lottie's side of the conversation came through clearer, although her tone struck him as a wee bit shrill.

Understandable given the circumstances. His caress along the back of her thighs was partly to reassure her that she was handling the situation well and partly for the sheer joy of touching her.

"Thank you ever so much, Mrs. Fitzwilliam. Lord Amesbury and I are glad you were able to join us this evening." A moment later, Lottie said, "I last saw him going, er, downstairs." Ethan bit his lip and pressed his face against her leg to smother the laughter, then nibbled a path back toward heaven, soothing each nip with a flick of his tongue. "Although, knowing Aunt Agatha, she's probably introducing him to friends. If you see them, do let him know I'm waiting." Her strained laugh sounded credible enough. With a lazy lick, he tasted the slit of her quim. She handled herself admirably under pressure.

"Yes, the man is *such* a dear." Lottie took one step forward—largely unnoticeable to the likes of Mrs. Fitzwilliam but effective in pressing his head back against the railing. He grinned at the silent reprimand, then held her hips in place, laving her core with the flat of his tongue.

Mrs. Fitzwilliam must have moved along to mingle with the other guests inside, because Lottie's body turned pliable under his hands once more. Skimming hands up toward her wet curls, he brushed her open to hint at his intention before sliding his finger inside. The soft curve of her lower belly quivered against him, and he would have given anything to have more than just a finger inside her. With a wee bit of luck, they'd have a lifetime to take their pleasure in each other.

And wasn't that just the damnedest thing.

Or he'd be left with just his hand and memories. The worry about her father tried to rise in his mind, but he ruthlessly squashed it to focus on the present moment, when once again, Lottie pressed him to the railing.

Holding his head in place with her glorious body, she set the pace against his mouth. The sound of her low, shuddery moan sang a song meant for only him. A rush of earthy sweetness flooded his tongue, and he swallowed her release, softening the pressure against her until his tongue grazed only the petals and curves of her flesh, avoiding the central bundle of nerves.

He gave her quim one last gentle, closemouthed kiss. Ethan traced his fingers from her ankles up to that ribbon garter, then back down again. The shakes of her body were quieting.

Under his fingers, her legs were smooth and strong. At last the quivering in her thighs settled, and the silence beyond this dark haven let him know it was safe to emerge. Ethan shimmied out from under the cover of a wide pannier and stood as if he'd been leaning beside her against the railing all along. Dragging a hand down his waistcoat, he tried to set himself to rights and hoped the erection tenting his breeches would abate soon.

Beside him, Lottie's fingers held the balustrade in a death grip. A flush covered her chest, visible in the light from the single flickering lantern nearby. Ethan covered one of her hands with his.

She cocked her head, then froze when the wig slipped at an awkward angle. "That was...marvelous. But what about your satisfaction?"

"I'm not worried about me. I wanted tae make it good for you. I promise I always will."

Lottie squeezed his hand, then straightened the costume ears he wore. "The Big Bad Wolf, indeed. If they only knew what a kind man you are."

Ethan grinned, letting her see his teeth. “I promised tae eat you up, didn’ I?” Lottie’s husky laugh loosened the lingering knots of worry in his chest.

She stood on her tiptoes to whisper in his ear. “Darling will let you in the side entrance after the guests are gone. Find your way to my room tonight and do it again.” Her hand slid up the line of his hard thigh to close over the length of his erection.

He glanced at her sharply. “Are you suggesting what I think you are, lass?”

“We’re going to be married. What’s the harm?”

It tempted the fates to say as much out loud. So many things could go wrong tomorrow, but tonight…she offered everything. And standing on that balcony, with her skin glowing from the pleasure he’d just given her, he couldn’t say no.

Chapter Twenty-One

The gaslights outside Lottie's window dotted the lane to the mews, which finally showed signs of settling after a busy night. Their last guest had departed over an hour before, but her body hummed after the assignation on the balcony. That orgasm had left her with weak knees and shivers under her skin whenever she'd spied Ethan's knowing smile throughout the rest of the evening.

Darling entered the room, singing to herself. "First things first, milady. You're probably ready for that wig to come off."

"I hope to never wear another wig for as long as I live." Finding the small bench at her vanity table with her skirts obstructing the view turned out to be a chore in itself. Behind her, Darling giggled, lined her up with the padded seat, then pressed gently on Lottie's shoulders.

"Thank you, Darling. What would I do without you?" Lottie removed her earrings while her maid withdrew one hairpin after another from the wig. When Darling lifted the heavy thing off her head, Lottie sighed. "I feel as if my head is floating somewhere high above my shoulders." Lottie fiddled with the clasp of the necklace, removed it, and ran her fingers over the bejeweled pendant. Darling motioned for Lottie to stand, then set about unpinning the bodice and removing the layers of the gown.

"I have a rather personal request. Do you have those French letters we discussed purchasing in Kent?"

Darling's smirk spoke volumes. "Aye, milady. I'll just set one out in a bowl by the bed, shall I? How's he getting inside the house?"

Lottie would bet her mother's pearl earbobs that her cheeks were twin flags of flaming pink. "I told him you'd let him in the side entrance."

"I'd be happy to deliver him right to your door. But after that it's your responsibility. I'll leave you to tie the bow on him." Darling's eyes were alight with humor as she folded away the night's costume for storage.

Lottie wasn't sure what Darling meant about the bow, but she really didn't want to ask questions right now. She stepped out of the pile of fabric, letting the petticoats and shift settle on the floor, then she shrugged into a pink satin dressing gown. Out the corner of her eye she saw Darling fill a small bowl with water and open a packet, preparing to soak the French letter so it would be soft for use later.

Lottie folded the remaining pieces of the costume, then began her nighttime routine.

"Shall I draw you a bath, milady?"

The clock on the mantel struck the hour. "Do I have time for a bath?" It did sound lovely.

With a shrug, Darling gathered the lemon bath oil that

had become a favorite. "If milord finds you naked in the tub, I doubt he'll mind. Might help you relax a bit. You're fluttering about like a nervous bird."

Leave it to Darling to find the perfect relaxation aid and seduction setting. After pinning her hair up, she sank into the tub in front of the fire. Lottie closed her eyes and took a deep breath, filling her senses with citrus-scented air. Hot water soothed her muscles. Dragging that heavy dress around all night had been a far more physical experience than the average evening entertainment, and her neck ached from the weight of the wig.

The soft swish of wooden door against carpet, then the *snick* of her key in the lock alerted her to Ethan's presence. She kept her eyes closed, waiting to see what he would do next. Having him near, knowing where the night would lead, sent a ripple of excitement through her.

A kiss as soft as a butterfly landed at the corner of her eye, above her cheekbone. "Good evening, my lord. Would you like to wash my back?" She smiled at his low chuckle, and she finally lifted her lids. The gold starbursts in his eyes reflected the firelight, and for a moment she could only stare. He was beautiful. With a wet hand, she smoothed a curl off his forehead, then cradled his jaw as he leaned down to kiss her.

Pulling back, he shrugged out of his coat, waistcoat, and shirt, tossing them onto a chair to land on the book she'd abandoned earlier. If she'd thought him beautiful before, the play of light on his bare skin made a mockery of the word. Beautiful? No, breathtaking. "Someone should sculpt you. Michelangelo's *David* is a puny weakling in comparison."

The flash of his grin had a roguish quality, sending a shiver of arousal through her. He knelt beside her and picked up a washcloth and the bottle of bath oil, then poured a liberal amount onto the cloth. "Do you have any idea how long I've wanted tae slick this oil over your skin, lass? This is the stuff of fantasies for me."

"You are easy to please, then," she said. With gentle but thorough strokes, Ethan covered her skin in warm scented oil and water, rubbing away tension in her shoulders and neck with his long fingers. The massage elicited a happy moan from her. "That feels so good. Your hands are magic." He took the encouragement as it was intended and continued his exploration, dipping beneath the surface of the water to cradle her breasts.

"No, *these* are magic. I've not seen you naked all at once before. I take back what I said before. This is the stuff of fantasies," he said, tugging gently on her nipples.

There'd always been the threat of discovery, so clothing had been shifted or lifted aside, not removed entirely. For the first time, they had all night, and she'd have all of him. Feeling like a seductress, she gave him a saucy glance over her shoulder and rose from the water, then stepped from the tub.

At his poleaxed expression, confidence coursed through her veins. The lush mounds of her breasts bounced as she pulled pins from her hair one by one, setting them aside in a bowl beside the tub.

Ethan swore in the guttural tone of a man nearing his edge. "Sweet bloody Jesus on a cross..."

"Do breasts usually trigger blasphemy?" she asked, dabbing at her skin with a towel. When she leaned down to nip the corner of his mouth, her breasts swayed forward. He caught a nipple, sucking it deep with a delicious drag of sensation. Snaking an arm around her waist, he palmed one of her buttocks.

"I'm having a wee bit of a religious experience. Your figure is the kind Scots immortalize in drinking songs. You're all curves. Everywhere. Dips and valleys...perfect." He set his mouth against her breast, working his way up as he stood, tasting her with a needy combination of tongue and teeth that sent her pulse pounding.

They stared at each other for a heartbeat. If only he could always look at her as he did now. Unrealistic, but a fine goal. At last, he reached her mouth and she welcomed him, tunneling one hand into his hair, as if to anchor him to her.

His hands traveled a deliberate path down her back, over her hips, and grasped her firmly where her thighs creased under her bottom. A gasp escaped when he lifted her off her feet, wrapping her thighs around his hips to carry her toward the bed. Everywhere he touched, a trail of pebbled gooseflesh followed. Sensation and desire tangled with a ribbon of joy, coursing through her. The way he looked at her quieted any lingering nerves.

Ethan didn't try to be proper or restrained. Thank God, because neither did she. She wanted the man who'd licked her into a passionate climax while under her skirt on the balcony and cornered her for heated kisses in the servant hallway.

The focused expression he wore was by far the sexiest thing she'd ever beheld. As if he didn't know where to touch first but was eager for every inch. She couldn't stop touching him—any part of him she could reach, which wasn't much when his clothes covered everything below his waist. The abrasion of fabric against her nakedness was its own kind of arousal. "You have too many clothes on. How is that fair? I want to touch you. To make you feel good."

"You had a head start. If I take my clothes off, I'll no' be able tae stop myself from finally being in you." Ethan knelt on the bed, between her feet, trailing fingertips over her. From her shoulders, down her ribs, circling feathered brushes around her puckered nipples, then marking a path to her waist and hips.

She blew a curl out of her face and shot him a look. "I fail to see the problem."

That dimple by his mouth flashed. "Ach, lass. You're perfect." He grasped her thighs and held her open to him. With a soft, openmouthed kiss above her belly button, he skimmed his lips down toward her mons. Lottie desperately wanted to close her eyes and feel, but watching his obvious bliss at every touch and taste was an aphrodisiac of its own.

"Hello again," he whispered with a smile in his voice, then parted her folds with his tongue. With steady pressure and gentle pulls, he focused on the point of pleasure near the top of her slit. Surrender had never been easier, as pleasure washed over her.

When he entered her with a thick finger, then curled it to find a spot inside her she hadn't known existed, Lottie moaned a curse under her breath. "Don't you dare stop doing that."

"Bossy," he teased, gently nipping the cluster of nerves, then sucking the sting away while that finger worked in and out, readying her body for his. Ripples of sensation pulled into a tight ball that seemed to wrest her body from her control. Her back arched, her hips rose and fell against his mouth, and her voice cried out over and over. Lottie wasn't sure what she said. His name and God's mixed with threats if he stopped, because fire flickered through her in the most delicious way.

Ethan rode out the climax with his mouth on her, gentling his pressure as she came down from the peak. He made one last pass with his tongue before crawling up her body, looking far too proud of himself. With twinkling eyes, he said, "My future wife swears when she comes."

"Did I? Should I apologize?" Her body clenched with aftershocks as she lounged under him, happily limp and wrung out.

He kissed her, hard and swift, in answer. "Like a sailor. Never stop. Don' doubt your instincts or responses in bed with me. No' ever."

She smiled, then purred when his teeth explored the slopes of her left breast. "My instincts demand you get naked. It's been too long since I've tasted you."

"That night in the library was forever ago. I've dreamed of you since. Wanted you every day." Kneeling over her, he paused to let Lottie unbutton his breeches.

It was like unwrapping the best present in the world, with layers of clothing coming off his large frame. The edge of the bed dipped as he removed his boots and breeches.

The shifting lines of heavy muscles on his back and arms enthralled her. His body differed from hers in so many ways, and she ached to explore every glorious inch. With one hand, she pushed him to his back across the bed, then crawled atop him. Skin to skin, she spread her fingers over the ridges and planes, finding the spots that made his breath catch.

With sure hands, he settled her legs on either side of his hips. Pushing his hardness against her, he paused against her center. "You're sure you wouldn' rather wait till after the wedding?"

She reached for the bowl by the bed and handed him

the French letter. "You're Scottish. Who needs official ceremonies, anyway? Didn't your country use to handfast? Now show me how this works."

"We have been known tae play fast and loose with the formalities, but I had tae ask." He made a noise deep in his throat when she stroked him. The silky-smooth hardness of his body was fascinating.

Her giggles began when he tied the ribbon around the base of his erection. Darling's earlier teasing came to mind, and Lottie finally understood. Another short laugh escaped as a snort, and Lottie clapped a hand over her mouth to stifle the sound.

Raising a brow, Ethan said sardonically, "It's heartening that you aren' intimidated by what we're about tae do, lass."

"How—" she gasped. "How could I be scared when your member is tied up like a little girl's pigtails?" She leaned forward, burying her face in his chest, trying desperately to contain her giggles. An answering chuckle rumbled under her cheek.

"If you're going tae laugh, at least humor me by calling it a cock and not my 'member.' We aren' meeting for teatime, lass. 'Tis a cock."

The body part under discussion remained hard and ready between them. Recovering from the absurdity of seeing a satin ribbon around it, she stroked him again and felt the arousal within her flare when she repeated the word. "I love your cock. It's a beautiful cock." Especially with its pretty blue ribbon, but she would *not* say that, for fear of collapsing with mirth again.

He'd liked it when she spoke during their previous encounters, and each time she said *cock*, his erection twitched against her. How novel. He wanted her to speak—apparently the less ladylike, the better.

With her hair over one shoulder, creating a dark curtain to separate them from the world, she slid her folds up his shaft. Her voice came out in rapid, breathy pants. "God, that feels good." The silky slickness wasn't a total mystery, but her body's response to this man made her marvel. "I loved seeing you come apart when I had my mouth on you in the library." Beneath her, Ethan drew one stiff peaked nipple into his mouth, moaning his encouragement. "Your thighs tense and shake right before you climax. Next time you come I want you inside me."

He groaned like a man on the cusp of something epic. Yes, he liked it when she said whatever was on the tip of her tongue. Ethan's fingers clenched her hips. There might be ten small marks on the curve of her hips tomorrow, and she'd be glad for the reminders of his strong hands. Those points of contact seared, guiding her against him in a rhythm her body desperately wanted to learn. Lottie whimpered, tugging his head closer, urging him to keep going. Forever, preferably.

"Lottie. Love, I need tae be in you," he said. The plump head of him notched her opening. They both held their breath for a heartbeat.

Willing her body to relax around him, she sighed, "Yes. Please. Fill me."

As she sank onto him, he choked out, "Fuck, you feel amazing."

This was a new dance—a push and pulling slide of coming together over and over until the ropes of the bed creaked in time with their groans. Heat came off his body in waves, and Ethan's hands moved over her once she caught the cadence of lovemaking. Finally, he anchored one fist in her hair, repeating her name like a prayer.

Drawing the mass of her hair aside, Ethan placed open,

wet kisses along her neck and rolled them over. Lost to sensation, Lottie stopped thinking and simply felt. With their fingers intertwined, he pinned her hands overhead and trapped her in his gaze just as effectively. Sparks built, tingling up her inner thighs to the point where their bodies joined, then spiraling up her abdomen like embers caught in the wind.

There was no other way to explain it. Fireworks comparable to the show at Vauxhall exploded within her, stealing her breath.

"Stay with me, lass. Watch me while you come."

Staring into his eyes was a new vulnerability, but she surrendered to the feeling. He'd brought her to the brink, and she had to trust Ethan to bring her through this pleasure. Ahead of them lay a lifetime of this feeling—this discovery of one another's bodies—and the thought set loose a flood of fierce happiness as she cried out.

She took him with her as they stared into each other's eyes with mutual awe. Lowering himself on unsteady arms, Ethan settled beside her. A place on his chest near the cradle of his shoulder seemed made for her head.

Stroking her back, he said, "I'll have tae leave this bed eventually. I hope my legs work by then."

She giggled. "I can't feel my toes. Or my knees. I had no idea my knees could go numb."

The vibration of his chuckle rumbled under her ear. Burrowing her nose in the side of his neck, she breathed him in. Contentment turned her bones to jelly, and she let the gentle brush of his fingers down her spine lull her.

"I'll never get tired of touching you, love."

She murmured sleepily, "Then don't stop."

Chapter Twenty-Two

The following morning's salacious headline "Mr. M Warns the Heir to the Former Princess and Her Brute May Carry His Blood!" would surely give her father apoplexy if he read it. After the powerful and tender lovemaking of the night before, the gossip rag was a cruel return to reality. Neither of them deserved this nonsense, especially Ethan. He was a good man. Lottie slapped the paper down on the table with a growl. That didn't satisfy, so she crumpled the newssheet in her fist, threw it to the ground, and stomped on it.

Agatha looked up from her tea with a benign expression, as if her honorary niece weren't throwing a fit. She lifted an inquiring brow.

"I hate the gossips." Lottie took her seat at the breakfast table once more and tried to emulate her aunt's calm. Taking a sip of her tea, she said, "May every one of them find eternal release in a frigid watery grave. There. I feel better."

"They shall settle soon. Mr. Montague seems to be enjoying his moment in the sun by drawing this out as long as possible. But even he will have to give way once you're respectably married. It will turn out. You will see."

Lottie wrinkled her nose and pushed her eggs to the other side of the plate. They were cold anyway. Her godmother was a mighty ally in this situation, and perhaps having her on their side would help sway Father. Her unruffled reaction to the slanderous headlines didn't soothe Lottie's riled sense of justice.

"You are not riding this morning?"

"Ethan will be by shortly. I wanted to sleep a little longer and recover from the late hour of the ball." He'd sneaked out as dawn had crept over the windowsill, leaving her in the warm blankets that smelled of them. She'd immediately claimed his pillow and breathed in his scent. "The ball was a smashing success, by the way. Well done, Auntie."

"Thank you, darling girl. It is always best to be the hostess who sets expectations in society, rather than the one who tries to meet others'. Now, perhaps we can discuss the wedding after your ride?"

"Already itching for a new project? Very well. Wedding plans begin this afternoon." Happiness bubbled up, but she pushed the emotion down and drained her teacup. "If a letter from Father arrives while I'm gone, please open it and then prepare me for the contents."

"I am sure your father will see reason. If you have moved past your history with the viscount, then I see no reason for your father to continue holding a grudge."

Praying the letter would be that well received, Lottie kissed her aunt's cheek, then left the room. She'd forgotten her hat upstairs, and Ethan would be here any moment.

Unfortunately, when Ethan arrived, it was clear their ride wasn't on his mind. He wore a small satchel crosswise on his body and practically ran into the room.

"I'm sorry, lass. A messenger caught me on my way out the door. Woodrest is burning. It was faster tae stop on my way out of Town than write a note." He grabbed her and gave her a fierce kiss. "I need tae go. I should have been there. Connor kept telling me tae come home," he said, then bolted from the room. Stunned, she stood in place for a moment before his words fully sank in. Woodrest was burning? The house or the estate—and did that even matter? His home was in flames.

Should she follow? No, if he'd wanted her there, Ethan would have said so. Perhaps sending a group of willing footmen to lend aid wouldn't be overstepping. She might one day be the mistress of Woodrest, but she wasn't yet, and she didn't quite know what she should do in this instance.

"Stemson!" Lottie called into the hall.

Ever the epitome of organization, Stemson soon had a group of the strongest footmen and grooms on their way to Woodrest to lend a hand.

Which left her with nothing to do. A pile of correspondence on her writing desk awaited her attention. Although referring to three letters as a pile stretched the truth.

A letter from Rogers with Stanwick Manor estate business sat at the top. After opening and skimming it to ensure there wasn't a note from Father, she'd set it aside yesterday. Now she read it in full. Shockingly, Rogers reported her father continued to regain primary control of things back home. While she was happy Father's mental state allowed him to be involved, years of disappointment held her back from fully embracing the good news as a permanent change.

The earl reclaiming his rightful place in charge of Stanwick meant things were returning to how they should be. Logically, she knew this. Once upon a time, he'd loved Stanwick as if the estate were another child. When Michael and Mother had died, his passion for life and all its responsibilities had died with them. So yes, her father paying attention to his tenants and land was a wonderful turn of events, albeit several years overdue. With her own future leading her away from Stanwick Manor, she should be thrilled to cut ties and focus her attention elsewhere. And she was. However, the tightness in her throat was an effective reminder that nothing involving Father was simple.

When Mother had died, he hadn't shared his grief with Lottie or shown concern for her own grieving process. In many ways she'd lost everyone that day. The old pain tried to surface, but instead of letting it take over, Lottie tried to imagine waking up to Ethan every day for decades—as her parents had woken up to each other—then one day, having him gone. Never to return. The thought was inconceivable, and she'd awoken to him only once.

No wonder Father had retreated from reality. But then, so had she in some ways. Work had been her hiding place. For five years Stanwick had been her world, sun up till sun down.

Exactly how Ethan felt about Woodrest. Was he there yet? How bad was the fire? She glanced at the clock on the mantel. No, he had another hour of hard riding.

Tension knotted her shoulders. Taking a deep breath, she counted. Inhale, one, two, three. Exhale, one, two, three. Like so many times before, to settle her nerves, she imagined the future she wanted.

Soon, she'd have her own lands. Her own house.

Would she and Ethan divide their time between the estates, as many others did? In those instances, the wife wasn't usually a manager of a different property, so the family traveled together. One more thing to figure out.

Last night he'd said he'd invested heavily in the brewery. Was that on fire too? What if he lost everything? Then they'd need her dowry to survive. To rebuild.

Lord, that letter from Father needed to arrive soon. Putting pen to paper, she scratched out a response to Rogers's letter.

While waiting for the ink to dry, Lottie stretched in the desk chair, pausing when her neck protested the position she'd held while writing and a tender area in her nether regions throbbed against the seat. Last night's delicious activities meant sore muscles today. A ride on Dancer would help work out the kinks. Besides, pounding hooves on turf and feeling the wind whip her face were excellent stress relievers. Nothing said she couldn't go out on her own later, but riding had become one of those activities she associated with Ethan. Yet another sign that she'd inadvertently stumbled into becoming part of a "we."

A glance at the clock showed he might be arriving at Woodrest in about a half hour. The view out the window revealed no surprises. Late October meant gray weather. Ezra was a solid mount, and Ethan a brilliant rider. No need for her to worry. He'd get there in time. He had to. Thankfully, Connor was more than capable as a manager, steward, or whatever other title Ethan might call him. Connor would have handled the situation before now.

What had Connor called her? A distraction. She crossed her arms and tapped out a rhythm on her forearm with her fingers. Before Ethan left, he'd said something on his way out the door. *I should have been there.* What did he mean?

Their engagement ball was last night. They'd agreed he'd stay in London until they heard from Father.

Or were they the words of a man who felt responsible—guilty that he hadn't been there when tragedy struck home? The tapping of her fingers slowed, then stopped. Were they the words of a man who knew he'd failed his people because he'd prioritized her? Focused on their relationship, had they somehow become just like her parents and ignored the needs of the people who depended on him? Ethan had mentioned that Connor's letters were full of calls to come home and deal with the brewery construction, reminding him of the need to be present for the large business enterprise he'd invested in. The feeling of being torn was real for Ethan, yet he'd chosen her. Over and over. Oh God, why hadn't she seen it?

Tenant cottages could be burning right now—tenants like the Thatchers. Their livestock might suffer, crops from this harvest could go up in smoke, and if their lord hadn't been in London chasing her, he might have been there to stop it. Or he could have caught it earlier.

Dread bloomed, shortening her breath. Connor had tried to warn her, but she hadn't listened. All she'd cared about were those depressingly dark blue walls in that breakfast room.

Agatha's voice cut into her spiraling thoughts. "Are you done, my dear? Madame Bouvier is expecting us soon. At this time of day traffic might be a snarl."

"The modiste? I thought we were discussing wedding plans today." Plans she really didn't want to pursue given her worry over Ethan and Woodrest.

"We are. You can't get married without a dress. Not just any dress will do. Your gown is the most important part of the wedding."

"I'd think the bride and groom were the most important part."

Agatha would not be deterred. "Your gown will set the standard for this Season's weddings. We leave in ten minutes. Please try to keep up, love." The subtle scent of expensive perfume lingered behind after her godmother.

"A dress. Thus, it begins." Heaving a sigh, she tried to shove down the panic and concern over Ethan, Connor's warning, and her father. Agatha wanted a gown, so they'd buy a gown. At least Madame Bouvier would offer tea for her trouble.

An hour later, Lottie wished for something stronger to drink than tea. They sat in the same parlor-style fitting room she'd entered months before, upon her arrival in London. Back then she'd worn a dress destined for the rag bin. Today Lottie was a beautiful example of a well-turned-out woman, dressed head to toe in Madame Bouvier's designs. Her wedding gown would be a work of art.

"Beaded chiffon overlay or a lace overskirt? What do you think, Lottie?" Agatha held the two fabrics. Not waiting for Lottie's answer, she turned to Madame Bouvier, who cradled the pale-blue silk they'd already chosen. "The chiffon, I think. But pearls, not beads. That much lace might look busy. We mustn't overpower the bride, after all."

If lace could outshine her, they had bigger issues to discuss, but Lottie held her tongue. Aunt Agatha was the arbiter of fashion, not her. If left to her own devices, Lottie would spend most of the day in breeches. Truth be told, while she loved the effect achieved by luxurious gowns, she missed the utilitarianism of her old dresses and work trousers. She'd never dream of sitting in the grass by a stream in the dress she wore now—or climbing a tree or chasing a lamb in a pen or any number of other activities that had once been her day-to-day life. She imagined how Ethan would respond to seeing her in breeches. Grass stains after that encounter would be a certainty, and they would both be happy afterward. She smiled into her teacup and sipped.

"The dress must show to advantage not only in the church but on canvas. Definitely pearls," Aunt Agatha said.

"Canvas? What are you talking about?" Lottie nibbled a small cake, picking out the dried currants with her teeth to relish first.

"Your wedding portrait, of course. Had you forgotten? I've already sent a letter to the artist who painted your parents."

The wedding portrait. Her mother's family immortalized their brides and had for generations. It was sweet of Agatha to continue the tradition.

That painting of her mother hung in the library, where her father could see it all day. He conversed with that portrait as if her mother might step off the canvas at any moment and answer him. It was too good of a likeness for her tastes—it had hurt to look at the picture for a year after Mother's death. The artist had captured her essence, right down to the bottomless love she'd held for the earl, shining from an eternally youthful face.

"Forgive me if I overstepped by commissioning the portrait. It's what your mother would have done. She would be over the moon for you." Agatha's eyes shone until she blinked away the moisture with a sniff. "As her best friend, it is my duty and privilege to handle this affair as she would."

The shards of grief surprised Lottie as they cut deep. Mother had condemned Ethan with the ferocity of a lioness after the Paper Doll debacle. Maybe she'd have come around these past few months and softened under Ethan's apologetic charm. Maybe not. Now that she found herself planning a wedding to the man declared an enemy by her parents, her mother's absence found new ways to hurt.

Silly, but she hadn't thought of it before now. Lottie would walk down the aisle, and her mother wouldn't be there. Emotions swelled until her chest felt ready to burst. The burning behind her eyes threatened tears that might never stop if the first one fell. The reality was that Mother would never have the opportunity to succumb to Ethan's charm or hear his apology or appreciate what a decent man he'd grown to be. The burn of grief made it tempting to run away from the discomfort, run away from the nagging worry over her father's reply, and definitely run away from the wedding planning. Everyone's lives would settle back onto their previous courses.

Maybe then Ethan would focus on the brewery and never again fail to be present for the ones who depended on him. Shaking her head, Lottie shoved the thought aside.

Squeezing Agatha's hand, Lottie grappled for composure. "Thank you for thinking of it. Pearls and chiffon it is."

Chapter Twenty-Three

Dawn crept into her room in increments. First, the sound of birds through the small opening in her window. She'd lifted the sash to allow for fresh air sometime during the wee small hours, hoping the chill would clear her head. The yeasty scent of fresh bread from the kitchens followed the chirp of birdsong as a new day greeted the world. It would probably be a beautiful day. One of the last before winter took hold.

Lottie's fingers clutched the edge of her blanket, as they had for the past countless hours. Sleep had been elusive. Grief was a funny thing. It lingered in places you didn't expect, appeared in situations you hadn't considered. She'd gone from the high of finally coming together with Ethan in bed, then kissing him goodbye when he raced home to fight a fire, to the reality of worrying over him and wondering if they'd be allowed to marry. Choosing a wedding gown while pretending all was well had been a challenge, but then grief ambushed her. Her mother should have been in that shop yesterday, deliberating between beads and pearls. It wasn't fair.

The corners of her eyes were crusty from the dried tracks the tears had left on their way to her pillow. She'd cried as if feelings were liquid and if she could only pour them out, she'd once again be happy and clean. Instead, she was simply hollow.

How many times yesterday had she heard that her mother would be proud of her? Happy for her? Perhaps her mother would have eventually forgiven Ethan as she had, but when Mother died, she'd hated him. That knowledge settled in her belly like a bowl of cold porridge.

The soft click of the latch of her door signaled the entrance of someone into the bedchamber. A chambermaid squeaked in surprise when Lottie sat up. "Apologies, Betsy. I didn't mean to surprise you."

Betsy bobbed a curtsy, then set about stoking and building the fire in the grate. "You're up with the birds, milady. Breakfast hasn't been laid out downstairs, but I can send Mrs. Darling up with a tray if you wish."

"Thank you, but I'm not very hungry. Just some tea in the morning room, if you could. I'd appreciate it." Lottie threw the covers off, then shivered when her toes hit the floor. The chilly morning bit at her bare feet. Perhaps the shock to her system would restore equilibrium after yesterday's ups and downs.

Betsy completed her work while Lottie changed behind the privacy screen. This morning called for comfortable clothing, not complicated gowns or riding habits. Poor Dancer was probably antsy for a good gallop. Maybe after tea, she would be up for a ride.

Ethan hadn't sent a note last night, and that was a worry of its own.

Three cups of tea later, Lottie's outlook on life had only slightly improved. Stemson brought the morning post, along with the papers. The newssheets could wait. One more awful headline and she might crack. A slim folded paper with her father's insignia pressed into the seal made her pause.

Lottie turned the letter over in her hand. Her father's sharp scrawl confirmed that this was the letter she'd been waiting for. She'd almost forgotten what his handwriting looked like. Looking around the empty room, she wished Agatha or Ethan were there to either provide moral support or celebrate with.

Except Ethan was in Kent, fighting to keep his home. Sitting in a freshly redecorated breakfast room, far from danger, Lottie felt useless and decorative. Like the paper doll he'd once called her.

Charlotte,

It would appear you have once again become the subject of gossip and speculation. Lord Danby tells me the papers are full of your exploits, the likes of which can only be interpreted as an effort to make your disdain for a proper match known. In addition, the letters from yourself and Lord Amesbury erased any doubt that your time in London has been spent finding the least acceptable candidate for a husband in order to force my hand.

Clearly, you are too old and set in your ways to be amenable to marriage, so I am prepared to offer a compromise. Rogers assures me he taught you well, so I will give you your heart's desire—property of your own to manage and the funds set aside for your dowry. Rogers has one in mind about which he's already written to you.

If you want to be an ape leader, so be it. That outcome, as distasteful as I find it, is preferable to marrying that Scottish upstart.

Should your desire to marry Amesbury be genuine—although I can't imagine how—then I can't stop you. You're of age. However, I can and will ensure not a penny of your dowry lines Lord Amesbury's pockets.

In short, if you continue with this engagement to Amesbury, know that you do so without the support of your family's wealth or title. Neither of you will be welcome at Stanwick Manor.

He didn't sign it.

All the air left her lungs in a wobbly cry. He thought their letters were a manipulation tactic on her part. Those prejudices and preconceived notions he held would be the end of them.

They'd expected a rejection while hoping for a blessing. Leave it to Father to take her by surprise and complicate matters further.

Cut off. Never allowed to go home. Disowned if she chose Ethan.

Or everything she'd wanted, handed to her.

The tears fell in earnest now while birds sang outside the window.

They'd repair the damage to the brewery, since it primarily consisted of stone. But the granary? Ancient timbers and wattle and daub had stood for over a century yet were no match for flames.

Ethan swore fluently until Connor stopped nodding along and just stared.

"Are ye done, Ethan?"

"Whoever did this stole food off the tables of my people." Ethan spit on the glowing embers of what used to be this year's grain harvest. "Find the bastard responsible. I'll have his guts for garters."

"I have men listening in the village, plus two footmen goin' door tae door askin' questions. Someone somewhere saw something. Macdonell is out for blood."

"Milord, message from London." A servant reined in his horse before handing over a folded piece of paper.

Glancing at the handwriting, Ethan smiled. Lottie. Memories of how she'd looked when he'd left her bed—soft and pink and well loved in the early morning light—were his bright spots in an otherwise wretched day. Or days, rather. Almost forty-eight hours ago, he'd kissed her goodbye, then rushed from London. Of course, the letter could be news about the earl's response. In which case, he had other pressing matters to deal with. If the earl said yes, they would celebrate. If he said no, another hour or two of ignorance wouldn't make a difference in the long run. His people needed him right now, and the earl would have to wait. Ethan tucked the letter in his pocket before nodding his thanks to the servant.

Acrid smoke lingered against the sun, while the blackened beam remnants of the granary stood as charred testaments of stubborn construction. He would update her via post this evening. She needed to know about this. While it could be the work of an unknown enemy, more likely than not, they'd eventually uncover Montague's hand behind this attack on his livelihood.

As he surveyed the damage with tired eyes, the anger that had been his constant companion since he'd come home battled to escape. How dare that worthless bastard set foot on his land? Hurt his people, destroy the fruits of their labors, endanger their livestock's food supply for the winter? Montague would pay. There wasn't a consequence severe enough to cover the damage done here. The niggling worry in the back of his mind asked how much more he could afford to economize in order to rebuild. He'd find a way. They'd make it and come out stronger on the other side.

"My worry is for whatever's next, aye?" Connor muttered.

It was a valid point. The day before yesterday, workmen discovered the destruction at the brewery site. Everything flammable had burned. Stone walls had been smashed and equipment destroyed. What should have been a boon for the village economy lay in ruins. That was when Connor had written, and Ethan had set off for home. They'd worked all day to set to rights what they could at the worksite. When the band of men arrived from Lady Agatha's household, he'd been grateful for the help. They needed every willing hand they could get. Yesterday, instead of returning to London, he'd canvassed the village, searching for answers.

Last night, as he'd settled in for the night, planning to write Lottie, the alarm had gone up. Another fire. In the summer it would mean devastation to fields. But on the cusp of November, it meant an estate could be beggared by the loss of the harvest, leaving tenants to struggle and possibly starve as the cold set in. They wouldn't be in such dire straits as that, but it would mean sacrifices and possibly pushing the brewery project back.

Montague would not win today.

"If the goal is tae exhaust us tae death, they might win yet. I'm weary tae the bone. How are you holding up?" He glanced down at Connor's wooden leg.

Connor waved away his concern. "Tae hit us again will be their undoing. They'd better pray we never catch 'em."

It was just like Connor to not speak of his leg, but with the muscles in Ethan's feet and thighs screaming, he could only imagine how much pain Connor endured to work alongside him. "I mean it. If you need a break, take one. I'll not have you overdoing it. We both know a raw stump is the last thing you need."

"I'm no' a child, milord." Connor's irritation cut through the fatigue to slap at Ethan's ever-present guilt. "I've taken care of this estate for several years an' done it with only one leg. How about ye let me decide what my own body needs, aye?"

"Yes, of course. I'm merely looking out for you."

"Stop coddling. Yer guilt is as plain as yer face, and I'll not have it. I could leave you in the dust an' work anywhere else if I wanted." Connor glared.

"God, how could I not feel guilty?" A wind stirred between them, hot with smoke and smoldering flames.

Connor rolled his shoulders and huffed. "Because 'tis a good life we have here, aye? We work hard, Woodrest rewards us in kind. This is better than the army would have ever been. An' the only one who'd baby me worse than you is me mother. I can' go back home. But you're clan. You are my family. An' as family, I'll level yer bloody lordly arse intae the dirt if ye mention my leg again. Let. It. Go."

The words repeated in his mind. *Better than the army would have ever been.* "Do you mean that? The life here is better than the one you'd planned before the accident?"

"Of course 'tis. Don' be daft." Connor dismissed the conversation to survey the damage once more, shaking his head. "Will take a lot of work tae clean up this mess."

The guilt he'd carried like a touchstone shifted, lightening. Ethan wanted to hug Connor, to thank him for forgiving the loss of a limb—although that level of acceptance defied understanding. From his body language, Connor wouldn't welcome a hug—even a manly one. Instead, Ethan turned to face the same direction. "Aye. Will take time and effort. Good thing I have help." He chanced one heavy palm against Connor's shoulder and squeezed.

Connor returned the gesture. "Ye need a nap, but we both know ye won' take one. Let's check in with the men. Maybe they 'ave news."

"Wait. What's that?" Ethan pointed.

Several dozen yards away from what remained of the brewery, a crowd had formed. As they approached, the tension in the air reminded Ethan of a boxing match. Angry cries of men and the occasional pained sound came from whoever lay within the makeshift ring. Connor shot him a worried look as they picked up the pace.

In the center of the circle lay a man making sounds like a wounded animal as he curled into a ball to protect himself from thrown stones and kicks.

"What's the meaning of this?" Ethan pushed through the crowd.

One of his tenants grabbed the beaten man from the ground to hold him aloft like a fresh kill. "We found him. If our children and livestock starve, it's on his head!" The man threw the arsonist at Ethan's feet. "Tell him what you told us."

When the bloodied man raised his face, Ethan's anger cooled as if splashed with icy water. Jutting cheekbones, yellowed skin, and hollow eyes wet with tears were not what he'd expected of the one responsible for all this destruction. A stump of a leg, amputated below the knee, told its own tale. "Is this true? You set the fires? Ransacked the worksite?"

A nod.

"Why? Are we enemies?"

"A gent sent me in a coach. Paid me in coin."

"Where's the money now?" Connor asked, cocking his head. Ethan knew that look. Connor was assessing the intruder and puzzling through the information. It reminded him of Lottie. No doubt she'd handle the situation in a similar way.

"I gave it to me wife for food. The kids never had full bellies till now. I ain't done nofink like this 'efore, I swear." There was no doubt the tears were real, although the thin stranger firmed his chin against them.

"The man. Describe him," Connor demanded.

"Clean. Fair hair. Made all them ladies coo like doves when 'e walked by."

Ethan nodded to Connor. That described Montague all right. Cal had been following him from gaming hell to brothel and back again, then visiting the men who had his vowels the next day. As of a few days ago, he and Cal were Montague's largest dun. Encouraging Montague's father to call him home to rusticate was supposed to get him out of Town and bring an end to the gossip columns. It would appear Montague had hidden depths of villainy. "Where are you from?"

"Seven Dials. Gent waltzed in like 'e was the bloody king 'imself."

Ethan squatted in front of the man and sniffed. He reeked, but not of alcohol. As Ethan stood, he towered over the man in the dirt, his shadow covering the arsonist, who shivered in the rags he wore. No doubt, those rags were all he had. And here Ethan had planned to throw away his soot-covered clothes. His abundance stood in stark relief against the man's condition.

Desperate men did desperate things. Ethan rubbed a palm over tired eyes. Heavens, he should have slept days ago. He shared a look with Connor in silent agreement. "What's your name?"

"Billings. John Billings." The man eyed Connor's peg leg, then his own. The look held such a weight to it, Ethan felt it in his chest. A plan came to him, fully formed, and the rightness of it fell into place with an almost audible click. Connor wasn't the only man needing a home and work despite a missing limb.

"Mr. Billings, I will give you a choice. You were hired tae perform a dastardly task, and you did it, which tells me you're good at following orders. I can walk away now, let you find your way back tae London and your family, as the man who hired you intended. But that assumes the other men let you get that far."

The man's eyes darted, taking in the angry faces around him.

Connor spoke up. "Or I take ye in a coach tae get yer woman an' bairns. Then ye return tae rebuild what ye destroyed."

John Billings froze, staring at Connor and Ethan. "Rebuild?"

"Do ye have any experience building things, or do ye jus' prefer tae set them on fire?" Connor cocked his head in challenge. The circle of men shuffled closer.

"I built some in the army."

Ethan offered the man a hand and waited until John grasped his palm before pulling him to his feet. He weighed next to nothing. Without releasing the hand, Ethan drew him close, until the man had to crane his head up to meet his eyes. "Your choice, Mr. Billings. Go back tae London and rot, or stay and make recompense."

The tears on John's face left rivers of mud in their wake. "Yer givin' me a job? But I hurt yer master. Burned the granary. The lord will never let me stay."

"Eh, the viscount does what I tell 'im," Connor said, breaking the tension when several of the group chuckled.

Ethan grasped John's hand. "You claim you've never done this before. Prove it. *This* is the hard path. I'm lord and master of these lands, and you've hurt my people, John Billings. I'm no' like tae forget it soon. The men hate you. None of us trust you. You've an uphill battle ahead. I expect you tae work an honest day's labor for an honest day's wage. But hear me now—if you betray me, I'll beat you myself, throw you tae the wolves, an' never regret it."

"Me wife an' kids? They'll have a roof? Food?"

"Aye. As long as you work without another issue like this, you have my word."

John collapsed his beaten head against their clasped hands and, after a shuddery sigh, wept with such force his shoulders shook.

An hour later John Billings and two footmen were London bound. The local men begrudgingly agreed to not kill the man when he returned. Their acceptance came easier after Ethan assured them no one would starve or suffer from the sabotage. Purchasing grain from neighboring estates would take profits from the year, but in the end they'd all live to eat another day. Rebuilding might have to wait until after the next harvest, but they'd figure it out.

Back in his room, the water in the pitcher hit Ethan's flame-toasted skin with all the gentleness of shards of ice, then trickled down his chest, rinsing away the soap. Drying with a linen, he searched for a clean shirt. The smoke-filled clothes from the night lay draped over a wooden chair, far away from any other fabrics they might destroy. It was when he donned a new waistcoat that he remembered the letter in his pocket.

> *Forgive me. Common decency demands I say these things face-to-face instead of writing. I suppose we shall add cowardice to my sins, listed below inconsistency.*
>
> *I cannot marry you. No, that is not entirely true.*
>
> *I will not marry you.*
>
> *My father has refused the match and I find myself unwilling to challenge him in this. Thank you for offering the protection of an engagement when I needed it. As per our original agreement, I am ending our arrangement now that your services are no longer required. I tire of London and shall soon be free of Montague's vile rumors.*

Consider your moral debt paid, since we both know that is how all this began. Your slate is clean, Ethan.

I wish you the best.

The edge of the bed caught him because his knees were useless. Like a punch to the gut, Lottie's words turned his vision to a watery haze.

The earl didn't approve of the match. He'd probably rejected Ethan without a second thought. Or maybe this was just the natural order of things correcting itself. A shepherd didn't marry a lady. A young man who hurt a woman from a place of damaged ego didn't eventually win the girl. It wasn't the way life worked.

His head weighed heavy in his hands, and Ethan's breathing echoed as a harsh gurgle in the room. So this was how heartbreak felt. Aptly named when the woman you loved walked away, breaking and stealing pieces of you as she went. No wonder it hurt so damn bad. Parts of him were gone forever, given away with a kiss to the lovely Lady Lottie, who lost control only when she was in his arms.

Ethan crumpled the letter in his fist, threw it to the floor, then stared at it. In a fit of pique, he stomped on the paper.

What a day. Hell, what a week. The highest of highs, the lowest of lows, and a lovely bit of arson in between. At least Montague no longer had John Billings in his pocket. John, who hadn't even realized he'd been speaking with the master here, because the lord of the manor looked like a common laborer.

The cream stationery's clean purity showed a sacrilegious blemish of a sooty boot print where it lay on the carpet. Ethan stared at it until the mark became more than a dirty blemish.

The sooty print proved he worked and fought and toiled alongside his people. But he did all those things because he *was* the master here. And not only here. No matter where he laid his head or tracked his filthy boots, Ethan would remain Viscount Amesbury.

All the Cousin Jeromes and Lord Bartlesbys in the world couldn't change that fact. It didn't matter that society hadn't fully embraced him, or even that there were merchants who looked down their noses at his rough ways. Ethan was a viscount, and damn anyone who'd try to shame him for the bit of wicked luck that had landed him in this position.

And a viscount would not retreat meekly from the presence of a damned managing lady like a shepherd boy would.

He loved her. He'd shown her over and over in that big bed after announcing to the *ton* that he was marrying her. "If she wants tae end things, she can do so tae my face. Connor! Whoever can hear me—saddle Ezra." Slamming the bedroom door behind him, Ethan stopped in his tracks, then returned to the room. With black-stained fingers, he plucked the crumpled paper from the floor and smoothed the letter back into a flat, smudged sheet. Although his hands shook, he carefully folded Lottie's last letter to him and tucked it away in his pocket. The ride to London would be brutal on his aching body, but the day had only begun.

Chapter Twenty-Four

"Please tell me it's poisoned. Put me out of my misery," Lottie croaked.

"Don't tempt me. You've wallowed half the day away already. That's enough, thank you very much." Darling held the teacup, waiting.

"Blast! Madame Bouvier has probably already begun work." Lottie shot up in bed, shoving her mass of hair out of her eyes. "I need to cancel the order for the wedding dress." She rested her head in her hands, wishing the day would end. Father's letter was written in permanent ink in her brain, she'd read it so many times. Even after sleeping on it, she'd been unable to find a solution.

So she'd ended it.

It had taken five tries to get the letter to Ethan right. The first version was weepy, laying out the whole process, her father's ultimatum, and her struggle with the decision. Bit by bit she culled the emotion from it until the final draft was crisp and businesslike. With this decision, she was taking her emotions back from his tender care, and it felt wrong to pour her pain into his lap to grapple with alongside his own. The giving of her trust hadn't been done lightly, so it came as no surprise that the taking back of it was just as deliberate.

A messenger carried the letter to Woodrest this morning while she returned to her room and huddled under the covers like a child hiding from ghosts. The pillow Ethan had used still had traces of his scent, and she'd cuddled it close, wetting the down fluff with her tears.

Darling sank onto the edge of the bed. "You're sure this is the right choice? We could send a message back to your father. Or let the servants take care of him—the earl deserves something for giving you such an ultimatum. A maid could put cat hair in his smalls. I have friends at Stanwick, you know. The man needs a lesson."

Despite herself, Lottie let loose a watery laugh. "Nothing so Machiavellian is needed. Although cat hair in his smalls is rather brilliant. I'm in awe and slightly scared for anyone who crosses you."

"There's more than one way to hit 'em in their stones, milady. The earl has it coming for sending that letter."

Lottie picked at a nail before catching herself. "It is a lousy choice to have to make, but it seems that at heart I am nothing but a jilt. An impure one, at that. A jade. As they'd say, 'I almost tied a knot with my tongue that I couldn't untie with my teeth.'"

"What in the name of all that's holy are you nattering on about? Who says that?"

"*Dictionary of the Vulgar Tongue*. Ethan gave it to me. I'm only in the *K*s thus far."

"Ah. Well, you'd best get up. Tell me what's next.

You always have a plan. Tell me all about it." Darling flung the coverlet back. "What you need is some fresh air. Wear the green wool today. Maybe we can take a walk. That'll put roses back in your cheeks." Darling held out the gown.

"As always, you are right. Thank you."

Today might have been awful, but she had a chance to reclaim her future—the original future she'd wanted before she got caught up in Ethan. Planning her return to Westmorland would keep her mind off how her letter would affect him. It was a cold comfort, but perhaps she was the one taking the brunt of the hurt. After all, if he loved her, he'd have told her. So maybe Ethan's anger or hurt would be short-lived.

Eventually, Ethan would return to his brewery and his people. And she would find her people elsewhere, while cherishing the one night she'd spent in his arms.

There was a chill in the air to remind everyone that winter approached. Leaves covered the ground in a colorful carpet created by Mother Nature at the expense of the naked tree branches reaching toward the heavens with bare bark fingers.

Darling raised her face to the morning sun. "'Tis easy to be grateful for the weather on a day like today. Soon enough, it will just be endless drab rain."

"Don't forget the wind that bites as if it has teeth. Best we enjoy the sun while we have it." Lottie left the path to wander through the grass toward a copse of trees. After several minutes of silence, she stopped, shaking her head.

Darling scanned the area. "What is it?"

"This is the route we often took on horseback. I suppose I'm following it out of habit." Tears threatened. Utterly ridiculous feelings. She'd had a choice, and she'd made it. Granted, it hadn't been a nice choice. Or an enjoyable choice. But given the circumstances, it was the wisest course of action. The logical, safe option. Ethan would need to rebuild whatever damage had been done, and for that he would need money. Money she wouldn't have if she married him. In lieu of money, he'd need connections. She couldn't even offer that. Father would disown her, which would leave her with no social influence of her own. Her peers laughed at her. Without a dowry, Lottie was a liability.

With this decision, she freed Ethan to focus on his responsibilities, even if that meant finding an heiress to marry. The thought brought a wave of bitter tears, so she didn't allow it to linger. She was doing the right thing for him.

Besides, there was no undoing that letter at this point. Even if her father came around, she'd broken something with Ethan that couldn't be repaired. To go from sleeping in his arms to ending things…there was no coming back from that.

"You'll miss him," Darling said.

Lottie blinked to clear her eyes, then turned back. "Everywhere I look, I see memories of him, and that will drive me mad eventually. We need to go home. I'll tell Agatha when we return to the house. If we are out of London by the end of the week, that should suffice. Then I can take all the walks I wish, but do it in breeches, on my own estate. The one with the view of the sea. It will be lovely, you'll see." She wasn't sure whom she was trying to convince—herself or Darling.

"I'll go where you do, as long as we bring Patrick." Darling tried to keep up with the rapid pace Lottie set as she scurried away from memories in the park.

"Without a doubt, if Patrick wishes to come, he's welcome. I'll need a coachman. Otherwise it would just be the two of us rattling around the property until we hire more staff. I don't know, though. All that peace and quiet? There are worse futures." Newgate Prison, for example. Or marriage to James Montague.

They were almost back to Berkeley Square. The steady clip-clop of hooves broke through Lottie's thoughts. "Let's move farther to the side. This carriage has been behind us for the last block. I fear we've been holding up traffic."

"Most drivers would have passed and splashed muck onto our skirts," Darling said.

"Ah, the rare considerate coachman. Here I believed your beau to be the only one of those in England." The flush that crept over Darling's face made Lottie grin. It felt good to smile amidst such hard days.

The coach drew alongside them, then stopped as the door swung open. Lottie barely registered surprise before a cudgel struck Darling's head, and her beloved maid fell to the ground at her feet. The horrifying sight froze her as she tried to come to grips with the brutal violence of it.

A strong arm grabbed her from behind and pressed a foul-smelling rag over her face.

Then she knew no more.

This was, without a doubt, the stupidest thing he'd ever done. When a woman gave you marching orders, you marched. It may have been a while since he'd enjoyed a woman in his life, but this one prickly lass was different.

She'd managed to get under his skin and stay there. And damn it, he'd taken her to bed. Did that mean nothing? Ethan shrugged his caped coat closer around himself, wishing he'd paused long enough to dress properly. Begging a woman to explain herself might have a better success rate if he wore a cravat. Instead, he'd galloped away from Woodrest with only the bare essentials. If Lottie's decision to comply with the earl's refusal stemmed from doubts of his suitability, this wouldn't help his case.

Late afternoon sun warmed his uncovered head, and the final colors of autumn crunched beneath filthy boots as Ethan thundered up the steps of Lady Agatha's stately Berkeley Square residence. Obnoxious birds chirped their greeting from a tree beside the steps, inciting his glare. Today was not the time for timid brass knockers. In his current mood, he'd be tempted to rip the decorative bit of metal off its hinges, so pounding a fist on the massive door felt bloody brilliant.

Where was the butler? What was his name? For the life of him, he couldn't recall the name of Lady Agatha's butler here in Berkeley Square. Dawson had stayed on with the rental house to serve the next tenant. Every now and then Ethan caught a glimpse of him going about his duties next door to Cal.

He pounded again, then tapped the knocker for good measure. Where was everyone? The footmen and maids? He raised a hand for a third time before someone finally answered the summons.

"Excellent, milord. Thank you for arriving so quickly. Lady Agatha is beside herself," the butler said.

Wait, what? "You sent for me? Has something happened tae Lottie?"

"Did the messenger not find you?" the servant asked.

"Lottie sent a letter tae Woodrest today. Are you telling me she's not here?"

"No, milord. That's the problem. Lady Charlotte is gone. Her maid arrived home by herself not long ago. It seems they were attacked in the street."

Already striding down the hall, Ethan called over his shoulder, "Lady Agatha is in her usual place, I assume? Is Darling with her?"

Trotting to keep up, the butler wheezed, "Yes, milord. Lord Carlyle only arrived a moment ago. We are organizing the travel now."

The scene in the drawing room didn't calm the worst-case scenarios whirling in his mind. Darling perched on a sofa, pressing a cold compress to her head, while Lady Agatha marched around the room, thumping a cadence with her cane, looking as battle ready as a geriatric woman could. Which, surprisingly enough, would intimidate the hell out of anyone.

Cal stood, his expression pained. "He took her, Ethan. Montague has Lottie."

This was Montague's rebuttal to their letter to Danby. Steal the fiancée of his largest dun. Bonus to Montague that she was an heiress. Ethan knelt before Darling. "May I?" The maid shifted the compress aside to show the point of impact, which appeared to have already stopped bleeding. "Did you lose consciousness?"

"Yes. I'm not sure how long I lay in the street. When I came to, the coach was long gone."

Ethan hung his head, grappling with his emotions. Lottie had been taken in full daylight. Heaven only knew how long Darling had lain in the dirt on the side of the street. Even in this posh area of London, a woman had been accosted and left for dead long enough that her wound stopped bleeding on its own. London could be a bitterly cruel place for most of its inhabitants and was home to more than one character with Montague's depravity.

He shied away from the thought before it fully formed. Imagining Lottie at the mercy of that bastard wouldn't help. There would be no coming back from the terror and panic. Better to focus on Darling. "I'm so sorry you were hurt, Mrs. Darling. Can you tell me anything that would help us find Lottie?"

Cal piped up, "We've determined she was one block away when attacked. The three of us were establishing a timeline when you came in. They have about an hour's lead on us."

Ethan turned to Cal. "How are you already here?"

"They sent a messenger to my house, not realizing you were at Woodrest. I forwarded the message to Kent but couldn't very well sit about with your girl missing. So here I am."

That made sense. Ethan asked Darling, "Do you remember anything else? Did you see anything? Was Montague driving, or did he have a coachman? Anything about the coach? Every detail is important."

Darling closed her eyes, appearing to sift through her memories. "He had a driver. Red carriage, flashy yellow trim. Big black wheels with yellow spokes."

"A traveling rig, then, not a racing curricle?" Cal clarified.

"Yes. This was made for longer distances," Darling said.

"Perfect. Most of the others on the road are yellow. This should stand out tae hostlers." Ethan turned to Agatha. "Have you already sent for your traveling carriage?"

"Done. It should be ready for us in a quarter hour." Lady Agatha turned to Darling. "Are you fit enough for travel?"

Darling winced when she shifted the hand with the compress but appeared determined. "Just try to stop me. I owe that man a few whacks when we catch up with them."

Lady Agatha nodded. "Brilliant. I shall lend my cane to the cause should you desire a weapon."

Calvin said, "Montague probably borrowed the carriage, which means borrowed horses. We might overtake them on the road."

"Do you know where he's taken her, then?" Darling asked.

"Gretna Green, of course. It is the only logical outcome if he has gone through the trouble to kidnap her," Lady Agatha said.

Ethan exchanged a look with Calvin. There were other possibilities. Less honorable possibilities that centered on revenge and ruination instead of marriage. The thought made a cold sweat break out on his forehead. If that rat touched one hair on Lottie's head without her permission…Ethan's clenched hands shook with a force great enough to unravel him. Closing his eyes, he forced calming logic into his head. Out with the horrific scenarios and creative punishments. In with the planning, decisions, and immediate rescue of his Lottie.

Lady Agatha was right about one thing. If they were to give chase, they must choose a direction in which to search. Might as well go north and hope for the best.

Chapter Twenty-Five

There were horses running over her head. It was the only logical explanation for the pounding rhythm of her pulse in her skull. Sunshine warmed her face, and light filtered through her eyelids, burning like pokers. The fuzzy film coating her mouth suggested that a small creature had died there—no doubt her breath could stun a dragon at thirty paces. But oh, her head. If only it were possible to take it off her shoulders and store it in a cupboard somewhere until the pain abated.

Alas, aching head and body remained firmly connected. The rumble of carriage wheels against stone and dirt beneath her thrummed in a steady vibration, punctuated by the occasional excruciating jolt, triggering nausea with every movement.

Keeping her eyes closed, Lottie attempted to piece together the bits of information working through her pained head. Although obviously in a carriage, she didn't remember getting into a carriage. When did she order one?

Where was Darling?

Why, oh why, did her head feel so horrific? Had she succumbed to one of her megrims?

Inhaling turned out to be a regrettable decision. This carriage reeked. Her throat closed against the roll of her stomach at the lingering taint of alcohol-based vomit and cloying perfume that clung to the squabs. And she sprawled on that seat.

That was enough inducement to attempt sitting, holding her head as if to keep her brain in her skull, and the whole throbbing mess attached to her neck. A groan escaped, but even that amount of noise triggered a whimper.

"Sleeping Beauty awakes." Montague lounged casually on the opposite seat, as if he hadn't a care in the world. She winced, dearly wishing to smack that smirk off his face. When she could move without pain, of course. Why was she with Montague? More pertinent still, why was she with Montague *alone*?

"What happened?" The raspy voice didn't sound like her. "Where are we, and why the hell are you here?"

"Such language, wife," he chastised.

"Wife?" Please no. The tempo of the pulse pounding through her head picked up. At the engagement ball, she'd promised Ethan that she would take a burly footman wherever she went. Of all the times for her to remember.

Montague shrugged. "Well, as near as. You have several days before we reach Scotland to get used to the idea."

Kidnapped. And where was Darling? God, why couldn't she remember? Alarm coursed through her, threatening to stampede over logical thought. Tamping down the fear, she struggled for control.

No time to panic. Not when escape must be the priority. Craning her neck to see out the window, she scrambled for clues. They were out of the city—how long had she been unconscious? A sign flickered past the window. They were on the Great North Road, and he'd just mentioned Scotland.

"Scotland? Oh dear God. Gretna Green?" Lottie palmed her belly to settle the roiling nausea.

"No, Lamberton. Scotland is Scotland, after all—we needn't romanticize this. Everyone else will do that for us. As it stands, you've been traveling for several hours in a closed carriage with a suitor."

"Former suitor." She gritted her teeth.

"I have your father's permission to wed you, and I made sure everyone knows it. In society's eyes, we are as good as married. Don't you see? I won." Montague laughed as he pulled the shade closed, blocking her view. "I apologize for the headache. If you'd behaved yourself and seen sense, I wouldn't have resorted to these measures."

"How is it *my* fault you kidnapped me?" Her voice rose with each word until they both winced.

The slap came as a surprise. Teeth rattled against each other as her head swung to the side. For a moment, the burn of her cheek overshadowed every other discomfort.

Montague brushed his hand on his breeches, wiping off traces of the offensive contact. "I am not marrying a fishwife. You will never again speak to me in that tone. Act like a lady, and I will treat you as such."

He'd finally gone insane. And not just the "Aunt Dottie is a bit touched in the head" kind of insane. No,

Montague needed a room at Bedlam. That was all there was to it. Hot tears threatened to spill through her lashes, but she dashed them away before they fell.

With each moment that passed, the memories returned—full of disturbing details. The sound the cudgel had made when it hit Darling's head now echoed in hers. They'd left her on the ground. At that thought, she was almost sick. "What did you do to my maid?"

"What needed to be done. I'll hire another. She's no longer important. What *is* important, my dear, is establishing the rules for our journey. We have many stops ahead of us before the Scottish border, and I won't have you making a scene."

Lottie sneered. "I am *not* your wife or your dear or anything else except captive to a madman."

"I thought you'd say that. You're so very predictable. That's why you'll be tied in the carriage until we stop for the night. I plan to drive as far as possible before we stop, so prepare yourself for long days. But what's a little discomfort when the prize at the end of the journey is so sweet?" Montague winked as if this were all a great game. He openly ogled her bosom, although the green wool gown covered everything.

By reflex, Lottie's hands shielded her chest. "You mean to jail me in the carriage with no breaks until we reach Scotland?"

"I have a hamper of food to fill at the inns. I'm not a monster. We'll share a room when we stop for the night."

There was no way she'd touch the topic of sleeping arrangements right now. Lottie rolled her eyes. "There are other necessities besides eating."

"I thought of that too," Montague said, offering a

narrow porcelain tureen with a handle. A bourdaloue. "For milady's needs." He offered it grandly, as if presenting the crown jewels. Lottie wrinkled her nose, so he shrugged and placed the portable chamber pot on the floor between them.

Rubbing her aching cheek, Lottie tried to plan. The circumstances grew more dire with every mile. The only opportunity to escape might be when they stopped, so she must focus her plotting on those breaks in travel. Otherwise, days of captivity loomed ahead.

Who knew if Darling lived or had been able to get help? Had Agatha thought it odd they weren't home yet? Perhaps her aunt would send for Ethan—her heart broke a little. Ethan, whom she'd jilted.

"Since I don't doubt you will attempt an escape when we stop at night, I'll tell you now not to bother. Our tale of woe is sure to entertain every innkeeper who will listen. You see, darling wife, we are on our way to a nunnery in the North, where the sisters will care for you during your frequent bouts of hysterics and heartbreaking insanity. I love you too much to admit you to Bedlam, you see. We are quite tragic."

"The Romeo and Juliet of our time," she sneered.

"Without the pesky dagger and poison, naturally."

Oh, her kingdom for a pesky dagger or dram of poison. If only she'd been born a man. She could challenge him, shoot him at dawn, and be done with it. Few men suffered through kidnapping and forced elopements to a neighboring country.

Montague laughed at her silence. The unpleasant sound grated on her nerves, but Lottie held her tongue. They appeared to be making good time if the swaying of the carriage was a clue. Fast horses were good for only so many miles before they would need to be changed out for a fresh team. May the next pair be swayback nags.

No obvious solution or escape plan presented itself, but perhaps if Lottie could get him to revert to his habit of talking about himself ad nauseam in the theme of villainous monologuing, he might let slip some bit of helpful information.

"How do you think you'll get away with this?"

Montague sneered. "I've already gotten away with it. You know, the carriage was so quiet before you woke up. If I choose, I can knock you out for this entire journey. Now sit there and behave like the lady you claim to be."

"Apologies. I must have missed my governess covering proper etiquette for being kidnapped and drugged on the Great North Road. Perhaps you *should* knock me out if what you wish is a silent, biddable so-called wife."

"It would make the consummation easier. A bit boring, though. I think I might enjoy it if you fought a little." His grin reminded her of a predator showing its teeth.

Intuition told her he spoke the truth. A man who would kidnap and slap a woman wouldn't draw the line at rape. A shiver shot through her system that had nothing to do with the chill in the air. If she were unconscious, she'd be without means of defending herself. Somehow, she must hold him at bay while not making him so angry he'd knock her unconscious again.

"Consummation will have to wait." Lottie forced a dismissive tone.

"Do you think I'm going to wait until we reach Scotland?" Even his laugh sounded cruel. "How am I to keep busy for the next few nights, except to roger what is rightfully mine?"

Blinking innocently, Lottie ignored the panic clawing

at her. "I thought men were put off by a woman's menses. I'm afraid you've made far more work for yourself by kidnapping me during this week of the month." Rumor had it he was an awful gambler. Let's hope he didn't know a bluff when he heard one.

Montague's laughter stuttered to a halt, and he raised his eyebrows. "Excuse me?"

"My courses began this morning. I've always been subjected to excessively heavy monthly cycles. Our first concern is procuring rags. Unless you want to see my gown and these lovely cushions stained with blood, you will have to ask for rags from the posting houses as we pass them. I go through rags quite quickly during these first few days, you see."

"How am I supposed to obtain rags for...that...at a posting house?" Montague's face would have been comical if she'd been capable of laughter at the moment.

"You'll have to ask around. My maid normally takes care of this for me. As I have no maid, because—oh yes—you knocked her out and left her in the gutter to die." Lottie did not try to hide her bitterness. Appearing to comply this soon would only make him suspicious, and her face hurt from the last point he'd made at her expense. "You will have to figure it out. Since you've already decreed that I stay in the carriage, you'll need to fetch them."

Montague looked uncomfortable, but Lottie kept her expression steady, maintaining eye contact. He must not suspect she was lying. "Ensure they are clean, please. I do not need to be dealing with someone else's stains." Montague looked a little green, much to her satisfaction. If at all possible, giving him a disgust of her could only work to her advantage. Thankfully, few men claimed a working knowledge of women's menstrual cycles, and even fewer were prepared to deal with the reality of them.

The carriage slowed at a posting house to change horses. They couldn't be that far from London. If she ran now, perhaps—

"Not so fast, little wife." Montague reached into the bag at his feet and pulled out a handkerchief, a rope, and a length of fabric. In the split second while Lottie calculated the chance of a successful escape, Montague lunged, twisting her and pressing her face against the seat.

He was not a large man, and she was by no means a dainty, delicate female, yet he pinned her easily, as though she were a recalcitrant child in need of a spanking. Kicking blindly but connecting with only air, she struggled to throw him off. Lottie's sound of outrage died against the revolting velvet cushion.

Above her, he muttered about feisty women, chuckling as he bound her wrists and ankles. Montague shoved a handkerchief into her mouth, securing it in place with another wrapped around her head, leaving her twisted and vulnerable. She lay trussed like a hog ready for the spit and fire.

The gag prevented screams and absorbed every last bit of moisture in her mouth. Lottie tried not to whimper. All the power she'd claimed a moment before with cheeky demands for rags leaked out her eyes as tears. Laughter tickled her ear, making her skin crawl.

Montague kissed one cheek and winked as if this were all a game. With a light swat on her bottom, he said, "I won't be gone long. Wait here. Be a good girl. If you don't make a fuss, I might even untie you when I return."

She glared ineffectual daggers and tried to roll away to dislodge his hand.

Montague whistled as he walked away. Whistled, for the love of all that was holy. Tears fell, only to be caught by the gag. Lottie rested her forehead on the cushion, refusing to think of the travesties committed on this seat before her arrival, and tried to batten down her mind against the wave of defeat cresting over her.

The rope chafed her wrists, leaving no wiggle room for comfort. This position strained her shoulders, and one calf cramped in protest.

To think, she'd briefly considered marriage to this monster. Like those venomous insects she'd read about in a huge book in her father's library, Montague enticed his prey with beauty. Most animals realized flashy colors and gorgeous skin meant danger. Obviously, there were things human women could learn from the natural world.

Outside the carriage, low murmurs of conversation kept her prison from feeling empty. Surely people would come for her, eventually. There had to be an end in sight. Her very sanity might rely on the notion of imminent escape or rescue. The trick would be somehow slowing Montague's progress enough for rescuers to catch them. Considering her current position, that seemed an impossible goal.

One thing remained certain—she couldn't manage an escape if she was tied up. Which meant building trust or making Montague believe she would go along quietly.

Montague returned a few moments later. With a lowered gaze and blazing cheeks, he shoved a small bag toward her, letting it fall on the floor by her seat.

"Your rags," he said, but made no move to release her bindings.

Lottie rested her cheek against the seat and closed her eyes. How was she going to get out of this?

Chapter Twenty-Six

Ethan had never pushed Ezra so hard. Lady Agatha's carriage was somewhere on the road behind them. Calvin kept pace beside him, although they didn't exchange much in the way of conversation. Lady Agatha's outriders surrounded them, breaking off at inns and posting houses along the way to ask after the red carriage. They were assuming Scotland was the destination, but he couldn't help thinking there was an awful lot of England outside London.

Gretna Green made sense. Montague had no property of his own. His father's hunting box lay somewhere to the north. Ethan could not recall where. Maybe Calvin knew.

If Montague's purpose was to get his hands on her fortune, a hasty marriage would be the most expedient way. Dragging her to a hunting box would not serve any long-term goals.

If he thought ruining Lottie would deter Ethan, then Montague didn't know his foe. Ethan would not leave Lottie to that brute. It did not matter what happened; he would happily marry her—assuming he could convince the woman in question. Damned managing female.

No matter how he inspected the situation, it seemed his and Calvin's financial machinations had driven Montague to this. Panic-induced kidnapping hadn't been considered as a probable outcome while hatching their plan. Applying financial pressure to Montague and convincing his father to pull him from Town should never have hurt Lottie. The whole point had been to protect her.

Beside him, Cal motioned to a posting house. Ethan waved him on, indicating he would continue on to the next one. Several days without rest were taking their toll, and his vision began to blur around the edges. No doubt as soon as he stopped, he'd collapse from exhaustion. The harried flight to London seemed to have happened a hundred years ago.

Another posting house loomed ahead. Tossing the reins to a nearby groom, Ethan slid off Ezra's back and brushed a soothing hand over the mount's heaving chest. "I need a new horse and information. Red carriage, yellow trim, black wheels. Have you seen it?"

"Aye, exchanged a team a while back," the hostler said.

"Which direction did they go? Did you see the passengers?"

The man stared, then spit on the ground. "How much is it worth to ya?"

Digging a coin from his pocket, Ethan slapped it into the man's hand, not caring about the denomination. "Now talk. Tell me everything."

Five minutes later he tore off down the road to catch up

with Calvin. Cold wind whipped at his face. The hostler claimed to know nothing about a female passenger, but his description of Montague had been accurate, right down to his obnoxious habit of mentioning the Earl of Danby every ten seconds. Discreet, Montague was not.

The information wasn't much to go on, but at least they were going in the right direction. Over the next rise the yellow of Agatha's livery stood out against the dull colors of the road. If the outriders were there, Calvin might be too. Ethan pushed the horse harder, murmuring words of encouragement.

He prayed that Lottie's remarkable brain was even now finding a way to stall her travel north. His strong, bullheaded love had a mind of her own and wouldn't appreciate this situation. Hell, Montague might be in pieces by the time they arrived. The thought gave him his first smile in hours.

Calvin nodded a hello when Ethan caught up to the group, and they set off. "You've looked better, my friend."

"I found a man who saw Montague, but he didn' see Lottie. They have a decent lead on us and are making good time."

"So they're on their way to Gretna," Calvin called over the wind.

"Aye. What if we're wrong, though? Doesn' his father have a hunting retreat up north? He may have taken her there." Montague wasn't the most patient of fellows, as this situation showed.

"There was mention of a hunting box one night at the gaming hells. Let me think on it," Cal said. Several minutes passed with only the thunderous hoofbeats between them before he called out, "Peterborough—the hunting box is near Peterborough."

"We'll check there first. Lady Agatha should be close behind us."

Peterborough. Please let them catch up to Montague that quickly. Exhaustion made Ethan sway in the saddle, but he somehow found the energy to stay seated. They had to find her.

By the time they arrived the last rays of sun cast amber and pink streaks across the rooftops of Peterborough. Lady Agatha's carriage had caught up shortly before the turnoff for the small town.

At the Earl of Danby's hunting lodge, all was quiet, dark, and closed up. The driveway's unmarred fallen leaves created a colorful testimony to how long the house had sat undisturbed.

Ethan hung his head. Cursing each mile they'd driven off the Great North Road, he calculated how long it would take to recoup the time lost to this detour.

"Might as well be certain," Calvin said, dismounting and tying his horse to a tree. They circled the house, looking for unlocked doors and signs of life. The dark windows and cold chimneys gave off a depressive feeling.

"Stable is empty. No livestock," a footman reported.

"I shall secure lodging for the night. We will meet you at that inn we passed in town." Lady Agatha knocked on the ceiling of the carriage to signal the driver. "My old bones are ready for a soft bed, and I imagine yours are too, gentlemen."

Lady Agatha opted to dine in her room, while the rest of the group ate in the taproom of the least questionable lodging to be had. The inn sat like a squat mushroom in the shadow of a great Gothic cathedral. But as inns went, it was clean, and the service hadn't given Ethan any reason to complain. Not that he'd be terribly picky in his current condition. Food, then a reasonably soft flat surface, and he'd be happily unconscious.

Unanswered questions rattled around his sleep-deprived brain. The dim room with its flickering lantern light only fed the exhaustion creeping through him. He ate without tasting the food.

Darling pulled out a chair and flopped into it. "Lady Agatha's tucked in for the night. You wanted to see me, Lord Amesbury?"

"Aye. I'm hopin' you can help fill in the blanks. There's much we don' know. Are you sure you've told us everything?"

Cal interrupted, "Before we get into this, have you eaten yet?"

Darling shook her head. "Maids don't dine with quality." Her incredulous expression cut through the tired fog, pulling a rusty laugh from Ethan.

"We're in the middle of nowhere after a bloody awful day. Proprieties can hang. You need tae eat, lass, so eat."

Waving a serving girl over, Ethan asked for one more plate.

Ethan turned back to Darling. "Now, back tae my question. Is there anything from the last few days that may help us? Lottie had promised tae bring a footman with her when going out. Where was he?"

"We didn't bring a footman. I don't think she thought of it. At least she never mentioned it. Milady spent the last few days upset. Crying a lot. She said she wrote to you, so I'm sure you know all this." Darling smiled her thanks to the serving girl and dug into her meal.

"I don't have the foggiest idea what's happening right now. Care to clue me in?" Cal asked.

Ethan motioned to Darling. He had a feeling there was much he didn't know about the situation compared to Lottie's maid.

"Well, it all started with the wedding gown. She and Lady Agatha went to the modiste, and Lottie wasn't the same after. I don't think she slept that night. Then the next day she received that letter from her father forbidding the match."

Ah yes, the letter. That at least he knew about. He didn't understand how a wedding dress might have set Lottie on a path of calling everything off. He'd love to know what the earl said in his letter, though. "The next day she wrote and ended everything."

Cal swung to look at him. "What? She ended it? What reason did the earl give for denying you? Doesn't the man know you love her to distraction?"

Before Ethan could answer, Darling wiped her mouth and said, "Well, she didn't have much choice, did she? When the earl says he'll cut her off without a penny if she marries you, she knows to listen. At least this way she gets to keep her dowry and family. It killed her to make that decision, but he'd backed her into a corner."

Cut her off? Ethan sat back in the chair as the air left his lungs. It made sense now. No wonder she'd ended things. With such harsh consequences on the line, finding a way to marry despite the earl would be too great a risk.

"I don't think she liked it, but milady is resilient. We were planning our return home when Montague attacked us," Darling said.

"Wait, she was going back to Westmorland?" Cal voiced the thought that made Ethan frown. She'd planned to slip from London without seeing him in person.

"We were to leave by the end of the week. She hadn't told Lady Agatha yet," Darling said.

"During this time, you never saw Montague or heard anything relevant tae today?" Ethan pressed.

"I'm sorry. That's everything." Darling set her fork down, then finished her drink. "If you think of any other questions, I'm happy to answer. But I'm as shocked by all this as you are."

"Thank you, Mrs. Darling. Get some rest. We need tae be on the road at first light." Ethan stood when she did and cut her a small bow. Looking bemused, she said good night.

Cal stayed quiet when Ethan took his seat and drained the mug of ale before him. Outside, night had fallen in earnest, with only small areas of the stable yard illuminated by lamps for late-arriving customers.

The church bell in the cathedral tower chimed the hour. Eight, nine, ten.

"I meant tae beg, you know," he told Cal. "I planned tae ride in all self-righteous and more than a wee bit desperate and do whatever it took tae change her mind. Didn' know the earl cut her off, though. I can't ask Lottie tae turn her back on her father. He's all she has left."

"I'm sorry, Ethan. I didn't know she'd ended it."

A laugh escaped him, the sound utterly without humor. "All this time I've been trying tae make up for the past, but it doesn' matter tae the likes of the earl. There's no going back or fixing it." Five years without hard alcohol or a woman. Five years of telling himself no, because he needed to be a better man—one who didn't hurt people with his careless words and bad decisions. And during that time, Connor had forgiven him. Over time, even Lottie had softened. She'd shared her body and her bed, but he didn't think he'd reached her heart.

The only ones hating him now were the earl and himself.

"No, my friend. There's no going back. Only forward. We can awake every day, determined to be good men, then follow through. That's as far as our control goes." Cal signaled the barkeeper for a drink.

Holding up two fingers, Ethan ordered himself one too. Five years of no whisky for a Scotsman was long enough. He'd spent each day living with the fear that he'd lose control. Well, he might not be able to control much, but he could reclaim this.

"Are you sure?" Cal asked when the drinks arrived.

The amber liquid reflected the light in the glass. Benign. Like so many things in life, something he could use for good or evil. A pleasure to enjoy or to over-indulge and suffer the consequences. Ethan didn't have the craving disease, like Lottie's coachman and others he'd known. These years hadn't been about making healthier choices for himself. They'd been a form of self-flagellation. Was he sure? "Aye. This all comes down tae fear and hating myself for what I've done. I'm tired, Cal. So bloody tired."

"So just like that, you decide five years of penance is enough?"

Ethan rested his head on his fist, staring at the glass. "Can you tell me what more I can do? I mean it. Name one thing I can do tae make everything right, and I'll do it. I'll do it standing on my head while shoutin' 'God Save the King.'" The words had to fight past a throat tight with regrets. "I used tae be an arse, but I'm no' that man anymore. People depend on me for their livelihood, see? Besides, turns out I can make bad decisions sober as well." Like giving his heart to a woman never meant to be his.

Cal's expression remained neutral as he raised his glass. "To doing all we can."

Ethan touched the rim of his glass to Cal's. "Tae being better men."

The whisky burned as it went down. He had no desire for another.

As the sun set, it became apparent that rescue would not arrive as soon as Lottie would wish. With no way to calculate how far ahead they were of whomever Darling had alerted, she kept her ears open but found the day wearing on her. Yes, Darling was healthy and raising hell on her behalf—Lottie could not contemplate the alternative. She must not give up hope.

Someone would come. Soon.

Tugging the thin blanket over her shoulders, she cradled her head on her arm and stared into the fire. Their small room contained one narrow bed, which Montague had claimed, and a table barely large enough for a washbasin of water.

Today had been hell. True to his word, Montague had trussed her like a piece of wild game at each change of horses. The shiny pink skin on her wrists glowed red in the firelight. No doubt her ankles showed the same marks of abuse, although her walking boots provided some measure of protection. By the end of the day, Montague believed her sufficiently cowed to stay quiet without a gag. And she had, since she'd been too busy plotting her escape.

Montague had shared their "tragic" story with the innkeeper, along with a coin. She'd stared at her feet, wishing the earth would open and swallow her, then meekly followed him upstairs. The bastard should count his lucky stars she didn't smother him in his sleep with a pillow.

With no money, transportation, maid, or protection of any kind, all Lottie could claim was her father's name. Unfortunately, the Earl of Brinkley held little influence this far east, and she had no way to prove the connection. Montague had a fat purse borrowed from someone with equally shady morals. The flashy carriage, the horses, the steady flow of coins—none of it belonged to him. Through circumspect prying, she'd determined that Montague owned nothing except clothing, debt, and a substantial ego. There could be a valid argument made that the clothing wasn't his, since she'd bet the tailor remained unpaid.

Montague's snores overpowered the snaps and pops of wood in the hearth. Did most men snore? During their one night together, Ethan hadn't made such a racket. The snoring paused. A bubbling gurgle of flatulence echoed through the room. The snoring resumed.

How could anyone think eloping to Scotland was romantic? Hours upon hours cramped in a carriage, barreling up the Great North Road, relieving themselves in front of one another, and now spending a night on a hard floor, listening to a man break wind. Ballrooms and lusty novels did not prepare one for this. Thankfully, Montague had turned his back willingly enough when nature's call had finally forced the use of the bourdaloue, and then she'd disposed of the "dirty" linens in the small pouch within the bag he'd fetched for her.

All a ruse, of course. A ruse that needed to continue if she was going to have any chance of Montague keeping his hands to himself. They were one day down, with several more ahead of them. Lottie prayed an opportunity for escape would present itself during that time. She could only natter on about bowel distress, nausea, and cramping for so long before the man knocked her out again.

This—by far—had been one of the worst days of her life. Lottie finally allowed her eyelids to drift shut.

Tomorrow. Tomorrow, she would escape.

Chapter Twenty-Seven

"Doesn't kidnapping and elopement strike you as rather melodramatic?"

"Blame your precious Lord Amesbury. He didn't leave me much choice in the matter," Montague said.

"What does Ethan have to do with this?"

"Ethan, is it? He and Lord Carlyle bought my gaming debts, then wrote my father threatening to ruin me. Father isn't happy. To add insult to injury, there's a rumor that Father cut me off. This last week men tried to collect debts left and right. Hounding me as if I were some commoner, instead of a gentleman. I'm not going to debtor's prison." Montague curled his lip in a cruel expression that fit him perfectly. "If I marry money, everyone is satisfied. You're conveniently rich, and the man who attempted to ruin me seems awfully attached to you. That's what I call a winning hand."

A winning hand. Something Montague must not be

terribly familiar with if his gambling debts were crippling. She studied her intertwined fingers instead of looking at his smug face. Funny that someone so vile could remain beautiful on the outside. Thanks to her actions that day by the pond, his nose had a distinctly crooked angle to it, forever marring his perfection. Good. No less than what he deserved for using his physical appeal as a tool, and his ego as a weapon. There wasn't enough room in the coach for them and his ego.

Catering to the third occupant of the carriage might be key. Pander to his ego. Make him think he'd won. Yesterday Montague had believed her willing to wait in silence, so he'd left off the gag by the end of the day. Perhaps if Lottie convinced him he'd converted her to a willing captive, he'd create an opportunity for escape through complacency.

While nothing appealed to her more than the thought of smashing the delicately painted bourdaloue over his head, she'd need to lie convincingly. "Let us call a spade a spade. I broke things off with Amesbury earlier this week." Lottie feigned earnestness. "You need money. I need a husband or else I'll be firmly on the shelf. I see no reason we could not lead entirely separate lives if we married."

Montague cocked his head. "How separate?"

"No heirs. No more contact than needed, and only then through a solicitor. You live the life you currently enjoy, while I manage the estate. An estate that's far, far away. You stay in London doing whatever you wish."

"You wouldn't mind if I used your piles of pretty pound notes to keep a mistress or two?"

Focusing her gaze out the window, she searched for clues to their location. "I don't care what you do with your man parts, as long as you don't do it with me."

"One woman is as good as another. I won't need any snot-nosed brats to carry on my name unless I somehow end up inheriting. If that happens, you'll need to do your duty and give me an heir. What you describe sounds like the perfect marriage." He laughed. "We are of an agreement, then?"

Even the abstract idea of bearing this man's child made her throat burn with bile. Lottie hesitated—because the idea of sex with a crazy man should be enough for any sane woman to pause—then nodded. Whatever she needed to do or say to pacify Montague long enough for her to get away, she would.

How ironic. She'd just manipulated her way into a man agreeing to everything she'd wanted when she arrived in London. A hollow victory, indeed. One thing her time with Ethan had taught her was to raise her standards. He'd shown from the beginning how wrong she'd been to want an uninterested husband—not that she'd listened. Throwing herself headlong toward disaster, all the while believing she knew best, appeared to be her strength these days. How ridiculous that it took an escapade of this scale to show her what a great nodcock she was.

Even thinking Ethan's name brought a spike of pain. Would that ever go away? She might forever compare men to a certain giant, rough-hewn Scotsman. They'd had one night to fully enjoy each other, and it would have to be enough.

It would never be enough.

She wanted more mornings waking up in his arms. More pillows that smelled like him. A child with his blue eyes. One hand rested on her belly. What if they'd made a child? The French letter wasn't guaranteed protection. Except then Ethan would marry her out of obligation instead of desire. And she'd be an even greater burden on him, penniless, with a ruined reputation and a child.

At some point her heart had slipped past affection and friendship into unknown territory where she didn't want to imagine a future without him. Due to her strong pragmatic streak, she knew he'd need money to rebuild Woodrest. Thanks to her father, money was something she couldn't offer. She'd been so sure it was the right choice to free Ethan. Noble, even. After all, Woodrest and Ethan's people were more important than her heartache.

Here she was, finagling and lying and doing what she had to do to escape this kidnapping. It was a hell of a reminder that she wasn't by nature someone who capitulated easily. Why, then, had she rolled over when Father sent his ultimatum?

Ignoring the headache brewing behind her eyes, Lottie tried to logic her way through the mess she'd made. If she gave up her fortune but had Ethan, would it be worth it? He'd never said he loved her. But then, she'd never spoken about her feelings either. Did she love him and not just desire him—as scary as that idea was?

Perhaps emotion couldn't be excluded in this matter. Logic coexisted with emotion, surely. Going forward, balancing the two might be the only way to fix the mess she'd made.

If Woodrest needed an infusion of capital to recover from the sabotage, she'd be the worst possible woman for Ethan to marry. But what if they could figure out a way? The situation would present a unique challenge to an estate manager—or a woman of her interests. Instead of being handed a property and a fat purse by her father, she could step out of that safety net and help Ethan re-build. Together they could make a difference. Really, that was what her dream always boiled down to—making a difference.

There wouldn't be the independence of being on her own. Risking a glance at Montague, she tried to imagine the future he demanded. She'd have independence. In fact, she'd have everything she'd initially wanted when she rolled into London with her stupid, detailed, narrow-minded plan.

Whether he'd meant to or not, Ethan had changed everything. If she were entirely honest, she didn't want to be independent of Ethan. She wanted to work alongside him. Hear the rumbly burr of his accent when he teasingly called her Princess and see the way his face lit up with laughter when she made a face at the nickname.

Objectively speaking, if her dreams could be fulfilled with Ethan, then Father's ultimatum held little weight beyond finances. Their relationship had never been terribly close to begin with, and almost nil since Mother died. It pained her to consider losing him, but it was killing her to imagine a future without Ethan.

So, new plan. First, escape this damned carriage. Second, find Ethan and apologize. Finally, explain about Father's letter in detail, then try to concoct a way to somehow rebuild Woodrest without her dowry.

The landscape outside the window hadn't changed significantly in hours. Everything whizzed by in a blur of brown and green, broken by gray stone fences. The mid-day light played over Montague's perfect features. Even on the second day of their journey, Montague managed to be clean-shaven with crisp linen and polished boots. No wayward curl to brush off his forehead, or scars with stories tucked away under his shirt. Montague would never dream of padding around his library in stocking feet. And no way would Montague let her cut his hair in front of the warm kitchen hearth late at night.

God, she missed Ethan.

Leaning her head against the padded wall, she closed her eyes and let the swaying rhythm of the carriage lull the tension from her bones. Nothing could be done right now. A huge yawn split her face until her jaw popped. "I'm exhausted. I'll take a nap if you don't mind, Mr. Montague."

"We established long ago that you were to call me James. Now that we'll be married, I insist," he said.

Lottie closed her eyes, exhausted on every level. "Yes, James."

Go to the devil, James.

Finally, she slept.

By the end of the day, he left her unbound, as she'd hoped. They stopped for the night at a cozy inn nestled beside the road, shadowed by the great limbs of a black walnut tree. An owl called from somewhere in the nearly bare, menacing branches silhouetted against the night sky.

With or without help, tonight she would escape. If rescuers didn't arrive, she'd steal clothes from a groom, then sneak into a nearby barn to hide until Montague left the area. Her mind buzzed with contingency plans and scenarios.

When they arrived inside, Lottie stood quietly, fixing a vacant, placid expression on her face as he repeated the lies from the previous night. Montague obviously relished explaining how unhinged his poor wife had become to necessitate a trip north to a convent, where he would leave her in the Lord's hands. He brought his hands over his heart when he said he'd pray she might find sanity once more and be returned to him—a farce worthy of the stage.

Lottie almost smiled. Let him have his fun now. She'd have the last laugh soon.

The innkeeper's wife, Mrs. Mitchell, clucked over Lottie, calling her "poor lamb." The burly innkeeper appeared less impressed, but as his pocket was heavier by the end of the dramatic spiel, he didn't ask questions.

As Mrs. Mitchell led her by the hand toward their room, Lottie said over her shoulder to Montague, "Why don't you relax with a pint? I'll speak to this kind woman about replenishing those female supplies you gathered for me yesterday."

A moue of distaste crossed his face, and he stayed behind in the taproom. Montague made a lousy fake husband. Not that she had any comparison, having only had a fake fiancé before this.

Fussing over the linens, Mrs. Mitchell sent for a maid to fetch water for the washbasin. "You mentioned feminine supplies. Are you on your courses, dear?"

There would be no better opportunity. Holding out her wrists so the woman could see the shiny red marks, burnt and rubbed raw around the delicate skin, she said, "I need help. My name is Charlotte Wentworth, and that man kidnapped me. That is why I have no luggage. I'm without a maid, because he attacked her on the street when he abducted me."

While Mrs. Mitchell didn't look entirely convinced, she didn't pat Lottie on her head and fetch Montague either, so Lottie continued. "He imprisoned me in the carriage, bound at the wrists and ankles, with a gag in my mouth. Please. If I were going to a nunnery for the *rest of my life*, wouldn't I have trunks? Gowns? I beg you, Mrs. Mitchell, help me."

The red marks on Lottie's wrists held Mrs. Mitchell's attention for what seemed an eternity before she asked, "What can I do?"

The relief nearly brought her to tears. "*Thank you.* I believe my family is somewhere on the road behind us. Until they catch up with me, I must do what I can to stall our travel."

"Smart, my dear. How do you plan to do that?" The innkeeper's wife appeared to warm to the subject. After two days of feeling so very alone, Lottie wanted to hug the woman.

"Do you have an herb garden or apothecary nearby? With lady's slipper, white willow bark, and hollyhock, we can make a draught. All we need do is upset his stomach and then induce him to sleep. As tempting as it is, I can't hurt the man permanently. I just need to make him too miserable to travel tomorrow."

"Perhaps some poppy syrup to sweeten the mix?" the lady innkeeper said. "Yes, I think I have everything you need."

Lottie cocked her head to the side. The woman's dark-stained fingers triggered a memory from the hours spent making rounds at Stanwick with the midwife. "Is that black-walnut dye from the tree out front?"

"Yes." Mrs. Mitchell hid her blackened fingers under the corner of her apron. "Today I mixed the darker pulp with wax to stain my wood floors. It gives a great shine."

"Have you any of the soft outer casing left from the walnuts?"

Mrs. Mitchell nodded. "I have plenty."

"Perfect. We'll mash some of that pulp into a paste. With the tincture of herbs and poppy syrup in his food, whatever he's eating has to have a strong enough flavor to mask the mixture. But that should do the trick. Black walnut will make him want to be near the outhouse for a while."

Mrs. Mitchell's eyes sparkled with mischief. "I'll gather what we need. Then let's see what we can do about poisoning your husband."

When the woman served them herself, Lottie sent up a prayer that everything had gone smoothly in the kitchen. "We have a hearty beef stew for you to warm your bones after a long day's travel. I hope the flavor isn't too strong for you, Mr. Montague. I use a nice dark ale in my stew. Mr. Mitchell loves it." She gave them each a bowl, handing Lottie one with two chunks of bread on top. "Mrs. Montague, I included some extra bread for you. Eve's curse is miserable, isn't it? The bread may make you feel better." She winked at Lottie on her way out of the room. The bowl with two slices of bread clearly hadn't been tampered with, plus it came with the bonus of extra bread. Bless the woman.

Lottie took a tentative sip of the stew. "This is delicious. The bread is perfect. Somehow, it's the small inns that have the best bread. Have you noticed?" Nerves made her chatter.

When he took a bite, he wrinkled his nose. "Whatever ale she used must be ghastly." He pushed the bowl aside, but Lottie stayed his hand.

"I would hate to offend her. She has been such a lovely hostess. She didn't even raise a fuss when you asked to have our meal in the room. It's been a long day of travel, and this is all we have to eat."

Montague sighed, then finished the bowl and took her second slice of bread with a petulant look. Lottie held her tongue about the bread theft and made idle conversation with her captor in front of the fire while she waited.

It wasn't long before Montague's gurgling stomach interrupted the conversation. He frowned, placing a hand to his belly. "I told you that stew was off."

Feigning concern, Lottie frowned. "I'm sorry to hear that. I thought it delicious. Strange that I am suffering no ill effects."

Montague's face contorted in pain. She almost felt sorry for him. Almost. "Oh dear. You don't look well. Perhaps you should find the privy."

Montague shot a glance to his bag with the gag and ropes. The desire to bind her while he was indisposed was so obvious, she almost made a grab for the bag herself. In the end, his bowels made the decision.

The heavy footfalls of his boots on the stairs rattled a small framed painting on the wall as he ran from the inn to find the outhouse. Although their room had a lovely floral-painted chamber pot, he must have decided that whatever was happening didn't need witnesses.

If she could thank him for that, she would. Instead, Lottie smiled into her teacup and enjoyed the crackling fire.

Mrs. Mitchell poked her head in the room through the open door. "Are you well, Mrs. Montague?"

"All is as it should be." The women exchanged a grin, and Lottie sat back to stare at the flames and wait.

The peace did not last long. Montague stumbled into the room, leaning heavily on the doorway. Using the wall for balance while one hand held his stomach, he groaned, "I don't know what's wrong with me."

"Maybe you should lie down until you feel better."

Montague whimpered as she tucked him into bed like

a small child. When he closed his eyes on a pained moan and rolled to face the wall, Lottie moved the chamber pot across the room, slipping it behind the curtains.

It would be a long night for some of them in this inn.

Dusk came and went. For the past half hour Lady Agatha's coachman had carefully picked his way through darkness, with only the moon and a hanging lantern to guide the way. No one spoke of stopping for the night, all of them acutely aware that Lottie and Montague were preparing to spend their second night on the road.

"We found them!" The outrider's cry pierced the repetitious clamor of hooves and carriage wheels.

Ethan sagged in the saddle. "Thank God."

They came to a stop and waited for the grinning footman to bring his mount alongside them. "The Wild Dove, just at the edge of Doncaster. I've left Georgie to watch their coach, but it seems they're stopped for the night."

When their party arrived at the inn, they didn't try to be quiet about it. No doubt Ethan looked a formidable sight, storming across the yard, with the many capes of his coat fanning out behind him. Theatrics weren't usually his style, but if Montague happened to be watching, Ethan hoped the worm quaked in his boots. The innkeeper's eyes widened when Ethan burst through the front door and skipped formalities. "A man and a woman arrived in the red carriage that now sits in your stables. Where are they now?" Ethan slapped a coin down on the bar. The innkeeper eyed the coin.

A squat little woman sidled up beside the innkeeper,

beaming at Ethan. "Goodness, you are a big one, aren't ya? She's in the parlor through here." She came around the bar and led Ethan to a door. "Safe and sound, she is. If you're wanting to dispose of the man, he's upstairs wishing he were already dead."

Wishing he were dead, was he? Curious. "I'll deal with him later. Thank you for your help."

Calling the tiny room a parlor was generous. After two days of imagining worst-case scenarios, Ethan thought himself prepared for anything. He'd never considered this.

A fire roared in the hearth, providing warmth for the couch that had been pulled close to the fireside. Lounging under a blanket, reading a book, was Lottie. Steadying himself with a hand on the doorframe, he let the relief roll over him as he drank her in. She was here. Safe. Reading, of all things.

An incredulous smile split her face before she threw the blanket aside and launched herself from the couch. "Ethan!"

He met her halfway, swooping her up in a hug and burying his face in her hair. Relief stole his breath, and the broken mess of his heart calmed somewhat when she clutched him as if afraid to let him go. She may not love him, but she didn't hate him, and he'd have this one last hug. He skimmed his hand up and down her spine in a soothing stroke, and she responded by tightening her grip.

Except, this was all wrong. No matter how strong the urge to hold her close and never let go, their relationship was a thing of the past. As if the letter had never happened, she'd slipped into place under his chin, where she fit like a puzzle piece. Those dark curls he loved frizzed in a halo around her head, then knotted into a tangled braid down her back. The gown she'd donned almost forty-eight hours before was a mess, yet she managed to be the most beautiful wreck he'd ever seen. But she wasn't his. With slow, measured movements, Ethan untangled her fingers from around his neck and stepped back.

Rather awkwardly, Lottie pushed her hair off her face and tried to set herself to rights, avoiding his gaze. "I'm not sure what's appropriate, given our new circumstances, but I am happy to see you."

The feet between them felt like miles. Speaking past a tight throat, Ethan asked, "It's no' my business, but are you...Did he—"

Staring at her feet, she shook her head. "Montague has much to answer for. But I am safe and relatively untouched."

Part of the worry nested in his chest unraveled. "Where is he?"

"Unwell at the moment. I planned to set off on my own at daybreak."

"Can't say I'm unhappy he's sick. Although it puts a wrinkle in my plan tae beat him tae within an inch of his life."

"He'll be back to his evil self in a day or so. We only poisoned him a little. Mrs. Mitchell made an excellent accomplice."

"Poisoned him? Of course you did." In spite of the heartache, she made him laugh. "You're brilliant, lass, but you're also a wee bit scary. Well done."

She wrapped her arms around herself instead of him. "I, ah, I didn't expect you to come for me. Not after my letter."

"Yes, your letter." Peeling his gloves off one finger at a time, he tried to find the words to address the situation.

"I'm not here tae press my suit, lass. We both know that's over. Darling told me you're going home, so I'll see you tae your father safely." The earl would probably love the opportunity to share his thoughts on Ethan's presence in Lottie's life, face-to-face. "I'll let the others know where you are." Turning to the door, he focused on the metal doorknob instead of her as he spoke. "Engaged or not, I'd come for you if you needed me, Lady Charlotte." Best to get back in the habit of addressing her properly. She wasn't his anymore.

Chapter Twenty-Eight

The next morning dawned with a heavy gray fog over the landscape. Lottie said goodbye to Mrs. Mitchell, thanking her again for her help, then joined Ethan and Lord Carlyle.

"He's under guard. Last time I checked he was a sweaty, foul mess, drooling on his pillow. The man snores like some kind of wild animal," Lord Carlyle said.

"Not all men make those noises when they sleep? I had wondered." They turned to her with twin aghast expressions. "I'll take that as a no. Ethan—I'm sorry—Lord Amesbury, I'm ready to leave when you are. Darling and Aunt Agatha are already in the carriage."

Amesbury turned to Lord Carlyle. "Three days. That should give him time tae recover sufficiently for travel. Hire a carriage and meet me in three days."

"Agreed. He wanted to go to Scotland so badly. Who are we to say no?" Lord Carlyle grinned.

"Where are you taking him?" Lottie wasn't sure why she cared in the grand scheme of things, with so many other issues to worry about. Ethan's gentle rejection last night still hurt. *We both know that's over.* She'd broken them.

"We'll bring him tae my village near the Solway Firth. I have a plan tae make sure he never touches another woman." Amesbury's thunderous expression would inspire fear in anyone. Anyone but her.

When he'd walked through that door last night, there'd been a moment when all was right in the world. The thump of Ethan's heartbeat had sounded like home, and none of the events of the last few days had mattered one whit. He'd smelled of cold air and smoke.

Then he'd stepped back, and reality had reared its ugly head. Ethan wasn't hers. He wasn't even Ethan anymore. And that was her fault.

"I'll see you in the carriage." Given the mad clash of emotions warring within her, retreat seemed the best option.

Her maid sat beside Agatha on the plush seat, which thankfully smelled worlds better than the prison carriage of the last few days. "Darling, how is your head?"

Lottie had learned last night that Aunt Agatha had supplied Darling with regular draughts of willow-bark tea to make travel slightly less torturous, since, surprising no one, the maid had insisted on joining the rescue party.

"They didn't manage to knock it off my shoulders. Hurts like the devil." Darling touched the spot on her head with a wince. Darling's pallor remained ashy, highlighting the livid bruise on her head, and a scabbed cut in her hair.

"Stop touching it, then," Agatha huffed. Her godmother

seemed thinner after the last several days of stress, although blessedly solid and, well, Agatha.

"Auntie's right. Don't touch it. I worried about you, you know." Lottie checked the doorway at the inn. Amesbury's shoulders filled the space as he paused to fasten his coat and run a hand through those curls she loved so much.

The carriage rocked under his weight. The only available space was next to Lottie, and judging by the smug look her maid and godmother exchanged, that wasn't an accident.

"One more night on the road, then we can part ways at your father's estate tomorrow before supper," he said.

Well. Heroic rescuer or not, he clearly couldn't wait to be rid of her. Not that she could blame him. Silence fell on the carriage for several miles. The longer they went without speaking, the sterner Agatha's face grew, until the woman's pointed looks at Lottie became uncomfortable. Try as she might, Lottie drew a blank, searching for a safe topic besides the weather.

"Does anyone else smell smoke?" She craned her neck to view the landscape. There wasn't a telltale plume in a field, or even a nearby cottage to explain why she smelled fire.

Beside her, Ethan shifted farther away. "That's me you're smelling. I didn' change clothing before I left, and then forgot tae bring a satchel for the road. Apologies. I was in a hurry."

Ignoring that last bit of sarcasm, Lottie laid a hand on his knee and said, "How is Woodrest? I was worried sick over the fire. Are the tenants safe?" Goodness, how had she not asked before now? The thigh muscle under her fingers tensed, and she snatched her hand away as if burned. Everything about his body right now screamed *hands off*, and she had to respect that. But Lord, how she wanted to touch him. To linger and soak him in.

"Our good friend Montague hired an arsonist tae wreak havoc at Woodrest. I was dealing with that when I got your letter. No one was hurt. The construction site will need tae start anew. The granary is a loss, as is this year's harvest. John Billings never made it tae the main house."

"I trust the fiend is now in custody," Agatha said.

"Nay, he's my newest tenant." He gave Agatha a tight smile. "After making such a mess, 'tis only right he cleans it up. Montague hired a desperate man tae do his dirty work in exchange for enough coin tae feed his family."

Lottie rested her head in her hand and propped her elbow on the window ledge. Sweet heaven, had there ever been anyone so *good* as this man? "That's a significant loss for you, and then you had to deal with my letter. How utterly wretched. I'm so sorry."

"Aye, the twenty-fifth of never would have been a much better day tae call off the wedding. I understand why you did it, though."

Silence descended once more, now laden with an awkwardness none of them could escape.

Agatha wasn't one to let such a thing stand. "I think we can all agree Montague has done irreparable damage to your reputation. Slinking back to London with a concocted story might work, but Montague borrowed the carriage from one of his cronies, and that gentleman will talk. Returning to Westmorland is logical, but I do not like it. Not one bit."

"I was planning to go home anyway. Not under these circumstances, granted. But in the end, it's all the same.

Spinsterhood may suit me after all. You don't have a husband, and your life is exactly as you wish it to be." Beside her, Ethan tensed, giving her hope. If he didn't like talk of her future without him, he might be open to an apology.

Her godmother rolled her eyes. "Darling girl, there is an ocean of difference between a widow and a spinster. To think otherwise is foolishness. Marriage to the right person can mean unbelievable happiness. It is finding the right person that is the challenge. You two nodcocks managed to bungle your way into happiness through pure chance and half-baked scheming. Why not see if the earl thinks kindlier upon the match when seeing for himself the depth of your attachment?"

"I'm no' worth Lottie risking her relationship with the earl. Having her own estate and the fortune with which tae run it means everything tae her," Ethan said.

Ouch. Lottie bristled. "Money is not *everything*. You sell yourself short, sir."

Ethan finally met her eyes. "Do I, lass? I think we both know I have the right of it."

The blue of his eyes deepened with hurt, turning a shade she'd only ever seen in the flash of a bird's wing or the reflection off a lake. Passion made his eyes a soft blue gray. But pain was a vibrant blue. She'd rather not know that.

Darling's wide-eyed expression implored Lottie to say something—anything—but all the words caught in her throat. Her emotions were a tangle, with guilt rising to the surface. When given the choice between Ethan or keeping her fragile relationship with Father and accessing her dowry, she'd chosen the money. Never mind that she'd had reasons for doing so.

The fact that Ethan needed her dowry now more than ever and she wouldn't be able to help didn't matter. That she'd decided he could have helped sooner with the fire if he'd been home instead of distracted with her was also irrelevant.

More than anything, she longed to rest her head on those shoulders that were wide enough to carry the world, and hear the rumble of Ethan's voice in her ear telling her it would be all right. First, she'd need to find a way through his anger and ask for forgiveness.

Ethan shouldn't have made a crack about her choosing her fortune over him. Regret slammed through him as soon as the words left his mouth. "I'm sorry, Lady Charlotte. That was rude. You were free tae end the engagement and did so for your own reasons. I apologize."

The adorable little wrinkle between her eyes showed up only when her considerable intellect pondered something. In the past he would have smoothed the crease away with a finger, then teased a smile out of her. Ethan clasped his hands tighter between his knees.

Lady Agatha studied them with pursed lips. Darling sat quietly beside her, no doubt wishing she'd stayed behind with Cal.

Ethan held his tongue against a flood of words. Wouldn't you know it, a big part of him wanted to beg. He'd thought there could be nothing worse than thundering up the Great North Road worried sick about her. He was wrong. Sitting next to her in a coach with their shoulders brushing at each bump and rut in the road and not being able to hold her could be a level of his own personal hell. As usual, Lottie was composed and keeping her cool, even after having to rescue herself from her kidnapper. There was an emotional boundary between them—her on one side and him on the other. To be held at a distance left him cold. She shifted beside him on the seat—*right there* and he couldn't touch her.

The carriage traveled at a sedate pace in order to keep their outriders and mounts as rested as possible for the journey, but he wished those wheels would turn faster. Ezra had arrived at the inn with a groom that morning and trotted alongside the coach. Even though it was kinder to let his mount travel without carrying his weight, it was tempting to escape the coach and ride outside.

They stopped in York for a meal and supplies. Near the posting house was a bookshop and small marketplace that provided everything they needed for the long day ahead—reading material for Agatha, Lottie, and Ethan, and knitting needles for Darling. At a stall near the entrance of the market, Darling had cooed over yarn and charmed a discounted price out of the wool merchant. With a skein of yarn in her lap, the maid now happily clicked the needles as she created something. It was anyone's guess what the mass of string would become.

An hour later, a pressure on his hip pulled Ethan from the story of Rob Roy. After so long in the coach, Lottie had finally reverted to comfort over comportment. With her legs on the seat, she'd pressed her back against the side of the carriage, then rested her book on her thighs. He smiled. Ethan had found her curled up sideways in the library armchairs at Woodrest, and it was a common sight to catch her in an undignified sprawl in Lady Agatha's drawing room. At last, his lady had found a comfortable perch, although the point of her shoe dug into his hip. Without a word, Ethan lifted his leg enough to slip her foot under his thigh and relaxed, pinning that small part of her beneath him. Maybe her toes were chilly inside the thin boot. Or maybe she missed touching him as much as he missed her. Whatever her reason for not moving her foot away, he absorbed the contact like a starving man hungry for her touch. Turning the page of *Rob Roy*, he stole a glance out of the corner of his eye. She smiled at the page in front of her.

Chapter Twenty-Nine

Agatha's words ran across the forefront of her mind like some kind of banner. Her father could reconsider. If she told him the full tale about Montague, Father might feel guilty for pushing the match and listen to reason about Ethan. Ironic that Montague might have done her a favor—not that she would send him a thank-you note anytime soon.

There might be hope. Father could change his mind. Ethan might forgive her if they were alone long enough for her to apologize and explain. The second day in a traveling coach packed to capacity was hardly the time or place for a private conversation.

Without letting herself overthink it, she held her hand out to Ethan, resting palm up on the seat between them. Bless him, he didn't ask for an explanation, just intertwined his fingers with hers, then went back to staring out the window. That he allowed her to touch him again sent hope barreling through her veins.

His hand was her tether as she wandered through tangled thoughts. The comfort of this simple contact with a specific person brought one word to mind. Love. The emotion of poets and stupid men who rode into battle—willing to die in the name of some fair maiden they probably had no right to in the first place. Love had destroyed more than one country. She prayed it wouldn't destroy her too.

Her parents had been so in love they'd talked only to each other instead of their children. So in love they'd chosen to spend their days secluded in their rooms instead of following through on long-forgotten promises of picnics by the pond. The carriage passed through the familiar gates of Stanwick Manor and continued down the drive. Soon, the pond in question would be visible over the crest of the sloping lawn to their left.

Whatever Lottie's own feelings, they bore no resemblance to the example provided by her parents. As she examined their relationship from the outside, given this new perspective on love, a tiny bud of happiness bloomed within the dark memories. Mother and Father were not perfect by any means, but they'd known love. Yes, their mistakes had shaped her childhood, but it was high time she took responsibility for the poor decisions she'd made, instead of laying them at her parents' feet.

Ethan's accusation the day before stung—that she chose money over him. The truth of it only made it worse, and she had to face that. Which left the question of what to do. Defying her father didn't scare her as badly as it had mere days before. Marrying whomever she pleased and riding off into the sunset sounded better every moment.

Stanwick Manor came fully into view, with its comfortably predictable lines that never veered toward frivolous or decorative. Woodrest's gargoyles, curves, and stained-glass windows appeared to have been designed by demented fairies in comparison.

She owed Ethan an explanation and apology, but they were mere moments from facing Father. Squeezing his hand, she faced him. "Please. I know there are things to say between us. But trust me one last time. Let's talk to Father together. Present our case in person, like Aunt Agatha said. He might listen."

"It's about bloody time," Agatha muttered. Darling clapped and bounced on the seat, but Lottie kept her gaze on the stone-faced man by her side. With a small nod, he squeezed her hand.

At last, the carriage drew to a stop before Stanwick Manor's great double doors. Ethan stepped down, then held out a hand for Lottie.

It felt great to hold his hand again. The way his long fingers wrapped so entirely around hers never failed to make her feel safe. He tugged her closer. Smoke, sweat, and road dirt made her nose tingle. The poor man needed a bath even more than she did.

"Lass, we're goin' tae speak with your father. An' then you and I will have a talk about that letter."

He'd once told Lottie that her brain was a dark and twisty place, and he stood by that statement. Only God knew what was happening in her head, but when she'd reached for his hand in the carriage, he'd taken it. At this point he couldn't help accepting every last touch.

That she wanted to talk to her father with him, showing a united front, sparked hope within him where there'd been only pain for the last few days. He didn't know if showing up together would work, or if her father would listen.

Back at Woodrest, Ethan had managed to wash only the bare minimum before reading Lottie's letter. Within moments his clean shirt had absorbed the lingering smoke clinging to him. After chasing a carriage up the Great North Road on horseback for two days, there wasn't a single bloody inch of him that was presentable. Without a change of clothes, a bath would have been a waste of time. And without a bath, purchasing clothing would be throwing good money away. Sure, he could have ordered a bath along the way at any of the inns, for an exorbitant fee. But at some point, he'd become too exhausted to care.

He was in traveler hell. And he still didn't have a damn hat.

Every bit of grime on his skin itched when the carriage doors opened. This wasn't how he'd imagined meeting the earl again. Nevertheless, it seemed he had the chance to meet her father and say his piece—in all his travel dirt and disreputable hatless state. Shortly after that, he'd likely be thrown out on his ear.

Lottie's fingers tightened around his as they entered the house.

The Earl of Brinkley's library was everything a library should be. The warmth from the crackling fireplace enhanced the perfume of leather, ink, and paper that greeted him like an old friend. Unfortunately, the earl himself was not as welcoming.

"Charlotte? What are you doing here? And Lord Amesbury in the flesh. I see you've brought half the dirt between here and London in with you. Is this how you pay a visit in Scotland?" the earl said.

Biting the inside of his cheek to stop the words he wanted to say, Ethan glanced over at Lottie to see how she wanted to handle this. With Lottie by his side, he took a wide-legged stance before the elaborately carved wood desk.

"We received your letter," she said. A bubble of hope grew within him. She'd asked for his trust one more time, and he had to wonder what she had up her sleeve.

"What, I wasn't clear enough? Why on earth would you bring him here?" the earl asked, then turned away to shelve the book in his hand. "I thought I made my opinion of you clear years ago, Amesbury. This isn't the first time you've asked for my blessing, and my answer hasn't changed."

Lottie wrinkled her brow and asked Ethan, "What is he talking about?"

"The day after the prime minister's assassination, when I told you I'd call—"

"I waited and you didn't come. Yes, I remember. But that's ancient history, Ethan."

"Lottie, I was there. The butler took me tae your father instead of you."

She looked between him and her father, clearly confused. "But Father knew I was expecting you. I told him all about how you'd helped me that day—saved me from the mob."

"I asked tae court you. The earl rejected my suit and sent me home with an earful."

The earl piped up, "He wasn't worthy of you. I wasn't going to give my daughter to some fortune-hunting shepherd."

Ethan bowed his head in agreement. “You were right tae turn me away.” The earl gave him a surprised look. “I didn’ love her. I saw Lottie as an easy, beautiful solution tae the financial mess I’d inherited.”

“I didn’t get a say in that decision, I suppose?” Lottie said, but her father ignored the comment.

“And you think you’re good enough now? What’s changed? My sources tell me your estate is still practicing economies and you’re sinking the title into trade.”

“I wish I could tell you all was right and prosperous, but Mr. Montague indulged in a wee bit of sabotage. We will need tae rebuild and find a supply of grain for the winter tae replace our losses.”

Beside him, Lottie said, “Then Montague kidnapped me and tried to force an elopement. The man is a villain, Father.”

“I hardly believe it. Why would Mr. Montague do such a thing? I gave him my blessing. He didn’t have to kidnap you.” Finally returning to his desk, the earl carried three books from the shelves.

“Why would you endorse such a man? Where is the consideration for my safety? What about what I want?” Lottie said.

“What you want?” The earl slammed a book on the desk, and the sharp clap made Lottie jump beside Ethan. “I am giving you what you want! Your dowry, that house by the sea—everything you want, handed to you. Just say the word, and I’ll have Rogers purchase that house today.”

“But I want Ethan.”

Such a simple statement, but it meant the world to him. Clearly, they had things to discuss, but the hope grew until it filled in the missing areas of his heart.

The earl talked to Lottie as if speaking to a child. "Charlotte, I've made my opinion regarding this young man abundantly clear."

Straightening his shoulders, Ethan took a deep breath. "Milord, I know there's history between us. I'd welcome a chance tae make it right, in hope that you'll eventually bless our marriage."

"No. I told her no. This is the problem with the younger generation. No one *listens* anymore." The earl flipped open the first book in the stack and began to read.

Ethan rubbed the base of his skull with one hand and studied his filthy boots. This whole thing had been a losing endeavor from the beginning. Huffing out a laugh devoid of humor, he said, "You never approved of me, milord. Is it Scotsmen in general or me in particular you hate?"

The earl gave him a withering glare. "Being a member of the peerage, sitting in the House of Lords, and ruling our nation is a privilege and should be about far more than clinging to the last branch of a noble family tree. To be a lord, one must be raised to do it—formed and shaped and trained to move about in society. One must attend the right schools with others of his class—nothing you've done, because your parents did not prepare you for this life. Your grandfather was a black sheep, but his brother was a good man who raised his heirs properly. You were never supposed to inherit."

There was little he could argue with there. "You're right. Fate put me here, and I often wonder why."

The earl gestured toward Ethan's clothing. "You don't dress like a lord, carry yourself like a man of quality, or think like one."

"I apologize for my informal dress. Two days on

horseback, then another two in the carriage tae get here took its toll." The tension from his hands spread up his spine to his shoulders. He glanced down at the dried mud he'd tracked onto the carpet. He was an absolute wreck, and now the library smelled vaguely of dried horse shite. Brilliant.

"Are you telling me that your dislike for Ethan stems from basic snobbery? Lord, Father, that's mighty narrow-minded of you. None of that matters."

"None of it matters? Charlotte, of course it does. Why do you think we trained you so tirelessly? Deportment lessons, dancing lessons, voice lessons. Not that it did much good, because look at you now."

An ormolu clock ticked on the mantel, filling the silence. Lottie caved first to break the quiet. "So that's it? You're going to look me in the eye and hold on to your judgmental attitude, even though it hurts your only daughter?"

The earl assessed Ethan with cool, dark eyes. The resemblance to his daughter was suddenly uncanny. "My decision stands. You can have him, or you can have your dowry."

They'd tried. She turned to Ethan, guilt eating her alive. "Montague never would have hurt you if not for me. I'm so sorry. I owe you an apology for everything else too. Can we rebuild without my dowry? If we leave now, will you still want me if I don't come with a fortune?"

His smile reassured her. "We may have tae change the schedule for a few things. But we'll make do, love. We can work together tae restore Woodrest."

He spoke with such unshakable confidence, she

believed him. They would make it work, and build something new from their efforts.

Father cocked his head, looking at Ethan. "If this isn't about money for you, then what is it?"

"I love her. Her money or lack of doesn' change that."

"You love me? Since when?" She stared up at him, trying to wrap her head around the casual way he shook her to the core with his words. As if it was a given and she should have known he loved her.

"Lass." Ethan smiled softly. "Did you really think I proposed out of the goodness of my heart?" From the beginning, then. Breath escaped her as she considered the implications. This changed everything.

"Lottie? Do you love him?" her father asked.

"I..." Lottie's voice trembled. Her mouth opened. She closed it, gulped, and opened it again. No words.

Stepping back, Ethan let go of her, ignoring the hand she held out. Words failed as her brain scrambled, reviewing their shared history through the lens of this new information.

He'd prioritized their relationship over his estate, just like her parents had. Yet she knew he'd move heaven and hell to take care of his people. And Lord, how she wanted to be by his side, watching Woodrest thrive, working with Macdonell to make the new brewery a success.

Ethan loved her. When she'd written that letter ending everything, he must have been gutted. The gross mishandling of this relationship on her part crashed into her with flashes of memory.

The look on Ethan's face when she said she'd marry him.

His hunger when he took her into his arms that night in the kitchen of Woodrest.

The relief when he arrived at the inn to rescue her—even though she must have hurt him tremendously by ending their engagement.

He'd left everything behind to find her. Everything. He hadn't even brought a hat.

As if it were echoing in a tunnel, she heard her father's voice say, "Charlotte, I was trying to make things right. If your mother was here, you'd have married by now. I just wanted you to move on with your life instead of taking care of me." The rest of what he said faded in her ears, because she couldn't look away from Ethan's face.

The love had been there for anyone to see all along, but she'd refused to acknowledge it. Too wrapped up in her plans, as per usual. She'd hurt him. Hell, she'd probably been hurting him one degree at a time for the last few months, but everything had reached a boiling point in this library.

Hell on a broomstick. All he'd done was love her, and she'd brought an arsonist to his door, then broken his heart.

"Ethan, I'm so sorry."

Chapter Thirty

The ground hit him as hard as her words had. At the last minute he remembered to roll as he came off the horse's back, but the air left his lungs on an "oof" and didn't come back. As he stared up at the gray sky, struggling to breathe, the first fat raindrop hit him in the eye. Ezra was throwing him over too, and now the heavens were taking a piss on his head.

Ethan, I'm so sorry. Her stricken expression had damned their relationship until the only feeling left had been a dull thud of his heartbeat in his ears. What was the use of staying to hear more? So he'd run as if the hounds of hell nipped at his heels.

All the broken pieces inside him had turned to ice. Ezra hadn't been unsaddled yet, so it had been an easy thing to ride straight out of the stable and down the driveway, putting as much distance between himself and that family as he could.

In his pocket, her goodbye letter, in which she'd absolved him of any lingering guilt, crinkled when he rolled to the side. Rain splattered the dirt by his face, and one of Ezra's hooves stepped into his line of sight.

Finally, a trickle of air leaked into his lungs. The broken buckle of the girth strap dangled from the saddle he'd taken with him in that not-so-graceful exit off Ezra's back at a full canter. He sat up and hung his head. Rain slid down the back of his neck and pelted his knees. The water brought out the smell of smoke from his clothes. If despair and hopelessness had a scent, this was it.

She couldn't answer a simple question. *Do you love him?*

Ethan sighed and raised his face to the rain. What a fool he was. A heartbroken fool who went back for more, only to get kicked down again.

Ezra nuzzled his ear, huffing hay breath across his face. He absently scratched the horse's cheek. "Yes, sir. We'll go. The village can't be far, eh?" Hauling himself to his feet required double the effort it usually did, but with a muttered curse he threw the saddle over his shoulder and took Ezra's reins in hand. It could be miles, and his boots were already squelching, but there was no way he'd return to that drab, squat manor house.

"Ethan, stop!"

"Not bloody likely, Princess," he muttered. "She doesn' know when tae stop, does she, Ezra?" Hitching the saddle higher, he kept walking, ignoring the sound of the approaching carriage.

Scotland beckoned. Cal would meet him there with Montague, and then he'd mete out justice to a bully and a coward—which sounded like a grand time in his present frame of mind.

"Please. Get in the carriage and let's talk about this." It was hard to miss her, hanging out the window of her father's carriage as it rolled alongside him down the road.

He marched on, staring resolutely ahead. The horse swung his head back toward Lottie's voice, knowing she was usually good for a treat or two. "Don' look at her, Ezra. You'll only encourage her."

"I'm sorry. You have no idea how sorry. But if I'd had another minute to think, I'd have said yes," she called from the window.

At that he whirled around and growled, "Another minute? Were you sent by God tae test my patience, lass? You needed *another minute*? You've had months tae figure out the answer tae that question. *Months.* Did you need another minute when I took you tae bed? Or when you encouraged me tae ask for your father's blessing—who's still a right bloody prick, by the way. I've loved you for months, but you couldn't answer one simple question when he asked." He shook his head, then set off again, pulling Ezra behind him.

The noise she made was somewhere between a screech and a groan. "Don't you dare act all high and mighty with me, Ethan Ridley. You've loved me for months? Well, that's just brilliant—wonderful information to keep to yourself, you coward. Because you telling my father—who, yes, is a horse's arse—is the first time I heard you say a word about love. So forgive me if I needed a *damned bloody minute* to absorb that information. If you'd waited for ten more seconds, I'd have told you that I love you too."

He stopped again, letting the saddle fall to the ground, and lifted his face to the sky. The frigid rain could wash his face of dirt and tears and whatever else. Damn it. It irked him to admit she was right about anything right now, but she had a point. He'd never told her how he felt.

The coach might not have been going fast, but when she opened the door and flung herself from it, basic laws of physics dictated she had few options but to land in a graceless stumble against him, nearly knocking them both over. He caught her before she hit the ground. He'd always catch her, even when he wanted to wring her neck.

"Only a lunatic jumps out of a moving carriage. You could have been hurt. What the hell are you thinking?"

As they stood toe to toe, Lottie jabbed at his chest. The carriage rolled to a stop about ten feet down the road. "I love you. I had this plan, where I'd apologize and we'd come up with a way to save Woodrest. Except nothing went right. We didn't have any privacy in the carriage, and then you told me you love me—in front of my father of all people. It hit me all at once. How much I've hurt you, without realizing it." Tears rolled down her cheeks before being washed away by the rain. "I don't understand how you could love me through all that or why you're even here helping me out of this mess *again*, but I'm begging you to keep showing up. Just show up. Love me, and I'll love you, and we will make this thing between us real. Please. You won't regret it. I promise."

Heartbreak and hope were a strange combination of emotions, but they poured out of him like a hemorrhaging wound. She'd asked for his trust before they'd dealt with her father, and then she'd let him down. Ethan turned his back on her to stare back at the gates of her childhood home, digging his fingers into his hair and keeping them there as he muddled through everything she'd said.

With his hands on his head, it was simple enough for her to duck under an arm to face him again. "Let me guess. You need a moment to think?" she said with a small smile.

A laugh bubbled up despite the emotions clutching his vocal cords. Tracing the lines of his reluctant smile with a finger, she tugged his head down to her.

Ethan joined her in the kiss willingly enough, although without his normal enthusiasm. Right away, something was different. It was as if she poured her soul into the kiss, trying to fill the void where the broken pieces of his heart lay, soothing the pain she'd caused. After a moment, her tongue nudged at the seam of his lips, and he opened to her. Desire rose from the hurt and anger, turning the kiss frantic. Gripping the back of her head, Ethan gave her everything she'd asked for without words—the hunger, the pain, the emotional burden of loving her without being loved in return, the roiling desire that never fully settled, and finally, joy at what her body was saying. This wasn't a goodbye kiss or an apology kiss. This was a kiss that fought for something. Fought for them.

"I love you," she whispered against his mouth. "I'm so sorry I hurt you. That's what I was saying. Go ahead and be angry with me. I deserve it. I'll still love you when you're done with the mad."

Their cheeks were damp, from either the rain or tears, he didn't know. "Say it again."

"I love you. I'm sorry it took me so long to say it."

"Do you mean it? This week has been hell on us both. I can't do it anymore."

"I need you to trust me one more time, and I know that's asking a lot." Rain clumped her lashes into dark spikes as she looked up at him. Her hands hadn't left him since that shattering kiss. She smoothed a finger across his bottom lip, leaving a trail of sensitized tingles in its wake.

"Just tae be clear, I want everything, lass. A real marriage. A life together. A home. Perhaps children. I want the right tae kiss you for no other reason than that it's three o'clock on a Thursday."

Lottie let loose a watery laugh as he drew her closer to his chest. "Is that what day it is? I've lost track."

The lump that had been in his throat finally went away, and he drew a shuddery breath. "I want tae hear you laugh every day."

"Even though I hurt you?"

God, had she ever. Moving past that moment of devastation in the library had to be a choice. The decision came easier with her in his arms. "I'm no' blind, lass. There will be hurt feelings sometimes. You're a bossy, managing sort, an' I'm a stubborn arse. Good thing we both believe in second chances." Ethan tucked a loose curl behind her ear, then caught one of her tears with a thumb.

"I feel I should warn you that I might not be good at this. I've never been a partner. All I've ever done is either take over or stay silent and feel trod upon."

"If you're willing tae bend, then I'll bend tae meet you."

"What if we butt heads all the time?"

He laughed—something he'd thought impossible a half hour before. "Oh, lass—we *will* butt heads. I guarantee it."

The buzz whipping through him must be how birds felt when they danced on wind currents. Free, confident they wouldn't fall. She linked her fingers behind his neck, then burrowed her nose under his jaw. A happy giggle escaped her, making him grin wider.

Ethan tightened his arms around her waist. "Marry me, Lottie? For real this time."

"Take me to Scotland. Let's get married where you grew up," she said.

"That sounds like the best plan anyone has ever had in the history of plans."

Ezra butted his head between them and whuffled in her face, making Lottie laugh again. "Hi, boy. Want to go to Scotland? I'm sorry that means you'll be tied to the back of the carriage again." They threaded their fingers together and headed to the waiting carriage. "Besides, there's still Montague to deal with. I don't know what you have planned, but I want to see it through to the end."

In the carriage, Lottie slipped into her place at his side. She'd done it—told him she loved him—and now she'd be married in a few short hours.

The coach dipped and swayed, and they fell into each other, riding the movement, hanging on to one another. Those dark curls she loved so much, damp from the rain, tangled around her fingers, tying them together. The taste of him was a welcome home. Heat rose within her, as it did each time they kissed, but this time she let it burn unchecked.

Need—that constant companion when he touched her—clawed, demanding she get closer, press harder, love deeper. When Ethan pulled her into his lap, she helped bunch the wet fabric of her skirts high up her hips so she could straddle him. A happy sigh escaped her, turning into a moan when the juncture of her legs—with that marvelous epicenter of sensation—rode the ridge in his breeches. The building tension brought heat, with a tingling that began at her toes and traveled up the back of her legs, to wrap around her inner thighs. With frantic, fumbling fingers, Lottie opened the placket of his breeches, reacquainting herself with his length.

Breaking the kiss, Ethan leaned his head against the velvet padded wall, groaning. "We don' have a French letter."

A bead of moisture pooled at the head of his cock before she spread it around the crown with a thumb. "Do we need one? Think of this as our wedding night, a few hours early. Didn't you say the Scottish were fine with playing fast and loose with the formalities? We can make our public declarations tonight with the minister but make private promises here. Just you and me making vows."

Ethan nuzzled her ear, placing kisses along her jaw. Before he reached her mouth, he pulled back. "Another excellent plan. I love you, Charlotte Wentworth. You have my heart an' my trust. I give you my hand, my name, my love, and my protection. All I have is yours. How do you English say it in the Book of Common Prayer? With all my worldly goods, I thee endow."

"I promise to love you—even when it's scary to do so. I vow to come to you with my fears." She wanted to memorize every hard angle and rugged plane. As she stared into his blue eyes, with their gold starbursts and burning emotions, the vows came easily. "I am bringing you all the parts of me that don't work well with others and am trusting we can figure it out. I vow to be your friend and partner. I can't in good faith promise before God to obey you. I think we both know that would be a lie."

Ethan laughed, wrapping her closer against his chest. It felt wonderful to laugh in such a serious moment.

Months ago, in that inn off the beaten path in

Warwickshire, she'd cursed how his scent affected her. Now he smelled like love, safety, and a warm future full of moments like this. Although he could use a bath.

With a grin she teased, "It's probably best that we aren't doing this in the Church of England. I don't think we could keep a straight face for that part of the vows. But the rest? The rest is there. I will honor you. Keep only to you, forsaking all others. In sickness and in health. Are we married now, by Scottish standards?"

"Close enough," he whispered, already bringing her close for a kiss.

Positioning his cock at her entrance, she moaned at the sensation of having him inside her again. With the carriage movement dictating their rhythm, they clung to one another.

Ethan helped tug her dress and shift down to free her breasts into his eager hands. Muttering expletives that sounded like praise, he lifted one breast to his mouth and drew heavily on the tip. Closing her eyes, she threw her head back and surrendered to the sensation.

"I've missed you, Ethan."

He moaned encouragements against her skin, then switched his attention to the other breast while his hold on her hip tightened to guide her along his shaft, building the friction they both needed. "Keep talking, lass."

"What's the rest of it? With my body, I thee worship."

"I think that's my line. With my body, I thee worship. An' all the rest that I can't remember right now, because holy hell, Lottie, you feel amazing."

As he met her stroke for stroke, they stole kisses, gasping for air that tasted of rain and pleasure. "Tell me again." His intense gaze fed her desire.

She knew exactly what he asked for. "I love you."

The carriage rocked beneath them, their bodies chasing pleasure as fast as the wheels could take them.

"I want you tae come apart in my arms."

Tremors began in her thighs, then her belly quaked. She lost the rhythm, so he carried her through as the tension within finally released and stars ran through her veins. Below her, his hips bucked, surging into her body, as he followed her over the edge.

Clutching her in the aftermath, he stroked her back, then down her arms and back up to begin again at the base of her neck. Touches to calm and cherish, not entice.

With a happy sigh, she said, "I love you. I know I said it a few minutes ago in the middle of all that, but my brain was spiraling out the top of my head at the time, so I'm not entirely sure I got my point across."

His arms tightened around her. Ethan buried his face in her hair. "I'll never tire of hearin' it. I adore every gorgeous, bossy inch of you." He squeezed one breast. "Especially these bits."

A growl rumbled through the coach. They looked down at Ethan's stomach. He shrugged a bit sheepishly.

"I can fix that." After setting her dress to rights, Lottie reached for the hamper on the opposite seat.

"You did this?" Ethan unpacked the basket.

"Of course not. I was busy having an emotional breakdown. Darling and Agatha are the heroes here. They packed the basket, sent for the carriage, and gave us their blessing. They're going to rest for a bit, then follow behind us." Lottie popped the cork off a flagon of wine and pulled out two metal cups. "I don't know what I'd do without the two of them."

Ethan swallowed a mouthful of food. "What does Lady Agatha think of the plan tae marry in Scotland? Won' she want the grand gown and St. George's?"

"She said—and I quote—as long as she's there to wish us happy, we could get married naked in the woods if we wanted. I can now testify that Scottish ceremonies are very loose in your wild country, so the naked thing is definitely an option."

His laugh warmed her to her toes. "And Darling? Did you suggest she come along and marry her coachman while there? Because that sounds like one of your plans."

Lottie gaped in mock outrage. "I'm not that managing—" He cut her off by shoving a slice of ham in her mouth. "Fine, yes. She and Patrick are coming with Agatha," Lottie confessed around the ham.

"You are nothing if not efficient, love. Did you ladies plan out the rest of Patrick's life?" He washed the teasing down with a healthy gulp of wine.

"Of course we did. They'll either move with us to Kent or breed horses in America." Lottie nibbled a piece of cheese, returning his sarcasm with her own.

"Either way, we'll always have room for them. They might be a good fit for an idea I had while home."

She brushed away a bread crumb stuck in his scruffy beard. "What have you been concocting in between fighting fires, catching saboteurs, and rescuing damsels who poison people?"

"The man Montague hired, John Billings. He worked against his conscience tae sabotage my home in exchange for barely enough money tae feed his wife and children for a week. He's a former soldier. Lost his leg in the war. How many more soldiers are desperately tryin' tae feed themselves and their families but can't find work because of a physical handicap? I want Woodrest tae be a place where men can work with dignity and raise their families outside dangerous neighborhoods like Seven Dials and the rookeries."

Lottie laid her head on Ethan's shoulder. She nibbled on a dried piece of fruit and offered it up to share. What he proposed made so much sense, especially when one knew his generous heart. Thank heaven he hadn't been raised to be a lord. Because of that, he was better than most of the aristocracy.

"I love it." She gave him a peck on the lips, pulling back before the sweet sentiment could build into anything more. "Thank you for riding across the country to save me. You were so dashing, ready to fight Montague."

"Aye, but you got tae him first, you little savage." The dimple in his cheek never failed to cause a flutter in her belly. "I'll always come for ye, lass. And I'll mow down anyone fool enough tae get in my way." Ethan let go of her hand to bury his fingers in her hair, holding her steady for his kiss as the carriage hit a bump. "Are you sure you don' want the society church wedding?"

"I told you, Agatha is joining us tonight. We have it all planned."

He sighed. "I'm surrounded by managing females."

"Get used to it, Lord Amesbury."

Epilogue

The river and nearby waterway of the Solway Firth carried men, ships, and silt to and from the sea with the temperament of a demanding mother-in-law. The air smelled like mud and fish.

Cal might be cranky with fatigue. Once he finished this task, he'd get something to eat. Maybe that would help. Lack of food made him irritable, and he was most definitely irritable.

A muffled sound came from the other seat in the carriage.

"Shut up," he replied.

Montague glared ineffectual daggers from behind his gag. No doubt the man was making a rude gesture behind his back, where Cal had tied his hands.

Justice was justice, after all. And Cal was nothing if not fair. Montague had been treated to the same tender ministrations he'd shown the new Lady Amesbury.

Ethan and Lottie's marriage over the anvil had taken mere moments. Glancing at his pocket watch, Cal checked the time. The lovebirds were naked by now. He'd bet on it.

Angus, an affable three-toothed man who'd known Ethan since birth, opened the door and climbed inside, carrying the smell of whisky and tobacco with him. "Time tae take out the rubbish, eh? 'E's beginning tae smell."

"You don't know the half of it. Let's just say this has been a very long trip," Cal said. Whatever Lottie had given the man was nothing short of foul.

Angus directed him to a pub near the docks that was suitably disreputable for their needs. In the farthest corner, drinking in the shadows, sat a man with his back against the wall. After years of friendship with Ethan, Cal would be the first to admit that his metric might be skewed. But judging by the man's shoulders, he was a bit of a beast. Easily as broad as Ethan, but without any layers of gentility. Definitely a rough character, although younger than he'd expected.

Angus doffed his cap. "Captain Harlow? Had a bit of trouble. Thought ye could help. Lord Carlyle, this here's the gentleman I told ye about."

Gentleman might be stretching the truth. *Pirate* was probably more accurate. Cal eyed the sketchy seafarer a moment before motioning to a passing barmaid for another round of ale. The woman eyed him up and down suggestively, then winked when he placed a coin in her palm.

"You'll get more than a drink from that one," Captain Harlow said, nudging a chair toward Cal.

"I'll just take the drink, thank you." Cal took a seat and waited for Angus to sit beside him before speaking. "I won't waste your time, Captain. A man kidnapped my best friend's wife."

"You need me to track him down? I don't find people."

"Your services aren't required for that. We have the kidnapper outside under guard. We need you to make him disappear."

"If you want him gone, he'll need papers. Papers will cost ya." Harlow paused when the barmaid came back to their table.

The pirate captain—there was no way Cal would ever think of him as anything else—smirked when the barmaid rested her generous bosom on Cal's arm while delivering their drinks. Her offer was clear, but Cal wasn't tempted to take her up on it. He was here for business. She walked away with a pouting flounce, and Cal returned his attention to the pirate captain. "Name your price."

"Not a good negotiator, are ye, boy?" Angus muttered from his glass.

"My one condition is you have to take custody of him now. I've been carting him around the country for days and want rid of him."

"He's beginnin' tae smell," Angus reported.

"He anyone important?"

"Good family. Not an heir," Cal said.

"Then I'd better get to work. First, gold." He named a price that had Angus choking on his drink.

It would be worth it if Montague disappeared forever. Without a second thought, Cal handed over the purse of coins he'd brought with him. He'd tell Ethan it was a quarter of that amount, should he ask.

Rolling the purse in his hand, sending the coins jangling against each other, the pirate captain cocked his head. "You're a good friend to do this for a lady who's not even your wife."

"This man is a threat to all women, and I have a sister." Cal drained his glass and rose from the table.

Eyeing Cal, the man said, "I might like to meet this sister."

"You'll never meet my sister. I guarantee it. Now, let's get down to business."

The coach awaited them in the farthest corner of the stable yard from the pub's entrance. Cal swung open the door, and there sat their coachman, happily holding a pistol on Montague. Their captive yelled through the gag, but no one attempted to decipher what he said.

"You're right, there is a stench about him, isn't there?" Captain Harlow sounded almost cheerful when he continued, "You are now prisoner 8792-39. Or you will be once I've forged your papers. You're charged with the crimes of kidnapping, being an arsehole, and generally making the wrong people mad. How do you plead?" He didn't pause for an answer. "Never mind, I don't care. You get a free trip to the penal colonies of Australia, courtesy of his majesty, the king. Come along, 8792-39."

June 1820

Ethan winced, pitying the young man who'd just stepped on Emma's foot in the middle of the ballroom. Spinning Lottie through the steps of a waltz to sidestep around the couple, Ethan held his wife close enough to garner a few censorious glances from the matrons off the dance floor.

"Poor lad. Not likely that he'll get a second chance to impress her," Lottie said.

Cal had claimed more than once that his sister's preference for rogues would be the end of his sanity. Most mornings he and Lottie listened to Cal lament his sister's suitors over breakfast, since they were conveniently located next door.

They'd leased the town house next to Cal's for the Season while Ethan attended to his duties in the House of Lords. Parliament had been in session since the king's death in January, and the government was busy preparing Prinny to take the throne. Ethan's and Lottie's weeks were full, split between Kent and the brewery, which was preparing its first batch of ale, and London duties.

The music came to an end with a trill of a flute and the gentle swish of silk skirts on the ballroom floor. Couples left the formation, and new ones took their place for the next dance.

Ethan tucked Lottie's hand into the crook of his elbow. "How long until we can leave, do you think?"

"We promised we'd stay for a few hours. Lord knows Cal might need to find you and do that wild-eyed panic routine if Lord Roxbury dances with Emma twice. Although I suppose Dawson could let Cal in later, should he stop by." Lottie had been thrilled that Dawson was still part of the staff in residence with the house, and yesterday she'd finally convinced the older man to move to Woodrest with them at the end of the Season.

The combination of Dawson and Connor would certainly make things interesting. Ethan had every confidence they would figure out a way to coexist, the same way Connor and Lottie had navigated their way to acceptance and mutual respect. It hadn't taken long for his clansman to develop an appreciation for Lottie's willingness to jump into the hard work of the estate.

Nodding to acquaintances, Ethan and Lottie headed for the refreshment table. Lady Agatha turned from her friends and greeted them with a wide smile. "Good evening, my darlings. Are you enjoying yourselves? No, of course not. Amesbury, you look like you are on your way to the gallows. Try not to scare the debutantes. Lottie, are we still leaving at noon tomorrow?"

His wife kissed her godmother's cheek. "Yes, Auntie. I'll come for you in the carriage at noon. Connor is expecting us by teatime."

Lady Agatha's regular visits had helped warm Lottie to Connor's good graces. Connor adored the older woman, needling her with shameless flirting—which she met with a half-hearted reprimand and a twinkle in her eye.

It wasn't chance that Agatha had been in residence at Woodrest when Lottie's father visited a few months ago. Tensions remained there, but Ethan was hopeful that with time the relationship between his wife and her father would heal. The earl did gift them with her dowry, although Lottie declined an additional property. She claimed her new home kept her plenty busy—especially now that she was helping Patrick and Darling establish a small horse-breeding operation on a corner of Woodrest's acreage.

They sipped glasses of champagne and surveyed the crush in the ballroom. Ethan turned to his wife. "What do you say tae finding the balcony and taking in some fresh air, love?"

Lottie leaned close and whispered, "I know you and balconies, and I doubt you'd fit under the skirts of this gown. Fancy a trip to the library instead?" She pressed her body against his side, sending his blood heating in anticipation.

Ethan drained the champagne in one gulp, set the glass aside, and offered his hand. "Library it is, Princess. We both know how much I love a woman who reads."

About the Author

Bethany Bennett grew up in a small fishing village in Alaska where required life skills included cold-water survival, along with several other subjects that are utterly useless as a romance writer. Eventually settling in the Northwest with her real-life hero and two children, she enjoys mountain views from the comfort of her sofa, wearing a tremendous amount of flannel, and drinking more coffee than her doctor deems wise.

You can learn more at:

BethanyBennettAuthor.com
Twitter @BethanyRomance
Instagram @BethanyWritesKissingBooks

Looking for more historical romances?
Fall in love with these sexy rogues
and darling ladies from Forever!

A DUKE BY ANY OTHER NAME
by Grace Burrowes

Lady Althea Wentworth has little patience for dukes, reclusive or otherwise, but she needs the Duke of Rothhaven's backing to gain entrance into Society. She's asked him nicely, she's called on him politely, all to no avail—until her prize hogs *just happen* to plunder his orchard. He longs for privacy. She's vowed to never endure another ball as a wallflower. Yet as the two grow closer, it soon becomes clear they might both be pretending to be something they're not.

THE TRUTH ABOUT DUKES
by Grace Burrowes

Lady Constance Wentworth never has a daring thought (that she admits aloud) and never comes close to courting scandal... as far as anybody knows. Robert Rothmere is a scandal poised to explode. Unless he wants to end up locked away in a madhouse (again) by his enemies, he needs to marry a perfectly proper, deadly dull duchess, immediately—but little does he know that the delightful lady he has in mind is hiding scandalous secrets of her own.

Follow @ReadForeverPub on Twitter and join the conversation using #ReadForever

WHEN A ROGUE MEETS HIS MATCH
by Elizabeth Hoyt

After clawing his way up from the gutters as the Duke of Windemere's fixer, ambitious, sly Gideon Hawthorne is ready to work for himself—until Windermere tempts Gideon with an irresistible offer. Witty, vivacious Messalina Greycourt is appalled when her uncle demands she marry. But Gideon proposes his own devil's bargain: protection and freedom in exchange for a *true* marriage. Only as Messalina plots to escape their deal, her fierce, loyal husband unexpectedly arouses her affections. But Gideon's last task for Windemere may be more than Messalina can forgive... Includes a bonus story by Kelly Bowen!

Discover bonus content and more on read-forever.com

Connect with us at
Facebook.com/ReadForeverPub

A GOOD DUKE IS HARD TO FIND
by Christina Britton

Next in line for a dukedom he doesn't want to inherit, Peter Ashford is on the Isle of Synne only to exact revenge on the man responsible for his mother's death. But when he meets the beautiful and kind Miss Lenora Hartley, he can't help but be drawn to her. Can Peter put aside his plans for vengeance for the woman who has come to mean everything to him?

ANY ROGUE WILL DO
by Bethany Bennett

For exactly one season, Lady Charlotte Wentworth played the biddable female the *ton* expected—and all it got her was society's mockery and derision. Now she's determined to take charge of her own future. So when an unwanted suitor tries to manipulate her into an engagement, she has a plan. He can't claim to be her fiancé if she's engaged to someone else. Even if it means asking for help from the last man she would ever marry.

Find more great reads on Instagram with @ReadForeverPub

THE HIGHLAND LAIRD
by Amy Jarecki

Laird Ciar MacDougall is on a vital mission for Scotland when he witnesses a murder—and then is blamed for the death and thrown into a Redcoat prison to rot. He never thought he'd be broken out by a blind slip of a lass and her faithful hound. He soon learns that Emma Grant is just as fierce and loyal as any clansman. But now they're outlaws on the run. And as their enemies circle ever closer, he will have to choose between saving his country or the woman who's captured his heart.